# God's Little Isthmus

## More Tales from Madlands

*22 agosto 2.004*

*Para Txentxo*

*Que pases muchos*
*años buenos*
*aquí en " Madlands "*

# A novel by
# J. Allen Kirsch

**𝑾p**

*Waubesa Press*
**The quality fiction imprint
of Badger Books Inc.**

© Copyright 1997 by J. Allen Kirsch
Published by Badger Books Inc. of Oregon, Wis.
Proofreading by James A. Nelson
Color separations by Port to Print of Madison, Wis.
Printed by BookCrafters of Chelsea, Mich.

**First edition**

**ISBN 1-878569-44-9**

*For Ellen and Brian*

*and*

*In Memory of Timothy H. Hosey*

*1954-1996*

# FALL SEMESTER, 1990

# 1

Cissy Pankhurst sat down with her old neighbor Roz to make a list of reasons why she wasn't going to get tenure:

*1) Dept. mad at me for taking leave of absence this semester.*

*2) Gave A's to 300 out of 340 students in Intro class five years ago.*

*3) Chair hates me.*

*4) Men in dept. mad at me because of my sexual harassm't complaint vs. Isaacson.*

*5) My book was my dissertation, sort of.*

*6) At 1 article per semester, I should have 10 published, not 8.*

*7) Sandra and I up for tenure at same time. Rickover pushing for her to get it, not me. Only one of us can possibly get tenure.*

"There," she said to Roz, repressing a shudder as she thought of her departmental chair, Vance Rickover.

"But you forgot the most important one." Roz stole the list away from her and scribbled. Finished, she handed it with a flourish back to Cissy, who read it:

*8) More men than women get tenure.*

There it was, the crowning blow. Roz was right. On the first day of her semester leave, Cissy had thoroughly convinced herself that she had no hope of tenure, thus negating the purpose of the leave itself, plus losing income in the process.

At least Evan was living with her now, thus making for cheaper — actually, dirt cheap — rent. Evan was the first good thing that had happened to her in years, five years in which she'd been bruised by the department and cheated on by Jeb, her long-term ex, at least for the last four. She'd had her own secret crush on Evan since the fall she met him. But unlike Jeb, she hadn't been unfaithful — plus, Evan had been married then, and was now only separated. It was a miracle that she'd been able to publish anything during the emotional chaos and routine blow-ups she'd weathered with Jeb. As to Madison... she was happily resigned to it, knowing there were better as well as far worse places she could have landed.

But tenure — the word itself had even acquired a magical ring to Cissy — meant life-long job security. Academic freedom to interpret and present ideas as she saw fit, without fear of reprisal. Acknowledgment by her peers that she was qualified to do so. And, perhaps more than anything, tenure meant never having to apply for another job again in her life.

"Items four and eight are blatantly sexist," Roz stated, bringing her out of her reverie.

"And number seven is an unfortunate coincidence," Cissy jumped back in. "The Old Boys' Club of Museum Studies isn't going to grant tenure to two women at once, especially not after they gave it to Ginger last year. If one of us gets it, it'll be Sandra." Sandra was married to Rickover.

"But there *is* a new chancellor pushing for minority hirings and retention," Roz said.

Cissy knew that Roz "knew" everything, whether it fell in her field or not, and this didn't. Cissy couldn't imagine that Donna Shalala's grandiose "Madison Plan" would trickle down to her.

Her second-floor window overlooked the intersection of Willy and Ingersoll Streets, and Cissy stared out, her brow furrowed, and stroked her long ash-blonde hair. It was a late August day and fall was not yet in the air, though in Madison, it would be soon. She shifted her glance and warily eyed the plaster ready to crumble from the ceiling.

Evan knew that it was for many professors the semester's most eagerly awaited, but feared moment: *The Insurgent's* semiannual UW Faculty Review. The radical newspaper had student informers size up the faculty, focusing largely on their political correctness and, where perceived, sexual sins.

He sat in his fifth-floor office in FAB — the Fine Arts Building — the newspaper spread in front of him, its timing perfect to coincide with Registration Week, now renamed "Welcome Week." His own entry simply read "Schultz, Evan: Impeccable politics; a fun instructor." He was glad that the students considered him *fun*. As for politics, his were hopelessly rooted in the sixties. A faculty member with a curatorial background, he'd been instrumental in bringing minority exhibits to Madison, even one of Frida Kahlo's memorabilia, long before "Fridamania" had swept the country.

Knuckles rapped on his door. Before he could get up to open it, Ginger burst in, her eyes incendiary. Today she was color-coordinated in aquamarine shoes and dress, the dress spangled with gold as usual. She brandished *The Insurgent* in front of him, pointing at the Faculty Review, and read her own entry aloud: "'Brilliant lecturer, though gender and class analysis somewhat weak.' "I ought to sue these motherfuckers!"

"Ginger, your race is showing."

"If they said my race analysis was weak, then I'd really have a case. As the only black woman — black person — in the department... How dare they! I'll track down the little bastard from my class, whoever he was, who told them this. Wait, I think I know! I bet it was that rich bitch from Chicago with the dreadlocks last spring! Even if she's graduated, I'll find her out..."

"Calm down, Ging. You've already got tenure. No one pays attention to this. What does it matter?"

"My honor is stained!"

"Look what they said about Cissy. And she doesn't have tenure." He'd have to do his best to keep the entry from her: "'A skilled and often overly demanding instructor. If Pankhurst has any politics, no one can figure them out.'"

Ginger began to read the list of her colleagues, as if for the first time. "You probably wrote your own entry," she snorted.

"Ginger, really."

"I'll track down the editor of this rag and wring his or her goddamned little neck!"

"Ginger, if you don't calm down, I'll have to force-feed you one of these." He extracted a small white envelope from his coat pocket, which contained a finely rolled killer joint. It was his last one, until Pepper came through with more.

Ginger spiked the floor with her high heels and sputtered unintelligibly. He hoped that she'd exhausted her tirade. "I don't do that," she stated, eyeing the envelope as though it contained fecal matter. "And, by the way, your hair's getting a little grey," she added, then walked out the door.

Evan had rarely seen her this angry. If he hadn't known she'd quit, he would have sworn she was coked up this morning. He decided to go to the men's room to see exactly how much grey had infiltrated his head of thick blond hair.

❦

"We'll call Irv right now," Roz said. Irv was Roz's husband, a lawyer, Cissy's landperson and, like Roz, her former neighbor.

"He'll help you out."

"Isn't this... premature?" Cissy ventured.

"You just made this list, you're up for tenure next semeter, and the Old Boys are out to screw over women, in particular, you. If I were you, I'd have my defenses lined up now." They both stood up — Cissy a whole head taller than Roz — and Roz grabbed the phone and punched in the number. Then, in an unexpected move, she handed the receiver to Cissy, just in time for her to hear, "Irv Barmejian here."

"Uh, Irv, it's Cissy. I'm sorry to bother you, but do you have a moment?"

"I'm with a client, but I always have a few minutes for the next person to get tenure in Museum Studies, even if it means I'm going to lose my best tenant."

What did he mean? That she wasn't going to get tenure and would have to leave Madison? No, he'd just said the opposite. That she'd buy her own house if she got tenure? If so —and it was currently a great big "if"— maybe she would. "Oh, I'll call back later, since you're with a client."

"No need to. I don't charge by the hour." From what Cissy had heard, he barely charged at all. "Is it the loose stair? I'll have someone come over today, or tomorrow at the latest, to fix it."

"It's not that. Roz came over to pick up the rent check and inspect the stair and we began talking. I was wondering... if you'd ever represented anyone in a tenure case against the university."

"Don't tell me you're expecting trouble." Irv's tone sounded appropriately worrisome.

"Roz and I have just made a list of eight reasons why I won't get tenure and three of them are sexist. If I go down, I don't want to go down without a fight." She wasn't sure if she meant this, but had to justify her call —no, Roz's call—somehow.

"I've never been involved in a tenure case. But I don't see why not. I've done every other kind of case in the universe."

Cissy remembered: the right to raise chickens in the city limits; the right to grow a prairie lawn in neighboring Sun Prairie, before Sun Prairie had outlawed them; and many stranger ones. If she remembered correctly, he often lost.

"I just thought I'd call and ask. I may end up needing your help some time this year. I just had a tenure anxiety attack. Sorry to bother you," she said, then hung up.

"Don't worry about bothering Irv." Cissy saw that Roz had lit up behind her back. "He never has clients. He's always free. I don't even know what he does in his office sometimes."

"He had a client today. I'll get you an ashtray, Roz." She couldn't believe Roz would light up without asking. She went into the kitchen, whipped open cupboards and drawers, but couldn't find one. "Evan has one somewhere around here."

"He must have one for smoking dope."

"Yes." Cissy gave the syllable a tinge of annoyance. She found the ashtray in the bedroom, walked out and handed it to Roz. Ashes at Roz's feet told her she hadn't made it in time.

"Thanks." Roz promptly extinguished her cigarette butt into it, stuck the ashtray back out to her and headed toward the door. "Now just don't step on the third step down and Irv will have someone here tomorrow. Hell, I could probably fix it myself, but I've got at least six commitments today. Your house was on the way, so I thought I'd save you the twenty-nine cent stamp for the rent." Never mind that the rent wasn't due for two more days, and Irv was as mellow as Roz was inflexible. "As for tenure, you talk to Irv again. He'll head a team of the best lawyers in Madison and fight the university tooth and nail. So long, Cissy." Roz flung the door closed behind her.

She made it sound as if a denial of tenure were a foregone conclusion; Cissy regretted even having broached the topic with her. She'd taken the semester off to maintain her mental health and, with Roz's help, had destroyed it on her first day off.

Carefully skipping the third stair, she went out and headed to the back of the house, the site of her herb garden.

Peppermint, spearmint, apple mint and pineapple mint threatened to overrun the parsley, basil, borage and dill. The mint, however, was the source of the herbal tea that got her through the day. She began to pick off leaves, then yanked off stems — no easy feat — and before she knew what she was doing, she was pulling up entire plants.

She stopped, stood back, and looked at the incipient destruction of her garden. Was she losing her mind?

She'd expected it to happen sooner or later this year, but not already.

❧

After attending a welcoming function for the new students in their Master of Fine Arts program, Evan had gone back to his office. Vance Rickover, as chair, had given a welcoming address, loaded with his usual military — especially, naval — metaphors. The result was so severe that the students must have thought they had embarked on the Titanic and the captain had just announced its imminent doom. They seemed either frozen in fright or by nature as austere as a cluster of Capuchin monks. Or both.

He was preparing to leave FAB when a barely audible knock came at his door. Cissy's secret knock it wasn't. He opened and there stood Pepper Isaacson: tall and dark, a physical replica of his father Sumner. The mere thought of Sumner was unsettling, but Evan was always glad to see his son.

"I was just down on campus doing research for Amelia, came over here to pick up my father's mail, and thought..." Evan hustled him in and closed the door before he could say more. "...I'd drop off your quarter-ounce now."

"Perfect timing, Pepper. I was down to my last joint. But I don't have the cash on me now." The truth was, Evan was desperate for dope. Since he'd moved out of the Mount Horeb farmette, left his wife and moved in with Cissy three months ago, what irritated him most was that she'd harvested all the pot a month early, for herself. And he couldn't take her to court for that. "You don't deal this stuff on campus, do you?" he whispered.

"One: I don't deal. I give it away to PWAs for medicinal purposes. Two: I do this as a favor to you and to no one else. If Juan thought I was actually dealing, he'd probably kick me out of the house and then I'd land back at my parents'."

"I'm glad you're discreet."

Pepper smiled slyly. "'Discretion,' that's my middle name.

Want to have a toke here in the office?"

Evan shot him an enigmatic look, until Pepper broke out in low laughter.

What Pepper didn't know was that in earlier times Evan would have said yes without hesitation.

# 2

"God, am I glad to be living back in the center of things again. I don't know why or how I lived all those years out in Mount Horeb," Evan said, as he hiked up King Street Sunday afternoon.

"Well, why did you?" Pepper couldn't imagine living in the middle of nowhere. After living in San Francisco, he felt at times that Madison was "nowhere."

"Good question. When I married Anne, we had to decide whether to be near-east-side hippies or country hippies. We figured it would be safer to raise kids and dope out in the country. I guess we envisioned some sort of mini-commune."

"Yeah," Pepper agreed, remembering his own commune experience. He looked up at the facades of the turn-of-the-century buildings and tried to remember which one held Irv's law office, hidden away in a small second-floor room.

"I just didn't expect that our carpenter would be the only other resident besides the kids, and that he and Anne would end up..."

"Bummer," Pepper said, as Evan trailed off. He didn't know how much Evan wanted to talk about his marital breakup, but enjoyed having a straight male friend like Evan, who would confide in him. At least he was involved and apparently happy with Cissy. "Cissy didn't want to come up here today?"

"Cissy?" Evan chuckled to himself, as if at a private joke. "It's not really her bag. She only likes to smoke before sex. Can you believe she never smoked in her life until I turned her on this year?"

Pepper pondered this. "Far out. I guess it is a little odd for people our age to take up marijuana, just like someone our age starting to smoke cigarettes."

"And get this," Evan went on. "She was afraid she'd see a student or someone from our department here today, as if anyone else in our department got high, as if they'd hold it against her when we're all here for the same purpose."

The purpose was the Great Midwest Marijuana Harvest Fest, taking place at the Capitol this afternoon. "Just as well I don't have my kids this weekend. I could hardly bring them here."

"I wonder where the crowd is," Pepper said, as they approached the southeast corner of the Capitol.

"At the top of State Street. Tommy's supposed to have his Capitol cops out everywhere today."

"Tommy" was the current Republican governor, who'd done his best to keep this year's Fest from being held. They were holding it despite him, permit or no permit, and he'd threatened arrests. "I suppose we'd better walk around the Capitol."

"We could light up a joint and walk right through." Evan tried to gauge Pepper's reaction and looked at him in complicity.

"Guess we wouldn't want to get arrested before it starts, would we?" Pepper said.

They reached the opposite side of the Capitol and saw the marchers, who had just finished the trek up State Street. The first speaker was trying to get the crowd's attention, with little success. The organizers didn't *officially* encourage anyone to smoke marijuana, but pot was in the air everywhere. It was as if the Dane County Sheriff's Department had just destroyed a half-ton of the evil weed.

"Let's not be in the minority." Evan pulled out a joint.

They stood among several thousand and puffed, while people passed out literature for NORML — the National Organization for the Reform of Marijuana Laws. The Capitol cops observed the throng from across the street and, Pepper noticed, from some of the Capitol windows. The crowd smoked blithely away. How, after all, could some twenty or forty cops start busting people in a crowd of thousands?

"If they started busting people, they'd have a regular riot on their hands," Evan said, echoing Pepper's thoughts.

"Yeah. Hey, look at that sign!" Pepper pointed at it. "'Hemp's a Harmless Weed. Tommy's the Evil Dope'." He craned his neck and saw others: "'Free the Heads, Jail the Feds'" and "'Pot: The All-American Herb'."

They finished the joint, as the sun shone down on them. "It must be in the high sixties," Pepper said.

"Oh, the sixties were high, all right," Evan quipped. "We were all in a good space back then. Did you know Madison voted back in the seventies to legalize marijuana? Only a referendum, of course."

"Guess I never knew. I was in San Francisco then." After Pepper had escaped from his parents' house to the commune, and the commune had died out, he'd gone to Stanford and earned his Ph.D. in geography. Like many Ph.D.s in Madison, he'd rarely used his degree in his field. "That was a cool scene out there too. Cool place for a guy to do his trip."

"Cool. Those were the days." Then he went from waxing nostalgic to waxing bitter: "Eight years of Nancy ruined that. The fucking country should've just said 'no' to her. Not to mention *him.*"

"Still," Pepper went on, "I think this is one of only a few places in the country besides Berkeley that'd tolerate an open-air pot festival." For all his complaints about Madison, he had to grant the city this.

"Look over there!"

"What?" Pepper turned around, mildly dazed, half-expecting to see a beefy cop with a billy club menacing them. Instead he saw a middle-aged man, whose chiseled looks exceeded ten on a scale of ten.

"Blake Abell," Evan said. "The new guy they hired last year in our department. Full professor, tenured."

"Heard of him, never met him."

"Looks like you're going to. He's heading straight for us."

A cigarette in hand, Blake Abell approached them. Evan introduced them, fortunately omitting last names. Pepper didn't appreciate being known as his father's son. Madison was a small town, and there were very few Isaacsons in it, none of them, likely for the better, relatives.

"Blake, surprised to see you here," Evan greeted.

"I guess I could say the same about you. But too surprised, I'm not." Blake smiled devilishly.

"Want to trade in your cigarette for something... tastier?" Evan asked. "I take it that that's not all you smoke."

"Where's your hemp shirt?" Blake asked.

On second glance, Pepper realized that Blake's own shirt was indeed made of hemp. Blake, obviously, was no novice pot-smoker. "We'll all smoke another?" Pepper said.

They sat on the Capitol lawn to smoke, tie-dyed teens holding a large bong whooping it up behind them. Sixties' types, some of whom looked as if they'd worn the very same clothes since then, milled about, glassy-eyed. Dogs wearing bandannas seemed as placidly stoned as their owners. Another speaker's voice from the Capitol steps strained to reach them.

"Where's Cissy today?" Blake asked.

"Oh, at home, working on an article. You know, she has workaholic tendencies, which just get worse as tenure draws nearer. And she doesn't even smoke."

"She should do fine. Cissy's getting tenure would be the best gift the department could get."

"I could groove on lying down in the sun." Evan stretched out, discontinuing this line of conversation.

Pepper supposed that, especially when Evan was stoned, he didn't feel like discussing Cissy's tenure with anyone, certainly not with Cissy, who was convinced that she wasn't going to get it, and probably not with Blake, even if he was going to vote in her favor. Pepper joined him on the grass and a minute later Blake did the same. Pepper was tempted to sniff Blake's hemp shirt, or his armpit.

"This is really something," Pepper said. "If my father could see me now, smoking dope with not one, but two members of his former department." The dope made him talkative, and he realized he might have given away his identity. Blake, either polite or stoned, didn't show it if he registered the comment. "And who knows how many others could be lurking about?"

"Ginger's the only one I could think of," Evan said. "But, one: I don't think she'd do it in public. And, two: she prefers, or preferred, coke."

Blake did register this comment. "That woman's hopped up on something. Never knew if it was speed, coke, or a natural high. I never would have guessed when I arrived that the department was so full of heads."

"I think even my Dad tried dope in the sixties," Pepper added, stoned. He had no idea if this was true.

"At least we don't have to worry about seeing Rickover here," Evan said.

"Let's not even think about that dude." Blake rolled his eyes and looked upward, as though studying cloud formations.

"Right," Evan agreed. "That bastard's always in a funk."

Pepper cupped his hands behind him as a head rest. At an angle below them, he could see one of the many spreads of flowers that adorned the Capitol Square. A bed of flowers to his left formed a map of Wisconsin. "I don't see why they couldn't include a few marijuana plants in one of the flower beds around here. Pot *is* native to Wisconsin."

"Yeah, pot for the people," Blake seconded.

"You used to be able to buy it up here at the Farmers Market." Evan stretched his arms out, as if to encompass the Square. "Under the table, of course."

"Pepper's right," Blake said, and Pepper perked up. "Smoke a little weed in the flower bed, then do your Farmers Market shopping. That should boost sales, especially of chocolates and pastries."

They lay in stoned silence for a while, Pepper watching Blake and other men, his eyes always propelling themselves back to Blake. He wondered which sex Blake was watching.

"Think I'd better go." Blake stood up suddenly and stretched. "I still have to finish up tomorrow's lecture for Exhibition and Display Design."

"You work stoned?" Pepper asked, avoiding a more obvious ploy to get him to hang around.

Blake got up and winked at him. Was it sexual, Pepper wondered, or simply a manifestation of pot-smoking solidarity?

Standing, Blake seemed disoriented, perhaps in renewed awe of his pot-filled surroundings, or maybe simply reacquiring his balance. Pepper watched him keenly as time seemed to go into a slow, delicious motion.

Finally Blake said, "Peace, guys," and wandered off.

"A nice, if somewhat enigmatic guy," Evan observed when Blake had ambled out of hearing range. "Didn't even know he turned on. Nothing wrong with keeping your life private, I guess. And he's got something to keep private."

"Oh, yeah?" Pepper said. He hoped it was that Blake was gay, but didn't voice this.

"Yeah," Evan said. "Something happened out in California. Something to do with why he lost his job or resigned and came here. But nobody knows what."

The news — or non-news — disappointed Pepper. If the department couldn't discover it, how could he? But, then again...

"Wanna head back?"

Pepper looked at his watch, his interest in hanging around diminished, now that Blake was gone. "Think I'll head on down to Sunday beer bust at the Bull Dog. "Wanna come?" he added jokingly.

Evan actually seemed to contemplate the invitation --to

Madison's biggest gay bar. Pepper couldn't imagine he was that liberal, that un-selfconscious, but apparently Evan was.

"I told Cissy I'd be home by six."

"OK. I'll go myself." Juan was driving cab today and Pepper could enjoy his freedom.

He wondered how Blake would have responded if he'd asked him to go to the Bull Dog. Maybe he'd find Blake at the Bull Dog, though he'd never seen him there before. He checked his shirt pocket to make sure he had another joint to smoke on the bar's patio.

❦

Juan parked the PC cab at the lot on the company grounds, as he'd done for ten years, in happy enough underemployment. He walked the six blocks to Irv's house on Orton Park, where he lived rent-free — as Irv's best and, once, poorest friend — in long-sought bliss with Pepper, with whom he inhabited the basement apartment of the renovated Queen Anne.

He tiptoed in through the back door of the apartment by Lake Monona. In the bedroom Juan touched the sheets, feeling his way in the dark, and Pepper woke up immediately.

"Is this an erotic sheet massage or what?"

"Could be." Juan forced a smile, not having expected the question.

"Well, jump in."

Juan shucked his clothes and hopped in.

"Hey, I got a something sort of sexy to tell you."

"Really?" Pepper sat up and rubbed his eyes into wakefulness.

"Yeah, my last call was to the Bull Dog and my passenger was this leatherman, with this blond guy in his twenties. They were practically doing it in the cab."

"Those two? Hell, they were practically doing it in the bar four hours ago."

"You went to the Bull Dog?" Juan said, in near-disbelief, but hoping not to sound upset.

"Yeah, man. Beer bust. *Carpe diem.*"

"Sounds good to me," he lied.

"Then, how about some *carpe noctem?*"

# 3

By eight o'clock, Irv had prepared supper and awaited Roz's arrival from wherever: the Labor Farm office, the Rape Crisis Center, Womynspace, a mere three of at least a dozen possibilities. She'd often start her volunteer work at one office and, without telling him, progress through several other offices during the course of the day, leaving him with no idea where to reach her and only the vaguest notion of when she'd return home.

Roz finally breezed into the house, shed her clothes by the door, sat down, plunked her breasts down on the dining room table. Although he'd got accustomed to her nudism, he still found it hard to look —as well as not to look— at her breasts across the table over dinner. He was sure that at nudist resorts, they at least dressed for dinner, though Roz would have none of that line of thinking.

"Irv, can you bring me a beer?" she called to him in the kitchen.

Irv had already taken the eggplant casserole out of the oven. "Point, Leinenkugel, or Miller?"

"Whatever."

"God, am I tired," he heard her mutter as he delivered a Miller Lite.

Irv went back to the kitchen, brought in the soup, then the casserole, and served himself. Roz proceeded to drink her Lite, had yet to fill her plate or touch the steaming soup. "I was at Labor Farm for four hours, then recycled their aluminum, glass and newsprint, schlepping all those bags and boxes into the car, then out again. Then I went to the Baltic States Independence Committee meeting, changed into my jogging suit and jogged past Womynspace and dropped off a stack of fliers for the Take Back the Night March, went on to the Rape Crisis Center and answered the phone for two hours."

It was at moments like this that Irv regretted having convinced Roz to quit her real jobs. He thought she just might take to her role as mother, but no. She deposited Dayne with Juan or Pepper in the basement apartment, or with Irv himself, even when he had work to do at his office, and had made herself into a professional volunteer *par excellence*.

"I thought I might get some rest while chained to the burr

oak, but it was already occupied and safe for another day, though I'm scheduled to be chained from noon to two tomorrow. We just can't let the city forestry crew cut it down. The only way that tree's going to die is if they kill us with it." She paused, as though tired from merely reciting her day's activities. "Otherwise I don't know when I would have made it home."

"Just make sure you dress when you chain yourself to it," Irv joked.

"Hey! If I chained myself to the tree naked, that might really help us get the publicity to save it!"

Irv could seldom be sure if she was joking or not. "That might not be..."

"Wait! I could be naked except for a green Labor Farm banner. Labor Farm, just like the tree, needs all the publicity it can get. We need to win the sixth district seat back somehow!"

"I'd suggest, uhm, some other route of publicity."

"I know! I can take Dayne with me while I'm chained to the oak and teach him the importance of environmental preservation."

Irv's look of faint amusement — she evidently hadn't been joking — turned to a glower. "Even if you're naked, which I truly hope you're not serious about, you're not going to have Dayne out there naked too. And don't say that just because he's only three and a half, it won't matter. And if you're chained to the burr oak, what's to prevent him from running out into the street?"

"I could hold him in my arms and breastfeed him. How's that? That's the most primal form of bonding."

Roz had to be joking now. Her attempts at breastfeeding had been sporadic and always short-lived, usually ending with cries such as "How can a kid have teeth like this at his age!?" She'd sorely tried to breastfeed Dayne, so she'd claimed. Though she'd given it up some two years ago, she was still complaining about its "aftereffects," by which she meant the "damage" done to her breasts.

"Roz, you don't think you might be doing too much? Just because you have the freedom to, doesn't mean..."

"Too much? There's so much to do. Besides, today was an exception." She took a swig of beer, finally heaped a small portion of casserole onto her plate, and blew on her soup. "Look at me."

All Irv could see were tired eyes, and tired-looking breasts — could breastfeeding really have "damaged" them? — dangling over her dinner plate. The truth was, Roz looked fragile, though she'd always been thin. Small of stature, she barely topped the table when seated, and her short, dark hair only seemed to underscore her diminutive size.

"One beer and now I'm relaxed. I'm not going to let stress get to me."

"I hope not." Irv finished his casserole and slowly began to sip his homemade lentil soup.

"No way." Roz gulped her beer, then attacked the ounce of casserole she'd served herself. Finished eating a few seconds later, she pushed the plate aside and went back to her Miller Lite.

"No soup, no more casserole?"

"Maybe some soup later. It's delicious, Irv. But I'm fine right now."

"With all the exercise you're getting — Remember those bags and boxes and bottles you lugged to recycling today? — you might need more calories than you think."

"If I'm hungry, I'll grab a snack before bed." She now lit a Camel filter, her idea of a snack, he supposed. Among other reasons, she claimed she could never have another child because she could never again go without smoking for nine months. Irv had hoped futilely that, after the long abstention, she might have conquered the addiction.

He was beginning to be truly concerned about Roz's overwork. At least, he had to admit, she got adequate sleep, accustomed as she was to go to bed at midnight, two or three hours after he did, and to get up at nine-thirty, four or five hours after he did. During the few hours they'd overlapped nightly for the last four-plus years of marriage, she'd never learned to cuddle. At best they stretched their legs to touch toes during the night.

"Oh, by the way, where's Dayne?"

He thought she'd never ask; lately the omission was not atypical. "I made him supper at six and an hour or so later he was ready for bed."

"So early?"

"Juan and Pepper took him for a walk this afternoon." Irv spoke with his mouth full. Swallowing, he added, "He rode on the Gay Liberation statue, so they cheerfully reported. Then they took him to the Co-op and walked down the railroad tracks."

"Sounds like a busy day. No wonder he was tired." She stubbed out her cigarette in the ceramic ashtray, a souvenir from their honeymoon to Nicaragua, back in the days before the Sandinistas lost power.

"Irv, I've been thinking... Though this may not be the best moment to bring this up." She looked up at the chandelier above them, then lowered her eyes to meet his.

God help me, she's not going to bring up a nudist vacation again, he hoped. It seemed to creep up every six months or so. Adamant, he was not going to parade nude nor take the family to a nudist resort, no matter what Roz wanted.

"I've been thinking," she began again, "about the city council seat. The third parties don't yet have a candidate and we have to get rid of Claypool." Claypool was the incumbent, liberal Democrat "scumbag" —to use Roz's word— who represented their district.

"Yeah." Irv planted his elbows on the table and rested his chin on his fists, always up for a good political discussion. "You're right about that, love."

"An idea's occurred to me." She contemplated the design on her pack of Camels for some ten seconds, then looked him in the eyes. "There's no reason why I couldn't run for the seat."

He felt his face whiten and his heart sink and thought immediately of ten good reasons why she shouldn't.

"I've been in the neighborhood and an activist as long as anyone. As you know, there's been no serious third party candidate interested or proposed so far." In reality, the elections were non-partisan and, in the sixth district, the "third" parties were more like a second party; Republicans were the third. "My support is grassroots-oriented and I have as much name recognition as anyone, which is a definite plus. I have the desire, I've certainly paid my dues, and now that I don't have to work, I have the time."

"You, who just rattled off everything that you 'had' to do today, have the time?"

"Well, if I were elected, I'd cut down on my volunteer stuff. I'd still do grunt work, like stuff Labor Farm envelopes when needed, but someone else can certainly cart off their recycling. In any case, the city's supposed to have curbside recycling by next year. Besides, serving on the Common Council..." — this was its official name — "...isn't a full-time job anyway. It's barely even a job. You know the money they give councilpersons is negligible."

Oh God. She'd thought this out in advance and was serious. He could only begin to envision the complications, and their married life together had been complicated enough, starting with Roz's artificial insemination. And she had yet to mention, if not to think of, the most important complication.

"Of course, there'd be a few little hurdles to jump, plus the typical hassle involved in running for any office."

Hurdle. Maybe she had thought of it. "Yes?" He lifted his chin slowly, hopefully, and locked eyes with her. She'd let her hair grow out just a little, but her face still looked wan, pale, even strained, though it currently sported a smile as wide as Lake Mendota.

"There'd be campaign financing to deal with. You know that Claypool and company are well-heeled."

That wasn't the hurdle that had occurred to him, so he stated the one that had: "What about Dayne?"

"Dayne?" She looked truly dumbfounded.

It was worse than he thought.

"You don't really think he's being deprived?" Her tone seemed innocent, vaguely shocked.

Irv didn't dare say yes. For better or worse, deprived of fathers he was not. Not to mention that because of his own sterility, Juan was Dayne's biological father, and he merely his legal one.

"Well?" Roz clearly expected an answer.

"There's a lot to sort through," he said, all diplomacy. "This all comes as somewhat of a surprise, springing it on me like this. Can we talk another time, after we've both had more time to think?"

"Sure, if you say so. But I really don't see what the problem is."

# 4

The next morning Roz struggled out of bed, having set the alarm for eight o'clock. The hour was ungodly, but she'd show Irv a thing or two, prove to him exactly how well she could manage. After her shower, she chugged a mug of coffee and took a quick dip into *The New York Times,* then went downstairs to fetch Dayne from Juan, with whom Irv had deposited him before going to his office.

"Dayne and I are going shopping," she announced upon seeing Juan's bewildered look.

"You? Shop? And at this hour of the morning? I've never known you to leave the house before noon." Juan spoke with his mouth full, cheeks puffed out like a chipmunk, as he noshed on a bagel. Crumbs littered the entire counter and kitchen floor and an empty bag of bagels was beside him. He hardly ever ate in public; this must be how be got his nourishment.

"I leave the house by eleven lots of the time. Where's Dayne?"

"In front of the TV."

Roz whirled around the corner, flicked the set off and pulled him up into her arms. "Mommy and Dayne are going to go shopping."

Dayne began to wail and, lest he kick her, she put him down. "See you in an hour or so," she said to Juan, who stood flabbergasted, cheeks still puffed out, and she pulled Dayne on up the stairs.

Roz walked him the four blocks to the Willy Street Co-op, where she bought Irv's favorite vegetarian foods: hummus, tebbouleh, tofu and soy burgers, a few things for herself and a Halvah bar for Dayne.

Outside on the street she saw Beth Yarmolinksy and her lover, the two young dykes that volunteered at Labor Farm. McSurely, that was the lover's odd surname that had stuck in her mind, but she'd be damned if she could come up with the first name. Snatching a glance at her watch, she realized she'd have to hurry, or she'd never make it to the liquor and hardware stores, then home, and arrive at Labor Farm by eleven to replace them.

But, what the hell? As far as she knew, they were students and didn't have jobs, so what if she was a little late? At least she'd be proving to Irv — with Juan and the purchases as her witnesses — that she could spend time with Dayne, get household chores and shopping done, volunteer all she wanted <u>and</u> run for city council.

"Well, it's eleven and she's still not here," Beth complained.

"Who's replacing us?" asked Verla.

"You know, Roz Goldwomyn."

"Don't know her."

"Yes you do." Beth vacated the folding chair and began to walk around the small Labor Farm Party office, its walls plastered with political posters, press releases, and newspaper clippings. She volunteered four hours a week, besides going to school part-time and managing Ho Chi Minh's. "She's that know-it-all dyke, barely taller than me, frizzy hair sorta like mine, early forty-something, who comes in here and acts like she owns the place."

"Oh, I do know who you mean. I always thought she was pleasant enough." Verla shook her long blonde hair and, with it, her long, lithe body, giving Beth sexual shivers.

"I suppose she's not that bad. It's just that, you know, she actually lived the sixties and she never lets you forget it. I can't help when I was born."

"At least you were never *born again.*" Verla referred to her own phase in the mid-eighties.

"Guess I wouldn't wanna be forty anyway, but still, she sorta irks me. I just hope she gets here, 'cause I gotta leave for Ho Chi's in a half-hour max."

"I have to go too. After my two organ lessons, I'll see you at Ho Chi's for a late lunch, OK? Then this afternoon I give a flute lesson, followed by that hopeless young thing on the oboe."

Beth arched her eyebrows. "C'mon, Verla. Don't call a woman a 'thing.'"

"You know what I mean." Verla again shook her hair and fluttered her eyebrows. The irresistible look made Beth feel nice and wet. Too wet for eleven a.m. in the Labor Farm office. "But I'm tempted," Verla went on, "to put in earplugs while she plays. At least it's money, so I shouldn't complain."

"Yeah," Beth agreed, still distracted by her dampness down below.

Money was always a problem, but they made ends meet, in large part due to their spartan, ecologically oriented, politically correct lifestyle, which still thrived on the near-east side of Madison. And they thrived with it; Beth couldn't imagine living in any other city, nor in any other part of this one.

"I'm going to go comb my hair. The eleven-thirty student is that upscale west-side woman who thinks she's going to be some high-church organist and I've got to look professional."

"You look perfect as you are." Beth was almost drooling.

"You look perfect too." Verla disappeared behind the bed

sheet that hid the mirror and sink. Beth took the compliment to heart and it went downward from there. Her wetness was now overpowering; she was tempted to feel herself. Instead, she got up impulsively and headed toward the hanging sheet.

She saw Verla's radiant reflection in the mirror before Verla saw her.

"Beth!" She'd obviously startled her.

"Verla." Beth now stood behind her and grabbed her around the waist with her arms. Verla pulled her comb through her hair one more time, then let it drop into the sink. Beth moved her hands up and caressed Verla's breasts through her blouse and bra.

"Beth," Verla sighed.

Beth pushed herself up next to Verla's backside. "Verrr-la." She felt herself begin to melt, abandoned Verla's breasts, and went for her zipper.

"Beth." The tone was clearly meant as a warning, but she didn't care. She turned Verla around and dove her hands into her panties.

"Verla," Beth gasped.

This time Verla didn't resist. "Beth," she moaned, stretching the name out for five seconds.

Beth knew they couldn't go all the way in the Labor Farm washroom. They were silent for some seconds before Beth reluctantly took her hands out of Verla's panties, zipped her up, and began to undo her blouse.

"Beth." Again the tone was cautionary.

"C'mon, it's OK."

Beth stepped back, pulled Verla into the hanging bed sheet with her, and unfastened Verla's bra. The sheet fully encircled both of them, their own private haven of lust.

"What if Roz comes in?"

"Don't worry. A dyke'll understand." Beth promptly put her mouth on Verla's right breast and she played with her left nipple. Verla threw her head back and let out a long, unabashed purr of pleasure.

"What the hell!?" Beth recognized Roz Goldwomyn's voice, full of shock or fright.

"It's OK, it's just us volunteers," Beth answered, still wrapped up in the sheet, as they quickly reassembled their clothes. As they hurried to escape their confines, Beth pulled in one direction, Verla in the other, and the sheet ripped loose from its hooks. Beth felt herself redden and saw that Verla's blush had turned to burgundy. Now truly embarrassed herself, Beth awkwardly lifted the sheet off them.

Roz Goldwomyn stood some six feet away, arms akimbo, awaiting explanations. As if there'd been any doubt what they'd been doing.

At least the woman who faced them was a lesbian. Beth quickly regained her composure and put on her best manners: "I know we shouldn't have gotten so carried away. But I knew it was you who'd be coming in and trusted you'd understand."

"I really have to go or I'll miss my lesson."

Without even pecking Beth on the cheek, Verla patted her clothes, spat out a nervous good-bye, and dashed out the door.

"You're damned lucky it wasn't someone else," Roz said. "You know it could have been. Other people come in here too."

"The last thing I'd want to do is compromise Labor Farm's integrity."

"Don't ever let this happen again." Roz's tone had yet to soften and it irritated Beth, confirming her belief that Roz acted as if she owned the place. "Sex in the workplace, a public place, is totally out of line."

"OK, OK, I'm sorry, damn it. I guarantee you it'll never happen again." Beth squared her jaw, staring Roz down.

Finally the face lost its stern look. "Good. I believe you. I was your age once, young and in love, or so I thought. I'm a confirmed nudist myself, but nudism and sex are totally unrelated things. When we're nude, we're all totally equal, accepting of our own bodies, and you don't even have to know your fellow nudists' last names or professions. And out in nature..."

"You're a nudist?" Beth interrupted Roz's lecture. "Hey, that's cool."

"There are several clubs in Madison and around southern Wisconsin." Roz was evidently warming up to the topic, which was, after all, preferable to a lecture on sex in the workplace. "And at home, I never wear a stitch."

"That's really great. Naked dykes on the Land. I always wanted to go to the Womyn's Music Festival and stuff like that, but money's always tight."

Roz contorted her face slightly at Beth's words. "Yes, well... I don't know of any all-women's groups in Madison." She paused, as though now wanting to change the topic, then did: "I'm totally accepting of all sexual orientations and I would have said the same thing whether it was two guys, or a man and a woman, wrapped in that sheet."

Roz's little speech exasperated Beth. "Do we have to go through it again? I said I'm sorry, all right? I'm just glad you're one of us. I know it could've been really awkward otherwise."

She saw Roz fingering a cigarette pack. "Hey, can we step outside and have a smoke? The phones aren't ringing. I stopped smoking four years ago, but every now and then I still get the urge. Especially after sex, you know?" She flashed Roz an impish grin. "Not that we went all the way in there," she added hastily.

Roz agreed halfheartedly, and they stood on the sidewalk, where a northerly wind was beckoning fall.

"You're not smokin' Marlboros or any Philip Morris product, are ya?" Beth asked.

As if taken aback, Roz shoved her pack of Camel filters under Beth's nose.

"Reynolds," Beth read from the side of the pack. "Good, you're safe." She took one of Roz's Camels, lit it, and inhaled with gusto.

"What are we boycotting now?"

"Jesse Helms," she said, assured of her correct lesbian-feminist politics, and proud to be one up on Roz. "Philip Morris is a major contributor to his campaign. So gays and lesbians aren't supposed to smoke them. I mean, no one should smoke them. I mean, no one should probably smoke, but... Just make sure you and your friends don't..."

"Deal," Roz cut her off. "Now you just make sure that you and your friend don't..." Roz stopped before stating the obvious. "And also, don't make assumptions about other people's sexual orientations, OK?"

Oh God, Beth thought. Did Roz Goldwomyn actually mean to imply she wasn't a dyke? Again Beth felt embarrassed, but, if Roz really was straight, she supposed she ought to appreciate her much more for her tolerance.

"And before you leave, go back in there and reattach the sheet."

It was almost time for her to be at work. She ground the Camel, half-smoked, into the sidewalk, and picked it up to deposit in the trash. Inside she gathered up the crumpled sheet and saw Verla's comb still beside the sink. Before Roz came back in, she quickly stuck it inside her panties.

# 5

Cissy speed-read the Faculty Review in the copy of *The Insurgent* that Sandra handed her.

"What I can't believe is that Evan didn't show it to me!" She was sitting on her downstairs front porch, anger at Evan and at *The Insurgent* battling in her mind: "What do they mean by 'overly demanding'? Asking students simply to attend their classes?" She paused and poured another glass of spearmint iced tea, having guzzled her first glass as though it were beer on a hot summer afternoon. "And my politics? What do they possibly have to do with courses like Archaeology or Anthropology and the Museum?"

"Oh, don't hold it against Evan. I'm sure he has your best interests at heart," Sandra said, distracting Cissy from her mini-tirade.

She supposed Sandra was right. She knew that the faculty not only paid little attention to *The Insurgent*, but for the most part actively hated it. But still, she was sensitive to everything written about her; if the written word could possibly fall into the wrong hands, in academia it certainly would. "Why did they even include me this semester in the Faculty Review? I'm not even teaching." Her "mental health" semester had had anything but a good start.

"But look what they wrote about me!" Sandra more or less wailed. "I *am* teaching, I'm up for tenure next semester just like you, and they had the nerve to write this!"

"Don't worry, Sandra." Cissy feared that Sandra had as much or more to worry about than she did. "Only students, and not even all of them, pay attention to this thing." She tried to convince herself this was true. Her eyes again fell on Sandra's entry: "Good early morning classes to sleep through. This instructor wouldn't recognize correct politics if they hit her in the face." From what she'd heard, the first part was probably all too true.

Sandra was digging in her purse — the size of a large carry-on flight bag. She was about Cissy's age, and her mousy brown hair fell limply around a pear-shaped, pleasant face. Finally Sandra extracted a roll of toilet paper and began dabbing at her eyes. If she aimed to wipe away a few tears, she only succeeded in displacing her mascara. The effect was one of a black eye in the middle of her cheek.

"Look at it this way," Cissy went on, half-jokingly: "The students read this, then you have lower enrollment and fewer papers and projects to grade."

"My enrollments are so low that if it hadn't been for Vance, my classes probably would have been canceled!" Sandra let the toilet paper drop to the floor of the porch and picked up her glass of tea off the wrought-iron table.

"It was a bad joke. Sorry." Cissy didn't know what to say, though she knew that, as chair, Vance —her nemesis, almost everyone's, probably even Sandra's at times— did do his wife certain favors. "What did Vance think of his own entry?" she asked, as eager to know as she was to change the topic.

"Oh, Vance doesn't read *The Insurgent,*" Sandra said simply.

"Just as well." Cissy knew fully well what students thought of him, without having to read it in *The Insurgent,* and took secret pleasure as her eyes again fell on his entry: "The less this jerk teaches, the better. Rude and intimidating to students. A misogynist with politics to the right of Somoza." She looked back up and realized that Sandra had been reading over her shoulder.

"So how's everything else?" Cissy prompted, as if she had invited Sandra over to talk and not vice versa. Today Sandra had taken the bus, gotten off at the wrong stop, found herself lost, and had ended up calling Cissy from the gas station almost directly across the street.

"Oh, so so."

"Tenure year usually is hell," Cissy said, hoping to push the conversation forward. She figured that, as they were going to go through the process together, they might as well commiserate.

"I'm afraid so," Sandra said lamely. Vance had engineered a spousal hire for her three years ago and her first three years of teaching at George Washington University counted toward her tenure, putting them up for it at the same time.

"Is anything particular wrong?" She looked at her yard, wondering if next year she should put in a front garden too, as Juan used to. If there was a next year.

"This is hard to say, but yes." Sandra had bitten her lip and had applied a piece of toilet paper to it. "It's Vance."

This itself didn't surprise Cissy — only the fact that Sandra would admit it.

"He's pushing me so hard. He wants me to begin to write my tenure lecture already. I was reserving this semester for my nervous breakdown and was only going to worry about tenure in January."

Cissy feared that this was not Sandra's idea of humor.

"When I'm not teaching, he thinks I'm at home working on my lecture, when in reality all I'm doing is biting my nails and watching the old 'Dark Shadows'. The whole series is now out on video, did you know?"

"No, I didn't." The next thing Cissy knew, she'd end up hearing details about Sandra's life in the attic, if indeed the rumor that Vance used to keep her locked there was true.

Sandra ruffled her dress, which hung as limply as her hair. It was loose enough that Cissy wondered fleetingly if she might be pregnant, then nixed the very idea. Vance certainly wouldn't permit that to interfere with her tenure. She wouldn't be astounded to hear that Vance had put their sex life on hold to give Sandra more time to write.

Cissy didn't know what else to say, and picked up Sandra's copy of *The Insurgent* again. "'Blake Abell'," she read aloud: "'New, but tenured. A political mixed bag. Reportedly canned from his last job.' See, Sandra, they damned everyone in the department." The entry for their distinguished senior professor, Bob Rothschild, read, "About to retire, about time."

"What about Evan?"

"Maybe they have a secret policy of saying something nice about one person per department." A duo of teenagers zoomed down the sidewalk on rollerblades. On an impulse, she ventured to ask Sandra what everyone had wondered about: "Do you think it's really true that Blake was fired from California?" Every rumor imaginable had been circulated: a drug ring, a female prostitution ring, a male one, a gang rape, falsification of credentials. To begin with.

"I don't know, Cissy." Sandra held her hands out, helpless, almost knocking over her tea with her elbow. "Even if Vance knew, he wouldn't tell me."

Cissy began to protest, then realized this was probably true. "And then there's Nick," she said. Many called him "Nick the Dick." Lamentably, he was Cissy's downstairs neighbor. She couldn't imagine that, with his salary, he'd chosen to stay in the cheap Willy Street house another year.

"Oh, poor Nick," Sandra said. "Did you see what they said about him?"

"Yes." Cissy stifled a chuckle, knowing that what they'd written was perfectly true. His *Insurgent* entry merely read, "Sexual harasser."

"At least they can't say that we women are sexual harassers."

"I wouldn't be so sure about that, Sandra." Sandra was slightly more out of it than Cissy had imagined.

Sandra gave her a befuddled look as Cissy heard footfalls inside. "Quick, Sandra, stick this in your purse." She shoved *The Insurgent* at her.

A second later, Nick Wren stood beside them. She knew he was forty-two, admitted he looked thirty-two, and judged his emotional growth stunted at twenty-two. He was new but tenured, divorced, and an Ivy League friend of Vance's. "'Afternoon, girls. A little friendly department bashing?"

Tongue-tied, she looked over at Sandra, whose mouth was frozen in an oval, a pear-shaped one at that.

"Don't sweat it," he continued, before either of them could form a response. "I myself am off to do some bashing. Ball bashing." He let the final two words dangle in the air before clarifying, "Racquetball."

"So I figured," Cissy said, not having figured.

"If you're ever up for a game, Cissy," he went on, blatantly ignoring Sandra, "let me know. I'm always up for teaching you."

"I will, Nick," she said, pulling herself together. "Though I think I get enough aerobic exercise as it is."

"Offer's still there, any time you change your mind."

He was off and down the sidewalk. She couldn't help but notice his hairy, muscular legs before he jumped into his Corvette. His money probably went for the Corvette and women shallow enough to be impressed by it or, God forbid, him. At least she'd never had to share the two-flat house alone with Nick, and was glad that Evan had moved in with her this summer, after Jeb had left her for Boston with the notorious punk-rocking Pep, the object of his long-standing infidelity.

"I might even take up racquetball, if I weren't so uncoordinated," Sandra said. "But Nick usually plays with Vance, and Vance would never let me play with Nick. Or anyone. He'd probably have a fit if he knew I was over here talking to you."

Cissy feared it was true. Sandra was as incapable of a lie as Vance was adept at it.

❧

"Just read *The Insurgent* entries for yourself!" Ginger screeched into the phone, shortly after Sandra had left.

"It seems Evan did try to hide mine from me..." Cissy knew he'd done it for her purported "good," but she was still a little miffed. "But now, thanks to Sandra, I've read them all."

"And you're not furious?"

"Evan could have shown mine to me, I admit, but it's hardly cause for a major argument."

"I'm not talking about Evan!"

"Well, what are you talking about?" By now, exasperation was creeping up on her; part of the reason for her "mental health" semester was to remove herself from Ginger's hysteria.

"What do you think I'm talking about? The entries for the women in our department. You, me, and Sandra. Didn't you read what they wrote about us? They didn't say one good word about any of us!"

"They were hardly flattering to the men either."

"I'm not talking about the men. Excepting Evan. They write about him as if he were God's gift to teaching."

"The students do like him..."

"They like me too. I suppose some of them even like you, Cis. Sandra, that's another case, but she can help bolster ours!"

"What case, Ging?"

"It's blatant sexism! We should file a class action suit against *The Insurgent!*"

At this moment, Cissy saw Evan come into the living room, gym bag in hand. "I don't know, Ging." Evan's eyes immediately perked up upon hearing the last syllable.

"I've checked out all the entries in every department. If my calculator works right, sixty-nine percent of the men's entries can be construed as negative, while eighty-four percent of the women's are negative."

"I don't know that a fifteen-percent difference is a basis for a lawsuit." Cissy was not going to involve herself in such a ludicrous scheme — right before tenure — even if Ginger pursued it.

"It's not only that. I've also rated the entries on degree of negativity, and the women's negative entries are much more damaging than the average man's negative entry."

Cissy couldn't believe she was hearing this. "Wouldn't you say that's a little subjective?"

"I would not," Ginger stated forcefully.

"Why don't you get Evan's opinion on this?" she said, motioning him toward the phone. "Here, I'll put him on," she said, handing the receiver to him before Ginger could protest. Fortunately, he didn't refuse it.

❦

Later that afternoon Evan and Cissy lay in bed, after Evan had spent some forty-five minutes trying to talk Ginger out of her litigiousness.

"She must have been on coke," he concluded.

"I don't care what, if any, drug Ginger was on. She's a pain in the neck. And even if it's unrealistic, I want to escape from all pain and unpleasantness this semester."

Cissy looked around the bedroom: crumbling plaster, chipped paint, windows that didn't open properly, uneven floor boards. Perhaps Irv could have the paint and plaster redone, but it would only be cosmetic. She had lived in the ramshackle house forever, it seemed, and had tired of it. The only move she'd made since coming to Madison was vertical, from downstairs to up, when Irv, Roz, and Juan had moved out.

"Oh, do that some more," she cooed, when Evan stopped caressing her left breast. From her left he went to her right, then nibbled his way up to her neck, licked strands of her long blonde hair. Cissy sighed, closed her eyes, then felt his mouth move downward, stimulating her. She did an involuntary pelvic thrust. "Ev, I can't take it any more."

"But you only had one orgasm."

"One longgg, mull-tiple one."

"Then what's wrong with another longgg, mull-tiple one?"

"It was so intense, I can't take another one. But that doesn't mean you shouldn't." She reached out to touch him.

"I already did."

Cissy opened her eyes, Evan rolled over, and she saw the evidence on the sheet. "Oh."

"Don't worry. With you it's so easy. I just lost control."

Evan cuddled up on the pillow next to her. She began to run her hand through his blond mane of tousled hair, then felt the remnants of styling gel on it and stopped, preferring it without the gel.

The late afternoon sun made a cameo appearance, bathing them in it briefly. Cissy felt his hand try to wiggle its way out from under and accommodated him. "After you get tenure, let's both take a leave and spend the semester in bed," he said.

"Sounds fine. Though preferably not a bed in this apartment."

"Come on. You're reliving the sixties you missed and you know you love it."

Until she'd moved to Willy Street, Cissy had never known exactly what she'd missed, but knew she was loving it now. With Evan, she'd even begun to smoke marijuana and now swore by it as an aphrodisiac.

"Yes, I love it. But I think I'd love it more on the west side. This year will be my sixth year in this dump, and I'm ready to go up in the world, if, that is..."

"...you get tenure." Evan had a rolling horizon contract as an instructor with *de facto* tenure.

"But at least the rent is cheap and I've been able to save."

"So you can buy a house on the east side."

"West side."

"Off the Isthmus, no way. The east side is cheaper. You know that, Cissy."

"West."

She knew they were playing a game and was content enough for the moment. She stroked Evan's chest with her finger, hoping he'd put a ring on it some day.

# 6

"Are you sure you boys eat enough at home?" Vonda Isaacson asked over dinner. The table easily held eight; she and her husband Sumner, plus Juan and Pepper, were spaced amply away from each other, as though physical contact at the table were verboten.

Juan looked at Pepper, then quickly assured his "mother-in-law" that they did.

"You're both thin, and, you," she said, piercing Juan with her green eyes, "really don't seem to eat much at all."

Juan wanted to shrink under the table. "I'll have another helping of fruit salad," he said, to pacify her. He'd mastered, so he'd thought, the art of eating little food undetected, but Vonda's watchful eye had caught him.

"Juan eats enough, Mom," Pepper said. "It was a wonderful meal. But after all, you wouldn't want us to get zaftig, would you?"

"Only women get zaftig," Sumner put in peremptorily.

"Your father's right, but only regarding the use of the word, which is used for women."

"I know, Mom."

"In any case, I'm sure you boys will never have to worry about that. Will they, Sumner?"

"No one in my family ever tended toward obesity." Sumner spoke from the far end of the table, barely making eye contact with them.

"Not in mine either," Vonda retorted, as if already on the defensive.

Juan finished his fruit salad as slowly as possible; perhaps the trick with Vonda was never to leave your plate empty. All he really wanted to do was go outside and smoke a cigarette.

"But you're the one whose uncles never married," Sumner said.

"My great uncles," she corrected. "Ira and Izzy."

"What's that got to do with anything?" Pepper asked, grabbing another slice of his mother's nut bread. Juan noticed Sumner ladling himself some more vichyssoise from the silver tureen. Didn't these people ever finish eating?

Juan watched Vonda flash a clinical glance at her husband. "Your father, in his infinite wisdom, determined that if it's ever proven that homosexuality is genetic, yours came from my side of the family."

"Jesus Christ, Dad. Don't you have better things to think about?"

"I read and think a lot." Sumner's tone was defiant.

It amazed Juan that they could even talk about the topic, though with Sumner and Vonda the talk rarely remained amiable for long.

"Eleanor Roosevelt was a lesbian," Pepper announced, for only God knew what reason, and all four parental eyes, plus Juan's, fell on him. Juan lifted a slice of kiwi to his mouth, hoping that he wouldn't break out laughing.

"I don't think so, darling." Vonda set down her water glass and fixed her eyes on her son.

"Bisexual, then. It's been in the gay press. A major biography is being written about her and when it hits the mainstream press, you'll see." Pepper winked at Juan.

"I've heard it myself," Sumner said gruffly. "Some people I knew thought the Roosevelts were Communists. Communism, homosexuality, it all goes together."

Juan assumed he was joking, or making fun of "some people." Pepper knitted his brow and shook his head. Vonda asked, "What do you think of lesbian romance novels?"

"I can see it now," Sumner said with derision, *"Eleanor's New Deal: A Bedtime Story.* A definite bestseller."

Vonda bristled. "Just be quiet, Sumner. I've never yet come across a novel like the one I'm thinking about. If anyone would know about lesbian romance novels, I just thought Pepper or Juan might."

"Never read one, Mom."

"Me neither," Juan echoed.

"You could go downtown to A Room of One's Own and see what they have," Pepper suggested. "Or you might be better off just asking a lesbian."

"I don't know any."

"Let me think. I bet you do." Pepper stoked up his smile. Juan looked on, enjoying Pepper's easy banter with his parents. "Remember Miss Nilsson, my high school calculus teacher? Well, she lived with Miss Goddard, the girls' phys ed teacher. For *many* years."

"I met the woman exactly once."

"She died anyway, I think."

"I was just thinking about a lesbian subplot in my next novel. Something to... let's say, revitalize the genre. I'm not one to take the same formula and duplicate it over and over again. That bores *me.*" She placed her cloth napkin back in its gold ring.

"Your novels are far out enough as it is," Sumner said.

"Setting my last one in Madison was not far out. Madison is a perfect setting for a novel. My new one is going to have an academic setting."

"Oh, you're going to mine Dad's experiences in Museum Studies?"

"Pep-per." Vonda's voice was a distinct reprimand. Juan figured it had to do with Sumner's assault of Cissy her first year in Madison.

"I'm sure there must have been all kinds of torrid affairs in that department over the years. That's all I meant, Mom."

"Don't bet on that," said Sumner, who had finally finished eating. "It was a very staid department."

Pepper rolled his eyes at Juan. Juan dug two more pieces of kiwi out of the bowl, perhaps having fallen into the proper eating rhythm at the Isaacsons' table, now that the meal was apparently over. It was the first time he'd gotten up the nerve to eat a meal there.

"Truthfully, Mom, if you've sold straight romance novels, I don't think you'd suddenly want to add lesbians. Most straight people don't want to read about them, especially if you're going to let them have sex."

"Or about gay men either," added Juan, surprising himself that he said the word in front of Pepper's parents.

"Some people do like to read about lesbians having sex," said Sumner. Juan couldn't tell if he was playing a sort of devil's advocate or if he really was a sexist creep.

"If I do it, it won't be a pornographic fantasy for men like you." Her tone pungent, Vonda glared down the long table at him.

Pepper shifted his glance from his father to his mother. "I think, Mom, you'd better leave lesbian romances to the lesbians, unless you're planning a later-life change in sexual orientation."

"Mid-life, Pepper. Mid-life."

"We hardly have sex anyway," said Sumner. "So you might as well give it a try." Juan had no idea how to interpret these words.

"Sumner, I can't believe you said that in front of the boys." This time Vonda's look of ire was unabated.

"Everyone here knows everything else," Sumner volleyed, now doubtless referring to the sexual assault, which had been reported in the newspapers.

"No you don't," Pepper piped up. "You don't know anything about Juan's and my sex life."

Now Juan began to panic; Pepper had toyed enough. He trusted that the Isaacsons' intellectual curiosity didn't extend that far.

❦

They reached their basement apartment, where all was silent upstairs. Pepper pleaded exhaustion and headed to the bedroom soon after. Juan didn't have to drive cab until the following evening, and decided to stay up to watch the local news. Even the headline stories were boring: It rained too much and the farmers couldn't harvest, it rained too little and there was nothing to harvest. Unless there was a murder or an election — and in Madison there were more of the latter than the former — agriculture dominated the news half the year.

Sluggishly, he got up and and walked around to the kitchen cabinets.

Even after a year he had still not got used to what were for him the luxuries in the kitchen: microwave, cast-iron double sinks, garbage disposal, dishwasher, breakfast bar with leather padded stools. He quietly opened a door, took out a bag of potato chips, and polished it off in a few handsful. Potato chips — all chips, for Juan — were designer junk food and hard to resist. After brushing the crumbs and wiping the grease off his hands, he removed a bag of tortilla chips and tore it open. He dipped the first third in hot salsa from the refrigerator, then consumed the remainder dry, the better to eat faster. The contents of the cupboards on display, he contemplated them, decided on the peanut jar, and tipped it to his mouth until his cheeks bulged. Then a pause for chewing. Hmmm. What else looked good? In the back he found a stale, nearly empty bag of Cheez-its, which he poured down, mixing them with the peanuts. Next to it stood a row of Wheat-Thin crackers, promptly devoured.

Where to next? He scoured more cupboards and located a bag of pre-buttered popcorn. Putting on the stove fan as background noise, Juan placed the popcorn in the microwave. From the refrigerator, he extracted a hunk of cheese, set it on the inlaid cutting board of the tiled counter, and reached for a few more peanuts as the corn started to pop. Within a minute the peanut jar was empty and he rolled it up inside the potato and tortilla chips bags and deposited them all inconspicuously inside the bottom of the garbage container. Tomorrow he'd replenish them before Pepper noticed. The popcorn bag filled to near bursting and he took it out just before the microwave could ping. He sliced off several pieces of the Swiss cheese to eat, then poured the popcorn into a large bowl. It disappeared within a few minutes.

Back at the refrigerator, he stuck his hand in an olive jar and stuffed a dozen or so into his mouth. Then a few dilled Brussels sprouts, and several tasty, marinated artichoke hearts dripping in oil. He wiped his hands on a paper towel, turned the stove fan off and scoured the cabinets mindlessly. Tofu burger mix might be worth a try. He plunged his hand in and brought it to his mouth; not that bad. Next to it rested Pepper's matzo meal, less tasty, but at this point Juan didn't care. Before he knew it, the entire box was gone. He tossed the containers into the trash and washed down the mazto mix with a glass of water. Little food that could be quickly eaten remained, except the cheese. He ate the slices he'd cut, then munched on a gargantuan hunk, which slowed him down. He sliced off the tooth-marked end of the cheese, ate these scraps too, and after a little more water, he opened the freezer. A container of frozen yogurt leapt out at him and he ate until his throat could no longer take the cold. His stomach began to ache as he opened the refrigerator door. His hand went for the butter and he broke off half of the stick. One greasy handful sufficed; at this point he barely tasted it. He closed the refrigerator door, and returned to the cabinets. Nothing tempting remained on top, so he opened the bottom ones and found a bag of little-used sugar. He stuck his hand in and the sugar clung to the butter still on it. Taking the bag in his hand, he poured the sugar directly into his mouth. When he'd had enough, he put the sugar and cheese back.

The kitchen intact, he headed to the bathroom and washed the sugar-and-butter mix from his hands, then went back to the living room and lay down on the sofa. He thought of Vonda's dinner, which seemed to have been days ago. Restless, he again turned on the television to take his mind off his binge and watched it in a blur. Then he rolled on his back, stared at the ceiling and patted his stomach gently. He knew he had a day or two before the fat would manifest itself, but... Now, while Pepper slept, was a good time. If he could manage to lift his bulk off the sofa.

He made his way sluggishly to the bathroom, a mild stomachache having set in, and quietly closed the door. As a precautionary measure for background noise, he turned on the shower, then took off his belt, and knelt before the toilet. Mere placement of the belt against his neck triggered the desired gag reaction. He felt the food begin to come up and removed the belt. Poised over the toilet bowl, he began to vomit. And vomited and vomited.

Once finished, he rinsed his mouth out with water, flushed the toilet, wiped off the edge of the toilet bowl with a wet rag, forced himself to tolerate thirty seconds of Listerine, then sprayed the room and the toilet with Lysol. He brushed his teeth vigorously and gargled with warm water in hopes of further eradicating vestigial vomit stench. A quick look in the mirror told him that he'd lost weight in the face, which he didn't know whether he liked or not. But lost weight was lost weight, and that was good. He ran his hand over his dark crew cut, and returned to the kitchen, which bore no trace that anything had transpired there.

He decided to take another breather in front of the TV before joining Pepper in bed, and felt an infusion of relief, a sense of lightness in his body, as he lay down on the sofa. Agriculture, sports, he didn't care what he watched.

# 7

Roz plodded *au naturel* down the stairs through the atrium in the southeast corner of the house, which offered natural light to go with her all-natural look. Though by now, any natural light was far gone. In fact, Roz didn't even know if the sun had shone this afternoon. She'd gone to the Rape Crisis Center, Womynspace, then to the burr oak this morning, and felt so good about her acomplishments that she'd decided to lock herself in this afternoon, ponder her conversation with Irv tonight, and take a nice long nap while Dayne was in Juan's hands.

Irv sat consuming *The Capital Times* in the living room, the arch of which led into the dining room, which in turn led to the kitchen and breakfast nook. She passed by him to make coffee. The coffeemaker was programmed to prepare her a nice strong pot of Costa Rican roast every morning at nine-thirty, but she'd forgotten to program it for her afternoon nap. She poured in the water and the coffee she'd ground and ambled back toward Irv.

"Women professors at UW earn less than their male counterparts," he announced what he'd evidently been reading.

"I could have told you that. In addition to the fact that fewer of them get tenure. Did Cissy ever call you back?"

"Cissy?"

"You know. She called you a couple weeks ago asking if

you'd ever had a client in a tenure case against UW."

"Oh, that," Irv said, laying the thin *Cap Times* aside. "I think she'll call on her own if she needs to. And she doesn't need you to put her up to calling."

"How did you know it was me?"

"Cissy doesn't leap at the hint of any crisis like you do."

"Pepper and Juan will be watching Dayne for us tonight, won't they?"

"He's down there now, but I didn't ask them about tonight."

"You didn't?" Roz sighed to herself, trying to avoid any outward manifestation of annoyance. Since Irv's anarchic law practice was mainly a hobby, one would think he'd have time to do a few things for *her*. She didn't see why she should revolve her important volunteer work — and occasional naps — around his very open, empty schedule. "OK. I'll go ask the boys," she said with forced cheeriness.

"You're not getting dressed?"

"I dressed for the burr oak today, what you do want?" she snapped, impatience getting the better of her. "And why bother for Juan and Pepper? They've seen it all before."

"But do they want to?"

The question took her aback. "Two gay men aren't going to view me as a sex object. And it's the most natural thing in the world for Dayne, at his age, to see his mother in the buff."

"Whatever you say." Irv's tone was inscrutable.

"Don't worry. I'll be sure to dress for Ho Chi's."

Downstairs, coffee mug in hand, she asked Juan, who readily agreed. She decided to give him a respite and take Dayne back upstairs.

"I want Daddy!" Dayne screamed, lunging at Juan.

"Your other Daddy..." She almost said "real" daddy; in any case, it wasn't her fault that Irv was sterile and that Dayne, therefore, had two fathers. "...is upstairs. Let's go see him."

She'd prove again to Irv that she wasn't shirking her maternal role, as he'd had the nerve to imply. Her breasts wiggled as she walked up the stairs. Just as well, Dayne had yet to show any curiosity in them, no matter how diligently she'd tried to breastfeed him. Thank God those days were over.

❦

"That's the one I told you about." Roz nodded toward a short, curly-haired woman who barely could be seen above the bar at Ho Chi Minh's. "The one I caught making out with her girlfriend in the Labor Farm office."

"I've seen her in here for years. Actually, I think she's the manager," Irv said, as the waitperson brought their Millers.

"Her? Well, I suppose she has to do something to pay the rent."

"Speaking of Labor Farm...," Irv was saying when the waitperson reappeared and he ordered gumbo.

"Sorry. We just ran out. We have the seaweed soup and..."

"OK, seaweed, then. And, not that they go together, but the Cajun meatloaf too." Ho Chi's had recently expanded to include various ethnic cuisines and more non-vegetarian foods.

"What's the most impure thing you have on the menu?" asked Roz. "I don't mean chemically impure, just something good and greasy."

"For meat-eaters," the waitperson said with a hint of scorn, "we always have brats. And fries. The brats come with sauerkraut too."

"A brat and fries. No kraut."

The waitperson whisked the menus away, leaving them in momentary silence, which Irv broke: "Speaking of Labor Farm... and the city council race. Have you thought more about it?"

"As far as the city council race, you didn't exactly encourage me, not even to bring up the topic again."

"I didn't mean to discourage you." This was an off-white lie. "You're just so overworked."

"I said I'd cut back on volunteer stuff."

"Another thing — person, rather — needs to be mentioned: Dayne."

"I thought we mentioned him." She lit up, inhaled and blew a jet stream of smoke. "Hell, he's got three father figures, counting Pepper, and a mother. I try to breastfeed him and you discourage me. Chain him to the burr oak with me, which, by the way, is a real photo op for saving the tree, and you say no. I give all I can. What more does he need?"

Roz had evidently lined up her arguments. The words wouldn't quite roll off Irv's lips: "A real mother."

"I know what you're thinking. A full-time mother. Can you imagine the kvetching we'd hear from downstairs, if I kept him all to myself? What's wrong with communal parenting? Dayne and I certainly bonded during his breastfeeding."

Irv had doubts about the breastfeeding, but Roz's breasts

had certainly bonded with everything else possible: the sun, the dining room table, her Lifecycle...

"I'm afraid of the strain it puts on Juan and Pepper." Irv stopped, realizing he was veering away from his focus: Roz.

"Juan and Pepper don't have to help any more than they want to." Roz was being logical, yet constantly thwarting his logic. "So if they can't take care of themselves, it's my problem?"

Roz repossessed her Camel while Irv fondled his beard, which he'd just cut to a short, dapper goatee, not about to touch her last remark.

"Oh, so I *am* the problem." More of her smoke assailed Irv and the neighboring tables.

"I didn't say that. No one is the problem. It's a combination of factors, which, when you throw in a race for city council, creates a possible problem."

"It's obvious you don't think I should run. I've never told you..." She thrummed the table with her fingers until it started to rock. "...that I thought of running two years ago, but put it off, since I knew that Dayne was too young. But now I think the situation would be manageable."

Puffing in between every few words, she seemed to have expelled smoke throughout the entire smoking and non-smoking sections before stabbing the butt — and almost the ashtray — to death. Irv didn't even attempt the futile task of trying to wave the smoke away.

"It might be," he said. "I just want us to consider all aspects of it."

"Well, what's it going to take to make you satisfied? A twelve-hour commitment of slavery to motherhood everyday? Hell, we'll be sending Dayne to pre-school next year."

They were going around like rats on a treadmill, getting nowhere, Roz countering or defeating his line of thought at every step, leaving them spinning endlessly.

"And if I'm elected, there would only be the interval between April and fall, when he'd go to pre-school. I never thought I'd hear myself saying this, but if you think we wouldn't have enough help..." Now Roz almost tittered. "...my mother could come to care for Dayne next summer. How's that for some female influence?"

"Your mother?" The thought was frightening. Irv had no stereotypical dislike for Rhoda, but knew well that she was

Roz's prototype.

"It could be for just part of the summer. Wait, better yet, she can come and help out during the campaign. That's probably when I'll be busiest."

Irv noticed the shift in verb tenses, as though her running — if not winning — were a *fait accompli*. On that note, he knocked back his beer, and saw Roz tip hers to her mouth too. "Do you know what you're saying, Roz?"

"Actually, it's a great idea, the more I think about it. We don't visit her that often. And with her heart problems, you know... It would be the perfect idea, a great way to spend time with her and let her really get to know Dayne."

Irv's stomach churned at the thought. "Roz, how long could you stand your mother for? Our last trip there lasted exactly one week, Rhoda woke you up at six every morning, put us on display for every living relative, and planned our itinerary against our wishes. You swore..."

"I know, but this time she'd be on *our* turf. Plus, things have changed. We've both mellowed."

Roz hadn't loosened up one bit, and he doubted that Rhoda had either. "Imagine inviting her for two months and then finding out she's making you crazy after two days."

"I'd be busy, and she'd be taking my place. I wouldn't see that much of her."

Irv said the first thing that came to mind: "But I would."

"You could work as much as you want, see her as little as you want. If worse came to worst, we could always ship her back home."

"Oh? Like a dog in a crate?" he said, but Roz seemed not to hear him.

The first time she'd brought up the council race, she'd already thought it out, and now had evidently explored it even further. There was going to be no easy way of stopping her.

Irv scoured the premises for signs of the waitperson, wishing the food would arrive. His head ached, either from food deprivation or their discussion. Or both. "All right, go ahead and run. I'm sure everything will work out. You have my support."

Roz seemed taken aback. "'Go ahead and run'? So I have your permission? Is that what I need? Don't say things you don't really mean."

"I haven't said..."

"Do you want me to stay home and be a homemaker and mother?" Her fingers hit the table like a drum roll. "Or perhaps I should go back to work. Just because we — excuse me, you — have the financial means for us to live comfortably doesn't mean I should forget what it's like to work for a living."

"Roz." It was all he could utter; a sinking feeling overtook him.

"I'm an independent woman. Or used to be. I see: I've bought into the male power structure, dependent on you and your money. Well, I can put an end to that. I'll go back to the Co-op, then look for a second part-time job. We'll farm Dayne out to daycare as necessary, and pay for it like most working-class families. There, how's that?"

Irv could only groan to himself. He looked out through the door and glimpsed the neighborhood pharmacy across the street. He imagined himself, Roz, and Rhoda all filling tranquilizer prescriptions in order to survive.

"In the evenings, we can get a childsitter. My meager council stipend would at least pay for that. You wouldn't be burdened time- or money-wise."

Roz's willfulness had overpowered him. "Run. I want you to run." He was almost sorry he'd brought the topic up at all. Roz's running or winning could be a strain enough; but having her mother with them... Doing *pro bono* work on an Indian reservation for the coming months gained a sudden appeal. "Run. I'll support you any way I can."

She seemed to ponder this, knuckling the napkin, then picking it up and twisting it. "I'll believe you when I hear that again under calmer circumstances. Let's not talk about it for a week or two, then have this discussion again."

That was the last thing Irv wanted to do. "Please. No. I consider it settled. Run, Roz, run."

"Well, if you insist." She smiled widely, one slightly crooked tooth standing out among the rest.

"I wanna go cab!" Dayne screamed. The first scream had been in delight. This second one was a shrill whine, now that Juan had told him that he couldn't take him along while he drove. At the moment, he was beyond grammar correction.

Pepper was late returning from Amelia's and Juan had to

be at the company lot in fifteen minutes. "Uncle Pepper will be here soon. He'll take you for a ride in his car." Juan had no idea if Pepper would be up to it.

"I wanna go cab," Dayne repeated.

"Here, let's play with your train." They were sitting on the backyard terrace, hemmed in by low clouds. "Let's make the train go choo-choo."

"Rollendert," Dayne uttered.

"What, Dayne?"

He repeated the same three syllables, which Juan now deciphered as "roll in the dirt."

"As soon as we pick all the vegetables, you can roll in the dirt, OK?" He'd have to tend to the vegetables soon.

He went up to Dayne and put his arm around him. Why Dayne was so cranky tonight, he had no idea. Irv and Roz had simply gone to Ho Chi Minh's for an early dinner, though they weren't due back for a half-hour.

"Rollendert," Dayne repeated as he lay down, ready to collide with the cages of two tomato plants if he moved.

"Now, Dayne, let's play with the train on the pier, and try to keep it from falling off the bridge." He pulled Dayne up, led him by the hand, and picked up his train in the other. Dayne stopped, gripped the cage, and yanked off a ripening tomato with his free hand.

Tempted to rebuke him, Juan said, "Give it to *Tío* Juan. I'll put it in the window and we can watch it turn red, little by little, everyday." He set it on a step by the pier. At the pier's end, he got down on his haunches, placed the train in front of Dayne, and put his hands firmly on his shoulders. As he bent his elbow to look at his watch, Dayne promptly gave the train a shove and it veered off into the water. A metal train, it sank, and Dayne pounded his fists angrily on the pier.

Juan heard a car pull into the side driveway. "Come on, Dayne. Let's go see Uncle Pepper."

Dayne sat as if glued to the pier and Juan ended up dragging him. Accidentally or otherwise, Dayne squashed the tomato under his shoe.

Pepper rounded the corner, looking slightly bewildered or amused.

"Where have you been? I called Amelia's, she said you'd left an hour ago." He tried not to let his frustration show.

"I stopped for a drink at the Bull Dog."

Juan refrained from comment on this. After all, Pepper hadn't promised to come straight home, though it was his normal pattern. "Here, take Dayne, will you? I've got to leave right now. Maybe you'd better drive me to the lot, or I'll drive myself, to make sure I get there on time. Roz and Irv should be home in a half-hour or less."

"I want Mommy!"

"No, Dayne. Uncle. You're stuck with your Uncle."

"See, Dayne. I told you Uncle Pepper would take you for a ride in the car."

Pepper shot Juan a quizzical look. "And when you get back, if it's not dark yet, you might want to go scuba diving for his train. It went over the edge of the pier."

"I want Mommy! And my train!" Tears streaked Dayne's face as Juan began to heft him into the car.

"What's this? A tomato on his shoe?"

"Don't ask."

"I'll get a rag and clean it off."

"No. I'll wipe his shoe off on the grass. We've got to hurry. Are you driving me?"

Pepper nodded. "Ah, the joys of unclehood."

"Downright avuncular bliss," Juan muttered cheerfully. Not that it bothered him, but at times like this he felt like Dayne's only parent.

# 8

After the lunch-time rush died down, Beth went to confront her boss, co-owner of Ho Chi's, along with her husband Ron.

"Oh, Beth. Come in." Emily, tall and thin and red-haired, looked up from her paperwork. "Sit down. We had a good crowd today, didn't we?" Beth nodded in the affirmative. "How's school going this semester?"

Beth was tempted to respond, "Same old drag." But to make a good impression, she said, "Fine. Four more semesters, part-time of course, and I'm outta there."

"It's great what you're doing, putting yourself through school with your own money. I don't know what we'll do for a manager when you finish." Emily was old enough to be her mother, at least biologically, but she treated her more or less as an equal. "...I know I don't give out many compliments," Beth heard her saying. "I guess it's just not my nature. But you are, you know, the best manager we've ever had."

The compliment took Beth off guard. "Why, thanks." She only hoped her boss wouldn't retract the statement when she heard what Beth had to say.

"Is there something particular you wanted to talk about? Please don't tell me that we've lost another busperson." Emily let out a small, nervous laugh.

"No, it's not that. It's, well, a question of certain products we have here."

Emily seemed unfazed. "You promised you wouldn't hassle me because of the new meat dishes, as long as you didn't have to prepare or serve them."

A strict vegetarian who was contemplating becoming a vegan, Beth had said exactly that. After all, she had a job to keep. But now... "No, it's not the meat."

"So who's the latest boycott target? Our grapes are politically correct. And we still pay the banana tax at the Co-op because of what's going on in Honduras and Guatemala."

"Oh, the fruit's all fine," Beth responded, doubting that Emily was going to like what she heard. "It's Jesse Helms. The Marlboro Man. See, the Philip Morris Company is a major backer of his re-election campaign. And Philip Morris owns Marlboro, Benson & Hedges, and Merits, for starters." So far Emily, a staunch anti-smoker, hadn't flinched. "But they also own Miller beer and Kraft food products."

"We don't exactly serve Kraft macaroni and cheese dinners."

"I think we're OK on Kraft," Beth said, dispatching with the sarcasm. "It's the beer and the cigarettes. I'd like permission not to order any more of any of these brands."

Emily sat as if dumbstruck, pencil still poised in her hand, as the information began to sink in. "You know we've never tried to push Mad City Suds on anyone." This was Ron's line of beer, which had taken off and made money. His microbrewery had now expanded and had a beer garden on Lake Waubesa. "We've always kept a wide range of beers to suit everyone's taste. I just don't see..."

"I don't see what the difference is between Miller Lite and Bud Light. Or Miller regular and Bud regular." The truth was, Beth indeed couldn't. When she drank, it was usually wine or the hard stuff. "As for cigarettes, well..." Emily had tried having two non-smoking nights a week in the bar. "An idea whose time has come," she had announced. And, soon after, as business plummeted those nights, "An idea whose time has come and gone."

"Marlboro, did you say? And Merits? Oh, dear." It had evidently now sunk all the way in. "And Miller and Miller Lite? We order more of those any other brand."

"I know. Quite a dilemma, wouldn't you say?"

"To say the least."

"I don't have to tell you what an enemy Helms is to lesbians and gay men and people living with AIDS. He was the major backer of a new law that permits restaurants to discriminate in hiring PWAs."

"We certainly don't discriminate here." Irritation crept into Emily's voice, as she made the unnecessary statement.

"Though in fairness to Philip Morris, they've donated money to AIDS research, but still..."

"Beth, this proposed boycott is really a shocker. I'll have to talk this over with Ron, of course."

"I understand. I just needed to inform you and tell you where I stand, sure you'd agree how important this all is."

"Sure, I agree it's important. But putting it into practice? What would we do next? Institute a cigarette-brand check at the door?"

"I just thought I'd plant it in your mind. There's no reason Ho Chi's shouldn't lead the way in Madison on this."

"It would be nice... if we could." Then suddenly switching tone: "Have you finished ordering for next week?"

Beth took this as the rebuke it was meant to be. By Tuesdays she usually had, but this week was an exception. "No, but I will." And, to get even for the rebuke, she added, "Don't let any Dole products in here either. They've been exploiting workers and forcing sterilizations."

"Don't worry," Emily snipped. "I read the Co-op's newsletters too."

"OK. Just makin' sure. But you'll talk to Ron, won'tcha?"

"Yes. But don't expect miracles."

"All right." Beth knew getting it past Ron would be easy; Emily was going to be the problem. And, if she didn't follow her suggestion, Beth no longer knew if she could continue in good conscience working in a job that indirectly harmed so many people. The meat expansion had been bad enough, and did no small amount of abuse to her olfactory sense, not to mention her political principles. "But do whatcha can."

She'd save actual threats for later.

Beth and Verla went to the ACT UP meeting held in a small second-floor room on State Street. A chapter of The AIDS Coalition To Unleash Power had finally been founded in Madison, though the group was small. She and Verla were the only women present, which gave Beth secret satisfaction, as if they were the only women in Madison who cared about fighting AIDS. She knew this wasn't true, but she did know that Emily Skinner-Rosenblatt, who'd been politically correct before Beth was born, hadn't taken long to make up her fascist mind and cross over to the enemy.

A mustached man in a black leather jacket wore a T-shirt boasting a pink triangle and the slogan "SILENCE = DEATH." Living in the most radical neighborhood of students attending a politically correct university, Beth had opted to take Spanish to fulfill her language requirement —before the Sandinista troubles in Nicaragua, not that it was no longer useful. After four semesters she knew enough to understand the shirt worn by a long-haired man that read the linguistic opposite: *"ACCION = VIDA."* Her once frightfully confident language skills had met a roadblock, however, when she'd tried to read the untranslated columns in Spanish in *The Insurgent.*

She was glad to hear that some bureaucrat had signed the necessary papers for continued free condom distribution at STD clinics in the state. This meant she could now bring up her own agenda.

"I'm Beth Yarmolinsky and this is my partner, Verla McSurely," she piped up. "I'm thinkin' about the Philip Morris boycott and what we're doin', or more exactly, what we're not doin', here in Madison." She unhooked her fingers from Verla's and explained briefly.

"Hasn't Philip Morris given money to AIDS?" asked Silence = Death.

"They can certainly find someone else, not so homophobic as Helms, who supports their tobacco subsidies," said an older man. "So there's no reason not to boycott the sons of bitches."

"All gays and lesbians who smoke can help by stopping smoking any brand," said *Acción = Vida.*

"So what do you propose?"

Beth jumped back in on cue: "I'm manager at Ho Chi Minh's. I talked to the owners, proposed they eliminate all Philip Morris brands and Miller beer, and they told me no. It would be a 'financial strain' on their one-time 'politically correct' business. I say bullshit. I say we start with them."

"What exactly do you propose?"

"I'm not quite sure yet. I just think that what had been, up to yesterday, the most progressive, radical bar and restaurant in the city should lead the way."

"We don't want to alienate our friends."

"They support the enemy, they're not our friends any more."

"We shouldn't do anything too radical."

"Then what the fuck are we here for?"

"I've already gone the diplomatic route," Beth said. "What's too radical?"

"Throwin' blood on walls."

"Sounds good to me."

"I think that's a litle extreme," Verla spoke for the first time.

"What's wrong with a plain old-fashioned picket?" asked Silence = Death.

"That's not what ACT UP's about," countered *Acción = Vida*.

"Read you own T-shirt, man. Any kind of action can help."

Beth hadn't envisioned exactly where the discussion would go, but liked where it was going. "The neighborhood people should know what Ho Chi's is supporting. In this case, Helms, AIDSphobia, homophobia, lesbophobia and bigotry in general. An informational picket could be just what we need. You know the near-east side. Most of those people have never crossed a picket line in their life, never will."

After a brief silence, the older man, whose gaunt aspect Beth couldn't help but notice, said, "It sounds just like the right tactic to me. Ho Chi Minh's is our ally in theory. With a little push, they could become our ally in practice."

Various murmurs went up around the room. No one seemed to dissent, at least not audibly.

"What about the Bull Dog and the other gay bars?"

Pro and con, everybody talked at once, except Beth and Verla. The majority wanted to do it, just because Milwaukee — home to Miller — certainly wouldn't. Finally the older man, Aaron, wrested the floor: "I'll talk to the gay bar owners. If we're successful with Ho Chi Minh's, maybe they'll follow the lead. We have the Ho Chi's connection right here."

He looked approvingly at Beth, who beamed, she hoped, without too much self-importance.

# 9

"Vance thinks I'm at the library," Sandra said over the phone.

"I thought you just told me you were," Cissy responded, now confused.

"I'm sorry. I am at the library. I was confused."

Cissy wasn't going to dispute this.

"I've got to get out of here. Vance let me take the car today."

"All right. Fine, Sandra." When Sandra had first asked her if they could get together this afternoon, Cissy had hedged. She was trying to finish the first draft of her latest article, in spite of the hubbub of the Willy Street Fair taking place outside, with one of the performance stages almost next door. The article had been solicited for a book and the deadline was in November. Like Sandra, she probably should have gone to the library today, and she could have just met her there, quickly and easily. But it was obvious that Sandra really did need to talk to someone. "I'll drive over and pick you up, is that OK?"

"Sure. But since you can't drive through the Willy Street Fair, you'll have to go around it, which means taking Ingersoll Street."

"I've been to your house before. I think I can manage that."

"Just give me an idea of when you'll be here." Cissy looked down at her notes despairingly. Maybe she'd need Sandra to return the favor sometime.

"I've only got to get the car out of the ramp." "Ramp" still struck Cissy as an odd Upper Midwesternism for "parking garage." "Fifteen minutes?"

"Great." Though it meant Cissy would have to hurry. Her hair was a mess, it was Sunday, and she hadn't planned on venturing farther than the Willy Street Co-op, safely isolated from the fair.

"Now, you're at 805 Williamson, right?"

"No. It's 1099. At the corner of Ingersoll."

"Oh. I don't know how I got 805 in my head." Cissy didn't either. "I'll be in Vance's Celica. Thanks, Cissy. Bye."

Evan was out of the house, having taken to exercising at SERF on weekends. It was part of his silent combat of the crisis of turning forty. She thought he was in great shape and looked just fine, but if he wanted more muscles, that was fine too. Cissy headed to the bathroom, looked at herself in the mirror and determined: less fine. She hadn't washed her hair, and didn't have time now. The only remedy was to hide it, so she pulled it all back and managed to tie a red scarf over the bulk of it. She scribbled Evan a note and saw that her nails needed a manicure.

Sandra appeared at the door twenty minutes late.

"Sorry. I got lost. I got onto Spaight Street." She pronounced it "spite" instead of "spate." "Then I couldn't find Ingersoll, so, since I knew you were on Willy, I got back on it, parked way down at the other end and walked through the Fair."

"Well, I guess we'll just walk back through it then." So what if her hair was a mess? She'd probably go unnoticed among the dressed-down and oddly attired multitudes.

Their ears were assaulted by the culture stage, a rock band, and music of indeterminate origin. Then they passed by the bubble-man's bubble-mobile spewing bubbles, among the many food, craft and political vendors. The fair finally behind them, Cissy recognized Vance's MENSA bumper sticker, though she was hard-pressed to tell a Celica from a Cadillac. Sandra unlocked it and they got in.

Sandra put the car in gear, loped into second, then third, both with a jolt. Cissy guided her back onto Willy Street on the other side of the Fair. The car died at the first stop light.

"I don't drive much. Especially not a standard shift."

"Where are we going?"

"We're headed east, aren't we? I have two poppyseed muffins I made last night and two cans of mineral water..."

"It's such a nice day..." It was mid-September and Cissy knew there wouldn't be many more of them. "...why don't we stop at a park and sit outside?"

"And have a picnic!" Sandra finished, almost giddily, as though a picnic were excitement akin to riding a giant roller coaster.

"Fine. We're headed toward Olbrich Park, which isn't too far."

Sandra hunched over the wheel. Williamson became Winnebago Street and, without turning, they found themselves on Atwood Avenue. In between stop lights, Sandra lurched into fourth gear and Cissy grabbed the dashboard.

"Don't worry. I've never had a wreck," Sandra said without facing her, concentrating, apparently, on the road. It reminded

Cissy of riding with her grandmother, who was a bad driver when she began at age fifty and had only gotten worse.

Before Cissy knew it, they were approaching the entrance to the park and Sandra turned just in time, veered into the parking lot, stalling the car, miraculously, in a parking place. Olbrich Gardens to their back, across the street, they headed toward the lake and found a picnic table. Sandra removed the cans of mineral water from her gargantuan bag and laid out the two muffins wrapped in paper towels. Thank God, Cissy thought, she hadn't wrapped them in toilet paper.

Cissy got a good look at Sandra for the first time: Bags under her eyes highlighted her face; her hair was gnarled in wild top knot; she wore a shiny, geometric print dress of some synthetic fiber. In short, she looked like an aging beauty queen run amok.

As Sandra continued to fumble in her bag, library books tumbled out and a plastic bottle of prescription medicine rolled to Cissy's side of the picnic table. She restrained an impulse to read the label.

"Oh, that's just my Valium."

"Oh." Cissy had always had a fear of tranquilizers and the like.

"It helps when you're under pressure."

Cissy supposed so. She hoped Evan would serve as her own tranquilizer for the harrowing tenure process. She'd considered getting a therapist, as a matter of form, for tenure year, but had rejected the idea.

"Vance got them for me, from his doctor, with three refills. Then I decided to get some from my own doctor. She gave me ten milligrams, thirty-four tablets, with three refills."

"Sandra, are you sure this is helping you? Valium has a half-life, doesn't it? It stays in your system a long time."

"I suppose it does. I had to take one before I could drive, then I took another when I had my anxiety attack at the library. It must be in me all the time, not that I don't need it constantly."

"Be careful. You can get hooked on those things."

"I know. But I'll never get through tenure any other way."

Cissy ventured one last cautionary remark: "You could really be addicted to those by the time tenure is over."

"Worse things have happened to me." Sandra's expression verged on woebegone.

Cissy didn't doubt her, almost betting that she was referring to her imprisonment in the attic. She munched on her muffin and said, "Sandra, this is really good. I didn't know you were such a baker."

Sandra ignored the compliment and Cissy took in the view of the Capitol, visible across Lake Monona. "I just don't know why I'm going through with it all. I don't think I have a chance."

"Nonsense. If you don't have a chance of getting tenure, I certainly don't," Cissy said, hoping it wasn't true, but, in spite of her accomplishments, believing it was.

Sandra drank from her can of water and set it back on the table. "But everybody likes you, Cissy."

"It's not just a question of 'like'." Cissy swallowed the last bite of her muffin.

"No, but... no one likes Vance."

Blunt but true. "They're judging you, not Vance."

"It rubs off."

Probably true again. Cissy sipped her water, waiting for Sandra to say something. In front of her, two teenagers sat on the rocks by the lake, skipping stones over the water.

"Except for John Rutledge and Nick, I don't think I have a vote in my favor."

"That's ridiculous." Vance, as chair, couldn't vote on his wife's or anyone else's tenure — except in case of a tie, and on Sandra's, probably not even then — and Cissy struggled to come up with an upbeat remark. "Bob Rothschild is very fair-minded."

"Compared to some of them, I suppose."

They both knew that Ginger wasn't. She hated Rickover and, if she had her way, would probably banish both Vance and Sandra from the department. "We all know Ginger has high standards and is very professional. I wouldn't count on her voting against you."

Sandra didn't protest, but the look on her face said everything: She didn't have a chance in hell of getting a vote in her favor from Ginger.

Cissy finished her water and, in the absence of something to say, looked idly around: an interracial couple holding hands across the nearest picnic table, the tricolored sail of a boat on the lake, occasional cumulus clouds above them.

"There's always Blake. He seems very fair," she said, as Sandra wasn't pushing the conversation forward.

"Oh, you don't know, Cissy," Sandra said gravely. She eyed

Cissy above her muffin, took a tentative nibble. "This isn't bad."

"I told you so, Sandra."

"Vance doesn't like anything I cook."

"But what about Blake?"

"Do you think Vance would ever tell me? Secrets, they just seem to spill out of me. Like the Valium. Vance prohibited me from telling anyone about that. But, then again, it just spilled out onto the table. Literally. So I guess I couldn't help that one." Sandra smiled at her own ingenious logic, as though relieved that she now had one less secret to keep.

"At least we have Nick," Sandra went on. "Thank God he's a friend of Vance's."

"With Blake and Rothschild being fair-minded, and Nick and John on your side, see, you do have a good chance of getting the necessary votes." Maybe she'd helped Sandra through her crisis, but it now seemed to Cissy that Sandra had a better chance than she did. And she persisted in her belief that only one of them could possibly be promoted.

Cissy saw that Sandra was rooting vigorously through her bag. "I have to take a Valium for the road. Actually, I think I'd better take two." Sandra popped them as quickly as she'd said it, before Cissy could protest.

She wondered if she herself shouldn't try to wrest the wheel away from her, even if she'd never driven a standard shift in her life.

❧

"I'm at my wit's end. I've had so many conferences with his teacher and principal that I feel like I'm the one on detention," said Anne.

"Tell me again what Todd's done." Todd was Evan and Anne's eleven-year-old son, this their first face-to-face conversation since Evan had moved out. George, the carpenter who had replaced him in Anne's bed, had left for the afternoon.

"Obscenities on the chalkboard. Kicked two girls during recess. Overturned a second grader's lunch plate in the cafeteria. Called his teacher a 'cunt.' *That* word, of all words. Oh, how I hate that word."

Evan stood watching her harvest green peppers before the first frost. He missed their country farmette and having his own garden. Cissy had her herb garden, but it wasn't quite the same. "Where do you think he picked up the obscenities?"

"Kids at school. Where else?" Anne's voice cut like a razor; she showed him her backside and long, cascading brown hair, as though she didn't want to face him. Evan remembered when they'd gardened in the nude, isolated as they were in the country. Today she was clothed. "And don't imply he learned them from George."

"And what did Todd do *this* week?"

She gave him a profile view, now on her knees. "He tried to organize a lunch strike. Then, on Friday, apparently he got drunk on his lunch hour. Simple as that. And now he's suspended for three days."

"At least he's got a budding streak of social activism. I'm sure the cafeteria food is awful. I deduce you stopped packing his lunches." Evan himself had always packed them in the past.

"Yes, I missed just a few days. Just like you did once in a while."

"Where do you think he got the booze?"

"Believe me, not from George." The words were emphatic and the tone defensive. Evan hadn't intended an accusatory question. Neither he nor Anne had ever kept, let alone drunk, liquor on the premises. "He said he got it from the Olson boy. But the Olson boy was not drunk, nor suspended."

"A definite streak of anti-social behavior."

"The principal — Everett, that bastard — had the nerve to ask me if there were problems at home."

Although distressed over his son's acts, Evan enjoyed Anne's discomfort just a wee bit. "Are there problems?"

"You bastard." She threw a pepper at him — not as a gift — and he caught it. He wiped it off on his sleeve and took a bite into it.

"I told Everett — not that it was any of his fucking business — that Todd most certainly had a father figure and that there were no problems at home."

"He has a father too," Evan stated pointedly, wondering if Anne had dropped the words "father figure" on purpose or by accident. "Who sees him as often as our separation agreement allows."

"You know what I meant."

"Todd never had a problem before I left. Separation and divorce are hard on kids." He knew it was particularly difficult for Danielle.

"Oh, really? I didn't know." She now ripped out a plant

that had borne all its fruit for the year and shook dirt from the roots. "Don't you blame me, Evan."

He didn't blame Anne directly, though if anyone, he blamed George. About all George was good with was wood. "He doesn't spank or paddle the kids, does he?"

"The principal?"

"No. Geo... The carpenter."

"What a ridiculous thing to say."

Evan harbored doubts about George's parenting skills, resented the fact that today Todd and Danielle were in George's unofficial custody — whisked away for a ride in the country — and not his, though next weekend he'd have them. "Well, it seems we have a problem on our hands, doesn't it?"

Anne turned around, sat flat on the ground, her hand-woven basket of peppers almost full. "I'm afraid we do. Just don't go assigning blame to anyone."

"I'm not about to." But Todd had never done such things in the past. He'd only been in school four weeks this fall, and now, all this. "I suppose we should take him to a child psychologist."

"Probably so."

"Take him — unless you want me to — tell me how much it is, and I'll send a check." Evan hoped they could avoid nasty financial and custody battles during the divorce, but nothing was auguring well. "I'd better be going. Cissy's expecting me for dinner." Since Anne had mentioned George, he made a point of mentioning Cissy.

"Fine. George will be back soon anyway."

Evan didn't want to run into him and he knew it was mutual. "I'll take some peppers with me."

"Oh, you will?" Anne pretended surprise.

"We both planted the garden in May." It was one of the last things they'd done together. "Unless you're going to give me some of our pot you harvested, I think I'll take some." He knew he had her there.

"All right. Take some. But you could have offered to help now."

"I could have, but you didn't ask. I think I'll take a few tomatoes while I'm at it. Cissy's really into vegetarian cooking."

"Goody for her."

"Let's not start."

"You know where the baskets are. Pick some for me while

you're at it."

"Why don't you put Todd to work in the garden?"

As she didn't respond, Evan turned away, headed toward the porch where the baskets were stored, wondering if they'd manage a more civil conversation ever again.

# 10

*T*hey *made their way to the camp in the swirling snow, crash ing through diagonal drifts as they saw the crimson sky where bombs dropped in the distance, splintering life and edifice in the Republican village that lay beyond chessboard hills.*

Pepper read and reread the sentence that Amelia had written. "Amelia?" he called down the hall.

"Just a minute." The lilting voice emanated from the distance, most likely the basement.

He looked out the window of Amelia's house on Lake Mendota Drive, glad for a change of scenery. Word processing Amelia's biography of her late husband held more interest than any of the other free-lance jobs he'd found.

She appeared a moment later in her gardening attire, strands of long grey hair having escaped their bun. The "garden" was the supply of marijuana carefully tended under grow lights in the basement and was Pepper's source for himself, Evan, and a half-dozen PWAs. Amelia had been a supporter of NORML ever since it existed.

"Amelia. Will you come look at this?" He pulled up a seat next to him at the computer desk, sat down, and pointed to her handwritten text.

"I'm sorry my penmanship gets a little shaky."

"No, it's not that." Though it did get shakier when she'd been smoking. "This whole sentence is more than a little long to start with." Pepper wasn't a professional editor, but he did know how not to write.

"Yes, I suppose it is."

"Please tell me, what in hell is a 'chessboard hill'?"

"I'd call it a metaphor."

"A metaphor written under the influence?" he asked, not totally joking.

"Let's see..." Amelia seemed to ponder an answer, or to reflect on the past. "This part comes straight out of Ned's war diaries." Ned, before coming to Madison and ending up as chair of Museum Studies, had fought in Spain with the Abraham

Lincoln Brigade. "I know there are stylistic lapses in the diaries."

"He really wrote 'chessboard hills'?"

"Yes, he did. I wondered about it myself. I assume he meant hills white with snow and black with destruction."

"I dont know if it's that obvious," Pepper ventured.

"We can change or delete it then."

"And what about 'diagonal drifts'? I don't know if I've ever seen, or know exactly what is meant by, a diagonal snowdrift."

"It was a little flourish of mine. I don't want to sound like Hemingway."

"Don't worry. I don't think you do. So you didn't write this part under the influence?"

"No, I didn't."

That made it even scarier, if it was true. She was seventy-five years old, her mind lucid and, up until now, her prose too.

"I'll save writing under the influence for the commune part, when we often all were."

"Great. I can't wait to read that part." He knew it would be interesting, but only God knew how she'd render the commune and the characters who populated it. Pepper realized that he himself would be one of the "characters."

"I'll be getting to it soon, I hope, since I started with Ned's middle years."

"Well, I think I'd better call it an afternoon. I told Juan I'd be home for an early dinner."

"You're not having dinner at your parents'?"

"It's not a weekly thing." Thank God.

"Use your judgment and if you think so cut the 'diagonal' and the 'chessboard'."

"I think I think so."

"You finish up the paragraph and I'll be right back up. How much can you use?"

"I'll take up to an ounce to distribute, but only on the condition that you don't pay me for extra work this week."

"Since you're now my editor as well as word processor, I think you deserve extra compensation."

"If you insist, but I'll only take it in dope."

Juan went into the bathroom to rid himself of the gigantic afternoon breakfast he'd eaten with Dayne: five pancakes, a dozen or so sausages, three bagels slathered in cream cheese, plus a gooey handful of it for good measure — after Dayne had gone back upstairs. He took the normal clean-up precautions, then went to change his clothes, as if they too bore witness to his behavior. Or disease.

He decided to take refuge back in the bathroom, the only safe, private place in the apartment, as much to get his head together as to doublecheck for any traces of his most recent episode.

He unbuttoned his shirt and looked in the mirror, face-on. Passable. He turned to offer a profile, first sucking in his stomach. That, he said to himself, was what it should look like, remembering its former natural concave shape, recalling when he weighed ninety-seven pounds, at his full height of five feet, eight inches. So what if he'd been an undiagnosed anorexic then?

Next he bloated his stomach. The convex image was gross, sickening, disgusting, but right there in front of him. He let his stomach resume its new shape, still convex, and turned away from the mirror, repulsed.

He distracted himself with thoughts of his driver's license. The last time he'd gotten it renewed, he'd told the truth and his weight was listed as 135. The next time, it was going to say 125, or else.

The moment of reckoning awaited him, as he pulled out the new digital scale — one of the yuppie possessions he found particularly useful — with the weight read-out in tenths of a pound. Yesterday afternoon he had weighed in at 137.2 and hadn't eaten last night. Since he'd rid himself of today's meal, he began to calculate... Hmmm. He should be down at least to 136.7, or with luck, 136.5. His immediate aim was 135.

He took off his Levi's, underwear, shirt and socks, and prepared to step bravely on. Eyes closed at first, he steadied himself on the scale, then looked down: 136.5. Satisfied. He told himself that if he abstained from two more dinners this week, and repeated this afternoon's episode on each following day, he could easily be down to 135 or less by the end of the week. Still on the scale, he thought of sit-ups, dreaded exercise that they were, and told himself that by doing one hundred a day, he might even tighten him stomach muscles. Since Pepper knew of his aversion to exercise, he'd have to do those in secret too. Clothes on, he got down on his knees to check the dial of the scale, making sure it was accurate, trusting his efforts had not been in vain. He placed a finger on the scale, watched it go up, then back down to 0.0.

He told himself that when he got safely below 135 and maintained the weight, he could simply stop all this. He'd have a more than a year to diet himself down, sensibly, to 125, when he renewed his driver's license. Then he'd stop it all and Pepper would never have to know.

※

Pepper made it to the Bull Dog, in spite of Madison's mini-rush hour traffic, in twelve minutes, straight from Amelia's. He calculated by the clock that he was two minutes early. The afternoon bartender worked his way down the bar to him and Pepper ordered a martini, extra dry. The martini came within two minutes and Pepper sat and waited.

A few minutes later, Blake appeared. "Hey, there. Sorry I'm a little late."

"That's OK." The truth was that they'd lost ten precious minutes. "How are you doing?"

"Fine. Rickover scheduled a three-thirty committee meeting and wasted our time until just now. By the time I got to the car... Hell, I could have walked over quicker, but..."

"No problem." Blake sat down, sidled up his thigh to Pepper's, and ordered a glass of burgundy. Pepper was glad he rarely went to bars, as he recognized not one of the fifteen patrons and hoped it was mutual.

"Relax a little," he said to Blake. Pepper was in a hurry, but didn't want Blake to realize it.

"I was going to say the same to you."

"Oh, yeah?" Pepper left it at that, momentarily nervous. How could he have known that when he stopped in innocently at the Bull Dog last week, that he'd find Blake there, proving his hope or suspicion right, and that they'd make a date to meet again a week later? This was just an innocent drink, wasn't it? "Spent the afternoon word-processing and editing. Got a little eye strain at the monitor, I think."

"After a whole day on campus, I'm shot. Two classes to teach, but meetings and consultations with students and colleagues end up taking the whole day."

"I know."

"You do?"

"Well, not first-hand."

"But you know the department, don't you?"

Pepper figured it was time to admit the truth. "So you know. Yeah, my dad used to be chair."

"He did? I didn't know your last name. I only meant that that day on the Square I already recognized you. I'd seen you at the beginning of the semester going into Evan's office."

"Oh. I didn't see you. Well, now we know all about each other."

"Hardly," said Blake.

Yes, sexually, we know nothing, thought Pepper. The truth was that he knew next to nothing personally either, except that Blake was a full professor in Museum Studies.

"I wouldn't mind getting to know more," Blake said, offering the words that Pepper had been hoping to hear, though Pepper was quite capable of offering them on his own. Now they'd have to do the "your place or my place?" routine. And Pepper's place was not a possible venue.

"Neither would I," Pepper said belatedly.

"Come back to my place for another drink?" Pepper saw that Blake's was indeed gone.

"I don't have that much time, but sure," Pepper answered, taking a swig of martini and leaving the rest.

# 11

Roz began the hike downtown and stopped at Willy Street Park to have a cigarette. She eyed the plantings, most of which had finished blooming for the season, and went to sit on the curiosity that passed as a park bench. Ergonomic it was not. It was a rock formation meant to blend in with the land but, to her, looked like an elongated tumor that had swollen up strangely out of the ground. The pieces of colored glass embedded in it gave away any illusion that it might be natural. She could imagine kids running on top of it, falling, and breaking their heads on the part ostensibly meant for sitting. This was one place *not* to bring Dayne, nor let anyone else bring him, to play.

At A Room of One's Own, she purchased a book of color photos of female genitalia. Her old friend Maria, a commune drop-out, had written — photographed, rather — the book, and had tracked Roz down by mail from where she was living in northern California. Maria probably didn't even know that Roz wasn't a lesbian any longer, but what the hell. The book cost a mere fifteen ninety-five. She and Irv could give it a look-over — trusting he'd not have too much interest in other women's genitalia — then pass it on to the young dykes who volunteered at Labor Farm. Beth and... Velva. Yes, that was it. Velva. Maybe it would spice up their sex life. Then again, she thought, remembering the day she'd caught them making out in the sheet, maybe their sex life didn't need any spicing up.

After leaving the store she turned onto State Street, headed toward Steep & Brew to meet Seth, her and Irv's old friend, and not a commune drop-out. She noticed a new sporting goods store here, a new restaurant there, and found herself amid an accidental cacophony of competing street musicians. One was having her hair braided as she played the guitar and sang. A smart woman putting her time to efficient use, Roz mused.

She realized she hadn't been on State Street in ages. Having bypassed Victor Allen's smoke-free coffee shop, two minutes later she was ordering a cup of Brazilian at Steep & Brew, where one could still safely smoke in the confines of the back room, even if it was... well, the smokiest 500-square feet of space in all of Madison. The smoke was almost enough to make her choke sometimes. No doubt Steep & Brew would probably soon be following others' lead, and end up banning smoking too.

Roz stepped into the smoking den, cup in hand. As she'd predicted, she saw no sign of Seth, so she sat down and lit up. She was a little late herself, but leave it to Seth to be a little later.

She felt a hand on her shoulder and started in her chair.

"Wrong table, Roz." Seth and his pony tail came around to face her, his bushy eyebrows arched, and strong, straight teeth displaying a smug sort of smile.

"What do you mean, wrong table? Don't tell me you stopped smoking and are going to make me sit in the front?"

"Roz." The tone oozed mock exasperation. "I'm sitting over there in the corner. I just stepped out of the men's room. You are, you know, some twenty minutes late."

"So are you, usually. I had to buy a book on the way."

"Come over and sit with me." Seth pulled her chair back as she got up, and she followed him to his table.

"As to my city council race," she began, wasting no time, "I need to talk to you. I know you live on the west side, and I'm perfectly aware that the only reason you lost all of your races...

How many was it, three?" Seth nodded. "...was that you're far too radical for the west side. In the sixth district, even the second, you would have been a shoo-in. Tell me everything you did wrong, so that I do it right and get shooed-in." She realized that her words had not come out at all right, but she sat back, essaying a tentative smile, while Seth grinned back at her, apparently amused, or hiding it if he wasn't.

"Roz, I'd like to believe that the only reason I lost was that I live on the west side, but I'm afraid it's not true. I had a chance the first time, when there was no incumbent. Problem was, ten other people had a chance too. I should have gone a little more mainstream, at least during the race, and I would've had a better chance. You have to be careful during races. Then after you win, you can do whatever the hell you want. At least for two years."

"You're certainly not suggesting that I mainstream my act in the sixth district!" Roz put out her Camel and saw Seth begin to roll one of his own. "Not for Labor Farm."

"You could run without any ties to them, you know."

"I guess I could." This hadn't occurred to her. "But I'm really upbeat about running and all I want to do is win."

"Races are taxing."

"I'm ready to be taxed." Roz's adrenalin was flowing; she was on a good political high. Just talking about it made her feel excited.

"Image, Roz. Image is the key. And personality too."

"Personality? I'd think that in the sixth district that politics are a lot more important than personality. Don't tell me that you mean I have to go out and smile at everybody." Roz realized that she was probably glowering at the moment.

"You can frown in private, but only in private. 'Appropriately concerned' is the look you want when someone addresses a problem, but you can't go around with a hard, mean look on your face, even if you have the perfect politics for your district."

Roz didn't focus on the end of the statement, but rather on the "hard, mean look." "Do I really look that way, Seth?" she asked, suddenly distressed.

"You don't naturally, but you can. And sometimes you do."

"Perhaps I'll just have to retrain my facial muscles," she said, aiming for levity and a bright smile. She sipped her coffee and saw that Seth had an empty cup. "Refill for you?"

"I finished one before you got here. This is the refill. Now back to politics..."

"Yeah," Roz said, still concentrating on her smile. "In the sixth district..."

"In any district, you simply have to have the right combination of politics and personality. Not to mention the drive and a little luck."

"You know I have the drive. As to personality, I can smile for the masses if that's what they require." What did he think she was running for, a beauty queen? "As to politics..."

"Before Claypool was elected, there was a Labor Farm councilman, wasn't there?"

"Councilperson," she corrected. "Yes. But do you think it's the changing times? Does Madison change?"

"The times do more than Madison, but..."

"But what?"

"How badly do you really want to be elected? And, before you answer, think about this: You're going to have to be a public person, public official, if you win. Constituents will call you from seven in the morning up until midnight, weekends included."

"What do you think answering machines are for?"

"That's not quite the point. You're going to have to be out in public, in meetings, talking to the press, always careful of your appearance, demeanor and every last word you say. Especially before you win."

"'Before I win'," Roz repeated, savoring the words. "That's right, Seth." She restrained an impulse to hug him from across the table. "I want it bad, Seth, I really want it bad. I *am* going to win."

"How bad do you want it?" he said, eyes shining mischievously.

"Bad, I said. Don't you understand English?" She noticed Seth's brown eyes staring deeply into hers; her smile became a flimsy imitation.

"Irv has to want it too. In my case, I don't think Sunny was all that supportive."

"She wasn't? Well, Irv is." As she spoke, Roz wondered if he really approved of the notion, if she'd actually badgered him into it. She didn't think so. Not that she needed his permission, but she was not about to reveal her lingering doubts to Seth.

"You have to be sure, be a team. Sunny and I weren't a good enough team. She didn't think my west-side constituency was worth having me represent them."

This struck Roz as odd. "She didn't?"

"She didn't say as much. But you can always tell, can't you?"

"Of course. But I can't tell anything from Irv. I mean there's nothing to tell."

"Irv will come around. You work on him a little and I'll do the same. And hey! In the meantime, I'll be part of your team." If Seth's face brightened any more, Roz would have to don her sunglasses.

There was nothing wrong with too much support; Irv would definitely come all the way around. Maybe he didn't want to get her hopes up too much, didn't want to voice the ugly possibility that she could... lose. "I value your advice, Seth."

"I always knew, even back then, that you weren't a lesbian, Roz. Running as a lesbian would be much harder."

Where the hell did this come from? Roz clenched her coffee cup and had to content herself with draining the last few tepid drops.

"How did you know I was straight if I didn't know?" she said, setting the cup down. "And in the sixth district, I don't know that that would be true anyway. But since I'm not a lesbian, it's a moot point, isn't it?"

"Quite moot," Seth said smoothly, eyes alighting on her as well as various other women around the room.

Could it be that he was actually coming on to her? Could his sex life with Sunny be on the wane? Those two had always been oversexed. She supposed it couldn't last forever.

"Yes, moot," she muttered uncertainly. Perhaps she should shove the book of female genitalia in his face to quench his extra-marital longings, if indeed that was what they were. She studied his face briefly, decided she'd overreacted. Seth had always been touchy-feely, hadn't even touched her today, and by now she couldn't even remember what had triggered this line of thought. "I think I'd better be going, Seth. Lots of work to do, you know."

"Oh, I know. I'll be there to help any time. Let's get together again."

"Sure," she said automatically, knowing she could use his help as much as Irv's. But was this help with strings attached? Or was her imagination on overdrive?

Overdrive, she determined, as she stood up. She'd simply have to prop up her best front and hold it in place until the election. When she would win. With or without Irv's help, or Seth's, if need be. She was a strong, independent woman, who didn't need the patriarchy to help her win. Well, except their votes.

The next thing she knew Seth was holding the outside door open for her. A dreary fall rain had begun. At least her meeting with Seth had brightened the general lackluster of the day outside.

"Let's get together again soon, Roz."

"Yeah, sure, whenever," she answered, wondering how much help he could really be. As well as touchy-feely, she also knew that he was the all-talk, little-action type.

"Come to Mommy, Dayne." Roz knelt on the living room floor. "Let's color in the book here."

Dayne was sitting on the floor across the room. Irv and Juan had abandoned him and now chatted *sotto voce* in chairs behind him.

She raised her voice, for the men's benefit, as well as for Dayne's. "We can color the cat, the dog, whatever you want."

Dayne smiled, leapt up, and ran into her arms. Roz pulled back after a few seconds and beheld her son. Dayne looked down at the coloring book and announced, "Gonna paint the cat purple."

"Purple? That's interesting, Dayne."

She watched as he pulled several crayons from the box and decided on a shade that appeared to be magenta. Juan and Irv got up and went into the kitchen.

Dayne colored away, soon combining magenta with gold and silver and producing the likes of a calico suffering from radiation exposure. Within a minute he had finished or gotten bored with the cat. "Very nice," she said, as he held up the art work. On the adjacent page, he next began to color a dog green. Whatever he wanted was fine with her.

Roz beamed to herself. She was feeling good about herself, about everything. She was going to win the election, with Irv, with Dayne, with Seth, and all their support.

Irv and Juan came out of the kitchen, each with a can of Miller — Lite, in Juan's case — in their hands.

"Miller?" she said, aghast, and stood up.

"Yeah, you want one?" said Irv.

"No. It's on the boycott list. Don't you two remember anything?" She swore she'd told them, and explained again.

"Are those the last ones left?"

"I think there's another six pack," Irv answered.

"I'll just take them and give them to the homeless, then."

Irv rolled his eyes dubiously. Juan said, "Getting the homeless drunk on politically incorrect beer?"

"I could just pour them down the drain and we recycle the cans," said Irv.

"Nonsense. The homeless, lots of them recycle cans for a living. I can watch until they finish drinking and then help them get the cans to recycling. And, Juan, I'm not going to get them drunk."

"Standing around watching the homeless drink beer," Juan said. "A great way to spend the day."

"Fuck you, Juan," she murmured.

"Next thing we know," he said, then paused to sip his Lite, "you'll be organizing a bag ladies' support group."

"I don't see why not," she said, simply to counter him. "I don't know any city councilperson who supports rights for the homeless."

"You haven't even filed your nomination papers."

"There's lots of time. Nothing wrong with thinking things out in advance. Right, Irv?" she said, sure of his agreement.

"Of course."

Roz beamed again. "Do you see what Dayne's been doing?" She pointed down to him and the animal coloring book. He had progressed to a rhinoceros, which sported a blue body and was getting the finishing touches on a yellow head.

"What's this, Mommy?"

"That's a rhino," she said. "From Africa. R-I-N-O..." No way was she going to attempt to spell the whole word.

"It's R-H-I-N-O-C...," Juan began.

"Enough, Juan!"

"You're not, I take it, going to teach Dayne creative spelling on purpose," he said, serious and brow furrowed. "It's hard enough to combat what they're doing in the schools."

"All right," she cut him off, considering her own dubious spelling skills. "You, Mr. SPELL, are now my official proofreader for all my campaign literature, as well as Dayne's official spelling tutor in English and Spanish." If Juan wanted to be a human spellchecker, that was his business. "I'll just teach him the important things in life. Environmental preservation, feminist history, politics, and how to win public office."

She looked for some sign of approval from Irv, but only met with an impenetrable gaze.

# 12

A CT UP decided to begin the picket at eleven o'clock, when Ho Chi Minh's opened, targeting the lunch crowd.

Beth arrived at work at ten and, within minutes, two waitpersons and the busperson joined her. It fell on a day when she had bartending duties until one, thus directly controlling the flow of Miller during lunch. None of the other employees knew anything and Beth could play ignorant. While they'd support the cause politically, they might resent their lack of tips. Beth prayed that one day's picketing would do the job on Emily.

Through the corner door and main entrance, she espied Aaron, Silence = Death, *Acción = Vida,* and three others arriving shortly before eleven. Then came Verla, a paper bag over her head, painted as a death mask, as Emily knew her and it was important that she not know Beth was involved. They hoisted their signs: "Jesse Helms is the Marlboro Man"; "Philip Morris Kills"; "Bigotry = Death"; and "Fight Against AIDS on Willy Street." Verla carried the "ACT UP Madison" sign, adorned with pink triangles. The October day was true Native American summer, good for the picketers, and normally, for business.

Beth pretended oblivion when the signs started moving at ten fifty-five.

"Hey, what's this outside?" asked Janelle, one of the waitpersons.

"Looks like we're being picketed," Beth said blithely. "Why don't you go look and see what for?" She remained stationed behind the bar.

Followed by Ed and Alba, Janelle went timidly toward the door. A nice-looking trio, thought Beth: African-American, Latina and gay male, though Ed wasn't "out."

"AIDS!" Janelle exclaimed. The other two hunched behind her and read the signs, seemingly putting the information together. "They have leaflets to pass out too."

They had printed two hundred, explaining in detail their purpose.

"Why are we being picketed because of AIDS?"

"Damned if I know," answered Beth.

"Oh, do I feel like a scab!" Alba said with revulsion.

"You're not a scab. You didn't cross a picket line and you haven't taken anyone's job who's on strike," Beth explained.

"No one's on strike."

Not yet, Beth thought.

"Who'll cross the picket line, I wonder."

"Probably no tips today," said Ed.

"Yeah, them's the breaks," Beth said, feigning annoyance.

"Emily's not gonna like this."

"I don't like this," said Alba. "I'm not working here to support a politically incorrect business."

"I don't like the idea either."

"Screw the idea," Ed whined, "'cause I gotta buy groceries."

"You eat here for free," Beth reminded him. "And you can come to my house for dinner, if you want. And," she added, perhaps maliciously, "you can bring your boyfriend along too."

Ed threw her a shocked glance, tinged with fury. So what if she'd just outed him to Janelle and Alba? If he was so damned cheap as not to support AIDS activism, he deserved to be outed.

"Look, there she is!" screeched Janelle.

Beth saw Emily outside talking to Aaron, who handed her a leaflet, while the others marched back and forth. A man Beth recognized as a regular customer, always in at eleven for his beer and lunch, stood next to Emily. They both entered clutching leaflets.

Staring murderously, Emily marched straight past Beth to her office. The customer shot Beth a perplexed look and sat down at the bar.

"What'll it be?" Beth asked.

"You know what I usually drink," he said, one eye on the pamphlet. "Miller Genuine Draft."

"Well, is that what you want today?" Beth asked in her best saccharine tone.

He pondered the question as Ed, Janelle and Alba looked on from nearby.

"Oh, why don't you give me a Rolling Rock?"

"Today's a very good day to have one." Beth turned around to face the cooler and extracted the green bottle, which she brandished innocently just as Emily came out into the bar.

Beth opened the bottle, served it and took the money. Emily stood with her hands on hips on the other side of the bar. Beth had no choice but to face her. She was eager to see, yet fearful of, her reaction.

"Beth, did you organize this?" Her killer glare hadn't abated one bit.

"No," Beth answered truthfully.

She hadn't organized it. She'd only proposed it.

❦

"Marlboro's gone, but Miller's still here," Beth said to Aaron, calling him from the phone behind the bar the following day. She was alone; Emily's office was locked.

"One out of two, so we've got half the battle won."

"Yeah, but I don't know about the other half." Beth had smelled the beginning of success this morning, when the cigarette distributor removed Philip Morris brands from the machines. The coolers, however, still stocked Miller and it flowed from the taps.

"We'll keep up the pressure till they cave in," Aaron said. Last night they'd agreed to continue the picket until the offending cigarettes and beer were removed.

"So you'll be sending two people over today?"

"I can't. But Ray and Sol said they'd come."

"Verla's got two free hours between lessons if you need her."

"Great. Can I get back to you if I need to?"

Beth recited Ho Chi Minh's public number. "I'll be here till six today. Thanks. Bye."

She turned around and saw Emily casually sitting at one of the tables.

"Oh, you will, will you? I must have arrived right before you. I went to the restroom before going to my office. Then thought I'd sit here and relax a few minutes to prepare for today's masses."

"You eavesdropped," Beth said, angered, as much at herself as at Emily.

"So you lied to me yesterday?"

Beth said nothing for a few seconds. Yesterday's picket had reduced Ho Chi's clientele to a total of three for the lunch "crowd." Infuriated, Emily had sent Ed, Alba and Janelle home early. Ron had arrived, conferred with the picketers and Emily, and had sheepishly ignored Beth. When Emily told her she wouldn't be needed the rest of the day, she'd wavered between elation at the picket's success and anger at her early dismissal.

She knew she'd now compromised herself. "No, I did not organize the picket, like I said."

"Then, do you care to tell me what you have to do with it?"

Beth wasn't going to back down, determined to stand firm on her principles. She explained. The truth.

"We support your position, of course." Emily's veneer was frighteningly calm. "And, as you know, we're willing to compromise. Ron and I talked last night and, as you see, Philip Morris cigarettes are gone. We almost decided to remove the machine. But..." She shrugged her shoulders at the seeming impossibility of this. "As far as Miller goes, it stays, we've decided. I've read your literature. Miller is a popular product, a Wisconsin product, that just happens to have a bad parent company. I don't see what good it would do..."

"Dump it so that Helms loses." Beth broke in, envisioning kegs of Miller flowing down the gutters of Willy Street.

"We're more than prepared to compromise, as I said. Here." She whipped out her checkbook. "Two hundred and fifty dollars made out to the Madison AIDS Support Network, to show we're on your side."

"And then what? Announce it in *The Insurgent?* If you're going to give away the bucks, you should give them to ACT UP."

Emily's glare deepened. "Give it to the group that, if I heard right, is going to continue to picket us?"

Beth didn't know quite what to say in the face of Emily's logic and conciliatory gestures. "I'm sure MASN will appreciate your token gesture, but I don't control ACT UP."

"That may be, but Ron and I have to take control here. As long as they're out there picketing, we don't need a full-time staff of four plus me, not to mention the part-time staff. So you might as well go home today. Ed will take lunch and dinner — not that we'll exactly have a crowd. He's called me three times since I sent him home yesterday.

"As long as the picket goes on, I'll do the cooking and I'll have one of you out here in front. It seems that the same person can tend bar and wait tables, what with our booming business. I've scheduled Alba for tomorrow, Janelle for Thursday, and you can come in on Friday. And if the picket continues, every fourth day after that."

Beth's principles now started to do battle with her finances.

"And for coming in to set up today, I'll pay you for four hours. I don't think we'll need anyone after two. It's the mid-afternoon lull, anyway." Emily tried to fake a smile, as though she had placated Beth.

Beth's blood rose to simmering, her finances shoved into some dim recess of her mind, the fact that she'd counted on being paid for eight hours forgotten. "If we're lucky," she motioned toward the outside, where the picket would soon assemble, "you won't need anyone before or after two!"

"Whatever you think."

"I'm afraid the picketers are going to stay though." She didn't care how many worthy causes Ho Chi's contributed to and felt undeterred by Emily's "compromise." Emboldened, she added, "And if they need an extra body, since I have less than full-time employment here, I might just have to join them."

"I don't see how you can both picket us and work here."

"Neither do I."

"I've got to have a schedule worked out, in case we have more than a customer or two. So will I see you Friday?"

Beth deliberated only briefly. "Why don't you hire a goddamned scab!"

Thank God for Ho Chi Minh's, Roz thought. Right in the neighborhood, and there she could eat meat, smoke and drink, if she wanted to, in a politically correct atmosphere. Unlike some of the newer restaurants nearby, which thought they were PC, but which were really nothing but vegetarian, smoke-free atmospheres for the yuppified. Ho Chi's was right on the way to the Labor Farm office, and Roz had neither the time nor inclination to stop at home and actually prepare lunch.

She rounded the corner and was met with an eerie mask. What was this? It wasn't even close to Halloween. Roz shrugged it off and pulled on the handle to Ho Chi's door.

"If you have a minute, please..." The arm attached to the mask touched hers lightly as she pulled the door half-open.

"What the hell's this?" Roz whirled around. She noticed belatedly that the mask held an "ACT UP Madison" sign with pink triangles. The door behind her banged shut.

"An informational picket," said the voice, a woman's. She handed Roz a leaflet and Roz read it. She'd known about the cigarettes and the beer, but the picket was news to her.

"If you support these causes, we'd appreciate your solidarity," said the voice, remotely familiar. "Though they've gotten rid of the Philip Morris cigarettes since we began the picket."

"Of course I support them, but I've got to eat," Roz blurted out, unprepared for this dilemma.

"There are other places within a block or two."

"Yes, I know. I've lived here forever." Out of the corner of her eye, Roz saw another picketer, who had accosted someone else.

"Thanks for letting me know. I've got to run and should eat. I just have one problem. Request, rather. I like to see the face I'm talking to."

"All right," the woman said, and Roz swore the eerie mask smiled. She took Roz by the arm, led her a few feet away from the main entrance, turned away from the restaurant, and lifted the mask.

"Verna," Roz said, recognizing the other half of the pair she'd caught making out in the sheet.

"Verla."

Verla, Verna, Verva. Thank God she was just plain Roz. "Can you spare a handful of leaflets?"

"Sure." The mask again covering her face, she handed them over.

"Thanks. Got to run."

Roz took off, debating where to go. She'd probably have to settle for the Crystal Corner, have a beer and whatever snacks they had behind the bar.

Wait. If Ho Chi's was carrying Miller, certainly the Crystal was too, as was every bar on the block, which meant she should be boycotting them all.

"Goddamned boycotts," she muttered to herself as she walked off, uncertain where to head.

# 13

"When do you want to face the firing squad, Pankhurst?" Cissy stood, practically at attention, in Vance Rickover's office, and had half a mind to say "now." A swift bullet and it would be over. If his aim were good, she'd save herself six months of agony before being denied tenure. If he missed, then she'd be safe, alive, and have a permanent job.

"Well, Pankhurst?" he barked like a drill sergeant, his looks as scary as his bark. He could have passed for a smallpox or car crash survivor who, in the latter case, had neglected to have reconstructive surgery.

"You need to schedule the date of my tenure lecture *already?* This is three months in advance." She realized just how much she hadn't missed being around Rickover and in FAB. Rickover treated all the faculty, especially the untenured, as if they were recruits in his own personal boot camp.

"Not if you do it at the beginning of next semester. Remember that you're going through the tenure process in one semester, not one year, and you and the department have no time to waste." Rickover snapped his fingers for emphasis. "I strongly suggest you do it the first week of classes."

"The first week of classes? Everyone knows that week's hell."

"So is tenure. You might as well start off appropriately. Sandra's lecture is scheduled for the first week."

Cissy wondered if this was in fact true, but was not going to agree to the first week. "Why don't we say the second week?" she asked meekly.

Rickover paused a brief moment in thought. "I suppose we could postpone your court martial one week. In any case, after that it will be out of your trembling little hands."

Cissy was accustomed to his rudeness, but she had no comeback to this. Involuntarily, she looked down to see if her hands were trembling. They weren't.

"Anything else, Pankhurst?"

She realized she'd been silent and he'd been waiting for her to speak, a reversal of his usual procedure toward others: "Do not speak unless spoken to." "No, I didn't have anything to talk to you about." She hoped she hadn't emphasized the "you" too much. On second thought, she didn't care.

"Well, I did and I'm done, so, ten-four, Pankhurst."

Outside his office she smiled weakly at Wilhelmina, the departmental secretary, who nodded in sympathy. They both knew from experience that Rickover's bite was as bad as his bark.

"How's Cissy's article progressing?" Ginger asked Evan, her voice low and tone secretive, as if Cissy had had an abortion and she were inquiring about how it had gone.

"Mailed it off and waiting for acceptance." Evan stared fixedly out his office window. Ginger routinely made high drama out of everything and this year she'd elevated it to melodramatic or operatic heights.

"Better hope they accept it, and quick. You know, when you take a semester off right before tenure, they expect more of you. You have to have really produced."

"Cissy's producing," he affirmed, now facing her.

"But women always have a harder time with tenure." Ginger seemed hellbent on pressing some point. "Just look at Sandra."

"Cissy's not Sandra. And with the new chancellor and minority recruitment plan, I don't know if that's true any more."

"Don't be so sure." Ginger, who lived by make-up and clothes, caressed her legs as though probing her pantyhose for wrinkles. "Recruitment and retention are not the same thing. I'd published a book and fifteen articles, had first-rate teaching evaluations, and had to get tenure on my merit alone. If you think it had anything to do with my being a woman or black, think again."

Evan hadn't meant to focus on this touchy point, but he did know that it had nothing to do with her "service" record to the department, the university and the community, as she resolutely refused to do anything but teach and publish.

"If I'd had only half the number of articles, no way would they have given a black woman tenure. Inequity is built into the system. I had to produce more simply because I'm a black woman."

Evan supposed that Ginger was making some sense, though he wished she'd go away. He also wished she had gotten the Fulbright she'd applied for, since then they would have been rid of her for the semester. If her credentials were really so vaunted, why did she constantly have to flaunt them?

"Cissy might get by with having only ten articles. How many did you say she had?"

"I lost track." He was not going to give her further ammunition by letting her know it was less than ten, counting the latest one, to be included in a book. "Quality counts too, Ging."

Ginger snorted, a vein of offense crossing her face. Of course, since she'd published fifteen, she'd think that only quantity counted. He wondered briefly if she'd been snorting something else again.

"At least I didn't have to go though tenure." Evan again peered out the window, where students slinging backpacks crossed the walkway above University Avenue over to Vilas Hall.

"And you might not have gotten it. Look where you are today. Merely an instructor. For life." She said it as though it were solitary confinement. For life.

"Hey, I'm content as I am, Ging."

"But you can never be chair."

"I wouldn't want to be."

Neckline plunging, Ginger tilted in his direction in the swivel chair. At least she wasn't making an effort to show him cleavage. That was reserved only for men who could help her career. "We can't have Rickover forever. And, frankly, I wouldn't mind being chair."

The thought appalled him. If the choice were between himself and Ginger — definitely hypothetical — he just might change his mind about the chairship.

"Ging, didn't you have a class to teach?" He heard a bell ringing in the halls two floors below and noticed just then that she still had on the white gloves she always wore to write on the chalkboard.

"I taught it."

"Yeah, but it wasn't supposed to be over until right now."

"I said everything I had to say in twenty-five minutes and let them out, as *they* had nothing to say." She clearly implied it was her students' fault.

Evan thought it better not to comment on this dubious admission. "Well, I do in fifteen minutes. I'm taking them to the Elvehjem." The campus' art museum was a frequent outing for his class on curatorial techniques.

"Just make sure Cissy produces. Crack the whip."

"Jesus Christ, Ging. You sound like Rickover talking about Sandra."

She seemed to debate whether or not to take this as a rebuke. "Maybe I do. But without Vance, Sandra wouldn't stand a chance. Not that she does anyway."

Evan trusted Cissy did, and wondered why Rickover had called her in for a meeting with him.

Ginger marched down the hall, spurned by Evan. She had two hours until her next class, though she had to admit that the time was flying by this morning. She gazed into the open door of the janitor's closet, expecting to find... she didn't know what. But why should the janitor's closet be open? Then she saw the answer down the hall: The "vinegar lady," part of the janitorial staff, was scrubbing down the water fountain with vinegar as part of her cleansing concoction. Ginger briefly considered making conversation with her, but opted against it: It didn't do to be seen chatting with the janitors, even if the old black woman was pleasant in her gruff, yet homey way.

She rounded the corner and smelled smoke coming out from under Blake's door. She stopped in her tracks, saw the fire alarm down the hall, deliberated, then caught herself. Blake's smoking in his disheveled office would probably cause a fire one day that would end up destroying everyone's class notes and research.

She banged on his door and stung her fist from it. Today, perhaps, Blake would appreciate her cleavage. All at once, he swung the door open.

"Blake. Just thought I'd say hello. Oh." In the corner chair sat Sandra. "You have a visitor." This was very interesting.

"Come on in."

Ginger eyed Sandra with suspicion —she was probably trying to curry much-needed favor with Blake— and stepped in hesitantly. "Sandra. What a surprise. *To see you smoking.*"

"Sandra and I decided to have a cigarette in my office," Blake said jovially, and closed the door behind her.

"But Sandra. You stopped."

"I started again." Sandra gave a dim facsimile of a smile. "You know, tenure year. It's getting to me. I can't smoke in my own office or Vance would find out."

"Want one, Ginger?" Blake asked.

She had stopped years ago. "I think two cigarettes in this cubicle are enough. Otherwise we'll all need oxygen masks." She aimed for a jocular tone, then, affecting disapproval, said, "The whole campus will be smoke-free by April, you know." The truth was, she was suddenly dying for a cigarette.

"I'll either have tenure or be dead by then," Sandra said, coming to life, which for Sandra was about as much life as Sunny Von Bulow's. Not only did Sandra's face and wardrobe need makeovers, her whole personality did.

"I'll just have to smoke outside when the time comes." Blake seemed happily resigned.

He was dapper today, always debonair, seemingly single, and never — *never* — talked about his personal life. Ginger bent over, exposing her ample bust.

"Sure you don't want one, Ginger?" His eyes met her face, not her breasts.

"Oh, what the hell?" She daintily removed a Marlboro and let Blake light it for her. She rather liked the taste and, as cleavage exposure obviously didn't work, it wouldn't hurt to let Blake think she valued camaraderie with her smoking colleagues. A loud knock at the door rattled her out of her thoughts.

Blake opened it and in the hallway stood Vance and Nick, gym bags in hand.

"What is this, an opium den?" Rickover snarled. Smoke hovered near the ceiling. Ginger's own cigarette stuck out, unable to be hidden. Ginger's eyes flashed to Sandra; she'd somehow disposed of hers.

"Sandra, if you've been smoking..."

As if playing a perfect catatonic, Sandra neither moved nor spoke.

"And you, Ginger. Since when...?"

"Just fuck off, Vance." The words were out before she realized it.

"We'll see how you do when you're all standing in the parking lot in January at twenty below zero, puffing away. Maybe that'll make you stop, if it doesn't freeze your lungs first."

"It's not until April," Blake corrected.

"We men are off to do some lunchtime calisthenics," Rickover said, and Nick grinned broadly and, Ginger thought, stupidly. At least he always availed himself of the view of her diving décolletage. "I can't believe it's the nineties and you people are in here promoting lung cancer!" Vance went on. "You, Sandra, get to work. And if you think I didn't see the cigarette you stuck into that philodendron, think again."

The long ash on Ginger's cigarette fell onto her high heels. She tried to remember how she'd ended up here, smoking in Blake's office, and wondered where to go next. There was ob-

viously nothing else to explore in the department; maybe she
could go out and work in the sun if they hadn't yet closed
the Union Terrace down for inclement weather. She looked
at her watch, counting down the hours to her... meeting early
this evening. Yes, her WA — Workaholics Anonymous —
meeting.

# 14

Juan was driving on Milwaukee Street past cows, corn and
a barn to his right — a lone bucolic pocket of rural life
right in Madison — when he got the call from his dispatcher.
He turned on East Washington, passed by the drab semi-sub-
urban sprawl and, just beyond East Towne Mall, pulled into
the dealership. He waited a minute for the  passenger to Willy
Street, glanced at the showroom of cars that cost as much as a
small house, and steered around to the side. A man exited from
a garage and approached the cab. His beard was scraggly and
translucent blue eyes sat deep in the handsome face. Juan rolled
down the window; the man resembled a typical Willy Street
resident, but Juan didn't know him.

"Williamson and Baldwin?"

"I'm the one," Juan said brightly.

The passenger got in, and Juan logged the address.

"Car's in the shop for today," the man said, resignation verg-
ing on annoyance.

Juan was glad he didn't have a car of his own, but  glad
Pepper did. "That's a hassle."

"Don't I know."

Juan turned back on East Washington and breezed along,
passing by Wil-Kil Pest Control, with its large neon cockroach
sign, one of his favorites, especially when lit up at night. He
rolled down the window a crack. It was another beautiful October day — certainly one of the last of the season — and fore-
casted to reach eighty degrees.

The passenger studied his watch. Juan swore he'd met or
seen him before, but couldn't place him. "Live on the near-east
side?" he asked, friendly.

"Work there."

"I live there. No longer on Willy Street, though just a few
blocks away. Great neighborhood, huh?"

"I suppose." The man gestured at the houses and businesses
along East Wash. "No atmosphere out here."

"You got that right." Juan stopped the cab at the Milwaukee Street light. Just up ahead stood Red Letter News, which reminded him of Cissy, who had thought for years that it was a *legitimate* newsstand. Then he looked over at Kohl's, and thought of all the gastronomic temptations the supermarket held.

"Though sometimes the near-east side has a little too much atmosphere," the passenger commented, as Juan turned off East Wash a few blocks up.

"I suppose it can." Juan enjoyed talking to people who knew and appreciated the neighborhood. "Everything can be controversial on Willy Street."

"You're telling me."

"Now the radicals are even picketing the radicals at Ho Chi Minh's. That's the last place I ever thought would be targeted."

"Me too."

"Strange times we live in." Juan carried on the bantering, as he turned on Winnebago Street.

"Yeah, you can never keep up with the times, so it seems lately."

"Hell, on Willy Street, I thought the idea was to stay behind the times. As in 1969."

"I guess once it was. Maybe it still is. I don't know."

"But with all this recent stuff going on, who knows? If Ho Chi's politics really aren't what they used to be, maybe they need a little pressure on them to get them back in line."

"So some people think."

"For anyone to picket Ho Chi's, I'm sure they have a really good cause. You know people on the near-east side don't cross picket lines. I definitely won't."

"Well, I'm afraid I'll have to cross it. I own the place."

"Oh."

"Co-own, actually."

Juan stopped the cab at the corner where Ho Chi's was one of four businesses. "That, uh, comes to nine-ten. Sorry about the picket. I was just in there the other day. Before the picket, I mean. Regular customer. I had no idea. I'm sure you don't discriminate or anything..."

"Nine-ten." Ron Skinner-Rosenblatt cut off Juan's babbling, and extended a five, four ones, and a dime pressed on top.

"Thanks." Juan took the money and avoided looking him in the face.

"I'd leave a tip, but, as you can imagine, business is slow these days." The owner got out and gave Juan a wry smile from the front window on the passenger's side.

"Good job, guys!" Juan yelled at the half-dozen picketers before Ron made it to the door.

He had a half-hour for lunch, zoomed home to grab a bite, and parked the cab next to Pepper's car. Rounding to the back, he was about to open the apartment door, when he looked toward the lake and saw Pepper lying on the pier, eyes closed, face down and naked.

Tiptoeing through the garden, he made his way down the terrace to the lake. His first step on the pier roused Pepper, who looked up and shot him a mischievous smile.

"What the hell is this? Did you and Roz form your own private nudists' club or what?"

"Private? Hardly. You're welcome to join. Take off your clothes and join in right now. It's probably the last day it'll be warm enough."

"I'm on my lunch break. You know the sun isn't good for you."

"And neither are alcohol and marijuana. But at least I don't smoke cigarettes."

Juan had to admit he had a point.

"Melanoma at age sixty or lung cancer at fifty, I'll take the former." With this, Pepper rolled over on his back.

Juan resisted the temptation to take off his shirt and throw it over him. "You shouldn't get sun on your crotch," he said, agitated. He didn't even feel comfortable being seen with Pepper nude on the pier and obvious in the bright afternoon, and who could say where Dayne was? "Did you know that men who expose their genitals to the sun have a rate of penile cancer two hundred times higher than those who don't?"

"I read the same article, you hypochondriac. It usually takes years and years of constant exposure for that to happen. So I think I'll expose myself before my body goes to hell."

Juan began to knead his hands and now voiced his other concern: "Dayne probably shouldn't see you out here like this." It was quite enough that Roz was a nudist, but now Pepper? It had been apparent from the beginning that Roz was going to pay him no heed on this issue and he wondered if Pepper would either.

"Jesus. Loosen up. Dayne sees Roz naked all the time and I expect he's seen Irv nude too. They're not uptight, I'm not, so why should you be?"

Juan took umbrage at the "uptightness" remark, but no appropriate retort came to mind. "Look, I've got to eat and run."

"Transporting passengers by ricksha this afternoon?"

It took Juan a second to catch his pun. "Yeah, I thought I'd build up my arm and back muscles." He rolled up his shirt sleeve, made a bicep, looked at it with disdain, and decided it best to keep his own clothes on. All of them. Especially over his stomach.

He spent the late afternoon driving in all directions, from the airport to Middleton, from north of Lake Mendota to Fitchburg. His last fare took him to University Heights, where he routinely got lost or failed to take the quickest way through the labyrinth of hilly streets. He found Frank Lloyd Wright's "Airplane House," one of his few reference points, and made his way out. Conveniently, his last passenger's destination was on East Dayton, near the company lot.

He made the walk home as the sun set. Pepper was still or again on the pier, apparently asleep, and covered by his sleeping bag. The temperature had lowered to the sixties.

Inside Juan changed his clothes, then went back outside to join him. Pepper stirred, indeed having been napping. Juan looked toward the house, which, from their low elevation, soared above the lake.

On the top floor, there were no curtains, and a light was on. Juan noticed a figure in the corner. It moved. He hunched himself up on his elbows.

"Pepper?" Juan put a hand on Pepper's shoulder. "Look. What's that in Irv and Roz's bedroom?"

"That," Pepper said, "looks like Roz. How was your afternoon?" He sat up and rubbed his eyes.

"Fine. And yours?"

"Oh, I played with Dayne, put my clothes back on, came back out here and took a nap."

"What do you mean? You played with Dayne and you hadn't put your clothes back on!?"

"Sorry. Wrong order. I put my clothes back on *first*. 'Played with Dayne,'" he scoffed. "Sexual assault, in case you don't know it, is not genetic. As a matter of fact, it was so warm that I jumped in the water and rescued Dayne's waterlogged train."

"Oh, thanks." Juan tousled Pepper's hair, then looked back up to the house. "Jesus Christ! Roz is naked!"

"Well, she is a nudist. What do you expect? There are no curtains up there, you know." Pepper appeared unfazed by it all.

"Watch this!" Juan pointed upwards. "She's moving into the middle of the window. As plain as day."

"I'd say it's more night than day, Juan-Boy." Pepper at times used the nickname that Roz had given him.

"Yeah, but it's bright up there."

"Well, so it is. I don't see what..."

Juan cut him off: "But this isn't just nudity, which is legal in your own house or, so Roz has told me, outdoors on your own property. This looks like exhibitionism, which isn't legal."

"Calm down. It looks more like she's doing calisthenics than engaging in exhibitionism. In any case, there's a technicality. Exhibitionism is only illegal if you know someone is watching. Same goes for masturbation."

Leave it to Pepper to know such details. He'd probably checked them out as soon as he'd moved back to Madison. Juan threw him an uncertain glance, which he doubted could be seen in the enveloping darkness. "What new perversion is this?"

"It's not a perversion, you pervert," Pepper said with a hint of exasperation, as if having to re-explain to a toddler the use of a toilet versus a sink.

"I just wonder about her sometimes. What the hell has gotten into her? She's thinking of running for city council and she's doing this? Maybe Irv isn't satisfying her enough. Maybe..."

"Maybe you'd better accept the fact that Dayne is getting older, Roz is Roz, and is not going to change, and Dayne will be end up mentally healthier than other kids, with his nudist mother."

Juan barely heard Pepper's words and didn't like the gist of them. "I wonder if Irv knows about this? Maybe we should tell him."

"I'd say it's their own business."

"I guess maybe we shouldn't tell him," Juan realized, then thought again. Maybe someone needed to inform Irv about this. Maybe Irv already knew about it. Maybe Juan himself should confront Roz. "At least she isn't doing anything lewd."

"No, she's not," Pepper agreed emphatically. "But that doesn't mean you and I can't."

"Out here??"

"It's only illegal if we know someone's watching and Roz sure isn't paying attention to us."

"Right, uh, but I don't think so."

# 15

"What do you think of that Goldwomyn woman planning on running for the council seat?" asked Verla.

"Oh, Roz?" Beth felt the new, plaid, pseudo-cushioned seats on the Meadowood bus. The last burst of summer had shattered, the day seemed unreasonably cool and was rainy, and they'd chosen not to make the walk to Labor Farm.

"Yes, her."

"That woman's got balls, that's all I can say. Ovaries, I mean. Frankly, I think she's a little weird." Beth still found it hard to believe Roz Goldwomyn wasn't a lesbian.

"Oh, don't be so harsh on her. She might be an excellent candidate. No one else in Labor Farm wants to run, do they? In any case, you have to admit that politicians are an odd lot in general, don't you think?"

"Maybe. I don't know."

"You have to give her credit for not totally freaking out that day." Verla spoke of her unspeakable embarrassment, echoing Beth's train of thought.

"Yeah, but I still think there's somethin' a little strange about her." Beth looked out the bus window at Ho Chi's with annoyance and longing. The day's picket had yet to mobilize; they'd vowed to continue right up until election day. Alba had quit and Ed had her hours and Beth's. Janelle was threatening to walk out. Beth was glad to see Ho Chi's employment and business picture in shambles, glad to contribute to its demise by picketing it herself. Gay men, lesbians, and others from the neighborhood marched, and no one crossed the lesbians' evening picket line. For the moment, Ho Chi's business was as effectively eliminated as Beth's job.

They got off the bus on Willy Street and rounded the corner to the Labor Farm office. Beth saw lights on inside. Evidently, some diligent volunteer had come in early. They walked in, but saw no one. Then Beth noticed that the light was on in the washroom and heard faint noises emanating from it.

They hung up their coats and Beth waited to see who was the volunteer. As Verla milled around behind her, she read old Labor Farm clippings on one of the many bulletin boards. She'd drunk too much coffee this morning and the urge to use the restroom had crept up on her. She finished reading one clipping, turned to look at the sheet closing off the washroom, and moved on to another bulletin board. Verla had sat at a desk, now going through the Rolodex.

The urge to go was getting stronger. Whoever was behind the curtain was certainly dawdling. Beth pretended to concentrate on another article, but could barely pretend let alone concentrate, so finally she walked over to the white sheet.

"'Scuse me. It's Beth. I gotta go to the toilet." The toilet was enclosed in a small cubicle on the other side of the sink.

"It's just me, Roz. I'm not finished here, but if you want to come in, the toilet is free."

Relieved, Beth pulled the curtain open. She stepped in, looked up, and there stood Roz, naked from the waist up. Beth saw her wide, toothy grin in the mirror.

"I know you're a nudist, but..." Was this some weird way of getting back at her for the day Roz had caught them in the sheet?

"Just my breast exercises," Roz said casually. Beth nodded, scampered past her, and closed the door.

A minute later, she came out, and Roz, still topless, moved aside for her to use the sink. Beth thought she at least would have put her T-shirt back on by now.

"Roz, You didn't think somebody might...?"

"I *knew* who was coming in. I thought a couple of dykes would understand."

So she was getting back at them.

"'Course, I understand, but... What's wrong with your breasts, Roz? They look fine to me." After the words tumbled out, Beth had doubts about how they'd sounded.

"Breastfeeding. Don't ever breastfeed. It makes you sag. Fortunately, I have small tits, otherwise these exercises probably wouldn't even work."

"Breastfeeding? I hadn't thought about it. Wasn't plannin' on it."

"I can at least firm them up. That's what they need, firming."

Beth stared doubtfully at her, trying to avoid eye contact with her breasts.

"Lots of women work their pectorals with weights. Me, I just prefer to do isometrics. I've got so little time to do everything, I figured I could do my exercises here in front of the mirror, and if the phone rang, I could still answer it."

Beth pictured Roz topless on the telephone. "I thought, as a nudist, you were comfortable with your own body."

"I am. But nothing wrong with wanting to improve it. The two aren't incompatible, you know." The tone turned to that of the condescending Roz who got on Beth's nerves.

"I know. I'm liberated."

"Then I don't know how you can be critical of my doing my exercises at work. It's very time-efficient."

"I suppose," Beth said. "Mind if I wash my hands?"

"Not at all." Neither Beth nor Roz had pulled the curtain back, and Beth noticed Verla standing in the main office, observing them with perplexity.

"Oh, by the way, good job on the Ho Chi's picket. Irv and I did like to eat there. We sent money to Helms' opponent, you'll be glad to know."

"Yeah, sure, thanks," Beth muttered, still a little weirded out by Roz's audacity. If Roz and her husband had so much money, Beth should set up a Ho Chi Minh's ex-employees relief fund for herself and Alba and let them contribute to that.

"We have a ton of work here, with the party placing candidates in all the statewide elections this year," Roz went on, as if all were normal. Beth didn't need to be told; Labor Farm had even forced a primary run-off for governor. "There are yard signs, campaign leaflets, press releases to go out," Roz enumerated. "Might as well get to it."

Beth wondered if Roz was going to "get to it" too. She slowly made her way over to the stack of mailings and leaflets, and Verla followed. Beth left the curtain open to see if Roz would close it; she didn't. The next thing Beth saw was Roz cupping her breasts in her hands — checking them for firmness? But now she was displaying them, not in front of the mirror, but, so she deduced, for both her and Verla.

Beth shot her a stunned look. If this was meant to be revenge, Roz was carrying it rather far. Beth didn't doubt that

Roz was having some sort of sexual identity crisis.

At that moment, a goateed man, perhaps fifty, walked into the office and looked straight at Beth and Verla. Then he turned his gaze toward Roz. "Oh, my God!"

Roz scrambled for her T-shirt. "Don't be alarmed, Irv. We women were just comparing sizes. I volunteered to show Beth that hers weren't so small."

How dare she, thought Beth, as the man — her husband? — shot all three of them a skeptical glance.

"Put on some clothes or get out of here! This is one hell of a way to get yourself elected to office. You'll be lucky if the party doesn't sever all ties with you and your candidacy."

"How did you know I was here?" Roz had now picked up her T-shirt and held it in front of her chest.

"Are you coming or staying?"

Roz looked at him, then at her and Verla, as though debating the lesser of evils. Apparently decided, she grabbed her jacket, zipped it up over her breasts, and let the man lead her out of the office, T-shirt dangling in her hand. She didn't glance once at Beth or Verla.

"How could she!? Claim that we were comparing sizes?" Beth demanded.

"I think she must have problems. And, really, her breasts aren't *that* small."

"That's for sure. I mean, that she's got problems. And didn't I just tell you I thought she was weird? And this woman is runnin' for city council!?"

"Stranger things have happened, I suppose."

"Not in the Labor Farm office."

"Oh, yeah? What about us in the sheet?" It was the second time Verla had brought it up this morning, having refused to talk about it before.

"Nudity may be natural, but what we did is just as natural. I'm afraid Roz is screwed up. As well as a pain in the ass."

The scene baffled her, somehow threw her off balance. Her whole life felt out of kilter. She suddenly wished she were out of the office and down at Ho Chi's working as usual.

❦

What remained to do now was the unpleasant task of finding a job. Beth's savings, since her exit from Ho Chi's, had begun to dwindle.

Politically correct jobs were at a premium in Madison, considering the high number who sought them out. Most positions required a college degree or years of activism in the appropriate field. There was always PC Cab, but Beth didn't relish the idea of transporting obnoxious drunks. In any case, her DWI conviction some years ago probably would have nixed that idea, if she hadn't.

She scanned the alternative newspapers. Madison AIDS Support Network needed volunteers, but what she needed now was cold, hard cash.

"Cat-sitter," she suggested to Verla that evening, having brainstormed all afternoon.

"We've already got three more than allowed!" A minute ago Verla had been sultrily sipping tonic water. Now she shot Beth an apoplectic stare.

"Here, look," Beth said, paying but a modicum of heed to Verla's words, and thrust at her the ad she'd composed. "See, it says 'Your House or Mine.' Hell, what's a couple more cats?"

"Food bills."

"I'll just have two rates. One: They supply the food. Two: We do, and of course make a little extra profit."

"Most of our lesbian friends have dogs. Anyway, I think most people count on friends for this. Cats don't need that much attention."

"That's the idea. Give me time to look for something better in the meantime. You got any other ideas?"

"I'm getting a new pupil next week. I know it's not much, but..."

"Great. And maybe by next week I'll get one cat, then two more the next week, and we'll be on our way."

"Yes, to cat chaos, if they stay here, Beth. Just look."

Beth peered at the cats lounging in the living room: Brooklyn, Ladysmith, Miami, Skokie, Wilmette, and Jenifer, the kitten. All were safely desexed but Jen, and all were named for their places of origin, the kitten having come from Jenifer Street, a block away.

"We'd probably have to get some sort of cat insurance," Verla said.

Beth turned up her nose and dismissed the idea. "Maybe I'll just take care of them at their own house. Actually, that's much safer. We won't have to worry so much about the landdykes that way."

The "landdyke" herself was indeed named Barbara Landman. Beth usually called her the "slumdyke," "Big Babs," or "Barbie Doll." Her partner was Kendall Savage, whom Beth called the Savage Slut or Ken Doll.

"They hardly ever come over to fix anything anyway," Verla said.

Which was true, but at least they kept the rent cheap.

"Let's just pray we have no major breakdowns. As long as we send the rent on time, Babs'll keep her fat ass away from here."

"What a way to talk. You'd never let me get away with saying that."

"Yeah, yeah. Well, I can put up my cat signs and see what happens, right? Nothing to lose, as long as Babs doesn't spot one and recognize our phone number. And, even if she does, I won't be sittin' 'em here..."

Verla sighed, as though too lazy even to shrug her shoulders. "I suppose not."

# 16

Caught up in reading Amelia's biography of Ned, Pepper skimmed ahead... While still living on the East Coast, Ned had been caught up in the HUAC hearings, had met Lillian Hellman, and had even known Dashiell Hammett.

"Don't doubt a word of it." Amelia had glided into the room and surprised him, reading over his shoulder.

"Uh, I don't. I just didn't know all these things."

"Neither do most people. That's why I thought a biography should be written. Ned was very modest."

"That's for sure."

"And, no, I myself never met Hammett or Hellman, if that's what you were wondering." Amelia was right; he had been. "If Ned worked behind the scenes, I was as good as cloistered. Though I always had my little projects."

"Marijuana, may I presume?"

"NORML didn't exist back then. African-American musicians in New York were the first to turn me on to it back in the forties. And I did research on the topic. Hemp was an important crop in colonial times; the Declaration of Independence was even drafted on paper made from hemp. But more than a century later, Hearst started fanning the fires with his yellow journalism. It was a racial issue too, often used against blacks who smoked it in the South and committed 'crimes' against whites. It was never even outlawed until the late thirties. But then came World War II and hemp was needed, guess by whom? The US Navy. It was the only natural fiber that could survive in salt water for a long time. There was even a 'Hemp for Victory' program promoted among US farmers, as the international market could no longer supply us during the War. And do you know where marijuana proliferated most abundantly in this country?"

"Wisconsin?" It was a wild, if not illogical guess.

"Right you are. I'd say it's late enough in the afternoon, why don't we indulge in a little of the once-patriotic herb? Wisconsin-grown, at that."

Peppper checked his watch, looked at the computer monitor.

"There's no reason Ned's biography shouldn't be word-processed the same way his life was lived. Ned was turned onto it at the same time I was, even though he never publicly advocated it like I did."

"I'll finish up here." The length of Amelia's monologue had him convinced she'd already been indulging.

"Sorry for the sermonette. I thought you might be interested."

"I am."

"And you won't read any of that in the biography, since it's about him, not me."

"I'll race you. I'll finish this paragraph, you get the dope, and we'll see who's ready first."

❦

"God, if it weren't for you, Amelia, I don't know what I'd do. This is the only, steady decent job I've had back here since leaving the university."

"You're simply just like the rest of us. You want to work on something socially redeeming."

"I guess. And it's not like I'm without company. You can't beat Juan with his Ph.D. and driving a cab for a worker-owned company. *My* Ph.D..." He gave an exaggerated shrug of his shoulders.

"You did what you could. When you came back here you were a lecturer for a year, right? Then taught part-time."

"And then got to finish off the semester for old Reinhardt, who keeled over in the classroom." Indeed, he'd had to continue teaching the class in the same room in which the man had expired.

Then had come the tenure-track job. He'd had his foot halfway — or at least a quarter of the way — in the door. Unfortunately, so did several others who'd taught part-time. Unfortunately for all of them, the Department of Geography had hired a woman from Penn State.

"At least you have your parents," Amelia said. It was a remarkably sane conversation, considering their state of mind. "And your inheritance."

"You mean my 'allowance' from them." Amelia was one of the few who knew of the allowance. "If it were an inheritance, I could do whatever I wanted with it. Not that I can't with the allowance. We both know it's to keep me here in Madison so I don't go off scouting out tenure-track jobs elsewhere."

"Juan wouldn't want to leave Madison anyway." Amelia picked up a roach and put it back down.

"Hell, Juan can hardly be dragged out of the city limits. If he didn't drive cab, he'd probably never even leave the Isthmus."

"With the others from the commune spread out all over the country, *I'm* glad you're here."

"I never should have moved to San Francisco. It makes Madison look a little dull in comparison."

"You just have to make your own fun here and get out of town as often as possible."

The latter suggestion made a certain gear start to grind in Pepper's mind. "Speaking of 'making you own fun,' let's say we smoke another, OK? I'm not as stoned as I thought."

"I never mind a little reliving of our commune years."

After chatting with Amelia for an hour that seemed only half the time, Pepper sped off, pleasantly stoned, to meet Blake again. Much to his disappointment, the previous time had not resulted in carnal knowledge. On the other hand, he was... What was the proper expression? Charmed by, delighted with, enamored of, Blake's personality? A cheap, passing trick Blake was not, though he'd showed every sign of interest in the same carnal knowledge that Pepper himself desired. Blake was the type of man to... fall in love with. Well, he wouldn't exactly let himself do that; maybe it would just be an affair, fleeting or otherwise. Or maybe it would be just a hot time in bed. Maybe they wouldn't be compatible. Maybe Blake would become a sexual addiction. Maybe... Pepper didn't know what, except that he was very stoned, his testosterone was raging, and he was late.

He pulled the Sunbird into the Bull Dog's parking lot, cursing himelf that he hadn't suggested another more discreet location. He might see someone who knew him or Juan, someone he or Juan knew, or, a chance in a thousand, Juan himself.

Hurrying up the stairs, he entered, and there sat Blake at the end of the bar, one of five happy hour patrons. God, how the Bull Dog could be dismal at off hours... What was he doing living in such a small town? But then again, that there were only four other customers was good; the fewer to recognize him. And as long as Blake occupied a stool at the Bull Dog, the Bull Dog could never be dismal.

Pepper jumped up on a bar stool and patted Blake on the knee. "Sorry I'm late. I was working out at Amelia's again, and well, we got a little stoned and I lost track of time."

"No problem. Great to see you. Now we're even, since I was late the last time." Blake laughed lightheartedly and Pepper let himself swim briefly in the version of perfect manhood in front of him: six-feet tall, black hair, strong nose on a perfectly sculpted face, and from all appearances, the lean body of a thirty-year-old, probably not even gym-built. "Martini?"

"Oh, I'm so high, how about just tonic water?" Pepper wanted to remain sexually functional when... or if...

"Tonic water it is." Blake called the bartender by name and ordered it for him. Blake himself was again drinking the house burgundy. The tonic water came and Blake insisted on paying.

"Thanks."

"My pleasure."

Pepper gulped the tonic water, as the marijuana had left his throat parched.

"So you're word-processing the biography of the man who, if he didn't found it, made Museum Studies the department it is today?"

"Yep. He did a lot more too. Abraham Lincoln Brigade. During McCarthyism, probably the most major blight on the state of Wiscosnin, counseled his fellow brigadiers on their testimony before the HUAC, met famous, and probably infamous, people." Stoned as he was, he was no longer sure of details. "Uh, sorry, I got off the track. Ned was a great guy but — now don't take offense — but from what I hear, it's not the department it was in his time."

"No offense taken." Blake now patted Pepper's knee — friendly, sexually, reassuringly? "I'm sure it's not the same as when Ned, Davidine Phipps, your father, and others were there."

"I suppose not." Pepper trusted that they weren't going to dissect the Museum Studies personnel.

"Speaking of getting high, as you were earlier, I thought maybe you'd like to get out of here and get higher. My wine's just about finished, your tonic is too, and I've got more of both at home. Not to mention..."

Not to mention what? Porno videos? Massage oil? Maybe something a little kinky? They hadn't discussed sex and he had no idea what Blake was into. Pepper smiled suggestively before he realized Blake meant marijuana. As if he needed more right now.

"Uh, sure. Sounds great to me." Being anywhere alone with Blake sounded great to Pepper. "I drove here easily enough. If anything, I must be a little less high than I was." Though he didn't know that this was, in fact, true. "So I can follow you to your place with no problem."

"Sounds good to me. Let's go?"

Pepper nodded and saw Blake leave the bartender a generous tip.

He followed Blake down John Nolen Drive, unsure if he'd remember how to get to the condo, stoned. The October day, which had started off sunny, before clouding over, was darkening. At least Daylight Saving Time hadn't ended; otherwise it would now be pitch black. He took a quick glance to the left, dimly making out the Olin Terrace mural facing Lake Monona. He realized he'd swerved out of his lane briefly while glancing at it and would have to keep his eyes on the road and Blake's car. He let himself fantasize about Blake, getting stoned with Blake, having sex with Blake, which they would certainly do this time, wouldn't they?

As they headed down Willy Street, he thought of Juan. Juan was driving tonight, but until what time? Was it eight or was it ten? And Blake didn't even know Juan existed, as far as Pepper knew. Evan wouldn't have told him, would he? But the truth was, at the moment, Pepper didn't care. If he got home late, he had at least a half-dozen perfectly plausible excuses to choose from.

Within fifteen minutes, Blake directed him where to park in the condo's lot. Pepper locked the car door and followed Blake inside.

"Make yourself comfortable." Blake indicated the sofa. "I'll get some more — and better — wine. Tonic for you?" Pepper nodded. "And a little pipeful. Or do you prefer a joint?"

"Either one's fine."

"Just make yourself comfortable. You can take off your jacket for starters."

Pepper removed his jacket and wondered about "finishers." Perhaps Blake was sexually shy. Perhaps Pepper should remove his pants now, to speed things along. No, even stoned as he was, he wasn't quite ready to initiate things this way with Blake. The sofa, however, did look inviting and he experienced an overwhelming urge just to sprawl back. One shouldn't put one's shoes on someone else's sofa, right?

So he took them off, lay back, and waited eagerly for Blake's return, all thoughts of Juan banished from his mind.

# 17

"Snow! I wanna play in snow!" Giving in to Dayne's numerous pleas, Irv bundled him up in his snow suit and mittened his hands. Juan joined them as they took him across the street to Orton Park to romp in the season's first snowfall.

"Look, Daddy! A snowball!" Irv noticed that Juan, as usual, looked up at the cry of "Daddy!"

"Want to throw me the snowball, Dayne?" Irv crouched down to Dayne's level. From ten feet away he aimed and, thankfully, missed.

"Did I tell you Roz's latest idea? To have her mother fly out to take care of Dayne during her campaign." Irv watched Dayne as he rolled in the snow.

"From what I've heard about Rhoda, the very suggestion is proof that Roz might benefit from a long stay at Mendota."

"After her angioplasty, I don't know that Rhoda's up to taking care of anyone but herself." Irv hoped that maybe, with

Juan's support, the two of them could dissuade Roz from the ridiculous notion. In comparison, it made her proposed council run seem the height of sanity.

Juan coughed and spit up phlegm. "My first cold of the season. With you, me, and Pepper, plus Roz when she's available, I'd say Dayne's well looked-after. I don't see that Rhoda's needed for childcare."

Although envious of Juan and Dayne's mutual attraction, Irv knew that Dayne was not lacking in parental figures. He also knew that almost anything or anyone was preferable to Rhoda. He stuck his hands in his pockets, having gone out without gloves. "You're right about Rhoda, but I still say Dayne could still use more of his mother."

"Imagine: Your mother and grandmother here at once. How'd you like that, Dani?" Juan gave the name a Spanish twist and knelt on the ground. Dayne wrapped himself in Juan's arms.

"Yeah, how'd you like that, Dayne?" Irv repeated with his son's correct name, not really talking to him. Perhaps, like Juan, he should be charitable. In the sphere of female care, perhaps his grandmother would be better than his mother. Or maybe he was as crazy as Roz for even thinking that Rhoda would be more help than hindrance.

"Neither of you ever told Rhoda you're not the biological father, did you?" Juan asked, as Dayne tottered away to roll in the snow again.

"No reason to." Rhoda had only seen Dayne three times. At first he had simply looked dark —quite plausible with his Jewish and supposed Armenian blood — but not really Hispanic. But now, the mischievous one-quarter of his Hispanic blood — Juan's Cuban half — was making itself frighteningly pronounced.

"Then maybe she'll never have to know," Juan said.

"Maybe she'll never live to know. She's survived one heart attack and now, this latest operation." Irv saw that Dayne had gotten up, having made an angel in the snow.

Dayne ran back to Juan, as if pointedly ignoring Irv, who studied the two of them side by side. "The second she sees the two of you together, she'll know," he concluded aloud.

"Does it really show that much?" Juan seemed both pleased and surprised. "Do you want me to go into hiding if she comes?"

"I'm afraid it does show." Irv said, as Dayne ran toward the gazebo. "Not so fast!" He suddenly wished he'd brought a hat and gloves. Juan, as usual in winter, had encased himself in apparel suitable for north of the Arctic circle, though winter's official beginning was six weeks away. "Who knows? Maybe Rhoda's health will stop Roz from the council run."

Juan creased the exposed fraction of his brow. "I wouldn't count on that."

"I suppose that was wishful thinking." Irv headed toward the gazebo and Juan followed. "But something's got to give. She's got a husband, a son, and now a mother..."

"I think she's always had one of those."

"Her energies are over-extended: volunteer work, the council race, her family. She... she has no energy left... not even for sex."

Irv saw Dayne climbing the steps of the gazebo. "The first year and a half it was great. Of course, good sex doesn't last forever, not without an effort. The next year and a half was still good. But since then it's been straight downhill. No, not so much downhill, as nonexistent. Especially the last few months. Maybe we need to see a sex therapist."

"I'm sure you two could talk it out."

"No snow!" Dayne yelled from the gazebo.

"Right, no snow inside!" Irv agreed in a loud voice, determined today to play his rightful role as father. "Come on down, Dayne. Careful, or I'll have to come pick you up." He turned back to Juan: "It's icy over there."

"I'll get him."

"I don't even think she admits there's a problem." Irv trudged through the snow, trying to keep up the pace and conversation with Juan. "I've dropped hints. I communicate. But it's like talking either to the Sphinx, or to a magpie that rattles on and doesn't hear a word you say. Roz has her agenda, talks her head off. How could Roz ever be a councilperson? She doesn't listen. Frankly — and I've never said this to anyone before — I think marriage might have more or less ruined it."

He couldn't explore this further with Juan. The main reason they'd married — as opposed to simple cohabitation — was Roz's alternative insemination and his own deep-seated, but remote concern that Juan might one day want to claim parental rights. The marriage had been Roz's idea and he'd consented to it quickly enough when he'd thought of custody.

"You're not thinking of... divorce?" Juan faced him, carrying Dayne, mouthing the last word.

"No, not at all." Irv hadn't meant to imply that their problems were that serious. He looked up at the trees, one hardy specimen of which had yet to shed its dead leaves. The burr oak still stood, having escaped execution, at least until next year.

"That's good." Juan seemed genuinely relieved. They headed away from the gazebo, continuing their diagonal to the park's northeast corner, Juan holding Dayne's hand.

Irv realized he had nothing to fear from Juan. But Rhoda was a different case, and Roz another. "Just because I was once chaste for nine years doesn't mean I want to do it again," he blurted out in frustration, trying to grasp something tangible. Lack of sex, however, was not the major issue.

"You don't have to worry about birth control problems," Juan said, and Irv acknowledged this sore point, to which Juan seemed oblivious.

Anger and confusion commingling in his mind, Irv said, "It's occurred to me — mind you, only *occurred* — that Roz could be involved, or wants to be involved, with another woman. One day I found her exposing her breasts to two women in the Labor Farm office."

At this remark, Juan's eyebrows went up, then down. Irv removed Dayne's hand from Juan's and put it proprietarily in his own. He realized he was jealous, hated his jealousy, hated this conversation he'd initiated.

As Juan was awaiting explanations, Irv clarified: "Her breast exercises, she claimed, though she lied about it at first."

"That's a relief. That must have been what Pepper and I saw her doing in the window last month. But why the window?"

"She can see her reflection in the glass. I must have been in the bathroom, where the mirror is. Don't ask me why, but we have no mirror in the bedrooom, and she says she needs a mirror to check for symmetry."

"I guess that's logical enough. But I don't think you have to worry about another woman. Roz was a lousy dyke in the sexual sense, so she told me. It was truly all, or almost all, political."

"An emotional attachment, then?"

"To a woman? I don't think so. But to a man? I couldn't

really say."

This was the last thing Irv wanted to hear.

"She hasn't given you any signs of anything, any reason to suspect?"

"Nothing more concrete than the Labor Farm episode."

They reached the Gay Liberation statue, on loan to Madison before heading to New York's Christopher Park at Sheridan Square. Juan brushed off the bench between the two standing male figures and the two seated females and swept Dayne up and onto the bench.

"Brrrr!" Dayne uttered, beating his mittens together.

"It's cold, that's for sure," Juan said.

"Brrrroaks!" Dayne exclaimed, and waved his hands in all directions.

"Actually, there's only one burr oak in the park," Irv said to his son, before Juan could. "You know which one Mommy's trying to save."

"Woman doesn't have underwear," Dayne said, slapping the sculpted woman beside him. "Just like Mommy."

"Juan, what have you been telling him?"

"Oh, you know, at the Parks Commission hearings where they voted whether or not to place the statue here, some homophobe got up and said the statue was indecent because one of the women wore no underwear and one of the men had a bulge in his crotch."

"I take it you weren't teaching Dayne all the facts of life."

"No, of course we didn't talk about the bulge, which, if you look at the right angle, you'll see is true. How someone got the notion of no underwear on the woman, I'll never know."

"Mommy doesn't wear nothin'."

"Anything, Dayne. Mommy doesn't wear *anything*." Juan turned to Irv: "Even at three years and seven months, it's not too early to correct his grammar. And only God knows what havoc will be wreaked when they teach him how to spell, if they teach it at all."

"At least if Roz runs for city council, that may keep clothes on her more often."

Irv began to sit down on another part of the bench, felt its wetness, so remained standing.

"I wanna ride the stach-oo," Dayne whined.

Irv flashed a questioning glance and Juan explained. "He likes to ride on the guy's shoulders. The one with the bulge.

I've let him a few times. He gets a kick out of it."

Irv barely heard, his mind still on Roz.

"OK, one last time." Juan hoisted Dayne in his arms and lifted him up from behind onto the figure's shoulders. Irv watched with mild concern as Juan supported Dayne from the back. Dayne put his legs over the statue's shoulders and his arms around its head.

"I'm a cowboy!" Dayne yelled.

"You're sure that thing won't break?" Irv asked, suddenly envisioning having to explain to a public official how his son had broken an expensive work of public art.

"I don't think so. I'm sustaining most of his weight. I keep telling him that every time is the last time. But still, I suppose it's not politically correct."

"Plickly kreck," said Dayne.

# 18

Beth came in the door with mail in her hand. "A personal letter for you." Verla seemed to brighten at the prospect. "From your parents, I'm afraid," she added, and saw all cheer fade from Verla's face.

When Verla had come out to her parents four years ago, they disowned her. But two years later they'd deemed her savable and now wrote regularly, wielding their evangelic words like a machete.

Verla tore it open, unenthusiastic, and skimmed it. "Want to hear a choice part?" she asked, and began to read: "'...condemned to eternal damnation if you keep living with this woman who has led you down this sinful path...' And listen to this: 'And you know you'll never see your little brother or your grandmother in heaven.' I can't take it anymore!"

"I told you, stop accepting their mail. Wait! I know. I'll mark 'Deceased: Return to Sender' on the next one. That oughta shake 'em up."

Verla's eyes narrowed to slits and she bore her eyebrows down at Beth.

"OK. Forget I said that. Just screen out the religion and homophobia."

"Then there'd be nothing left."

"Oh, here's another envelope," Beth said with an ominous tone, noting the return address. Deciding that Verla had had enough unwanted news for the day, she opened it herself. Verla's eyes turned to inquiring ovals. "The landdykes."

"What do they want now?"

"An extra twenty-five bucks because we didn't pay the rent by the fifteenth!" Vague mental calculations had told Beth they could buy groceries for the rest of the month, but she hadn't counted on this. "And, they want us to remove the banner from the porch. Well, just fuck them. I forgot about the late clause in our lease."

"I'm afraid I did too."

Clearly, it was a "bad mail day" for the household.

"If I had money, I'd put a lease out on *them*," Beth said, seeing the meager pleasures of life, if not the necessities, swirling down the drain.

"I think you mean 'contract'."

"I know. I was makin' a pun, or at least tryin'. And tryin' to cheer you up."

"Don't worry about me. I'm fine."

Beth went over and caressed her shoulder. "I wouldn't want one of your parents' letters to upset you and make you fall off the wagon or anything."

"Beth. After more than four years, I'm not going to 'fall off the wagon,' as you put it, just because of a letter from my parents." The tone wavered between amused and vexed.

Beth removed her hand from Verla's shoulder, the better to look her in the eyes. "Have you been to an AA meeting lately? You haven't said a word if you have been."

"Beth." Vexation won out over amusement. "I go when I feel like it. Or rather, when I think I need to. You know that. And what about you? Have you been to classes lately? I haven't heard you say a word about them."

Verla was obviously as vigilant as Beth's mother had been, not without reason.

"Beth, you're not answering."

"All right. I skipped my social gerontology yesterday. Who cares about that anyway?"

"Sociologists, the elderly, and the students in the class, I would think."

"How about two out of three?"

"How about what you call 'precious' tuition money spent on classes? Classes that you don't always go to."

"OK. You made your point. But just 'cause I'm poor, does

that mean I always have to go to class?"

Verla rolled her eyes, and Beth found the reproachful look sexy.

"Things'll be better soon. After all, next month's Hanukkah. And you know what that means."

"Checks."

"You got it. Hanukkah gelt. Too bad you Christians don't have that same tradition."

Thanksgiving day came and the banner remained on their porch: "EATING TURKEY ON THANKSGIVING IS MURDER." At least Thanksgiving dinner was cheaper, if more meager, without a turkey. Beth had been once involved with PETA — People for the Ethical Treatment of Animals — when she'd spent a summer in Washington, D.C., as a self-proclaimed intern in their national office. It was upon her return that she'd urged Emily and Ron to ban all meat from the premises. Now that the Ho Chi's boycott was over, she'd become active in the cause again, the local organ for which was the Alliance for Animals. Fur and turkey were the most obvious and definite no-no's.

Having failed to make a passable latke, Beth was preparing whipped potatoes. Verla worked on the cranberry sauce, made from the Co-op's organically grown berries, which they'd bought and frozen earlier in the fall. For protein and calcium, they had hummus from the Co-op and a cottage cheese salad. And, if that didn't suffice, there was always a big container of yogurt in the refrigerator.

"And now," Verla abandoned the sauce and made a flourish with one arm, "a pumpkin pie!" She pulled it out of the back of the refrigerator and displayed it for Beth.

"Hey, great! But wait. That must have cost money. You didn't go buy it at Kohl's or Sentry, did you?"

"I did not go to a supermarket. I bought it at a bake sale. Probably baked in someone's kitchen right here on the east side."

"I trust the pumpkin was organically grown." Beth moved the cranberries to the table.

"Oh, I'm sure it was," Verla said too quickly. Liking pumpkin pie as she did, Beth wasn't going to quibble if it wasn't.

Dinner laid out on the table, they sat down. Wilmette strolled up to the table and promptly vomited at Verla's feet, as the other cats lolled in the background.

"Not again!" Beth said.

"That's three days in a row."

"He can't be noshing on plants all the time, can he?" All six cats were failed vegetarians, which, Beth supposed, was just as well, as she'd later learned that cats were, essentially, carnivorous, and tofu treats little to their liking. Nonetheless, her feline sextet retained their passion for plant tasting, which routinely made them sick.

"I don't know. We may have to take him to the Petinary."

"You know how much the vet can cost. We won't be able to eat for a week."

Verla stole a look into the living room. "Look. The papyrus is on the floor. Obviously, he tried to drink the water out of the pot, then chomped on the stems."

"I'll go clean up the plant. They're my cats."

"You can do that later. But the vomit at my feet is another matter."

Having had no luck with cat care or finding another job, Beth found herself volunteering more than usual in the Labor Farm office, when not studying or in class. The day after Thanksgiving, she had the luxury of being alone for two hours in the Labor Farm office before — who else? — Roz Goldwomyn breezed in, unscheduled.

"Hi, Beth." Roz took off her coat and revealed an old Earth Day T-shirt underneath. She was half-surprised Roz even remembered her name. "Where's Wilma this morning?"

Wilma? That had been Wilmette's nickname before his sex was discovered. "Oh, you mean Verla?"

"Sorry. You know me and names," Roz said, sitting down and pulling out a sixth district map in front of her. Beth looked on, imagining her plotting election strategy. Roz seemed determined not to meet her eyes. Then, without glancing up, she said, "Sorry about the other day in the office here."

For Roz Goldwomyn to apologize about anything was, in Beth's experience, astonishing. "If that was an apology, I accept it. I'm perfectly comfortable with my breast size, you know."

"It's just that... nudism is perfectly natural to me, and when you and Verla arrived that morning, I suppose I should have put my T-shirt back on when I finished my exercises. And when Irv, who has some hang-ups that some of us don't, came in, I had to explain things somehow. Since I'm running for city council, you know... It isn't easy to keep marital harmony and run for political office."

An idea began to mushroom in Beth's mind. "Hell, any two people both havin' jobs and maintainin' a good relationship at the same time isn't easy. The Ho Chi's picket was sure a strain."

After Helms won the election, the picket had slowly disintegrated. Beth blamed the fifty-four precent of the North Carolina electorate who had voted for him. And the Philip Morris Company, who had contributed to his campaign. And Ho Chi Minh's, who had supported the product of his contributor.

"But it was successful, no?"

"Oh, it kept away almost all of their business." Although business would probably gravitate back in, Ho Chi's politically correct image was justly tarnished, for which Beth was glad.

"Irv and I certainly won't be back, picket or no picket, until something's resolved. I suppose you no longer work there?"

"You suppose right. Couldn't work there and picket it, so I quit on principle. For the sake of the Movement."

"Quite admirable."

Beth could tell that now she was talking Roz Goldwomyn's lingo. "Yeah, but findin' a new job, a socially correct one, is a real bummer."

"Have you tried the Co-op?"

"Yep. Not hiring right now." The truth was that she'd been enthusiastically rejected. "You know, I can volunteer for Women's Transit Authority or dozens of places, but that doesn't pay the bills."

"I guess not."

"You happen to know of anything? Political, social, environmental?" Beth knew little about environmental causes beyond recycling, but she figured it sounded good.

"Not offhand. But I'd be one of the first to find out about anything in the neighborhood that comes up."

"Thanks anyway."

Beth saw that this was as far as the conversation would flow naturally, so she made the leap, having nothing to lose: "Hey, you wouldn't need a campaign manager, treasurer, community liaison person or anything, would you?"

"I should think I can be my own community liaison." Roz now resumed her know-it-all, condescending tone. Then she stopped, as if in thought. "I've hardly considered staffing," she began slowly, pondering if not softening. "I haven't even announced officially. But I should have a staff in order before I announce. What are your credentials?"

Beth recited her community activism and educational background, conveniently omitting, in case Roz needed a treasurer, that she'd flunked Math for Humanists and had a hard time adding double-digit numbers on paper.

"Not bad," Roz said. "I'll need a treasurer and a campaign manager. It would only be temporary, obviously, and these jobs usually don't pay."

"But it could pay maybe a little?" she asked in a tiny voice, hoping to sound financially bereft, or economically deprived by wicked parents.

"We could pay something, I suppose, for a good treasurer. It would be somewhat odd, but perfectly justifiable. I'd have to ask Irv. I've got so much to do. Yes, who knows, you might be just right for the job."

"That'd be great."

"Don't get your hopes up too high. Irv's been my ex-officio manager up until now, but — this is just between you and me — I don't think he's that excited about my running."

Beth hadn't been either, but now saw everything in a brand new light.

"As I said, I can't guarantee anything, but I can get back to you probably by next week."

"That'd be great. I can't get unemployment, since I quit. Principles don't count for shit in the unemployment office."

"I'm sure they don't."

"Hey, but thanks in advance for anything you might be able to do. Verla and me, not to mention our six cats, are just barely scrapin' by."

"Sure thing," Roz said, and paused again. "Yes, maybe I can do something for you."

"I'd really appreciate it."

The truth was, she didn't really want to have to blackmail Roz about her topless episode anyway.

# 19

Juan and Pepper were in their dining area, looking out over greyish Lake Monona, eating turkey and stuffing for lunch, the remains of the holiday dinner. Juan considered Thanksgiving eating habits shocking. People would eat plate after revolting plate, and actually keep all that food in their system. If they all wanted to turn into miniature whales, that was their right, he supposed. He himself had eaten with moderation.

"You know, Madison can be awfully boring," Pepper said out of the blue. "Growing up in Madison's one thing. You've got to grow up somewhere and Madison's better than most places. Living in a commune and going to college here? That can't be beat. But coming back here after graduate school, facing the rest of my life here, having to deal with my parents..."

"There aren't that many troublesome holidays with your parents," Juan said, passing over the rest of Pepper's words. It was easier to focus on holidays — even if they were a problem — than on his other complaints. Thursday they'd had to move up the dinner hour at Rutledge Street, so that Pepper could dash off to his parents' dinner, inflexibly set at four o'clock. Juan had chosen not to go; after his first meal there, there was no way he was going to put himself under scrutiny again at Vonda's table. "At least Christmas won't be a hassle."

"You know they don't really celebrate, but they'll want me there because I live here now, and make me the reason for a celebration."

"But after Christmas you'll be home free. They won't want you there for Hanukkah, will they?"

Pepper frowned and waved this concern away. "You don't understand," he said with unexpected aggressiveness. Then, mellowing his tone: "It's just that I don't want to be in Madison as much as I thought I would."

Juan's heart skipped a beat, his first thought being that Pepper wanted to go off alone. "Of course, Madison's not perfect," he conceded. For Juan, however, the truth was that it almost was.

"You didn't grow up here. You don't have your parents here. It makes a difference."

"I suppose it does." He didn't quite know what Pepper was

aiming at.

"Now don't get me wrong, but, I know that for you Madison is an idyllic little paradise. But after living in San Francisco, on the coast, for me it's just so small, not quite provincial, but... blah."

"There's lots to do here. I don't see what you mean by 'blah'." Juan knew perfectly well that he meant "boring." "Awfully boring," to be specific. "You're just living on the 'Third Coast'."

"What?"

"You know, back in the sixties and early seventies, Madison was called the 'Third Coast' because it was such a hot spot of anti-war radicalism, and so liberated."

"But just what coast is it on?" Pepper asked smugly.

Juan gestured toward the window. "What else? Lake Monona. I suppose Mendota would do too."

Pepper had had these minor crises before. But Juan himself had actually chosen Madison. His family had escaped from Havana to Miami, before his mother died. Then his father had taken him to his native Quebec, where Juan had spent ten years feeling and looking alien. Since coming to Madison, he hadn't wanted to relocate.

"I mean lots of things. Eric and Rick, for one. I thought by leaving San Francisco, I wouldn't have to live in the midst of AIDS. Of course, that was erroneous thinking." Juan's best friend, Eric, had died the year before, as had Rick, a good friend of Pepper's.

"Don't let that get you down so much."

"That's not really even it." Pepper paused over a forkful of stuffing, then put it down on the plate. They both looked out at the big dreary mass of lake, more than at each other. "In Madison, it's like... not living in reality."

Juan jumped in: "We've all heard that before. 'An island surrounded by reality.' 'Madison: 55 square miles, or however many, surrounded by reality.' 'Madison: An Alternative to Reality.'" He could have gone on and on.

"No, that's not exactly what I mean. Go ahead. Light up your cigarette." On edge, Juan lit up. He wondered if he could ever kick what had become his very politically incorrect addiction. Chances were, Madison, being Madison, would end up banning it before he could kick it. Now that might be a reason to move... But smoking helped suppress his appetite and he couldn't envision quitting.

"Madison, after San Francisco, it's... peaceful, safe, inexpensive, manageable," Pepper continued. "But lacking life. Lacking excitement. The only way to live here is to leave frequently and make your own excitement when you're here."

"I never found it that way." Juan had little doubt his words came out defensive. "You've already said that before anyway."

"You know what I mean. Culturally, sure, there are things to do, but fewer. At least after you've been spoiled by a larger city. In the gay community, of course there are lots of opportunities *for a city this size,* but it can't compare."

"Of course it's not New York."

"Or San Francisco."

Juan drew on his ultra-light, and pushed away his unfinished food, planning on having a secret snack later.

"When you met me in the commune, it was different. I spent seventeen years with my parents before I ever escaped to Amelia and Ned's. The commune was great, but I can't live in the past, even if I'm helping Amelia write about it. Madison became the place I had to leave. I did, got my degrees, stayed in San Francisco, then came back and barely used them. I came back because of you.

"But I have to play dutiful son with my parents, who live seven fucking miles away. It's stifling." Pepper's raised voice vented frustration. "They put social demands on me, they don't give anything much back, except my 'allowance.' I feel like a toy of theirs, a marionette whose strings they pull."

Did Pepper merely mean "purse strings"? No, probably a lot more. They simply lived nearby, Pepper was their only child, and they fixated on him. Which was more than Juan could say about his own father. Juan too had no siblings, had never met and didn't want to meet his step-siblings. Instead he'd created his own family in Madison.

"I know, it's a hassle," he sympathized. "They don't really call here that much, though."

"Oh, they call when you're driving, when I'm working at Amelia's, get the answering machine, won't leave a message, then kvetch endlessly about it. There are lots of things you don't know."

Juan ground out his cigarette, trusted the conversation had come to an end, yet wondered what it was that he didn't know.

"I'm serious. I'd like to get out of Madison, like for *us* to get out of Madison. Don't look so startled. I'm not  talking about tomorrow. And you know I want you to go with me wherever I go. I don't mean to spring this on you out of nowhere —not that I never hinted about it before— but it's been creeping up on me. You haven't traveled that much in this country. And there are places I'd like to see, and I can't believe you wouldn't too. Key West, New Orleans. Maine, Montana. Who knows, we might like one of them."

"Maine? Montana?? Sure, and I might like to winter in Greenland. You think Madison's dull and you're talking about Maine and Montana?"

*"Just to visit."* Pepper wiped his mouth clean with a cloth napkin. "New Orleans or Key West might even be livable."

"Key West. Ninety miles from home."

"Back to your roots," Pepper joked. "More or less."

"Yeah, but how would we get by?"

"We'd work. Plus, I have some money stashed away."

Juan assumed Pepper's allowance was adequate; he'd never asked and Pepper had never offered. Sumner and Vonda, by no means rich, had come from mildly monied families.

"I'm sure I could find another job." Juan decided to feign cooperation, though he had no intention of moving and expected this would all come to naught.

"We could start by taking a vacation this winter. "I've done a little research. I'm thinking of one of those all-gay cruises."

The rejoinder was automatic: "We couldn't afford that."

"There are several this winter, in February and March. Leaving out of New Orleans and Miami for the Caribbean, or from San Diego for the Mexican coast. Got a preference?"

"They're not cheap."

"OK, they're not the least inexpensive vacation on earth. But I'll just take you as your birthday present a few months early."

"I suppose I could think about it." He'd have to get off from PC Cab, knew it could be arranged, but would lose income. "You just want to meet all these upscale gay men," he said, aiming for levity.

"I imagine the group would be cosmopolitan. It should be fun. And besides, getting out of here in the winter would be good for both of us. You never take a vacation. All you do is complain about the cold."

Juan couldn't counter the former and didn't feel like arguing about the latter. He supposed a little vacation couldn't hurt;

it might even be enjoyable.

"And now, I think I'll stuff myself with some more stuffing. If you'll pass it back."

Juan passed it back. What was it with the Isaacson family? All they seemed to do was eat, and they never gained a pound. He, on the other hand, swore he could gain weight by osmosis.

Outside it had begun to rain, a bleak late November day. Late October and most of November had been bleak. Perhaps getting out of Madison for a week wasn't such a bad idea after all.

No, but definitely not on a gay cruise, he realized. He could never show himself in a bathing suit around a group of good-looking gay men.

Unless he lost at least ten pounds.

Lying in bed in Blake's condo, Pepper stared at the lights across Lake Monona and located the approximate site of Roz and Irv's house, his and Juan's apartment.

"Someone waiting for you to come home?"

"No. He won't be home for a few more hours."

"Hey, if you feel guilty, we don't have to keep doing this."

"I don't feel guilty." This was untrue. "It's that I just can't stop myself." This was very true. Each of the first three anatomy sessions he'd sworn would be the last. "You're so... good." This was an understatement: Not only were Blake's looks striking; his sexual prowess rivaled or exceeded that of anyone Pepper had ever met.

"It's not just me. It's the combination." Blake ran his finger-nails down Pepper's back, while he smoked with the other hand. Every single thing the man did was erotic, even smok-ing cigarettes, which Pepper had never liked. Though it seemed to be his destiny to keep meeting up with smokers. As much as he didn't want to admit it, he'd had to conclude there was some truth to it: Cigarette smokers were definitely a more interest-ing brand. In today's climate, an educated smoker was more like a maverick, an untamed stallion. And Blake was definitely the latter.

Blake's fingernails stopped just in time to keep Pepper from reinitiating physical contact. Pepper had resolved that this evening they would talk, at least a little. Two orgasms with Blake should be enough for one night. Though, if prompted,

Pepper couldn't swear that he wouldn't go for a third. But he was quite content just to lie next to Blake, anything to maintain their electric contact.

"You're awfully pensive."

Pepper had a million things to say, yet didn't know if he could say any of them. Blake was right, had seemed to intuit the situation: They didn't have to keep doing this if Pepper felt guilty. Pepper did feel guilty. Pepper couldn't stop himself. Pepper was falling in love.

It was possible to be in love — emotionally polygamous? — with two people at the same time, wasn't it?

But, no. He hadn't intended it and this was just sex, wasn't it?

"Shit," Pepper said, no longer feeling stoned. At the moment he felt like nothing more than getting stoned and fucking again. He scratched Blake's neck, and said, "Give me a hit of your cigarette?"

Blake passed the cigarette silently, Pepper puffed on the first tobacco of his life, and Blake said, "Keep it." Pepper took one more puff and ground it into the ashtray next to a used condom. He noticed that Blake kept ashtrays on the nightstands on both sides of the bed.

"Here I am. Madison in November. This weather's enough to make everyone go out, or rather, stay in and commit suicide. What the fuck am I doing here?"

"Here here? Or Madison here?"

"Madison, I mean," Pepper said, though the other question was equally valid. "I'm trying to make my life interesting in Madison and you're helping a lot. Too much. This is too good."

"*I* don't want to put an end to it."

"You know, we could have met in San Francisco when we were both living there. I mean, maybe we did, and never knew it."

"Oh, even if we met in the dark, I think I'd remember you."

Pepper took in the compliment. "I don't understand why you left the Bay Area. I know you came here for the job. But, besides that. I came back here because of Juan. At times I've regretted it, nothing to do with him. I'm just wondering how you could leave behind all that and how you can endure this."

"You're helping me endure it and you don't know what kind of question you've asked. But I'll tell you what the whole Department of Museum Studies has been wondering."

Pepper saw Blake reach for another cigarette and light it in the dark. He remembered Evan's saying something about Blake's "mysterious" background.

Blake inhaled, gazed out above the lake, and began speaking: "It was right before Magda and I got divorced. Student of mine. We invited him over to the house. The guy was beautiful, like you. It was obvious to me he was gay and, I suppose, vice versa. Magda even encouraged it, for my sake, you know, to ease the separation anxiety. I waited until he was no longer my student, even waited until he graduated before we began the affair. I was the one who forced him to seduce me, just to make sure he was sure. Steven was so... enamored, let's say, that he came out to his parents and told them all about me."

"Oh." Pepper feared he was getting the drift. Blake raised the cigarette to his lips again, and went on:

"His parents didn't take it well. Couldn't have taken it worse. They went all the way to the university president. They were major alumni donors themselves. There was nothing they could do, legally, but they were threatening to stir up a hornet's nest. And, I admit, it didn't look great: a forty-five-year-old professor with a twenty-three-year-old former student. Worse, they alleged it had started when he was in my class. In short, the pressure came down from above and my chair asked me please to resign. I said, 'Give me a stellar letter of recommendation and two years to find another job.' Jobs in the field being few, I took the one in Madison when it came along the first year."

"Glad you did."

"Here they all wonder why I left; not even Rickover knows. If it weren't for all that, I'd be much more open about being gay. And here I go, again. This time, involved with the former chair's son."

Pepper focused on one word, and one word only, which reverberated in his head: "You said 'involved'?"

"I guess I did." Pepper saw Blake's flickering smile in the dark of the bedroom. Sexily, he inserted a cigarette into the smile and blew a smoke ring in Pepper's vicinity.

"I feel like I'm levitating."

# 20

From the hallway Evan extracted a handful of mail from his box. About to return to his office, he heard escalating voices inside the main office.

"I need to have these hand-outs done before ten this morning," Ginger was demanding.

"But Professor Rutledge gave me these exams yesterday to have copied and stapled by ten today," Wilhelmina countered in distress.

Evan edged closer to the door, the better to eavesdrop.

"Why couldn't you have copied them yesterday?"

"Because with a faculty of nine, plus grad students, and only me to answer the telephone, I can't do superhuman feats."

"This is... ridiculous!" Ginger sputtered.

"I agree," Wilhelmina said coolly.

"That's not what I meant!"

"I simply agree that the situation is ridiculous."

"I meant it's ridiculous that you can't do this for me for my nine fifty-five class!" Evan swore he heard Ginger stomp her high heels.

"What this department needs is a student worker. Then maybe we could keep on top of things. We've requested one. Now, if I don't go copy Professor Rutledge's exams, his work won't get done, let alone yours."

"See what you can do!"

"Have you read all your memos this year?"

"What are you implying? Of course I have."

"One went out at the beginning of the semester stating that I need to have all faculty work twenty-four hours in advance, or I can't guarantee it can be done on time."

"I'm certain I never heard of any such memo."

"I'm sorry, but the memo went out."

"Well, you missed my mailbox!"

With that, Evan heard Ginger turn on her heels and come marching toward the door. He moved nonchalantly toward his mailbox. Slamming the door behind her, she bustled down the hall. He turned around and glimpsed the back of her pink dress and matching heels.

He gave the doorknob a pull and, as it was locked, knocked gently. "Wilhelmina? It's Evan." A few seconds later, the secretary opened the door.

"You shouldn't have to put up with abuse like that from Ginger or anyone."

"I know. All this work is too much for me. I've got to have help."

At that moment they heard raised voices inside Vance's inner office. Sandra emerged from behind the closed door a second later, tears on her face, make-up streaked. Rickover appeared on her heels and stopped, as though momentarily stunned to see Evan and Wilhelmina. Sandra turned to him and screamed, "I can't take this any longer!"

"Now see what you've done!" Rickover barked back, pointing at Wilhelmina. "It's contagious! You don't have to be listening in!"

Sandra looked woefully at Evan and Wilhelmina and, amid a new wave of tears, fled the office.

"Wilhelmina wasn't listening in," Evan said. "Ginger was in here verbally abusing her."

"I'll verbally abuse you all if you don't..." Rickover stopped, as though unable to come up with an appropriate threat.

"Sounds like you've already had a start at it with Sandra."

"Mind your own damned business, Schultz."

"I was just in here apologizing to Wilhelmina for Ginger. She's out of control this morning."

"So is this whole department."

"Professor Rickover, do you remember the memo that you and I agreed to about faculty giving twenty-four hours' notice for work they want me to do?"

Rickover hesitated, seeming or pretending to remember. "You've got to be flexible!"

"I'm as flexible as I can be, but I have very little time in which to flex." Her short, squat bulk quivering below her greying hair, she pulled her arms in, straightening and composing herself, then went on: "We have to have a student worker and we have to have one now. I can't do all this by myself and neither could anyone else."

"You never could."

"She's right, Vance. This department needs a student worker desperately and soon," Evan bolstered her, undeterred by and inured to Rickover's rudeness.

Ginger stormed back in and stopped in her tracks. "Look at this!" Wildly, she waved in the air a magazine, which, judging by the snippets of flesh he could see on the front cover, Evan concluded was pornographic. "Not only has someone been Xeroxing pornography, but now the goddamned machine is out of paper and I have to have my hand-outs done now!"

Evan wondered if it had been Rickover or Nick photocopying porno. Only faculty had a key to the room.

"Let me see." Rickover almost yanked the magazine out of her hand and began to peruse it, at more than necessary length. "Yeah, it's porn all right."

"Why would anyone photocopy pornography?" Wilhelmina asked innocently, facing away from Rickover and the magazine.

Evan looked at Ginger, then at Rickover, and said, "Could be they didn't have money to buy their own and borrowed it."

"There's paper right by the machine," Wilhelmina said, motioning toward Ginger, as though her hand were a wand that could make her disappear.

"I don't know how to put it in!"

Evan almost hoped that Ginger was back on coke. If this was her new personality, cocaine-free, the thought made him shudder.

At that moment John Rutledge stepped into the office, wearing a new toupee, whose fit left something to be desired. "I didn't find my exams in my mailbox yet," he began, tentative. "Do you think there's any chance...?"

"Not a chance in hell!" Ginger directed a malevolent gaze first at Wilhelmina, then at all of them. "My hand-outs have to be done now!"

"Vance, what are you doing with... that?" Rutledge asked.

"Ginger brought it in." He foisted it back on her.

"This is sexual harassment!" she screamed.

"She's right." Evan, and everyone else, turned around to see Blake standing in the doorway. "You heard me. Ginger's right," Blake repeated.

"Men leaving pornography in the Xerox machine for women to find!" She thrust the magazine out toward all of them, and tottered on her high heels. "Thank you, Blake," she said demurely. "It's nice to know there's one gentleman in the department."

"Pornography aside, I'd say my exams take precedence over your hand-outs," Rutledge said.

"I'll copy the exams, then the hand-outs. They should both

be ready for your nine fifty-five classes. Someone else will have to answer the phone now." Wilhelmina paused, surveying them as if a brood of ill-bred second-graders. "After all this, my nerves are so truly upset that I might have to go home for the day. And I might not get better until this department gets a student worker!"

Wilhelmina took a folder of papers and left the office. The faculty eyed each other warily; Evan wondered who was going to snap at whom first.

"She wouldn't dare!" Ginger spoke as if Wilhelmina had bodily threatened them all.

"The way you treated her, Ging, I'd say you're damned lucky she's copying your hand-outs at all."

"I've got to have my hand-outs now!" she screamed, still clutching the porno magazine.

"Just pass the magazine around," said Rickover. "That will keep the students entertained until Wilhelmina gets done."

❦

Cissy was stoking the woodstove when a knock came at the door. She went to open it and there stood Pepper, grinning.

"UPS. Delivery for Evan Schultz."

"Hi, Pepper. Evan's not home from school yet," Cissy said, not comprehending.

He slyly lifted a bag of marijuana from the pocket of his leather jacket and Cissy understood. "Oh, come in." She quickly ushered him inside.

"It's not the best idea to deliver to Evan at school. And by bringing it over here, we can try it out."

"You don't mean you and Evan tried it out in FAB?" Cissy asked, incredulous.

Pepper gave her a wily smile before saying no.

"Have a seat." She pointed to her new sofa, then to her rocking chair. She felt awkward being in this circumstance, never having been involved in a "transaction" before. Pepper took the rocker and began rocking. "Let me finish with the stove here before we freeze."

"Want any help?"

"No, that's OK." The truth was she hated firing up the stove in the morning and stoking it periodically throughout the day. She swore this would be her last winter in this house and never again would she cohabit with a wood-burning stove. "There.

Finished."

"The temperature seems fine in here to me."

"I forgot and let it die down and the next thing I knew I had gooseflesh. It'll be toasty in here in a minute."

She sat down on the sofa, relieved to be done with the stove, but unsure of drug-purchasing protocol. "Uh, am I supposed to pay you for this now?"

"Since I get it for free, Evan doesn't even have to pay, but he insists on it. So the answer is no. He'll pay me later."

"Can I get you something to drink?" She decided she could afford to relax. It was already three o'clock and she'd been working steadily since eight-thirty, when Evan had left for school.

"No. I'm fine. But I thought we could try out some of this, if you'd like."

"Oh."

"People usually like to, so they know the quality of the stuff they're getting. Hey, it's not a requirement or anything."

"I'm glad it's not a requirement." She stared, as she always did when she saw Pepper, as if to discern a resemblance between father and son.

"It's up to you. I don't want to interrupt your work." Pepper was every bit as gracious as his father wasn't.

"Well..." She'd never smoked without Evan and only before sex. But she had worked hard today, was feeling just frisky enough, and could surprise Evan, who would be home soon. "Sure, why not?"

"Great. I've got a pipe in my pocket."

In a post-acceptance pang of guilt, Cissy reprimanded herself. But she'd worked enough today and she was a specimen of health except for this one occasional vice. She saw that Pepper had inserted the pipe into the bag and was carefully tamping a bowl.

He extended the pipe and a lighter to her. "The honors are yours."

"I'm afraid I don't know how to light a pipe. Evan always rolls joints."

"No problem." Pepper lit the pipe himself and inhaled deeply, then passed it to her. Cissy drew in heavily, and coughed. "I'm afraid I've never smoked out of a pipe before."

"Now you have."

"No, I haven't. I didn't get a thing out of it."

"Try again. I'll get it going, then you just inhale, neither gently nor greedily, until you get your lungs full."

Cissy tried again, and at least didn't cough. They passed the pipe back and forth. After four hits, she felt a buzz, and the bowl was gone.

"Very good, I think," she said.

"Glad you like it. Amelia's stuff usually is."

"Amelia?"

"Yeah, Amelia Raitt."

"I never imagined..."

"I thought you knew. It's not exactly a secret. Grows it right in her basement."

Cissy knew of the downstairs "refreshment" at Amelia's annual departmental Christmas parties, but hadn't imagined she also grew it there.

They chatted some more and Pepper departed. Cissy, now higher than expected, barely remembered what they'd said and hoped Evan would come home soon. Then she realized she'd forgotten to pay Pepper. Then she remembered she didn't have to.

The telephone rang. She trusted it was Evan, held up at school, and hoped she could manage not to give herself away.

"Hello?"

"Is Evan there?"

Cissy didn't recognize the woman's voice. "I'm sorry. He's not. He should be home soon. May I take a message?" She thought she'd got it all out coherently, then saw that she didn't have paper, pen or pencil nearby.

"Yes, you can." The voice was not cordial. "Can you tell him that Anne called?" Oh, God. It was Evan's soon-to-be ex-wife and Cissy had never spoken with her before. "Tell him that his son is at the County Sheriff's Department."

"Oh, no." Cissy's response was instinctive.

"And that he'd better get over there right away. It seems that someone overheard a call between Todd and a friend supposedly plotting to kill their sixth-grade teacher and they've held him for questioning. This is an emergency, do you understand?" Anne shrieked into the phone, obviously hysterical. Cissy now held it at elbow's length. "You tell him to get himself out there the second he gets home!"

"I'll tell him. Or you could call him at school. He may still be there." She already felt less high.

"Just tell him when he gets home!" Anne shrieked again and hung up.

Cissy realized that she'd gotten stoned for nothing, and sat on the sofa, trying to order her thoughts. Only one came to mind: She was glad she'd never had children.

Evan's son plotting to kill his teacher? Could it be true? Next, could he be plotting to kill his mother? His father? Mass family murders were a not unusual quirk in Wisconsin, an otherwise placid state.

She got up and checked that the door was locked, then remembered that Todd was in the Sheriff's custody and probably didn't even know the exact location where his father lived. But there was Nick downstairs. He'd never approached her sexually, but he was creepy. She wouldn't want to be alone in the same room with him. She hadn't suspected Sumner Isaacson, after all. Nick could come home drunk, knock at her door or break in...

She stopped; the marijuana had made her truly paranoid. She calmed herself down, then, thinking of Evan's son, broke out into a guffaw after a few seconds.

"Plotting to kill the teacher!" It now struck her as hilarious. But then she found herself wondering if any of her students had ever plotted to kill her. She sat back in amazement that Rickover was still alive and burst out laughing again.

Evan appeared, having unlocked the door silently. "Cissy, are you on drugs, or what?"

"As a matter of fact, yes. I was planning a surprise for you, but Anne called. It seems she's got an emergency."

"What? Is one of the kids sick?"

"No. It's just that Todd tried to kill his teacher," she said, and tried to stop laughing.

"I hope this is a joke. What kind of drugs did you take?"

# 21

Roz wandered to the exercise/laundry room in the portion of the basement not taken up by the downstairs apartment.

"Too tired to talk?"

"At... the... moment." Irv plunked himself down on an unused weight bench, obviously having just got off the Lifecycle, a present from him to her last Christmas.

"I think I'll hop on." Roz debated getting on the cycle nude, then rejected the idea. Exercise itself made her feel awkward enough, let alone exercising naked. "Irv, throw me your shorts, will you."

She flung off her robe and stood nude except for Nikes and socks. He looked at her baffled. "Don't you have any clothes in the dryer?"

"No. Your shorts will do fine. You've got a jockstrap on underneath, don't you?"

"Between the jock and my shirt, you could probably wring them out and fill a beer bottle."

"But I didn't ask for *them*."

"No guarantee on the shorts either." He leaned back to pull them off. She helped him get them over his tennis shoes and put them on herself.

Currently bent on exercising more often, she jumped on and started pedaling. She decided to go for twelve minutes, then shifted the dial up to eighteen, and compensated by lowering the level of difficulty from ten to eight.

"I'm going to circulate my nomination papers tomorrow."

Irv only grunted in response.

The truth was that she'd come downstairs to talk about her campaign; the Lifecycle was an afterthought. "The sooner, the better, I figure. Don't you think?"

"Yeah." Irv was still winded.

"In any case I want to be the first to announce already. Don't you think?"

"Yeah."

"Though it's just a formality in Claypool's case." It was understood that the incumbent would be her main opponent, but she also hoped that an early announcement might forestall a third candidate, thus eliminating the necessity of a February primary. "You feel all right?"

"Yeah." He seemed less winded, but still remained stationary.

The back of his shorts was now sliding off her. "How long were you on for?"

"Twenty-four. The maximum."

"Maybe better go for eighteen the next time. Do you really think Dave will work out as my campaign manager?"

"Yeah." Having volunteered his services, Seth had been her first choice, but Irv had argued strongly against it. He didn't live in the sixth district, he'd lost three elections of his own and, although he was an old friend, a good friend, he was un-reliable and off-the-wall when it came to politics. Roz had had no choice but to relent, lest she lose Irv's tenuous support. At Irv's urging, she'd decided on long-time Labor Farm member Dave Offenbach. They'd never been close friends and had fre-quently disagreed, but it was a good tactical move, she sup-posed. Everyone respected him, as opposed to Seth, who'd still be there for her, on whose shoulder it was easier to cry than Dave's or even Irv's. Not that she'd need to.

"Do you think we can pay Beth to be my treasurer?" She sped up the revolutions, still feeling fit, determined to outdo Irv, to show off her boundless energy.

"It would be irregular."

"But not impossible, right?"

"Right. But only if..."

"I know. You said it before. 'Only if this is a big-time, major campaign. Otherwise it would be irregular.' Of course I'm go-ing to run a big-time, major campaign!"

Irv nodded agreement and slowly stood up. A small paunch, not bad for his age, rested above his jockstrap. He'd given her campaign its first donation, the maximum allowed, and she'd earmarked that amount for Beth. She'd been pleased to know that Beth had been an accounting major before switching to social work. Seeing her revolutions per minute increase, she smiled over at Irv, then looked downward. The bulge in his jockstrap had grown; he stepped over toward her.

She removed one hand from the handlebar, pressed her fin-ger into his T-shirt, and hit his navel. "Not now. I've got exer-cise and politics on my mind." And, she noticed, eleven min-utes to go. She put her hand back on the bike after gently touch-ing Irv's shoulder.

"I didn't know that I'd made a... sexual overture."

"Well, if you didn't, don't. Maybe later." She pretended to concentrate on pedaling, all the time thinking of her announce-ment, her news conference, and the race. She wanted to be alone, didn't know if she'd hold up for another ten minutes. Then she remembered that she'd promised to show Juan how to use the bike. As if it were some technological challenge... And as if he needed to burn off calories...

She looked over her shoulder, saw Irv beginning to ascend the stairs, his buttocks bouncing cutely. After eating lunch, she still had to call Beth, talk to Dave, return Seth's call and fit Juan in, if possible.

"Irv!" she screamed over her shoulder. He turned to face her as she went on pedaling, slower; she was beginning to feel winded herself. "If you're into it, how about we make love at three? Would that fit your schedule? I think I'll be free by then, if I'm not too tired."

Again, he seemed only to grunt in response.

Fine. If he didn't feel like it, she could certainly wait.

The news conference was set for noon Friday at the Labor Farm office. Roz hoped to get one reporter from both of the mainstream local dailies, even if it was a long shot. She'd tried to assemble as many people as possible — friends, plus Labor Farm regulars that she hadn't alienated over the years. This was, after all, more than a minor media event.

She'd slept until nine-thirty and was now relaxing on the chaise lounge in the sun-filled atrium with her coffee and newspaper. Irv was gone for the morning, but would appear with Dayne at noon. Just as well; she didn't need them underfoot now. She merely had to appear and read a prepared statement. Dave had rewritten it for her, eliminating epithets such as "Bushified warmonger" that she'd called her opponent.

Soon she panicked: What to wear? Panic turned to anger: Why the hell did she have to wear any clothes at all? But she needed to present the proper working-class image and part of her strategy was to present herself as a working mother. Irv's inherited millions remained a well-kept secret. Their house, however, one of the most opulent in the neighborhood, was an unfortunate matter of public record. She'd simply adopt a fuck-you attitude, were anyone to bring it up, or worse, to try to make an issue of it.

She surveyed the contents of the large walk-in closet, then stomped out, still nude, and lit a Camel. Spitting out a string of obscenities, she marched back in to contemplate her clothes. Even if the media showed up, her picture probably wasn't going to appear in the newspapers tomorrow. She stepped into blue jeans, not bothering with panties, and walked back into the bedroom. From the dresser drawer, she put on a pair of wool socks, then found her Nikes.

There, she was finished from the waist down.

She pulled open dresser drawers, found a stack of T-shirts,

finally coming up with a Labor Farm one, and pulled it on tight, without a bra, the better not to appear as if she'd undergone a double mastectomy.

She scampered down the stairs, threw on her winter coat and checked the lapel for politics. Although the election was officially non-partisan, she was going to be the official-as-it-got Labor Farm nominee, so she removed all other buttons. There might be some idiot present who didn't believe in "Pot for the People" or objected to the notion of "Let's Go Quayle Hunting."

It was almost noon when she skittered out the door and over to the office. From the outside, she could see it was packed — granted, it couldn't easily hold more than twenty-five people, and that was pushing it.

"Hey, Roz. Maybe the City Hall steps would have been more appropriate," Seth said into her ear as she entered.

"Hey! That would have been a great idea. Why didn't you suggest it before? I shouldn't have listened to anyone else. You should have been my manager." Of this she was sure now, and mentally cursed Dave and Irv.

"Better go do your thing, Roz. Good luck." He put up his hand and spread his fingers in a sort of peace sign.

She moved on, saying hellos to people she knew and by necessity elbowing others to get to the podium, where Irv and Dave stood nervously. Dayne sat on the floor crying.

"It's about fucking time," Dave whispered as she approached him.

"Good to see you, Dave. No need to worry. Now where's my fucking statement?" In her hurry, she'd forgotten her own copy.

He shoved it at her, and hissed, "Lower your fucking voice."

"Let's both watch our language," she said, now nervous herself. "Irv, what's wrong with Dayne?"

"He's upset, as you can see."

"What happened?"

"Nothing major. You'll find out soon enough."

Roz decided not to fret over this, but rather to put on a good motherly face. She walked over to Dayne and said, "How's Mommy's little boy?" He only howled in response.

She stalked over to Irv, and whispered, "Can you pick him up and shut him up?"

"It looks like Juan's doing that, or trying."

Roz glanced over, saw Juan and Pepper for the first time. "Well, just be sure his eyes are dry in time for the cameras."

"This isn't exactly a media blitz."

"It looks pretty full to me."

Dave had now asked for silence and, Roz realized, was in the process of introducing her.

"Thank you, thank you." She eyed her supporters and smiled, seeing everyone, but no one, and stared down at her prepared speech. At the top of it, as well as between each paragraph, Dave had written "SMILE," just as he had on hers. She began to read:

"This election year it's time to give government back to the people. We, Labor Farm, are the party of the people, the people's party outside the two-party system, the true party of the working populace, the majority of those who have populated our country, the true progressives and populists, outside the two-party..." Who the hell had written this? Was she reading correctly? It sounded downright surreal. But, before she could finish the paragraph, the assembled group applauded.

She saw her cue to smile and, in spite of syntactical dizziness, followed it, then continued: "After years of representation by the insiders' party and their machine, it's time to give your government back to you." She enumerated the key problems of the district, skipping over a drug problem and traffic concerns that Offenbach had put in. Who the hell cared about traffic patterns? And just because there had been a crack bust on Willy Street was no reason to talk about drug problems. Skimming fast, she went on to damn the proposed civic center, condemn the construction of the proposed public swimming pool that would ruin a woods, finished the paragraph, and was applauded again.

Thank God for applause, which gave a body time to catch its breath. She thanked those present. The speech stared up at her, and she again followed its cue to smile. As the clapping ended, she added, "I especially want to thank my family for their support. First, Irv Barmejian, and, though I don't know how much help he'll be, our son Dayne." She turned her glance to Irv and he hoisted him up on cue.

"And..." She saw Juan and Pepper standing next to Irv, and was considering a spur-of-the-moment notion to include them in the family, when she heard an unmistakable voice: "Irving, don't do that!"

The crowd silent, she directed a dumbfounded glance at Irv, who shook his head. The worst possible feeling permeated her as she turned in the other direction, where, from behind the washroom curtain, stepped a member of her real family...

"And to surprise Roz for the occasion, I'm her mother, Rhoda Goldmann." Rhoda gave a flourish of her hand to the masses, as if they were her subjects. She was draped in gold jewelry and a gilded cocktail dress and carried in her arms the disgusting miniature poodle she'd had the nerve to name Irving. Then, to Roz's horror, she saw that her mother was sporting a murdered mink around her neck.

"Hey, lady. You wear that mink on State Street, you'll be as dead as it is."

Roz craned her neck to see who the heckler was, then recognized the voice of her treasurer, who was still pointing a finger at the murdered mink. Fine. It was just as well that someone else reprove Rhoda. Roz marched over to Irv for an explanation.

"She called last week and said she wanted to surprise you. I tried to talk her out of it, but... I figured it would only upset you and that it was better for you not to know beforehand. I picked her and Irving up at the airport this morning."

"I didn't invite her to come this soon!"

"She evidently thought she had a standing invitation. As soon as we got to the office, Irving snapped at Dayne, almost bit him. That's why he was crying."

Roz stole a glance over her shoulder at her mother, who, for better, or more likely worse, was chatting with curious onlookers.

"I can't believe she wore a fucking mink. She could cost me the election!"

"Quiet, Roz. People will hear you. You're in the public eye now."

"Roz, darling!" Her mother greeted from behind. "Oy! Your tush is showing. You've got a hole behind. You've given up underwear?"

"That's not all I've given up, Mother."

# 22

Classes would soon be ending, giving Beth more time to look for a job and to serve as Roz's treasurer. Roz had promised her one hundred and twenty-five dollars a month, for up to four months. No one had yet to take up her up on her cat-sitting services. It was probably a dumb idea anyway, she concluded, as she stared out at the snow-covered roofs, dotted with chimneys, small pipes and solar-heating panels. She lowered her glance to a row of sparrows perched on a telephone wire. Bored, she got up and threw some bread crumbs on the porch to see if she could entice any of them to come down.

She couldn't attract a cat to sit or a sparrow to feed.

Verla had acquired a new pupil and was giving an oboe lesson this afternoon. They'd come up with one hundred and seventy-five dollars of the rent, on top of which Beth had painfully added three-quarters of her Hanukkah gelt. With the twenty-five-dollar surcharge, they still fell eighty short.

A knock came at the door. She peered through the curtains and made out the forms of the landdykes standing among the bread crumbs on the porch. Beth half-expected one of them to bend over and scoop them up to feed to their own birds, or to each other.

The cats were sleeping all over the living room. She scooped up Skokie and Lady, and trotted off with them into the bathroom. A surplus of one illicit cat remained. She picked up Jen, the baby, and deposited him or her with the other two. It wouldn't do well to let the landdykes see a kitten as evidence of the growing menagerie.

Back in the dining room, she heard the landdykes rapping again and trudged to the door and opened it.

"Beth, hello." Babs spoke with hollow warmth. "We thought you weren't here."

"Oh, I'm here all right," she said airily, then added, "bein' unemployed." She might as well go for sympathy, if Babs knew the meaning of the word. "You know the Ho Chi Minh's boycott left me jobless. But Verla, she's out earning the rent. Somethin' I can do for you?"

"Well, besides the rent, you could let us murderers in." It was Kendall, who spoke demurely, yet clipped, in some sort of phony British accent.

Murderers? she thought. She regularly applied other un-
flattering terms to them, but... "Sure, come in." The cats were
hidden; she saw no danger.

They stepped inside, shrugged off snow, and Babs scuffed
the rug with her work boots.

"We ate turkey on Thanksgiving," Babs clarified. "I belong
to PETA too, you know."

"You do??" This Beth found extremely hard to believe. Obviously, her landperson had become very, very lapsed.

"Yeah. P-E-T-A." Babs cracked a wide smile, showing the
gold in her teeth. "People Eating Tasty Animals."

"People... Eating..." By now Beth's mouth was agape. She
couldn't begin to utter the last two words.

"Hey, it's a joke." Babs moved as if to slap her on the shoulder, but Beth backed away, not about to go along with this.
"No hard feelings." It was definitely not a question.

"The Ho Chi Minh's boycott was certainly unfortunate,"
Kendall, the Savage Slut, jumped in.

"Sure was," Beth managed, gambling that this was safe to
agree with.

"For your own financial state," said Babs. "You quit your
job and picketed the place, I understand, and all for what?"

In Beth's mind the two of them turned into a lesbian Phyllis
Schlafly and her sidekick Eva Braun. "But they were
discriminatin' against lesbians and gay men and people with..."
Babs' footwear distracted her from her speech. "Hey, those boots
aren't leather, are they?"

"I believe they are," Babs answered as though it were obvious.

"You know, cows were killed for those boots. Rubber and
other synthetic materials work just as well." She shook her head
hopelessly; there was no educating some dykes.

"Mind if I smoke?" asked Kendall.

"We suspected you were having financial problems," said
Babs. The grooves in her face accentuated themselves as she
spoke.

"Sure, smoke as long as you give me one." Kendall extended
a pack of Virginia Slims Ultra Lights to her. "Yeah, you could
say we're havin' money problems, but we'll get the rent to you,
penalty and all."

Babs pulled out a Marlboro. "Actually, we're thinking, only
thinking, of selling the house. It's barely profitable. Your lease

says we can terminate it to sell with sixty days' notice. If you can't pay the rent, we're willing to let you out of the lease any time. This month's rent could be paid by your security deposit and you could move out January first. Or if you can pay the rent this month, February first."

Kendall eyed the dining room, as if scouting out excessive picture hooks on the wall. "Of course we'd have to do a thorough inspection to make sure you deserve the whole deposit back before we could let you use it for rent."

"We know some things need fixing and aren't your fault, especially in the bathroom. We'd be very fair in returning your deposit. But if we're going to maintain the house properly — a real expense — the bathroom is going to need major work." Babs sucked down her Marlboro. "Got an ashtray?"

"Aw, use the floor." Beth watched all four eyes bulge at her suggestion of ashing on their own property. "That was a joke too." She knelt down and dug one out of the kitchen cupboards.

"I know we haven't given you the twenty-four hours' official notice, but were wondering if we could take a look at the bathroom," Babs said. "We need to check for ceiling and wall damage around the shower. We'll probably need to put in a sliding door to keep water from further damaging the adjacent wall."

"The bathroom? Uh, someone's takin' a bath in there." It popped out before she could think, and she'd already said Verla was at work.

Kendall looked quizzically at Babs, then at Beth, eyelashes and eyes galloping with sexual innuendo, or a facial tremor.

"It's a friend from work." Oops, what work? "She hurt her back and has to take hot baths and she's only got a shower at her house."

Kendall rolled her eyes one final time. "Oh, we see." Her long ash detached itself neatly into the ashtray. "Well, you two have fun. I hope her back gets better."

"Yeah, yeah, it will, don't worry." Beth moved in closer, edging them toward the door.

"And when do you think you'll have the rent?" asked Babs.

"Got most of it right here, but one hundred bucks of it is my Hanukkah gelt," she added pointedly, for the benefit of her Jewish landperson, whom she considerd a money-grubbing slumlord.

"We'd like to inspect the bathroom tomorrow or Monday.

Let's say Monday. Do you think it might be free by then?"

"Yeah, and we'll do what we can about the rent." Beth reined in her anger; she definitely didn't want to move out. "Anything else?"

At that moment, she heard growling and wailing, the beginning of an all-out cat fight.

"Better go tend to your friend in the bathroom. Sounds like she might have scalded herself in the hot water," said Kendall.

"Well, we pay for the hot water." The next thing she knew, they'd be putting limits on the number of allowable showers per week.

"Think about our proposal. Staying or moving," said Babs. "Of course, it's up to you, unless we sell."

"Yeah, yeah." Beth ushered them out with a hand gesture, cat fights, poverty and homelessness overloading her mind.

The rent had to be paid soon. She wondered idly if the Savage Slut would take it out in trade.

Classes ended, the landdykes came and went, and with Beth's first check from Roz, they paid the rent. They told Kendall and Babs that they preferred to stay and hoped they didn't sell.

Beth was going to dedicate the weekend to the first of her final papers for her two advanced classes. At least she didn't have any of the pricks who gave both a final exam and a paper.

Juvenile Delinquency would be a relative snap. If necessary, she could title the paper "High School Memoirs." Social Gerontology was going to be the problem.

She made a pickle and tomato sandwich for lunch and sat down with it and the sad prospect of writing her paper. Her mouth was full and her mind empty when the phone rang.

"Beth? Hi, this is Roz. How are you?"

"Here, waiting for money to come in," she answered, swallowing. "How are your campaign contributions going?" She faked a chipper tone. The only contributions she cared about right now were to her own bank account.

"Oh, who cares about contributions?" Roz sounded clearly displeased by something. "I've got my mother on my hands."

"Oh yeah, her. She's not doin' somethin' dumb like makin' you drop out, is she?"

Roz groaned at her remark, which Beth now regretted. "But I might have to if we don't engage in some damage control.

My mother wearing that murdered mink at my press conference!"

"You're not lettin' her strut around the neighborhood in it, I hope."

"No. But I've got to get rid of her. That's why I'm calling." The voice turned suspiciously sweet: "To ask if you could take her off my hands for the afternoon."

"Gee, Roz. I'd be glad to..." This was not quite true. "But I got this paper to write."

"On what?"

"Don't know yet. It's for my Social Gerontology class."

"Great. You can write it on my mother. She's certainly a unique gerontological specimen, but I can't vouch for her sociability."

"I didn't think this was part of my job as treasurer."

"It isn't. There's forty dollars in this for you. I deliver her to you in an hour and you keep her until some time this evening. She's already managed to alienate two entire households. What the hell, I'll make it fifty."

Beth's heart leapt into... whatever organ was above it. Social Gerontology could wait until tomorrow. "Deal. I'll take her. But, what am I supposed to do with her?"

"Anything except let any voter in the sixth district know she's my mother. She knows you're my treasurer. You just tell her I'm going to win this election and what a wonderful person I am."

"That sounds easy enough," Beth hedged. The "wonderful person" part *was* stretching it a little.

"Oh, there's one more thing," Roz said shakily. "She comes with her dog, Irving, the hateful little poodle you saw the other day."

Beth began to envision the complications. "But Roz, I have cats. Six of 'em." Since the fight, she had them quarantined by twos in all three rooms with closable doors.

"Oh, dear. Irving doesn't like humans, let alone other animals."

Beth said nothing, letting the dilemma weigh on Roz's mind, as it did on her own. But she'd be damned if she was going to let the cats cost her fifty bucks.

"All right, sixty dollars. Otherwise she and I could end up pushing each other off the pier and then there'd be no council race for me and no job for you."

"OK. We got a deal." The money was making Roz sound more "wonderful" by the minute.

"And one more thing. In case she asks, listen, get a pencil, write this down. One: I am not a lesbian."

Yeah, and Jodie Foster's straight too.

"Two: Irv is Dayne's natural father." This was odd; Beth hadn't known that he wasn't. Further proof that Roz was a dyke — she'd gone and got herself alternatively inseminated. She waited for the next lie, savoring each statement, and not writing a word.

"Are you writing? Three: You're not a lesbian either. Got it? Lie as necessary. Make me look good. What the hell, if she comes back satisfied with the visit, I'll give you a hundred dollars, I'm so grateful."

"Jesus! Thanks, Roz." Now she could buy Verla a Christmas present and she might even have enough money for a few bottles of wine for the rest of the month. "Oh, one more thing. Does your mother drink?"

"She's got a heart condition, but yes, a little wine. If she wants to go out for a cocktail, just take her some place nice. She'll pay for the cab and the drinks. You'll just have to keep Irving at your house while you're out."

"Fine. See you when? About one?"

"I'll schlep her over by twelve forty-five if I can make it."

"Just make sure she's not wearin' that mink of hers. I know you got your own hassles with her, but I got my own reputation too, and I don't go out with minks."

Sixty dollars minimum, maybe even a hundred! If the old lady was a pain in the ass, she'd simply get her drunk, and hope she passed out.

# 23

"Is he really a hunk?" Cissy asked Evan as he drove his anemic car to school. It was one of her rare forays into the office this semester. It seemed that the department could function well enough without her. Almost too well, she feared.

"Ask a woman." He slowed down for a patch of ice on John Nolen Drive. "Oh, I suppose so," he relented. "He's in ROTC, comes to work in his uniform. Muscled, short blond hair..."

"Then he's probably a hunk."

"And probably a right-wing 'patriot' pig. After all, it was Rickover who hired him."

When they arrived at FAB, Ginger was sitting *on* the student worker's desk in the main office. She was obviously getting her work done by the cadet — whose name was Lee — probably leaving him little time to do anyone else's. She was so engrossed in him that she didn't even see them arrive. Just as well, Cissy thought. She grabbed her mail in the hall, greeted Wilhelmina through the open door, and she and Evan scurried away to their offices.

Within ten minutes, Ginger came in and shut the door behind her.

"Sorry, it's my office hour." Evan got up to open it back up. It was the end of the semester, when his office hours usually became overloaded.

"So how is Todd?" Ginger asked without preface, beginning her weekly interrogation of her colleagues about their professional or private lives, or both.

"Back in school." One particularly harried morning, he'd revealed the problem to her.

"What I don't understand is, how was his conversation overheard?"

"It was on a cellular phone. Someone else managed to overhear part of the conversation and thought he might have heard a real murder being plotted, and reported it to the sheriff."

"Hmmm. I've never had that happen on my cellular phone," Ginger mused, preoccupied. "It's almost like having your phone tapped."

"Not quite, Ging. This was a sort of fluke. In any case, Anne never should have bought the thing." He'd told her so and an argument had ensued.

"At least he's back in school."

"Yeah. They realized it was a kids' prank. Really, it wasn't even a prank. They were just fantasizing about how they wished they could knock off their teacher. Now they've switched him and the other boy to a different class. So, in a way, he got his way, via the Sheriff's Department and the principal." The original teacher had refused to have the two boys back in her class.

"But they must have mandated counseling or something. You know, he has to get help. Children at that age..."

"Ging, what do you know about children that age?" he

asked, teasing her.

She sat pouting, staring down into her cleavage. Perhaps her ample bust was her own personal source of consolation. Evan wondered what she'd done before she'd grown it. "I was one myself once," she said, meeting his eyes in defiance.

"He is getting counseling." With this, Evan hoped to end her probing.

"At least they let him back into school," she repeated.

"Thank God for that." And thank God it wasn't a reform school.

"And if it doesn't work out, you just put him in a boarding or a military school." Now she sounded like Rickover, not for the first time, lately.

"Hi, Cynthia," Evan said, seeing a piece of one of his ex-students pass in the hall. "You can interrupt us if you're waiting to see me."

The young woman ventured timidly up to his door.

"Sorry, Ging. It *is* my office hour. I have a student. We'll have to talk later." He'd think of some pretext to converse with Cynthia.

"Well, I'll just go down and see how Cissy's doing." Ginger didn't bother to tame her anger at the interruption.

"You do that." He trusted Cissy had already escaped, not really surprised that Ginger's radar eyes had taken in their arrival.

The hunk, he thought with a tinge of envy followed by a wave of nostalgia. Could a forty-year-old man be a hunk too? Perhaps he'd go exercise at SERF on his lunch hour, or after classes. He looked up at Cynthia, who was waiting for him to say something.

❧

Cissy was going through her files, looking for a bibliographical reference that she couldn't find at home. It had to be here somewhere. Evan had volunteered to look for it, but she'd said it would be easier to find it herself.

Before she found it, Ginger planted herself in the doorway. "Hi, Cis. How's it going?"

"Just trying to find a footnote," she said, her head still poised over the open filing cabinet drawer. She figured she might as well get Ginger's obligatory grilling out of the way before she traipsed over to the library.

Ginger slipped in and closed the door.

"How have you been?" Cissy asked.

"I'm fine, the department is running again now that we have a student worker, but Sandra... Oh, I'm not too sure about Sandra."

No one ever was. "What do you mean?"

"I'm afraid she's not going to get tenure."

Cissy doubted that Ginger was "afraid." The true word was probably "happy."

"What's happened?"

"Besides her losing control of the Intro class...," Ginger said, not explaining, "she doesn't look well. She might as well have 'failure' stamped across her forehead. She runs around the fifth floor in tears..."

Cissy remembered that Evan had told her how Sandra had emerged in tears from Vance's office last week. "If you were married to Vance..."

Ginger ignored Cissy's protest. "Blake is certainly going to vote against her."

Knowing Ginger, Cissy didn't doubt she'd probably polled every member of the department on Sandra's tenure vote. "One vote..."

"Oh, it's not just one." Ginger's tone oozed gravity. "She won't even make it through the departmental vote. She'll lose, three to two, at best, since Vance can't vote."

Cissy was glad that Vance, as chair, wouldn't be able to vote on her own tenure either. "Well, I'm going to go work on mine," she said, using one of Ginger's old lines, before she'd been tenured and promoted to associate professor. Now she was working on becoming a full professor before she turned forty.

"But you didn't find your footnote." The tone said that she was miffed at being dismissed.

"My files are so disorganized..." It was a half-truth. "It's easier just to find it at the library. I have to go over there anyway."

❦

Cissy sat on a stool in front of a computer terminal in the library, trying to come up with the proper entry. "SEARCH WAS UNSUCCESSFUL," the computer told her on both her first and second attempts. She looked up and saw Blake facing her from behind the terminal.

"Congratulations on your article," he greeted her.

"My article?"

"The one you sent to *Archaeology in the Museum*. A friend of mine is on the editorial board and told me they'd accepted it."

"W-wonderful," Cissy stuttered. "But no one's let me know yet."

"Oh. I suppose I did let the cat out of this particular bag. But since it's a good cat and not a bad one, I didn't think you'd mind knowing."

"Of course not. I'm thrilled. Thanks for telling me. That's one less thing I'll have to be worrying about before..."

"Before you come up for tenure," Blake finished. "You don't have anything to worry about at all." He winked at her, conspiratorially, and walked off down the library's wide hall.

As she was walking to the bus stop, in a hurry to get home, Nick pulled up in his Corvette. "Hop in, I'll drive you."

After vacillating briefly, Cissy got in. She *was* in a hurry and, in any case, couldn't easily turn him down. Besides, he would be voting on her tenure.

"Making tracks this semester?" Nick said.

"Through the snow. From home to the library today," she quipped. "I've just gotten an article accepted."

"Great. An Ivy League journal, I hope. Those are the ones that look best when everyone goes over your file."

Why was Nick saying this? He knew perfectly well what her specialty was, and that the most important journals in her field were located in the Southwest, or in Mexico.

"I know, your specialty is Mexico." Nick sped out East Johnson Street. "Just trying to give some friendly advice."

Cissy wondered if this was true, or if he was just trying to rattle her delicate nerves. She supposed that any advice couldn't hurt, though at this point it was too late to write another article, let alone to have it accepted by a "prestigious" Ivy League journal. She had to turn in her tenure materials in just over a month.

He cut over on Paterson to East Washington, turned on Ingersoll, and at Ingersoll and Williamson parked in front of their house. No way was Cissy going to invite him up even for a cup of tea.

"Remember what I said," Nick reiterated. "People are go-

ing to be looking at *where* you've published. You have published something in an Ivy League review, haven't you?"

The truth was no, and Nick would end up knowing it, so
she told it.

"Well, good luck," he said with an oily smile, as though she
might be needing it.

Upstairs, she decided to make the fatal list: who in the department would vote for her tenure and who wouldn't.

She put down Ginger's name on the yes side and added
Blake's below it, then put a question mark by Ginger's. Although Ginger was a "friend," Cissy judged her about as trust-
worthy as a food-deprived rattler. Blake was a sure vote, she
thought. But could he have been the one person who voted
against Ginger's tenure last year? Someone had and, if Ginger
knew, she wasn't saying who. She added a tiny question mark
next to Blake's name.

On the opposite side, she put Nick's name with a question
mark and John Rutledge's. Because Rutledge, like Nick, was
an ally of Vance's, she didn't trust him.

That left the enigmatic senior professor Bob Rothschild, who
had high standards and could be prickly. She deliberated putting him in the yes column, then the no column, and left him
in the middle, with a big question mark.

She tried to resist drawing a conclusion that would cause
her to crumble, to fall apart like Sandra. The only votes she
thought she had were Blake's and Ginger's, and this wasn't
even certain. She needed three definite votes, even to stand a
chance.

She thought of calling Irv again, but for what? She decided
it was time to go over the National Museum Association's job
list for next year, just in case.

She tried to convince herself: It was *just in case.*

Upstairs, she decided to make the fatal list: who in the de-

After leaving the library, Blake had returned to FAB, where
his accidental fifth-floor encounter with Pepper had taken him
aback. Pepper had been outside the main office, collecting his
father's mail. He'd asked Pepper to meet him tonight at his
condo, a day earlier than planned and, as he'd hoped, Pepper
readily agreed.

Now Pepper sat in his living room with a martini. Normally, after Pepper's martini, Blake would pour himself a second glass of wine and they'd head upstairs. But tonight... Blake didn't know if they'd go upstairs at all.

Pepper seemed relaxed and Blake could tell he was as eager to be upstairs as was Blake himself. He dreaded spoiling the moment, but he had to say something, better sooner than later. He considered postponing it until after sex, but feared that by then it wouldn't be said at all.

Pepper was smiling, as comfortable as Blake with the silence, which he now had to break. There was no way to do it except directly. He lit a cigarette, savored wine on his palate, slowly swallowed it, then spoke:

"Pepper, I have a problem. You and I have a problem."

Suddenly Pepper bore into his eyes, uncertainly, perhaps fearfully, perhaps guessing more or less what was to come. The dark eyes widened, almost piteously, reminding Blake of a wounded deer, either pleading for its life or waiting to be put out of its pain. He had to plunge ahead now — or never — though he had no idea how his feelings were going to spill out.

"Im afraid I'm falling in love. And I don't know if we can continue doing this. You've got a partner and I'm not... I can't... I didn't expect this to happen."

"Neither did I," Pepper said, poker-faced, then walked over and put his arms around Blake.

Blake pulled back, stared into Pepper's dark brown eyes, and now saw that he was valiantly attempting to keep them unmoistened.

"But I'm so glad it did." Pepper pulled him into a bear hug.

"But how can we...?" Blake pulled back once more to stare into Pepper's eyes, as if he might discover some secret meaning in them, the answer to his — to their — dilemma.

"We can do anything we want, if we really want to."

"I guess we can." Blake found himself suddenly relieved, his resolve having melted straight away. Maybe he'd try to state it more forcefully another time; he didn't see how he could go on like this.

Or maybe he wouldn't. Maybe he'd found, at long last, what he'd always been searching for.

Pepper... Isaacson. He was sure of it. And Pepper's behavior gave every indication that he too was just as sure.

"Pepper, do you have a middle name?"

"Only in Hebrew. If I get a speeding ticket, they write it up as 'Pepper NMI Isaacson'."

# 24

A friend of a friend had heard of Beth's cat-sitting offer and, after a personal interview, had agreed to pay her one hundred dollars for two weeks of cat-care, outdoor bird-feeding, and indoor plant-watering. Eva Drake had given her a half-page of instructions for the bird feeder, two pages for plants, and three for the cats, detailing at length their personality quirks. Did she think Beth was going to bunk with them and cater to all their neuroses, or what? Beth quickly understood why Eva had no friends who'd volunteer for this job. Maybe cat-sitting hadn't been such a good idea, if this was going to be the typical job. Still, it was a paying job, and it couldn't be too difficult to keep the cats and plants watered, fed and alive for two weeks. In any case, she had little else she had to do, except to write her final paper for Juvenile Delinquency and to serve as Roz's treasurer.

She made the short trek over to Riverside Drive, where the houses faced the Yahara River, connecting Lakes Mendota and Monona. She opened the door, and was greeted by two of the three cats, to whom she'd already had lengthy introductions. Victor and Diablo purred at her feet and followed her with gusto to the kitchen and the sound of the can-opener. As Beth spooned out their food into separate dishes, the third cat, a female calico named Ron Reagan, meandered in, as if groggy from a nap. As the plants didn't yet need care, she scooped food from a bag for the bird feeder, which stood near the house. She decided to venture into the snow without her boots, deposited on the living room mat. As she opened the back door, a scoop of bird-seed in hand, Ron Reagan darted out under her feet.

"Damn you, Ron Reagan!"

At least the yard had a fence, and Ron Reagan would be hemmed in.

Beth deposited the food in the feeder and saw Ron Reagan laboriously trudging through the snow, which was up to her fat, pampered belly. Perhaps she'd leave Eva some notes of her own on healthy cat feeding.

"I can run faster than you!" she challenged the cat playfully, putting down the scoop, and dashing out into the snow after her. As Beth approached her, Ron Reagan made her way to the cover of an evergreen. She hoped the cat couldn't climb it.

"Here, kitty, kitty, kitty," she called out, and bent down on her haunches. Her shoes, socks and the cuffs of her blue jeans were now wet.

"Out from under there, Reagan!" She made a swipe with her arm and the cat took off, Beth in pursuit.

Thank God for the wooden fence; Ron Reagan had nowhere to go. Beth trusted the fence was too high for her to climb. She had the cat cornered and would simply scoop her up and take her into the house.

She spread out her arms, one in each direction, covering her bases. As she reached to the left, Ron Reagan darted to the right, then, vice versa.

"Enough of this, kitty." She grabbed Ron Reagan by the scruff of her neck. As she stood up, the cat hissed, writhed and scratched. Beth proceeded cautiously toward the house, Ron Reagan resisting. About to lose her, she put her other hand under the cat's back feet, which clawed her deep.

"Goddamn you!" Beth still had twenty feet to go to the door. She sped up and tightened the grip on Ron Reagan's neck, both hands in pain. The next thing she knew, the cat had dug her teeth into Beth's fingers and bitten several times. She dropped her on the spot and ran into the house.

Inside, Beth washed her wounds and found rubbing alcohol and bandages in Eva Drake's medicine cabinet. Outside, Ron Reagan was not to be seen. It would serve the damned cat right to spend the night outside. Beth wondered briefly at what temperature obese felines could die of hypothermia.

More Hanukkah gelt arrived belatedly, from her grandparents and her mother. It seemed she would get through December without excessive money worries. The landdykes hadn't booted them out and, to show their financial trustworthiness, Beth and Verla planned to send the next rent check early. Beth had put in her name at a temporary services agency and, lacking good clerical skills, was going to spend next week at a Kmart, demonstrating a popcorn popper and passing out low-fat popcorn.

The following day she returned to Riverside Drive. Out-side, she called and called, then searched the yard, but there was no sign of Ron Reagan. Still smarting from her wounds, she felt just guilty enough to leave a dish of cat food outside before going her way.

Back at home, Verla demanded to examine her hand. Be-grudgingly, Beth took off the bandages.

"Look, it's swollen. See? You've got no choice. You have to go to Student Health, like I suggested yesterday."

"Sorry, I value my life."

"Here's cab fare. Go."

"I ain't dyin' and we ain't rich. I'll take the damned bus."

"You need someone professional to look at this, just to be sure."

"S'pose you're right. But I still have to finish my Juvenile Delinquency paper. Ought to write it on 'Feline Delinquency.' Motherfucking cat." She looked at her own brood. "You guys wouldn't do this to me, would ya?"

At Student Health's Urgent Care Clinic, she waited an hour, then was asked by a nurse if she'd had a tetanus shot in the last five years. As she wasn't sure, the nurse gave her one. Her hands were rewrapped, antibiotics prescribed, and she was told to return in three days if she saw no improvement.

The next day not only could she see no improvement; her nibbled digits — in fact, her whole right hand — had swollen like a gigantic marshmallow.

"You go to Student Health now. Give me the keys and I'll feed the cats before I give my lessons this afternoon."

"I won't be able to finish my paper on time."

"It won't be the first time, you've got a legitimate excuse, and you can't type anyway in your condition. I'll type up what you've got handwritten and you just go."

"All right, already!" She gave Verla a quick kiss and left to catch the bus.

"Emergency room," decreed the clinic doctor as soon as he saw her hand. "We'll call a van to take you to UW Hospital."

"What's wrong with it?"

"You've got a serious infection. Don't worry. They'll take care of you there."

She sat in the emergency waiting room for what seemed like hours. Finally, her name was called and a nurse had her lie down on a table. The doctor would be with her in a few minutes.

A doctor soon appeared, followed by a team of four interns or residents. Having examined her hand dispassionately, he said to the group, "The first thing you have to do in a case like this is try to save the patient's hand."

"Save the hand?" Beth echoed loudly, her voice reverberating down the corridors like a moribund yodel. She began to hyperventilate, sensed she was losing control. At this point, they administered a sedative to her.

She woke up, not knowing how many hours later, with her right arm in a splint and both arms attached to poles. An IV line went into her arm. "I'm dying. I'm a juvenile delinquent and I'm dying. How much time have I got?" she asked someone she didn't recognize, and sank back under.

When she awoke again, she saw Verla. "What happened to me? Am I dying?"

"No, you're not dying. You've got a deep cellulitis infection, whatever that is." Verla kissed her forehead.

"Cat scratch fever?" Verla turned her palms upright, then caressed Beth's leg through the sheet. "How'd you find me?"

"I called Student Health and they told me you'd been sent here. Oh, you poor dear."

"Did you finish typing my paper?"

"I'm afraid there wasn't much to type. I typed up what I found in your yellow notebook. It came to a page and three-quarters."

"Shit. Fifteen-page minimum." Beth observed the contraptions attached to her. "Guess I do have a good excuse for an 'incomplete' this time."

At that moment a doctor came in. "Just a few questions," he said, and Beth nodded. "When did the bite take place?"

"Two days ago, in the morning."

"Where's the cat?"

Beth looked to Verla. "Couldn't find her again this morning."

"Does the cat have all its shots up to date?"

"I don't know," Beth said, again looking to Verla. "We don't know," Verla said.

"This could be touchy." The doctor gave her one of those caring looks that only boded bad tidings. "We've got to produce the cat or prove it's had a rabies vaccine in the last two years."

"No can do," Beth said sourly, and realized it was about time to shell out for her own cats' vaccinations.

"Well, it might be worth the try. After a bite like this, you have seventy-two 'safe' hours. After that, the rabies shots won't even do you any good, if the animal was infected."

"Oy veh," said Beth.

"'Oy veh,'" repeated the doctor, "is right." She saw that his name was Feinberg. "Unless we have evidence of a non-rabid cat, you'll have to begin the shots tomorrow morning."

"This can't be happening to me," Beth said, in between a cry and a wail.

"I'm sorry, but I'm afraid it is," said Feinberg. "You don't, I take it, want to take the chance that you'll be the second person ever in medical history to survive rabies, now do you?"

# 25

Cissy noticed a few snowflakes hit the windshield, then evaporate, as she and Evan descended the steep driveway to Amelia's house, site of the annual departmental Christmas party. By the time they walked in, everyone was there except Sandra and Rickover, the Big Cheese — limburger, in his case. Before they had hung their coats up, he arrived with Sandra, greeting them, "It's starting to snow like a son of a bitch out there."

"Sure as hell is," Nick agreed. "Vance, you got snow in your hair."

"Boxer shorts," said Davidine, the retired Dean of Fine Arts.

"What the hell sort of expletive is that?" said Rickover.

"My dog wore boxer shorts and maybe you should too."

"Oh, he does," said Sandra, and Rickover stood with his eyes as wide open as his mouth. For once, nothing came out of it. Cissy and her colleagues stifled giggles.

"Davidine, how nice to see you." Cissy hadn't seen her since last year's party. "How are you?"

"When I took a cruise of the Nile in October, my sister Ralphetta took it upon herself to put my dog, Boxer, 'to sleep'."

"Boxer was eighteen, wasn't he?" Amelia inserted into the conversation. Behind her Cissy saw a spread of Christmas cookies, pastries, turkey, salads, sauces, dips, appetizers and a smattering of unrecognizable concoctions.

"He had a few more good years, at least as many as I do," Davidine said, and Cissy thought she heard her begin to sniffle.

She turned to Cissy and Evan, who flanked her: "He was the cutest thing. He wasn't a boxer. His name was Boxer Shorts. He was black, with a white rump. That's how he got his name, Rickover!" She barked the vocative across the room at him.

"The real party's in the basement," Amelia whispered to Cissy. She saw through a window that the snow was falling ever more heavily.

In years past Cissy had never indulged, much less at a departmental party. She knew that Evan had brought several joints with him.

"It could be time to head down," she said to Evan and Amelia. A few minutes around the three R's — Rickover, Rutledge and Rothschild, four if you counted Nick Wren — had been enough. She'd nodded at Vonda and Sumner across the room, figuring this showed sufficient politeness to the man who had sexually assaulted her her first year on campus.

She lowered her voice to Amelia: "Is something wrong with Davidine?"

"She's a little bit high and got sentimental."

That Davidine got high was news to Cissy. And when Amelia said "got high," there was no mistaking her meaning.

"We just had a little refreshment before the onslaught. Davidine's doctor doesn't let her drink any longer, so she's found a new outlet. I'll stay up here. You two go on down."

At the bottom of the stairs, she saw Juan stretched out on the sofa, head in Pepper's lap.

"I think Juan's had a little too much here," Pepper said.

"He's not the only one zonked out," replied Evan. "Davidine's stoned out of her gourd."

"And going on about people's underwear," Pepper added.

"I've got a couple of grade-A joints," Evan said.

"Just what we don't need, but be our guest."

Evan lit the joint, and he and Cissy smoked it, while Pepper watched in stoned silence. Cissy had more or less melted into Evan's arms when she heard the familiar rat-a-tat-tat of heels gouging the stairs.

A second later Ginger descended on them. "I knew I smelled something down here."

"Leave it to you to smell anything out," said Evan. "Check out the breath of all the guests yet?"

"Vance could use a mouthwash."

"Have a hit, Ging?"

She seemed to contemplate, then announced righteously: "I've been clean for a long time now. I knew you were all doing drugs down here, but I didn't expect to find an orgy!" She turned on her heels and marched back upstairs. Cissy disentangled herself from Evan, fearing Ginger would soon be embellishing on the details of the "orgy," for which she'd no doubt find a willing ear.

A few seconds later, Blake took her place, a bottle of wine in one hand. "Amelia said the real party's down here." He pulled out three fat joints of his own and laid them on the coffee table.

Juan struggled up to the bathroom, locked himself inside and peered out the window: The snow was for real. It was almost ten o'clock, and a contingent of the men was outside, trying to get the vehicles up and out of Amelia's driveway. When he walked back to the living room he saw that the TV was running a "Severe Weather Warning" along the bottom of the screen. Amelia smiled, beatifically blitzed, while Davidine snored. Vonda and Wilhelmina chatted animatedly, oblivious to the surroundings. Ginger scowled at large and Sandra looked at the TV, as though dazed. It wasn't from marijuana, he assumed; perhaps it was her normal state.

Amelia came to life, focused on him, and said, "I'm afraid we might be stuck here for the night. It's snowed a half foot since six o'clock and up to eight more inches are on the way."

"I'll let them know downstairs." Juan took another peek out the window. Pepper's car was blocked by at least four others, which would have to get out first. He'd either have to call in stranded to PC Cab or to find out if one of their cabs in the vicinity could pick him up. He shoveled food onto a plate in the dining room, took it downstairs and announced the news.

"We could go outside and play in the snow," Blake said, as though to deflect the difficult situation. Juan saw again that he was strikingly good-looking and that, with or without help, he had emptied the whole bottle of wine and was making his way through a second one, which had appeared from somewhere. Juan wondered fleetingly if he might be gay.

"I haven't seen such a good storm in years, and don't think I've ever enjoyed the snow when I'm stoned," Blake went on, and gulped more wine.

"I haven't either," Cissy said, obviously buzzed, smiles careening across her face. "Anything's better than having to shovel it."

"Crazy Californians." Evan shook his head at the two of them.

"We didn't grow up with it," Cissy said. "When was the last time you played in the snow stoned?"

Evan hesitated before answering. "Oh, twenty years ago."

"What do you think, Pepper?" she persisted.

"Sounds fun to me. If we're stranded because of snow, we might as well enjoy it. Juan?"

"No way. You people go." It sounded like an invitation to hell.

While they were outside, he could fill up several more plates, consume the Santa Claus on top the cake, then lock himself in the bathroom again. Cold and snow were facts of Wisconsin life, but one didn't have to go out and play in it.

❦

Cissy led the way upstairs, pulling Evan by the hand. She hadn't ever had this much fun at a departmental party. Along with Evan, Pepper, and Blake, she bundled up by the coat closet off the living room.

"We already tried, you fools," Rickover snarled at them, then rammed a drumstick down his throat. "If we men can't move those cars, you sure can't."

"Yeah," Nick seconded gruffly from in front of the fireplace, nursing a bottle of Johnny Walker Red. Rutledge and Rothschild sat in arm chairs, legs stuck straight out, their expressions disgusted. Sumner more or less hid in a corner, his nose in a book.

"We're going to play in the snow," Cissy announced gleefully.

"I always thought you were tetched, Pankhurst. Now I *know.*"

"Vance, be nice for once," Sandra admonished. "I think I'll join them."

"I'd go, but...," Amelia began. "As host, I think I'd better stay in. You all be careful of the hill. It's windy and snow's still falling. You could slip and end up at the lake's edge." Amelia's house was nestled in a deceptively small tract between Lake Mendota Drive and the lake itself.

"You're as crazy as a loon," Vance said to Sandra.

"At least this loon is going to have fun."

Cissy quickly took Sandra by the arm — the better to spare her Vance's rebukes — and led the five of them out Amelia's side door.

The snow was coming down hard and the wind swirled it around their heads. Cissy figured that the temperature must be about twenty, but didn't mind. She squatted down, extended her arms to Evan, who swung her around in a circle. She closed her eyes to the wind and snow and let the snow batter her face pleasantly. All at once, she landed on her bottom.

"Sorry. It's not like you're Danielle. You just slipped out of my hands."

"That's OK." She wrapped her hair around her ears into a pair of makeshift earmuffs. To her right she saw that Pepper was swinging Sandra in similar fashion.

"Wheeee!" Sandra screamed.

"Tiptoe through the tulips!" She looked over and saw Blake goosestepping through the snow and singing. She began to giggle. Laughing himself, Evan pulled her up. "You can't sit in the snow like that, Cissy. You'll catch a chill, or worse."

"Tiptoe through the tulips, with me!" Blake continued the song, hopping and flinging his arms in the air.

"And meeee!" Sandra screamed through the wind.

"I think Amelia does grow tulips out here in the summer," Pepper said.

"Let's slide down the hill!" Cissy suggested.

"That could be fun." Sandra came over to her side. Her face, in the path of a floodlight, glowed with childlike excitement.

"Your legs aren't even covered. Neither of you," said Evan.

"And you might not be able to climb back up," Pepper added.

"You men have no sense of playfulness," Cissy said.

"I do," Blake said.

"Right. None of you men but Blake is any fun." She let her hair fall back and the wind nipped her nose. "I'm all wet."

"Surprise, surprise," Evan shouted through blowing snow.

"These must be almost blizzard conditions," said Pepper.

"I'm wet too. Vance will think I'm an idiot, but I don't care!" Sandra announced.

Pepper threw a snowball at Blake. Cissy saw it disintegrate in the air. Blake ran toward Pepper, rammed his head at Pepper's stomach; both fell down laughing, and ended up practically wrestling in the snow. Cissy looked into the cozy house and saw the fireplace. If there was any collective holiday cheer, it was outside and not in there.

The inside, however, began to gain appeal, as Cissy realized she was not only wet, but shivering. "I think I've had enough," she said, and Sandra agreed.

"Pepper? How about you?" She almost didn't see him; he was lying in the snow next to Blake.

Pepper dragged himself up and stood. "I don't feel so stoned anymore."

"I still do," said Blake, who sat up hatless in the snow.

"Let's go in," Evan said.

"Stoned?" Sandra said. "Is that why you decided to come out here? You all got drunk in the basement?"

"Yep. Drunk in the basement. That's what we got," Evan said quickly.

She brushed off snow, tilted her head toward the sky, watching snowflakes diving at her in all directions, and stuck her tongue out to taste them.

"Come on, Cissy." She felt Evan grasp her hand. Sandra and Pepper walked over toward them. "Coming, Blake?" Pepper asked.

"Coming!" Blake screamed through the wind, and they went back inside.

❦

"We'll all just make the best of it," Amelia said, when Ginger reappeared. She'd ensconced herself in Amelia's bedroom, calling every cab company in the city, and even a limousine service, all to no avail.

By now, she didn't really care about the sleeping arrangements. All she really wanted was a few lines. If she merely wanted to fall asleep, she could have smoked with Cissy, Evan and, apparently, half of her pot-headed department. But if she was going to do drugs, she wanted good drugs.

She was to bed down in the dining room, of all places. Amelia had apologized profusely for the arrangements, taken special care to supply her with a sleeping bag, blankets, sheets, and pillow. She cursed Melvin — her husband — for being out of town and not being able to accompany her. That would have guaranteed the two of them a bedroom, she was sure.

As soon as the lights were out, she got up, took a Christmas napkin from the table, and wrote "DO NOT DISTURB" on it.

She took her bedding, minus the lumpy sleeping bag, and spread it on the bathroom floor. She taped the napkin to the door and closed it. No way were the rest of them going to see her in the morning with yesterday's make-up, smashed hair and wrinkled clothing. She hung her dress over the shower curtain rod, removed her high heels, and lay down to sleep.

The first knock came soon after. "Read the sign. It's occupied!"

"Ginger? I have to get in there!" It was Rickover.

"Go do it outside. I'm not budging!"

She answered the same to various other knocks during the night. Could it be something racial? Did white people have small bladders? She herself never had a problem getting through the night.

At six o'clock she awoke. As the "household" might be rising soon, she showered with a cap of Amelia's, dressed, applied her make-up and touched up her hair.

Once put together, she went to survey the sleeping arrangements. She'd seen Amelia take Davidine and Wilhelmina to her own room, where there was a private bathroom. She peeked into the spare bedroom and saw the Isaacsons. The study was locked, but she brushed against the door, making vague wake-up noises until she heard Cissy mumble something. The four R's were laughably sprawled around the living room. Sandra, stuffing her face, sat in the dining room. "Sleep well?" she forced herself to ask, not knowing where, or if, Sandra and Vance had slept.

"It's about time you're out of there!" Sandra, no happy camper, snapped at her, and made for the bathroom.

Ginger tiptoed to the basement, the only place left, and found Isaacson's kid and his boyfriend. That accounted for everyone but Blake. She tiptoed back up the stairs. Hmmm. Blake couldn't be sleeping in Amelia's room; in the Isaacsons' was equally unthinkable. That left Cissy and Evan's room. Evan had always been a little kinky, but bisexual? She didn't think so. She'd suspected that Cissy might be a repressed slut, and with a little marijuana... No, even that was hard to imagine. She crouched down to see what she could, only to discover there was no keyhole to peer through.

Frustrated, she returned to the basement. She looked around corners, checked for storage rooms. Nothing, except one padlocked room, which, she guessed, was the site of Amelia's not-so-secret marijuana garden. She scampered back up the stairs, rushed down the hall, uncertain where to head, and tried to discern shapes through the frosted window pane. It was just starting to get light; the snow had finally stopped. Then she remembered: she'd seen the five of them skipping around like fools outside last night. She went back through the living room, saw Nick Wren open his eyes groggily and exited through the side door.

There were no tracks in the backyard; they'd evidently been covered. She herself was in snow almost up to her knees, knew she looked ridiculous, but pushed through it anyway. At the edge of the hill, she saw two feet at the bottom protruding from the snow.

"Blaaake!" she screamed. No response. She yelled again, without result.

She plodded back through the snow, aiming for her recently made indentations. She reached the side door, flung it open and shouted, "Blake's asleep in the snow at the bottom of the hill!"

Rickover shot her an astounded glance and the other men sat straight up.

"Oh my God!" Amelia screamed in the background. "I thought he was sleeping in the basement den!"

Ginger darted past her and grabbed the sleeping bag she'd abandoned under the dining room table. By the time she'd made it back outside, Nick, Rickover and Rutledge were at the top of the hill and, one by one, slid down it. Ginger dragged the bag through the snow, positioned herself on top of it, and went down the hill with a slow, snowy whoosh.

Rickover caught her at the bottom and glared at her. Nick and Rutledge were brushing snow off Blake, who lay motionless.

"Frostnip?" she asked uneasily, and stood up on the bag. "Maybe we'd better wrap him in this."

"Frostbite, at least. Move off." Rickover practically grabbed the bag out from under her.

"More like hypothermia," said Rutledge, as Nick put his hand to Blake's neck, then under his shirt and coat.

"More like dead," said Nick.

# SEMESTER BREAK

# 26

"Mother, you are not going to be in the photos!" They were in the middle of the "family sitting" shoot for Roz's campaign literature.

"You yourself said this was the *family* photo. I suppose that, here in Madison, acknowledging one's mother is un-American!"

"Mother, it would be... like false advertising. Like implying you were a resident of the sixth district."

"But I can vote here. You tell everyone: 'You only have to have been here for ten days at the same address and have the intention to stay.'"

"The key words, Mother, are 'intention to stay'."

Irv looked on at the spat, an almost daily occurrence, and turned away, fending off despair. Rhoda's three-week stay had jolted the household nerves. Although they never observed religious holidays, they'd had to celebrate Hanukkah, then Christmas, all because of Rhoda's insistence, "for Dayne's sake." Dayne had liked it, but Irv was sick of it, sick of...

"We don't know exactly how long I'm staying, do we? But it will be at least through the end of your campaign."

"It's still deceptive. You're going to leave sooner or later."

Irv prayed that it was sooner. If Roz were less stubborn or minimally diplomatic, she'd let her mother stand in on one photo, and then not use it. Diplomacy at home, however, did not figure among her fortes. He wondered whether, if elected, she'd develop any when dealing with the public.

"Now, out of the way, Mother. If you refuse to understand, that's your problem. We have to shoot these last few."

"Irv, what do you think?" Rhoda asked him.

"I don't know what to think any more," he said, determined to stay as neutral as Switzerland, and looked hopelessly at the photographer.

❧

Roz whisked breezily down the stairs an hour after dinner, not a stitch of clothing on. She strode past her mother, who was watching TV, fetched a beer from the refrigerator and returned to sit down in the living room. Dayne was asleep in his grandmother's lap, and Irv reading in the adjoining den.

During a commercial came the reaction, not unexpected: "Rosamond! What on earth...?"

"Nudism, mother. I've abstained for three weeks because of you, but I'm not going to any longer. It's the most natural thing in the world."

Rhoda got up, with more than usual verve, setting Dayne on the floor and throwing her own sweater on Roz's lap.

"Mother, I am not going to put this on. Since you plan to stay a few more months, I figured I'd let you get used to it."

"Used to it! This is totally unnatural. It's... It's... perverse!" The TV program, an environmental one on a cable channel, resumed.

"What's unnatural? Irv sees me nude, Dayne sees me nude, you've seen me nude. It's as natural as it is for those animals, whatever they are, on the screen."

"Mommy's always naked," Dayne said, rubbing his eyes as he woke up.

"Do you mean to say you let Dayne see you like this?"

"All the time," Roz said aloofly, and sipped her beer.

"Roz, please put that on!"

She tossed the sweater back to her mother, who stood in the middle of the room, hands on her hips.

"The child will grow up to be..."

"What, Mother? Say what you mean."

"Say what?"

"Say... what... you... mean."

"You know what I mean." Rhoda paused, then gave a flick of her wrist, which left absolutely no doubt to her meaning.

"Mother, that's ludicrous. Are you implying that by seeing

a grown woman's body, he'll be turned off by it and start liking men?" Roz smiled broadly, and let herself laugh at the absurdity of it. "If anything, he'll come to accept a woman's naked body as the most natural thing in the world and will have no desire to tear some woman's clothes off when he's fifteen, just so he can see what it looks like. If he's interested and is in fact heterosexual."

"Don't lecture me, Roz! And in case you think otherwise, and I hate to say this, but there's no other way to reason with you: Your naked body, at age forty-two, is none too pretty a sight."

"That's right. Boost my ego, Mother. I happen to think that Irv would differ with you."

Both women threw a glance toward the den, and Roz hoped Irv would appear. But to no avail. Of course, he'd refuse to get involved. He was never there when she needed him. Seth, Pepper, and maybe even Juan would stand up to her mother.

"What would you think if I took off my clothes right here and exposed all of you to it?"

"That would be wonderful, Mother. It's so liberating."

"Roz, you're impossible. Worse than your sister."

"At least I've given you a grandchild."

"Yes, to warp in God knows what way. I know what did this to you, and don't try to argue with me. It was that phase of yours. Going to those festivals in the woods and marching around in the all-together with all those naked women. Don't tell me that's not what did this to you!"

It was true, Roz had gone to various music festivals, but only occasionally had she shed her clothes. "Mother, I did not do that."

"You did too. You told me so yourself."

Well, so she had. "That had nothing to do with it. I simply came to the point where I couldn't be bothered to be burdened with clothes in my own house. It's very healthy, sexually and physically."

"*Vey is mir.* Now I've heard everything." She lowered her voice and spoke in disgust: "Sexually healthy! I hope they have psychiatrists here in Madison."

"No, Mother. We're in the hinterlands here. We even have to order our toothbrushes from New York."

"Don't get sarcastic with me."

"As you reminded me, I'm forty-two. At my age I know

what I'm doing. I'm perfectly healthy. Mentally, and physically and sexually."

"Roz, will you stop...!"

"Your problem is you're afraid of sex, you're afraid of your own body."

"My body has enough problems at this age and I at least have the decency to cover it up. The next thing you know, you'd have your whole family walking around nude!"

At this moment, Roz noticed that Dayne had wiggled out of his pajamas and sat up, observing the conversation with apparent interest. At least he hadn't discovered how to play with himself yet.

Rhoda turned around, her eyes falling on Dayne. "See what I mean!" she said, not bothering to lower her voice.

"He's not even four yet. There's no harm."

Rhoda took the sweater and now attempted to wrap it around her grandson.

"Girls' clothes!" Dayne screamed, fighting off his grandmother's advances.

Roz determined that this was enough for the night. She stood up defiantly, arms stretched forward. "I'll put him to bed." After a second, Rhoda relinquished him and Roz grabbed him up, then tossed the sweater back at her mother.

"I'm going to have a nightcap and try to forget this whole scene," Rhoda said.

"Mother, remember your health. No more than two glasses of wine a day, maximum, and not every single day. You yourself said so. And you've already had one today." She was still angry at Beth and her mother for Rhoda's getting tipsy two weeks ago.

"I think I can conduct my own life at my age!"

"And I'll do what I please in my own house!"

Having reached this stand-off, Rhoda marched into the kitchen and Roz hefted Dayne upstairs, leaving it at that.

"Damn you, Irv," she muttered.

"Damn Daddy or damn doggie?"

"Damn 'em both!"

"Mommy, do I have to wear jammies?"

"Wear whatever you want!" she snarled, then realized she was no longer talking to her mother. In a gentle, maternal voice, she repeated, "Yes, wear whatever you want, darling. We don't have to pay any attention to your crazy old grandmother."

# 27

"If only I'd..."
"I feel so guilty, so negligent."
"I don't care what anyone says. I'm taking the blame."
"You're all blameless!" Davidine erupted. "You can't control yesterday nor predict tomorrow. You have to move on with
your lives today! Of course you're sad, but you shouldn't feel
guilty. *Read the clipping! Look at his alcohol level!*" Davidine brandished it in front of them. Cissy, one of the "guilty" ones, reread it for the first time since she'd seen it in the newspaper:

*UW-Madison Professor Freezes to Death*
*By Cynthia Ostrow*
*Capital Times Reporter*
      *A UW-Madison professor of Museum Studies died of car-*
*diac arrest due to hypothermia, the second casualty of the city's 14-*
*inch snowfall Friday night and Saturday morning.*
      *Blake F. Abell, 48, was found Saturday morning at approxi-*
*mately 6:30 a.m. near the lakeshore behind a private residence on Lake*
*Mendota Drive. Witnesses said he had disappeared from a Christmas*
*party at approximately 10:30 p.m. Friday night and that the disap-*
*pearance had gone unnoticed.*
      *Paramedics pronounced Abell dead at the scene. Given the*
*blizzard conditions and a below-zero windchill factor during the night,*
*Abell probably succumbed within two hours, the Dane County*
*Coroner's Office said.*
      *The toxicologists's report submitted to the Coroner's Office*
*showed that there were drugs in Abell's body and that his alcohol*
*level was .18 percent. The alcohol likely quickened his death, the Coro-*
*ner said.*
      *Abell had been in Madison for one and a half years after mov-*
*ing here from California. He had no relatives in the Madison area,*
*and the body was sent back to California for burial.*
      *(See related story on page 2B: "Frostbite Can Be Prevented.")*

      Cissy put on her coat, ready to descend to the lakeshore for
the memorial service that Amelia had organized.
      "Feel better?" Evan hoisted himself into his down jacket.
      "I suppose I do." Cissy didn't know how she was feeling.
"I couldn't have felt worse."

They filed out the side door silently, Davidine having stayed behind, unable to negotiate the hill.

"I had the gardener shovel," Amelia said. "Just follow the path."

Evan led the pack and Cissy followed right behind him. They reached the edge of the hill; Cissy felt as though they were walking a gangplank.

"Amelia, how do we get down?" Evan yelled, breaking the solemnity.

"To the right, there's a winding path I've had shoveled through the trees. There's sand and gravel on it, plus the trees to hold on to. You all go on ahead."

Cissy let Evan hold her hand and she, in turn, held Sandra's, behind her. The zigzag path turned out to be easy enough to navigate. Sandra continued to cry, her make-up streaked. Cissy would have liked to see Ginger here, just to see if she could maintain her flawless appearance and, especially, to see if she could show a trace of genuine emotion. But, as opposed to the four 4 R's now at the National Museum Association Convention in Indianapolis, Ginger had stayed in town and resolutely refused to attend.

Cissy ducked under a branch, held it up for Sandra, then lost her footing, and slid into Evan's arms. He held up the next branch for her, and the sinuous path wound to an end. At the bottom, Lake Mendota's ice-covered expanse stretched in front of them. Cissy felt as though she might have been in Antarctica.

To her astonishment, she saw that Amelia had beaten them all to the shore. "How...?"

"One of the grandchildren's sleds I keep for when they visit." Amelia seemed the type of woman who would be hiking through the Himalayas when she was in her nineties. "I've been doing it all morning. Slide down on the sled, then walk back up the path carrying it."

"Amelia! All of this trouble...," Cissy protested. Amelia had fashioned a golden sunburst on a piece of cardboard and stuck it in the snow. In the middle, in purple letters, she'd written, "In Memory of Our Friend, Blake. 1942-1990." Shiny gold sequins dotted the yellow background. It was a nice gesture, a bright note of color on the cloudy, cheerless afternoon.

The six of them stationed themselves around the sunburst: Cissy, Evan, and Sandra facing the lake; Pepper, Juan, and

Amelia with their backs to it.

"As I asked you to," Amelia began, "just say something that you remember about Blake and offer a memento if you have one. I'll start." She paused only a second. "I remember a man with perfect manners, a sense of humor, who gave lots of life to the two parties of mine he attended. And who, this year, brought me as a gift some of the best weed I'd ever smoked."

"I only met Blake that night, briefly," said Juan. "But he seemed to enjoy life. Perhaps a little too much to aspire to longevity." He attempted a faint chuckle.

The wind blew off the lake, and Cissy huddled further into her coat. Evan spoke before she could: "I remember when Pepper and I saw him at the Harvest Fest on the Square. How totally at ease Blake was, how he put others at ease. I think he was always at peace with himself. Blake was with us only three semesters. There was some resentment, at first, over this new hotshot colleague who was a full professor. But he was fair and ethical. Which made him a rarity in the Department. We'll miss him."

"Vance won't," Sandra muttered through tears.

"I remember how just a few weeks ago," Cissy jumped in, before Sandra's frankness got the better of her, "he told me that my article had been accepted. He didn't have to tell me, but he did, and went on to..." She wondered if she should reconsider her words, given Sandra's presence. "He went on to tell me I didn't need to worry about tenure. It was nice encouragement."

They all looked up at Sandra. What with the cold and the wind, Cissy hoped she'd hurry up.

"I'm glad..." Sandra stopped and stared out to the ice on the lake. She seemed transfixed by it, or numb, physically if not mentally.

"Yes, Sandra?" Amelia coaxed, after a ten-second pause. The cold was obviously getting to all of them.

Sandra's mind seemed to wander back to grim reality. "I'll always remember hiding from Vance, smoking cigarettes in Blake's office. I'm glad Blake and I sang 'Tiptoe through the Tulips' more or less together that night. And I'm glad Blake died with his secret." Several questioning glances landed on her. "And, in case you're wondering, I never knew what it was."

Sandra produced a plastic tulip out of her coat pocket and threw it on the "grave." "It took me forever to find this."

"Herb," Evan said, and everyone smiled or repressed a

laugh, breaking the tension, as he tossed leaves from Cissy's indoor pineapple mint into a circle from which the snow had been shoveled around the sunburst. The wind blew most of them away, but at least one hit the spot.

"Real herb." Amelia said, throwing a marijuana bud on top of the plastic tulip. "Don't any of you dare scoop that up."

"This is for the child in Blake," Juan said, and dropped a red rubber ball — a child's or dog's toy — into the middle. It bounced over the tulip, rolling to the edge of the snow.

"This is a personal memento," Cissy extracted a sealed white envelope. "It's just a private memory that I wrote out." She bent down and placed the envelope under the gaudy plastic tulip so that it wouldn't blow away. "It" was Blake's tenure vote in her favor.

"Pepper," Amelia said. "You haven't said a word."

Cissy too had noticed his silence, inside the house and out. Now he seemed frozen to the spot, stiff, his eyes closed, as dead as Blake, only vertical instead of horizontal.

"Pepper," Amelia prodded, and was met with silence. "Just say a few words. Everyone else did. You'll feel better."

Pepper opened his mouth and out came a string of words in what she imagined was Hebrew — the Jewish prayer of the dead? The deep baritone voice cut itself off as quickly as it had begun. Pepper drew his eyes closed.

"Let's all hold hands for a minute," said Amelia. They outstretched their arms, barely reaching each other around the mementos in the circle. Cissy closed her eyes, opened them, saw that the others all had their eyes shut.

"Now, Let's cover Blake up," Amelia finally broke the silence. "I mean, our mementos for Blake. Over there's a shovel."

Evan stepped over to the shovel, and piled snow onto the mementos, as some of the others brushed snow into the space with their hands. Pepper grabbed a handful and slowly let it trickle onto the spot.

"And when we're finished," Amelia continued, "all who want to are invited to come back up to the house and eat Guerrilla cookies and to consume Blake's legacy — the gift he brought me last week — in his memory."

Cissy noticed that Pepper continued to stand still, eyes closed, as Juan held his hand. Then he pulled his hand away and his eyes moistened. The sobs grew loud, then louder, before turning into a full-fledged wail. Juan, sporting a look of utter incomprehension, put his arm around his shoulder. Amelia came up and steadied him from the other side.

Cissy watched as they finished covering up the mementos. She turned to Evan and fell into his arms, among sobs, Pepper's having proved contagious. She'd spent days weeping for Blake, but was now weeping for herself.

"My tenure vote died," she moaned to Evan, as a shiver went through her body. A favorable decision on her tenure, she concluded, was now every bit as dead as was Blake himself.

"None of you knew him!" Pepper interrupted her reverie, astonishing everyone. "None of you fucking knew him one fucking bit!"

Cissy dared to turn her head slightly and saw the other five of them totally immobile, at a loss for words. Pepper stood still next to Juan, mouth agape, as though shellshocked. Juan's eyes had rounded into bewildered orbs, approaching the size of Pepper's open mouth.

# 28

Cissy and Evan stood contemplating the invitation to Roz's benefit at the Cardinal Bar. "I haven't seen Roz in a couple of months. It'd be nice to go support her."

"You know we have to get rid of Claypool. Roz is the only choice."

"I suppose she is."

"We'll vote for her and give her our five bucks at the door."

"Do you mean we pay to vote for her, and not vice versa?" Cissy joked.

"There are free hors d'oeuvres too."

"You can vote for her."

"What do you mean, I can? You can't vote for anyone else."

"Well..." Cissy demurred, not wanting to tell Evan the truth. He was right: She couldn't vote for anyone else. "Why are you so interested? You just moved into the district."

"And promptly registered to vote." He paused and eyeballed her. "And I'd like to stay here a while. Provided *you* would."

"Oh, so you *would* like to stay here?" she said, pleased with any topic, anything to take her mind off Blake, off tenure.

"As I once said, 'Buy a house here on the east side of the Isthmus'."

They hadn't talked about it in depth in some months. She

knew that problems with Anne and Todd had overly preoccupied him, and was resolved not to push him. "Sounds good to
me." She turned around and pulled every facial muscle she
had into a wide grin.

"Now, just tell me one thing: Why won't you vote for Roz if
you're going to her fundraiser? It doesn't make sense."

She supposed he could survive hearing this truth: "I never
registered to vote in Madison."

"Five years and you've never voted?"

She couldn't tell how appalled he genuinely was.

"Not only that. I never voted in California either. I've never
voted in my whole life."

❧

"Pepper, you've got to get out of the house."

"You go to Roz's benefit. I can always claim I'm sick."

"You feel OK, don't you?"

"Physically, yeah. Just depressed, that's all."

Blake's death had overwhelmed them both, and Juan knew
Pepper still felt guilty, even after the "grief session" and "funeral." Pepper had felt guiltiest of all, being the last one to go
in that night and not having insured that Blake was following
him. It still didn't quite account for Pepper's strange outburst
at the memorial service. Juan supposed he was just beginning
to learn the true meaning of "Jewish guilt."

"Roz needs bodies there tonight. It could even be fun. And
what could go wrong?"

"Roz's mother." Pepper was lying on the sofa, reading a T.
Coraghessan Boyle novel. "That's what could go wrong."

"We haven't had to deal with her that much since the shock
of the first week wore off. Besides, as Roz said, she needs us
there to occupy Rhoda, to keep her away from people who don't
know her."

"Precisely," said Pepper, "why we shouldn't go."

"Come on. Do it as a personal favor to Roz."

Pepper sat up and put aside *World's End*. "It seems we've
done lots more favors for the people upstairs than we've gotten in return lately."

"We do live here rent-free." Juan immediately regretted his
words, which had just slipped out.

"I'd much rather babysit Dayne. But if you insist, I'll go.
But you owe me one for this. You'll be repaying the debt soon

enough."

⚜

"Roz will let us in for free," Beth explained to Verla. "I'm her treasurer, after all."

Verla sat caressing Jenifer in her lap. "But did she tell you that?"

Beth let out a trace of exasperation and admitted the truth: "No, she didn't, but I'm sure she will. She knows we don't have money. Ten dollars total, that's cat food for almost two weeks."

"I don't know." Verla was rubbing Jenifer's tummy, determined to teach the kitten how to lie on its back in her arms. "What about Roz's mother?"

"Aw, give her a couple drinks and she gets real loose."

"That's not what I meant." Jenifer had fallen asleep, and purred lightly. "Roz was none too pleased with that outing." Roz had been so angry at Beth and her mother that day, that she refused to give Beth the full hundred dollars, and offered only sixty. Beth haggled until Roz gave up and gave her seventy-five.

"Well, if she gets drunk again, it won't be my fault. Like you're always sayin', no one else can make you drink. And if you want to drink, no one can stop you." She knew Verla couldn't argue with this and, indeed, she didn't.

"Now that I finished my Social Gerontology paper, I feel I deserve a break. A night out on the town."

"We could have an intimate 'night out the town' at home."

"Yeah, well, we can do that any time, right?"

"I suppose." Verla's words lacked conviction.

"Besides, Roz said she wants a multicultural presence there."

"What does she mean by that?" Verla looked up and the kitten opened its eyes and yawned. "I take it she's not talking about the physically challenged." Verla indicated the large bandage and arm splint that Beth still wore from her accident. Ron Reagan was gone and Eva Drake was back, but Beth had the upper — and swollen — hand. Ron Reagan's shots were not up to date, Beth could have threatened a lawsuit, and Eva Drake grudgingly paid her the promised sum. Beth's student health insurance had covered the hospital stay.

"I'm physically challenged right now and that counts. But I think Roz means lesbians. Hey, I could..." She tried to think of a substitute for "kill two birds with one stone," as PETA had sensitized her language in this area. No substitute came to mind.

"All right, I suppose," Verla gave in. "Just so I don't have to dress like one."

"Like one what?"

"Lesbian."

"The worst that could happen is Roz might show us off, me bein' her treasurer and all."

"Show us off as what?" Jenifer jumped down off Verla's lap.

"Dykes, what else?"

Cissy and Evan arrived promptly and each paid the five dollars at the door. Attendance was still sparse, Roz on top of them in a second.

"Cissy, great of you to come! And Evan, wonderful to see you!" What new public persona was this, Cissy wondered. Obviously, one of a would-be politician trying to hide her more abrasive character traits. In the distance stood Irv, talking to a pony-tailed man.

Cissy saw an elderly woman making her way to them, a wine glass in her hand. She looked conspicuously out of place. Cissy thought she might be an old-time east-side radical, a sort of counterpart to Amelia on the west side.

"I'd like you to meet my mother, Rhoda Goldmann. Cissy's a good friend, who used to live downstairs from me in our old house."

"Pleased to meet you," all three chimed.

"The two of you look like regular people," said Rhoda, casting a less-than-subtle look of disdain at the rest of the small crowd of offbeat east-side gurus, radicals and political meddlers.

Tongue-tied, Cissy saw Roz take off in a flash, and realized that she had purposely palmed her mother off on them. "We live in the district," said Evan.

"It's good to see that Roz has some nice normal supporters like you."

Cissy was again without words; she turned and saw a stream of others now lining up to pay their donation.

"I've never seen so many white faces and blond heads in my life," Rhoda stated. It was hard to tell if this was a neutral observation or a judgment. "I guess you expect it here on the prairie."

"I'm originally from California," Cissy put in, to say something. People often took her for Scandinavian in this part of the country.

"That's nice. I'm from New York, did you know?" Rhoda said, as if her accent weren't obvious. "Aren't there any minorities in this city?"

"Lots of them," Evan said. "To start with, the Cardinal's owner is Cuban."

"And, there are lots of Germans, Swedes and Finns, but especially Norwegians," Cissy added.

"I don't think that's what Mrs. Goldmann meant."

"Oh, do call me Rhoda."

Juan and Pepper waited in line to get in, holding the outer door, half-inside and half-outside.

"See, Roz doesn't need bodies, The place is going to be jammed."

"I don't think there's such a thing as a political benefit with too many people."

They finally moved up and paid their money, went in and got drinks at the bar. Juan saw Cissy and Evan talking to Rhoda. "See. Rhoda's occupied."

A minute later, they saw Roz whisk Rhoda away and straight over to them.

"Rhoda!" Juan conjured up enthusiasm at seeing her, as Roz stole away. "Nice to see you." He calculated it had been twenty-eight hours — maximum — since he'd last encountered her.

"Juan, Pepper, how nice. Could one of you boys get me another glass of wine? I'm afraid Roz is monitoring my consumption tonight."

"Sure, Rhoda." Juan escaped Pepper's condescending smirk and turned to the bar and the bartender. A minute later, Rhoda had her wine, for which Juan had paid.

"Thank you, Juan."

"Sure thing, Rhoda."

"Can I ask you boys a question? Are you aware of this new phase of Roz's?"

Juan trusted she didn't mean lesbianism. "No, I don't think so."

"Nudism, can you believe it? She actually walks around the

house with all of her parts hanging out. The truth is, her breasts didn't sprout until she was fourteen and stopped growing when she was fifteen." Juan tried to keep a straight face, no easy feat, and looked at Pepper, who was evidently enjoying this. "I hope I'm not shocking you. I think that any topic is good for conversation, but you just don't have to put it all into practice like Roz does. And the marijuana!" Rhoda waved her hand, as if dispelling smoke. "The smell comes out of her bedroom, and she thinks I don't know. Of course, she'll have to straighten herself before she's elected. Now, you two don't smoke marijuana, do you?"

"I smoke cigarettes," Juan hedged.

Rhoda craned her neck. "Oh, Juan, can you give me one while Roz is at the other end of the room? She knows I'm not supposed to smoke. But I don't see how one or two a day can hurt."

Juan pulled out his pack — Camel Lights, since Roz had prohibited him from smoking his Merits — and offered her one. He lit it, and one for himself.

"Now, if Roz comes by, I'm just going to hand this to you, Pepper."

"Not to me. Roz knows I don't smoke."

"Fine, I'll deal with it myself. Now tell me, you didn't answer my question. You two wouldn't smoke marijuana, would you?"

⚘

Beth talked her way past the volunteer taking contributions at the door, not without explaining several times. It involved a few white lies and a whopper, but they got in, their ten dollars intact. She was glad that, as treasurer, she didn't have to be taking the money and that Roz had found a volunteer.

"Great!" Beth exclaimed, making for the bar. "Now we got ten dollars to drink with."

"Beth, like you said, that's cat food money for two weeks."

"I'll only have one, don't worry." Beth ordered herself a glass of burgundy and a mineral water for Verla.

They went to the back of the bar, Beth seeing no one she knew except for a few Labor Farm volunteers, then she made for the hors d'oeuvres. "The money we drink up, we save by eatin' free tonight." Beth piled a plate with vegetables, cheese and crackers, fancy little sandwiches impaled by toothpicks, and some sort of Mexican pizza that didn't appear to contain meat.

"Hey, look! There's my old Museum Studies prof, Cissy Pankhurst." Beth pointed at her, none too subtly.

"Which one?"

"The one with the long blond hair and that big old skirt, next to the blond-haired guy."

"Oh, I see. She's the one that flipped out and gave you — and everyone else — an A that semester?"

"That's the one. If it wasn't for her, I could've flunked out freshman year."

At that moment, Beth saw Roz leading her mother out of the restroom, a mere two or three yards away from them.

"Looks like she's gonna dump the old lady on us," Beth said, and inhaled more pizza. Roz approached promptly, her politician's smile affixed to her face.

"You two have met," Roz said to Beth and Rhoda, "but I don't think you've met Vera."

"Verla," Beth corrected.

"Sorry, I always get it wrong. And tonight, with all these people, I don't have a chance. Now mother, you just have a nice chat with Beth and Verna."

"Sorry 'bout that day a few weeks ago, Rhoda," Beth said.

"Oh, I enjoyed myself. It's just that Roz thinks her mother is a shikker."

"Shikker?" Beth asked. She put down her hors d'oeuvres — her dinner — and took her glass of burgundy in hand.

"Your parents didn't speak any Yiddish at home, darling?"

"A little. I only know 'meshugge' and some swear words."

"Shikker means 'a drunk.' We all know there are almost no Jewish alcoholics, but the goyim, now that's another matter." Rhoda gave a deprecating stare at the room, or the goyim. Beth looked over at Verla, who either hadn't understood, or took no offense. "But speaking of meshugge, I'm sure you never gave your mother problems like Roz and her sister gave me. Roz went though a lesbian phase and would have me believe that half the women in Madison are that way."

"Oh, not quite half." Having played "straight" for Rhoda for one afternoon was enough, and Roz hadn't asked her to tonight. "Though on the near-east side, I'd say it's a little higher than elsewhere."

Rhoda eyed them questioningly for a second. "I think they

should have their civil rights and all, but how one could make that choice for herself, I'll never understand. It's the worst disappointment a daughter could give her mother. It took fifteen years for Roz to get over that." Rhoda made an elaborate hand gesture to emphasize the number. "And now, this new phase, nudism."

"Yeah, we saw," said Beth.

"Pardon me?"

"Oh, nothin'." Rhoda stared at her and Beth wondered how much the old lady knew.

"I don't know what was worse, the lesbian phase or this nudist phase. I just don't know about Roz. Her personal life, that is. Mind you, I think she'd make a marvelous politician. After a few years on the city council, I'm sure she could be mayor if she wanted. Of course she's going to have to clean up that nudist act of hers, and I certainly trust that her lesbian phase is gone for good."

"I wouldn't exactly call it a phase, Rhoda. If it's a phase, it's usually a real long one."

"Roz's was fifteen years," Rhoda repeated. "She threw it right in my face."

"Sorry to tell you this, but in my case, I think it's permanent."

"You?" Rhoda's eyes bulged to golf balls. "A nice little Jewish girl like you?"

"Yeah, and married to a nice shiksa — Verla, right here."

"I think I'm going to go freshen my wine."

"Your choice, Rhoda. If you get shikkered, Roz can't go blamin' it on me."

"No, but Rhoda can," Verla said. "It's not nice to shock an elderly woman like that."

# SPRING SEMESTER, 1991

# 29

Beth duly appeared at eight o'clock Tuesday morning at the Museum Studies departmental office, but found it locked. A work-study job had finally come through for her, twenty hours a week, scheduled around her afternoon classes.

She roamed the halls, saw Cissy Pankhurst's name on a door and remembered not only the saving A, but the adolescent crush she'd had on her. She wandered back toward the main office. Nameplates on the door read: "Vance R. Rickover, Chair" and "Wilhelmina Wiggins, Administrative Secretary."

Still no sign of life. Beth was both irked that she'd gotten up early for nothing, and hopeful that this might turn out to be a real easy job.

A few minutes after eight, a heavy, fiftyish woman came nervously down the hall, fumbling with keys. "Oh, you must be the new girl."

"If you mean the student worker, that's me."

"Yes, student worker," the woman muttered. They introduced themselves and Wilhelmina let them in the office and turned on the lights. Beth was making a point of letting everyone know where she stood this first day; buttons on her jacket read "SILENCE = DEATH" and "ACT UP." She left her coat on and let Wilhelmina get a look.

"You can hang your coat up over there." In any case, under it Beth wore her "I'm Not a Lesbian, But My Girlfriend Is" T-shirt. She let Wilhelmina get a look at that too, before pulling it off over her head. In any case, she wore another button, "YIKES

DYKES!" — the lesbian group on campus — on her blouse underneath.

"Just so you know, Professor Rickover teaches Tuesdays and Thursdays from seven forty-five until eight thirty-five, so those days if we arrive a little late, there's usually no one here to notice. But believe me, he's up here by eight thirty-six and we'd better be here and looking busy." Beth was liking the sound of this. "And at about nine o'clock, the place really starts to buzz." The secretary cast a glance at Beth's "YIKES DYKES!" button. "And speaking of Professor Rickover, he's not going to like what you're wearing on your blouse."

Rickover had interviewed Beth, who had prudently hidden her politics that day. The department was in a pinch, he'd told her, the secretary had threatened to quit unless they got another student worker right away, as they'd just lost their last one, an ROTC cadet, to Desert Storm preparations. Obviously desperate, he'd hired her. She'd sensed he was a reactionary creep.

Although not creepy or reactionary, Wilhelmina could use a little educating, Beth figured: "You must know the university prohibits discrimination against minorities, and with the new speech code, he can't even verbally insult me for anything."

"Oh, dear." New lines of worry seemed to etch themselves into Wilhelmina's face. "I don't think it's exactly a 'speech code.' Anyway... I'd better show you what to do. We'll go down to the service room first and make coffee."

"That sounds good." She'd need something to keep her system going at this godforsaken hour.

In the service room Wilhelmina began to show her the routine. She didn't know that she'd be preparing coffee —not listed in her job description— but supposed if she was going to drink it, someone had to prepare it.

"Oh, your hand!" Wilhelmina noticed belatedly, probably at first distracted by her sexual politics. "How will you ever work?"

"A cat bit me. Laid me up in University Hospital for five days. Had to have five rabies shots in the arm." Unlike the old days, the doctor had informed her, when they gave you twenty-three in the stomach. "Had to wear a splint on my arm, all kinds of shit." Wilhelmina winced. "Oops, sorry."

"How will you ever type? There's stapling, photocopying and collating to be done. I don't see how..." By now the secretary herself had made the coffee, which began dripping into the carafe.

"In any case, you can't discriminate against the physically challenged. But not to worry, the bandage'll come off in a week or two."

"Thank goodness for that. I mean, I'm sorry about your injury, but this department..." The secretary threw up her hands, as if already conceding defeat. "It's getting to be too much for me, and now we've lost a faculty member. Here, you and I can both have a cup, if you want."

Beth wanted. "Black," she specified.

As though she were an invalid, Wilhelmina poured it for her, then sugared and creamed her own. "There, that will leave more than enough for Professor Rickover."

They took their cups back to the office and Wilhelmina had her sit behind a desk. "I suppose you can at least answer the phone. I'll give you the faculty teaching schedules and their office hours. That accounts for half the calls. Though I'm afraid you're going to have to do some one-handed copying, collating and stapling too."

"I'll manage. I'm not paralyzed or anything."

"Oh, there's Professor Rickover coming now. You can always recognize his step, not to mention his jangling keys."

Through the doorway came Rickover, tall, lanky, and a face that could star in a horror flick. He carried notes in one hand, a coffee mug in the other. "G'morning!" he greeted the secretary gruffly. Then he saw Beth.

"Off with the button, shrimp!"

With that, he slammed his office door behind him.

Beth's first thought was to file a complaint for the "shrimp" remark. But maybe it was better to hold on to her newfound job. Wilhelmina shook her head warily.

Cissy went into the main office and saw the new student worker, who wore a lesbian button, and thought she recognized her.

"Hey, Ms. Pankhurst? How ya doin'? You probably don't remember me. I'm Beth Yarmolinsky, was in your Intro class five years ago this semester. You gave me an A."

"Ah, yes." Cissy recalled Spring Semester, 1986. After Isaacson's assault of her, she'd passed out 300 A's to the Intro

Class, in total frustration and a sort of misguided revenge. A few stellar students from her Intro classes had stuck in her memory over the years; this one wasn't one of them.

"Hey, you still live in that place on the corner of Willy and Ingersoll? I'm just down on South Dickinson."

"I do, as a matter of fact." Cissy didn't exactly mind student chumminess, but was already beginning to feel leery of this one.

"Thought I'd seen you around there. I used to work at Ho Chi's, was manager, in fact, till I resigned over the boycott. I'm sure you heard about that, didn't ya? That place used to be PC, but they went down the tubes, from politically correct to politically challenged. I'd say it serves 'em right, wouldn't you?"

"Yes, I suppose." She'd only known of the boycott through Evan.

"Then I saw you at Roz's benefit last week at the Cardinal."

"Ah, yes."

"So you been here a while? Just like me. Sixth-year senior this year, part-time, so it's gonna take me a couple more years to finish. I suppose you have tenure by now, huh?"

"No, I don't. Look, I'm sorry to interrupt you, but I teach in..." She glanced over at the wall clock. "Thirty-five minutes. And I need twenty copies of this run off and stapled before class."

Beth held up her bandaged hand. "I'll do my best. Especially for a kindred soul. Hey, don't look startled. I didn't mean to imply you're a lesbian or anything. I just meant a neighborhood groupie, that's all." Beth stood up, hollered in Wilhelmina's direction. "Hey, can you show me where the Xerox machine is? Here's my first job."

Wilhelmina flashed a distressed, apologetic look at Cissy, and led Beth to the photocopy room. Cissy could see it would have been easier to do it herself.

Beth attended her first Death and Dying class. The students looked comatose and the professor moribund, as though he soon might have to be dealing with the topic personally. Beth seemed the only bright-eyed one in the room. Rounding out her course work this semester was AIDS and Ethics. Lethal class subjects if she'd ever had them, but as she was finishing her advanced course requirements in Social Work and hoped to work with PWAs one day, these two choices seemed the most appropriate.

The prof passed out the syllabus and list of texts, then droned through the course requirements. Beth had already purchased the texts or checked them out of the library, when possible.

"There are twelve texts and thirteen of you. I take it at least one person will be dropping." The prof paused, came to life and met each student with suddenly fierce eyes, as though to scout out the drop-out, if not to scare one of them out on the spot. No one was moving; how could they in their collective coma? "So I'll assume there will be one student to lead the discussion for each text. Or maybe we can have two students doing each text and that way you can all lead two discussions."

Beth's hand shot up. "I'll take *A Death of One's Own*," she blurted out, referring to the book by her former history professor. She'd read it a year ago, found it quite moving and might be able to get by with skimming it this time. After five years, she'd finally learned it wasn't true that "nothing happens the first week of class."

"I wasn't going to have you choose until Thursday, by which time someone will usually have dropped, but if there are no objections..."

Beth stared down her classmates, as though daring them to speak. As if near death themselves or taking a post-lunch snooze, they didn't.

"All right. You're..."

"Beth Yarmolinsky."

The prof fumbled with his glasses, stared down at the papers on his desk. "Ah, yes. Here you are on the roster. *A Death of One's Own* is yours. Although I've listed the texts alphabetically, I've scheduled us to begin with Lerner's book. So you'll lead that discussion next Thursday."

"Not in two days!?" she raised her voice, panicking.

"I didn't say this Thursday, but *next* Thursday, as in a week from Thursday." He drilled his sharp eyes into hers, driving the point in. "But on second thought, there's no reason why we *couldn't* do it this Thursday."

Beth trusted that he was bluffing, still trying to scare someone away.

"It's one of the shorter texts and you could all read it in two days."

"No, please. We wouldn't want to fu... I mean, screw up

your syllabus or anything, would we?" She looked around at her classmates, hoping for a shred of support. It was hard to get back-up from the dozing or the dead.

"All right. Next week. You have your nine days." He looked down at the roster again. "Ms. Yarmolinsky."

"Now..." The prof stood up, not without effort. "Lest any of you think you're getting out of here after ten minutes, you'll write me an essay on your own personal experiences dealing with death and the dying. If you don't have any... Oh, of course you all do! Five hundred words minimum! These will count as your participation grade for today. You'll be getting one every single class day. An absence equals an F. Two absences and you're out! Unless, that is, you've been near death and you can prove it. Here, take these blue books and start writing!" He more or less flung them at them, forcing them out of their slumber to pick them up off the floor.

Shit. This was the first and last time she'd attend the first day of class. But maybe it wasn't so bad to get her discussion leading out of the way. Especially with her new job, she'd have to buckle down. And there was no way she was going to miss the Desert Storm protests, discussion to lead or not.

Now she had to sit back and think. She had two living parents, four living grandparents, and all her high school and college friends were alive. Then she foused on ACT UP; although some of her fellow members had been ill, none that she could think of had died. Hmmm. It seemed she'd have to write about the death of a childhood pet, not, perhaps, the best fodder. Or maybe, she mused, it was time to try her hand at fiction.

# 30

"I don't even think her name's legal," Roz complained to Irv as she sat naked on the bed. She was irate to read that a third candidate had filed in the sixth district, forcing a February primary. The house was, for a change, quiet, both Rhoda and Dayne in bed.

"She changed it legally, according to the newspaper. And your legal name is what goes on the ballot."

"Maddie Son!" Roz scoffed, and scratched her armpit. "It's... I don't know," she sputtered, looking for a fancy word that wouldn't come to mind. "Devious, that's what it is. People shouldn't be allowed to change their names to crazy ones like hers."

Irv cracked the slightest of smiles.

"Don't even say it! 'You sound like your mother.'" Rhoda had taken years to get over Roz's name change from "Goldmann" to "Goldwomyn."

"I wasn't going to." Irv's voice was so kind and gentle that she couldn't contradict him. "The only name I know that's been successfully challenged in court for purposes of a ballot is 'None of the Above.' In any case, she's only a fringe candidate."

"You can say that again." She'd heard of the strange couple —not a unique phenomenon in the sixth district— that had popped up out of nowhere two years ago.

*According to court records,* Irv read from the newspaper, *Son legally changed her name from Madeleine Quackenbush in September, 1989. Her husband, Dane County, changed his from Daniel Pierce at the same time. Son describes herself as a "street performer" who acts along with County and their "children," a dog named "Mad Dog" and a cat named "Rabid Cat."*

"God forbid they have real children. They'd probably name them 'State Capital' and 'County Seat.' Or 'Mendota' and 'Monona.' I still say that 'Maddie Son' is illegal. I think I should challenge it in court."

"Roz, don't be so litigious."

"I thought litigation was your business." She lay down and covered herself with a blanket.

Irv slipped out of his boxer shorts and under the covers. "Even if I thought there was a chance, it would only show that you consider her a serious opponent, which she isn't." ·

"I suppose you're right."

She rolled over next to Irv and let him take her in his arms. She began to relax, tried to put the election out of her mind. Irv kissed her lips, her neck, then her breasts.

They hadn't made love in... how long? Could it have been since her mother arrived over a month ago? Roz feared that it was. Poor Irv. She abandoned herself to his caresses and tried to block out all else, though Maddie Son kept trying to pop back into her mind.

Roz felt relaxed the next morning and looked with astonishment at the clock: ten twenty-two. She must have slept ten hours straight, and needed it; she hadn't even heard Irv get up. After her shower, she put on her flip-flops and padded downstairs.

She walked into the kitchen and stopped dead in her tracks. Rhoda sat at the table reading *The New York Times,* with her murdered mink around her neck.

"Mother!"

"Yes?" Rhoda replied blandly, eyes still on the paper.

"What do you think you're doing?"

"Giving you a taste of your own medicine."

Roz marched to the coffeemaker and poured herself a cup. In the living room she saw Dayne romping with Irving.

"God, this stuff is strong! Who made this?"

"I did. I thought you liked it that way."

"Mother, this coffee is thoroughly baked. What time did you put it on?"

"Six-thirty, when I got up."

"The coffeemaker's programmed to make mine at nine-thirty."

"I know. I didn't want to be wasteful, so I deprogrammed it. I thought you could drink this."

"You thought wrong." She began to prepare a more potable brew and realized she'd left her cigarettes upstairs. She reached a new pack from the carton on top the refrigerator, and discovered an opened pack of Benson & Hedges Menthol Lights.

"Mother, the doctor told you to stop smoking. I can't believe you're doing it on the sly. If you're going to hide your cigarettes, you could do a better job than this." She poured water in the coffeemaker and flicked it back on.

"Fine. Next time I will." Rhoda sat unruffled. Roz lit one of her own Camel Filters.

"And what do you mean, 'giving me a dose of my own medicine'?" Roz asked, fearing she knew the answer.

"I believe I said 'taste.' At least I'm not *draped* in mink, like you're draped in... your birthday suit. You, I presume, are making your own fashion statement, and I'm making mine."

"But your 'fashion statement' is very politically incorrect!"

"So would yours be in most circles."

"And that particular stole of yours. It even shows the poor little mink's head!" It was the head that revolted Roz more than anything.

"I read in last night's *Capital Times* that Wisconsin leads the nation in mink production."

"What does that have to do with anything?"

"I'd assume it means that minks should be in fashion here."

"Mother, this is Madison, not Wisconsin! And I'm running for public office and you're my mother and you're impossible!"

"Impossible?" Rhoda said coolly. "At best then, it's a case of like daughter, like mother."

Roz looked over and saw that Dayne had removed all his clothing.

"Dayne, where did you put your clothes?"

Dayne pointed off into the distance. Roz stood up and saw Irving chewing on them in the living room.

"Jesus Christ! Mother, Irving's chewing on Dayne's pants. I told you, Dayne, you can take off your clothes in the house any time, but you have to pick them up. You can't leave them on the floor."

She strode into the living room and bent down. Irving attempted to engage her in a tug-of-war over the pants.

"Mother, get these clothes away from this mutt of yours!" The dog nipped at her ankle. "Goddamn you, Irving!"

"Don't talk to Irving that way. He's probably more sensitive than you are." Rhoda came over, bent down on her knees and petted the dog, Dayne observing from behind.

Roz marched into the kitchen and took the local paper and a newly brewed mug of coffee upstairs. She lay down on her stomach on the bed and began to read. On the front page of the Metro Section she found a story about none other than Maddie Son.

"Filthy media whore," she muttered, as angry at the candidate as at the *State Journal*. Photos of all three candidates appeared, Maddie Son donning a turban and mirror sunglasses. She'd seen her before with her husband, who dressed identically. While she and Claypool received a mere mention of their names, the article focused on Son and her ridiculous proposals: to eliminate prostitution downtown — not even in their district — by creating a floating brothel on Lake Monona; to have horse racing with legalized betting on Willy Street; and to create a cow-petting garden in Orton Park. Never mind that the park had been Madison's first cemetery, before it was moved because of cow droppings on the graves of the departed. Roz knew a little Madison history, and suddenly wondered if Maddie Son did too. Hadn't Willy Street once been used for horse racing?

It was all ridiculous and Irv was right. She had absolutely

no reason to worry. Except, perhaps, about what was going on downstairs at this very moment. She decided to brave the day once again, and walked back downstairs with the paper. Her mother should get a laugh out of Maddie Son's proposals.

As she rounded the stairs into the living room, Rhoda stood at the open front door, the mink still around her neck.

"Mother!" she screamed and walked up behind her. A flash went off in their faces before Roz could steal a look at who it was.

Rhoda slammed the door shut and turned around, flushed and flustered.

"Mother, why did you open the door with that mink on?"

"Because the bell rang. I was dealing with Irving, Dayne, and Dayne's clothes all at once, and Irving had carried Dayne's pants right over here to the door. Then the bell rang, I stood up and pulled the door open, a young man mumbled some political nonsense and something about a survey. I was about to close the door on him, when you yelled and startled me and he took my picture."

"Oh, blame it on me." Roz ran to the window to see if she could get a glimpse of him. Glances out both front windows produced nothing. *"Our* picture, you mean. What exactly did he look like?"

"It was hard to see. He had those crazy reflecting sun glasses on and some floppy white hat. Actually it was more like a towel on his head."

"Oh, God!" Roz brandished the newspaper in front of her mother. "Do you mean he looked something like this?"

"Yes, except it wasn't a woman. Not that you can tell that's a woman by the picture. Or the person at the door might have been a woman with a gravelly voice."

"Do you see who this is? My opponent! Well, now I've got reason to sue! Invasion of privacy."

"I'd say it was my privacy."

"That son of a bitch could have been a rapist. I can't believe you opened the goddamned door."

"Roz, your language is so... unbecoming this morning."

"You're lucky I didn't say 'fuck.' Just take that mink off, will you? I can't take this any longer."

"As soon as you put your clothes back on, I will."

# 31

"You look awful," Evan said upon his arrival home.

"Just what I need to hear." Cissy covered her face with a pillow, then promptly sneezed.

"Gesundheit. I didn't mean it that way. How are you feeling?"

She lowered the pillow and wondered if he could tell. "Pleasantly drunk. Don't kiss me."

"Drunk?" Cissy consumed as little alcohol as he, a borderline diabetic, did.

Cissy's cold was so severe that she didn't even feel like working at home. Though Evan had brought up the wood as usual, she hadn't bothered with the stove all day; her fever itself was sufficient to keep her warm. She lay propped up on pillows in the bed; her knees made a tent under the blankets. A stranger might have assumed she was pregnant, if not ready to give birth. The nightstand beside her looked like an incipient pharmacy: Nyquil, decongestant tablets, nasal spray, aspirin, lip balm, cough syrup.

"There's alcohol in the Nyquil and in the cough syrup. You know I have no tolerance for it."

"What you need is a good hot toddy and what we need in here is some more heat."

"Hot toddy?" She was unsure exactly what one was, and thought people only drank them in the South, in the past, or in novels.

"Tea with honey, lemon and whiskey or bourbon. Best remedy of all."

"I'm already woozy. I think I'll pass, thanks. How was your day?"

"Well... After Anne called and informed me that Todd burned up all his textbooks in the wood stove at home and now we owe the school district over one hundred dollars, it got better. I took my advanced class to the Elvehjem. But yours..." — Evan had taught it for her — "...I had to rouse out of a mass bout of narcolepsy. Oh, there's a letter for you among the junk mail." Evan stepped out to the dining room, came back in and handed it to her.

She made out the return address from Monica, a friend from graduate school now on the faculty at Cornell. She picked up her glasses from the nightstand, put them on and ripped it open. By the second paragraph, her mouth slackened. "This is unbelievable!"

"What is it?"

"Monica didn't get tenure. Monica, with her book published to great reviews, scads of articles, and editor of a prestigious journal that she's killed herself working for! The department voted unanimously in her favor, their equivalent of the divisional committee split down the middle, and some mean dean himself broke the tie."

"C'mon, Cissy. Cornell's the Ivy League. It's different. You'll come through fine."

"'You'll come through fine,'" she mimicked, nervous about own own tenure talk next week. "What do you know about it? You're not a woman, you never went through tenure, and you don't have to publish!"

"But I do publish," he protested. "A little."

"You don't know what it's like having it hang over your head for six years! You do everything right, get your book published, then the Old Boys' Club gets together and plays politics with your life, bouncing you around like a balloon, flicking you back and forth with their fingers! And my mind, body and emotions are inside that balloon, and I can't take it any more! Look at me!" She stretched out her arms, knocking the open bottle of aspirin to the floor. "This cold is probably the result of the strain of tenure!"

"Have you been talking to Ginger today?"

"So what if I've been talking to Ginger? We women need to unite! We're tired of being screwed over by the system!"

"I never expected you to become such a feminist overnight."

"It's not feminism and it wasn't overnight. It's just equality that I want!" Cissy let out a long, deep cough. He bent down, patted her back gently and, when the cough subsided, stroked her hair.

"I thought feminism was about equality. But don't worry. You'll be the exception."

"If I live," she said in a hoarse voice, and burst into another spasm of coughs. "And if I don't, you know whose fault it will be!? The patriarchy's!"

"I know. You've been talking to Roz."

By Friday Cissy felt barely well enough to teach her classes. Rickover appeared promptly at her office door, a rarity now that he was chair. Those he wanted to see he usually commanded to appear in his own office.

"May I come in, Pankhurst?" It was the first time she'd ever heard him use these first two words, though she noticed that he had already crossed her threshold.

"Do you mean come in *and* shut the door? Be my guest."

He looked at her as if to upbraid her for flippancy, but pulled the door closed. Feet planted wide apart, arms crossed in front of his chest, he towered over her. "Heard you've been sick. Glad you're hale and hearty again. And I know you've been talking to Sandra."

"Why, yes. I talk to all my colleagues. Doesn't everyone?" She knew this was anything but true.

"Of course," Rickover snapped, undoubtedly knowing the falsity of her statement. "But I understand, uh, that Sandra has been confiding in you."

Confide. Cissy knew that Vance's use of the word meant trouble. Sandra hadn't revealed any deep secrets —only the Valium. No one had ferreted out Blake's secret, and the memorial service was nothing to hide. "Is something wrong?"

"I'm not here to grill you — that'll be happening soon enough — but what I want to say is this: Sandra's under so much stress, what with her lecture, that she's having psychological problems. She's not rational. Just beware: You can't believe anything she says."

"Anything?"

"All right. You can't believe *everything* she says. Her perception of reality is skewed."

"All right, Vance. I'll remember that." She smiled to herself, not adding that almost everyone in academia had a similarly skewed perception.

"That's all, Pankhurst. I know she talks to you. I'm glad she has someone to talk to." Cissy doubted his sincerity. "But just watch out what she says. Take everything she says with a grain, no, a shaker of salt. Got it?"

By the time Cissy attended Sandra's three-thirty lecture and took the bus home, it was after five. Evan had stayed home, laid up with a replica of Cissy's cold.

"How'd Sandra's lecture go?"

"The lecture was superb. But she was so nervous. She trembled like you wouldn't believe."

"Who wouldn't? You would, at least a little."

"Don't joke. I get my turn soon enough." She'd gotten a two-week "stay of execution" from Rickover before she had to give hers. Evan stuck his palms out, as though to keep her at bay. The next thing she knew, he'd put a mask over his mouth, as if he were quarantined, worried as he was about her catching his cold or having a relapse right before her tenure talk. The truth was, so was she. "But if I perform like Sandra, I'm out of here. Her content, her ideas, were masterful. But she shook so badly, she could hardly read it. I've never seen a case like it."

"Poor Sandra. Even with Vance as chair, I don't think it's going to be easy for her."

"Vance is hardly any help." Cissy remembered the morning's odd conversation with him, and inched up to the foot of the bed. "But that's not the worst: She totally fell apart during the questions afterward."

"Those are always nerve-wracking."

"I can sympathize, but this was... incredible. She shook like there was an earth tremor outside, and she couldn't answer."

"Everybody can botch a few questions."

"No, I mean she didn't say a thing. She'd mumble a few unintelligible words, start to stutter, then shake, and end up saying absolutely nothing. In response to all three questions."

"R & R's?" Rutledge was writing Sandra's tenure narrative to submit to the divisional committee and, one assumed, supported her. Rothschild, although friendly with Rutledge, smartly kept his distance from the rest of the department.

"Right. Rothschild's questions were predictably tricky, but Rutledge's and Nick's, which were easy, also seemed to baffle her. She didn't say a word."

"At least you'll look good in comparison."

"I hope."

❧

The following Monday afternoon Cissy attended an undergraduate studies curriculum meeting with Ginger, Rutledge and Nick. Nick had been put on the committee to replace Blake, and none of them had uttered a word of remorse about his death, since none of them — for that matter, no one in the department — had had to teach his classes. Luckily, one of his advanced classes had failed to materialize, and the one that had was given to Rutledge, who'd lost a class of his own for insufficient enrollment. The meeting, as Cissy expected, was a tedious and time-consuming bore.

On the way out, she saw Rickover leaving the dean's office. He cornered her in the seventh-floor hall, the other committee members safely dispersed. "Has Sandra talked to you?"

"I haven't seen her since the lecture."

"Yes, the lecture." His tone fell between lugubrious and disturbing. "She hasn't been her right self since. I think she may have to take a medical leave." Rickover pointed to his head, circling an extended finger.

"I'm sorry. I'm stunned." Could it have really affected Sandra this badly? Yes, she promptly concluded to herself. Tenure was hell, and it could. She herself felt lucky to have stayed more or less in one piece.

"Well, of course I'm sorry too, Pankhurst. But if she does talk to you, you can't believe a word she says."

"As you've told me," she retorted, disbelieving. Rickover was protesting a bit much.

He marched toward the elevator. Instinctively, she went in the opposite direction and descended the two flights of stairs to her office. It was at the far end of the floor from Rickover's and the departmental office, conveniently "hidden." As she headed toward it, Sandra's door, also hidden from Vance's, opened tentatively.

"Cissy, can you come in?" The request, especially considering the timing of her conversation with Vance, took her aback. Sandra look wretched; today she hadn't even bothered with make-up. Cissy stepped in and silently closed the door.

"I feel so awful since my lecture. I don't know what to do, Cissy."

She moved in closer, but stopped just short of patting her on the back; congratulations were hardly in order. She touched her shoulder lightly in support, thinking that she herself might need some soon.

"It can't be that bad. Your lecture went fine. So you stumbled on the questions. Big deal. Everyone had to agree that your talk itself was first-rate." She had to bolster Sandra's ego however she could.

"That's the problem."

"What is?"

"The lecture."

"Nonsense, Sandra. As I said, and as everyone knows, it went fine."

"That's the problem."

"What is, Sandra? I don't understand."

"I have to tell someone, Cissy."

"Tell somewhat what?"

Sandra sniffled, hesitated, cried softly, sniffled some more. Finally, in a barely audible voice, she said, "Vance wrote it for me."

# 32

"Happy birthday. Three months early." Pepper held out the present to Juan.

The present looked suspiciously like tickets of some sort. Opening the outside flap, Juan confirmed this: They were to leave on a Caribbean cruise in two weeks.

It was more like Pepper giving a present to himself, in which Juan happened to be included. He had to agree to go, as he'd be damned if he'd let Pepper sail off alone on a cruise with six hundred other gay men.

"Hey, we're going to the Caribbean! You could at least look happy."

"Yeah, you could too, one of these days. You've been depressed since Christmas. Frankly, I still think you should see a psychiatrist, or at least get counseling. You've got to talk to someone and you won't talk to me."

"I don't want counseling!" Pepper was adamant as he stood up in front of the window, making a late-afternoon silhouette in front of the frozen lake.

"Then maybe I do! Or we do! Do you know what it's like living with your being depressed all the time? Not easy."

"It's this godawful winter."

At least Pepper had said something, though Juan had a hard time believing it was only this. Since he'd returned, the previous winters had never seemed to depress him.

"I suppose we do need a break in routine," Juan admitted, still mentally resisting the idea of the cruise. He had just enough advance notice to request a week off from PC cab without causing chaos. In any case, enough part-time drivers would gladly take his shifts.

Laboriously, he'd binged and purged himself down to 130 pounds in the last half of December and first part of January. Now, he only had to do one thing: to lose five more pounds in the next two weeks.

In Miami they boarded the SS Lamprey. Food was laid out in a gargantuan buffet on the main deck. They each consumed a plateful — Juan eating only fruits and vegetables — and retired to their cabin.

Juan read aloud the list of the events as they lay on the bed: "Advanced and Beginning Aerobics, Afternoon Bingo, Pool Games, Dancing Under the Stars, Midnight Buffet, Captain's Reception, Masquerade Ball... Hey, we didn't bring any costumes."

"Tell me you'd want to dress up. We can participate in all or none of the activities."

There was nightly entertainment by musical groups that Juan knew vaguely, plus various activities and speakers, including gay celebrities such as Quentin Crisp.

The program advised them to "dress" for dinner. "This doesn't mean tux, does it?" Juan asked.

"No. That's only for the Captain's Reception and dinner that night. Tonight we should probably just put on jackets and ties."

"Whatever you say, mate." He was glad to see Pepper in such an improved mood. Maybe this cruise was what they both needed.

At dinner a waiter brought them menus and the tablemates began to get acquainted. Of the eight, four others obviously formed couples: Gene and Glen, from San Francisco; and Mike and Bob, from Buffalo. Two apparent singles joined them: across the table, Dex, a seven-foot Texan, and Edwin, from New Orleans. Both looked too attractive not to have lovers, Juan thought.

"Madison," Pepper said to the San Franciscans, seated to his left.

"Oh, the 'Berkeley of the Midwest'," Glen commented. "I went to Berkeley myself. The real one."

"I went to Stanford," Pepper said. "Lived in San Francisco for ten years. Then moved back to Madison, where I'm from originally."

Pepper conversed easily with strangers, unlike Juan. He looked to his right, where Edwin sat, awkwardly alone. Pepper and the San Franciscans were now going on about particulars of the city that held no meaning for Juan. Across the table, the Texan conversed with the Buffaloes.

"First cruise?" Juan found himself breaking the ice with Edwin.

"No, actually."

"It's our first."

"Jack and I went two years ago, different itinerary. But he's gone now. I enjoyed the first one enough, I thought I'd go again, even if on my own."

Juan deliberated offering condolences, thinking the conversational opening had already taken an unfortunate turn.

"These cruises seem to be a mixture of singles and couples," Edwin offered the answer to what Juan might have asked. "I'd say it's maybe sixty-forty in favor of couples."

Juan agreed as he played with his appetizer. He sipped his wine and let the waiter take away the uneaten food. No way was he going to make a pig of himself in front of this company. He felt almost too nervous to eat at all, but finished off his wine, then poured another glass.

"What do you do?" Juan felt as awkward as if he were cruising in a bar, something he hadn't done in ages.

"Oh, I'm a physician."

"I drive a cab." Juan volunteered the embarrassing information before it could be asked. "I have a Ph.D. in sociology, but never used it. I wanted to stay in Madison, so I ended up driving cab."

"No need to apologize," Edwin said, as their entrées arrived. Both had ordered Coquilles St. Jacques.

"I'm not." Juan saw Edwin's penetrating eyes, then admitted the truth: "OK, I am, I guess. I just wanted to stay in Madison for the culture. Counter, that is." Edwin seemed to take in his meaning perfectly.

Pepper had now progressed to animated conversation about leather bars with Gene and Glen. "Originally from New Orleans?" Juan asked.

"No. Mississippi. Like half the gay men in New Orleans," he added laughingly. "When you're born in Mississippi and are gay, you've got to go somewhere. I've been in New Orleans eighteen years." Juan guessed him to be about forty-five. He was blond, fit, with only a slightly receding hairline.

"I've got you beat. I've been in Madison twenty."

"You must have moved there when you were young." Edwin forked dinner into his mouth. "Eat up, it's going to get cold."

Juan took the hint and dedicated himself to serious eating for several minutes. Eating alone was preferable; with people he knew, acceptable; with strangers, difficult.

After the entrées came sorbet, then dessert. Juan had ordered spumoni, simply to have something to do. He took one bite and left the rest.

"Not hungry?"

Juan had momentarily forgotten that Edwin was a physician and was appalled that he had noticed his eating habits. "I guess not."

"You must exercise."

"Some."

"It shows."

He wondered, what shows? All that showed was his concave stomach, which he promptly sucked in. "What's your specialty?" he asked, quickly changing topics.

"Eating disorders."

He had to tame an urge to flee the table and would make sure never to sit by Edwin again. Perhaps they could finagle a change of tables or even switch to the later dinner seating.

"Going to be 'dancing under the stars' tonight? You and Pepper, that is?" Edwin inquired before they departed.

"I, uh, I don't know."

At the same time, he heard Glen ask Pepper if he'd be at the leather disco party that night.

"Sounds good to me," Pepper said, without consulting him.

"Who knows? Maybe I will be dancing under the stars," Juan said.

❧

They debated evening plans in the cabin. Pepper, clearly unenthusiastic about dancing "under the stars," said they could go to both. Juan, even less interested in the leather disco party, agreed they could.

"Look, why don't you go out on the deck and I'll go to the leather party? Then we can meet for the midnight buffet."

"Sounds fine." Juan, determined to hide his irritation, wanted Pepper to enjoy himseldf. There was no harm in letting him be on his own for a few hours, was there? It could only cheer him up, he trusted.

Pepper put on chaps over blue jeans, a leather vest over his white shirt, and black leather boots. Juan dressed casually, in baggy white pants, and wondered what in hell he was doing.

Upstairs, more than a hundred men occupied the dance floor, some shirtless in the humid Caribbean air. A gentle sea breeze caressed him, just enough to offset the humidity. In the middle of the group he saw Edwin dancing shirtless, his blond chest hair glistening under the disco lights that had been elaborately assembled. He seemed to be dancing with two younger guys, then with one, then by himself.

As the DJ mixed tunes, Edwin spotted him and sauntered over. Alone, Juan was suddenly petrified. Edwin pulled a white T-shirt out of his pants pocket, wiped the sweat off his chest. He looked, Juan had to admit, very sexy.

"How's it going?"

"Fine." Juan pretended to sip his vodka and tonic indifferently.

Edwin made small talk as he caught his breath, Juan half-listening and enjoying the slight rocking of the ship. The starry night was... romantic. And Pepper had deserted him for a leather party.

"Want to dance?" Edwin asked.

"Sure," Juan answered without hesitation, glad that Edwin had asked him first.

# 33

Cissy met Ginger in Evan's office, from where she could see the banner reading "FIGHTS AIDS, NOT IRAQ" stretched across University Avenue. Beth had proudly informed her that she'd helped erect it. Evan himself had marched in a recent Desert Storm protest, but Cissy lacked time to be thinking about Desert Storm, much less protesting it.

"Ready to go?" said Ginger.

"Ready." Cissy felt eager to escape the confines of FAB. The two of them, plus Evan, walked down the hall toward the elevators.

"Hey, guys!" Beth greeted them. "Been watchin' the goin's-on?"

"Goings-on? What goings-on?" Ginger asked urgently, as if there a SWAT team had appeared in the main office and she'd missed out on it.

"Didn't you see the cow?" All three shook their heads no. "Me and Wilhelmina had a perfect view from the main office. Guess it was slated for slaughter, or thought it was, and escaped from the Stock Pavilion. Made its way all across campus and charged down Bascom Hill. Tried to cross Park Street and made it, but a couple cars ended up in an accident. The cow got to Library Mall and they finally herded it into some sorta paddy wagon. Poor thing."

Cissy laughed, more at Beth's recounting, than at the incident itself.

"Hey, it ain't *funny*. The university's got no business keepin' poor animals locked up, killin' 'em, doin' tests on 'em. You all wanna join me in some sorta protest? Somebody's got to do somethin'."

"Not today, Beth," Evan answered.

"Then join me for lunch? I don't have a class for two hours."

"We, uhm, have some departmental business to discuss," Cissy said politely. "And we're not going to have lunch anyway." She and Evan had eaten theirs in her office; Ginger claimed she no longer felt like eating at midday.

"I bet I could tell you all a thing or two about departmental business, seein' and hearin' what I do down there." Beth threw back her head to the main office.

"Oh, another time. We're always anxious for tidbits of departmental gossip, aren't we, Ginger?" Evan said pointedly.

They rode the elevator down together, and Beth headed toward Memorial Union. Cissy, Evan, and Ginger walked through Library Mall, cleared of snow, toward State Street. The food vending carts that had populated the Mall from late spring to early fall were gone. To their left, Memorial Library's three new stories towered above them. They combated the winter wind up State Street to the Café Espresso Royale.

At a table by the window, Ginger wiggled around in her crimson dress, smoothed her necklace, which held a garnet pendant. Neither her mode of dress nor her personality had changed one iota since the day Cissy met her, though she seemed to grow new cleavage by the year. For the first time, Cissy wondered if she'd had enlargement surgery.

Neither she nor Evan had known what exactly to do with

the truth about Sandra's lecture, except that they couldn't simply hold on to such damning information themselves. Confronting Rickover directly was out of the question, and Cissy didn't want to make things worse for Sandra. So they had decided, not without trepidation, to tell Ginger, making a point of playing with her before spilling it.

"We know something you don't know," Evan teased.

Ginger immediately raised her eyes and jerked her head around, as if she were being spied on or about to be the object of ridicule, and seemed to scour her mind for what it might be. "Well, it's not Sandra's tenure vote." The executive committee had voted to postpone it until Cissy's came up. "And I'll eat my coffee cup if you tell me you've discovered the secret Blake died with."

She sat defiantly, daring to be told.

"Sorry, Ging. You'll have to dig that one out of the grave."

"But we can tell you something else of interest," Cissy said, straight-faced. "And it's serious."

Ginger paused perhaps one second, then gripped the table and leaned over it. Cleavage hovering over her coffee cup, she looked them both in the eyes, and said with gritted teeth, "Tell me, damn it!"

"Control, Ging, control!" Evan reached out to steady her.

"It's about Sandra," Cissy said, not liking, but not surprised by Ginger's rumblings of eruption. She could well blow her volcanic top when she found out.

Ginger leaned back into her chair, with an already smug expression on her face. "I knew. I knew."

"Then tell us what you know," Evan prodded.

Ginger paused, pouting. "You know I don't know a damned thing! So tell me!"

"Quiet, Ginger. Don't make a scene. We brought you here to talk in private."

"What is it about Sandra? You know how I am. I'm sorry. Tell me, please."

While Evan took a sip of coffee, Cissy envisioned making her get down on her knees and beg. Then she said: "She came to talk to me the Monday after the lecture."

"Probably crying about it all and bemoaning how she wasn't going to get tenure," Ginger said, as if she could still divine the information before it was revealed.

"Not quite," Cissy said. "She cried, yes. But what she told

me was this: She didn't write the lecture. Vance did."

Ginger's eyes seemed prepared to desert their sockets. "I knew. I knew."

Evan looked at Cissy, and simultaneously they said, "You did *not.*"

"Did you?" Cissy added in a high-pitched squeak.

"All right. I didn't know exactly, but I knew something was strange, the way she couldn't answer a single, simple question. Now it all makes sense. Why'd she tell *you?*" Ginger glared at Cissy, as if she were a entomological pest best eradicated from the planet.

"I don't know. I suppose she didn't trust you."

"The more important thing," Evan interjected quickly, "is now, what do we do?"

"God! Think of the ramifications, the repercussions..." Ginger fell back, legs spread, mouth wide open, all sense of poise having evaporated. "Not only is Sandra guilty of plagiarism, or academic dishonesty, but Vance too! Accessory to the fact! Accessory to plagiarism!"

"He didn't quite plagiarize, Ging." Evan twirled a spoon around the rim of his coffee cup. "He's more like the plagiarizee, if anything."

"You know what I mean. But this is... a bombshell!" Ginger herself seemed ready to detonate. "Vance is as guilty as she is! Well, we never wanted a department run by Rickovers. And now we can get rid of them both!"

"You mean get rid of Vance." Cissy already regretted they'd told her.

"This is super-serious!" Ginger, recovering, seemed to begin to plot. "What do I do now?"

"Ginger, we're not going to *do* anything for the moment," Evan said firmly. "We're going to think this through first."

"Sandra might recant, under pressure from Vance," Cissy added. "And deny she told me anything."

"Are you sure you heard Sandra right?" Ginger threw a doubting glance at Cissy, who nodded affirmatively. "Then this is the biggest coup since I've been here!" Cissy could almost see the gears moving in her Machiavellian mind.

"Look!" Cissy pointed at the window. Vance and Sandra were walking down the sidewalk right in front of them, Sandra's hair aloft in the wind. "And they're coming in here!"

Ginger gasped, then paled. "We've got to hide."

"You're right, Ging." Cissy panicked, as though, if they were seen talking, Sandra would guess the subject. And she well might.

Vance and Sandra came in and went up to the counter to order.

"Now we're all going to put our coats on and walk out of here as nonchalantly as possible," Ginger instructed, and Cissy and Evan followed her lead.

"To the Capitol," Ginger pointed, though they needed to head back to FAB, in the opposite direction. "We can't let them see us."

"You'd think we were suspects for a murder or something." Cissy felt uneasier than ever that she had violated a confidence. But then again, Sandra hadn't told her to keep it secret, and what had she expected her to do with the information?

"Who knows, we might be," Ginger said lightly. "If Vance found out that Sandra told Cissy and Cis here blabbed it to the world, Vance could..."

"Right. You *are* the world, Ging," said Evan. "You have to promise us you won't say or do anything yet."

"Just trying to add a little drama to things."

"I'd say we've got quite enough," Cissy countered.

"I guess we have, at that." Ginger seemed perversely pleased.

❧

The next morning Cissy sat drinking carrot juice and reading the *Wisconsin State Journal* while Evan showered and the wood stove roared.

The phone rang at seven fifty-five and she moved to the living room to pick it up. Who could be calling at this hour? The departmental office didn't even open for five more minutes. Her mother tended to call when rates were cheap, but it was five fifty-five in California, and her mother had never been an early riser.

"Cissy," came the abject voice she recognized. "It's Sandra. I hope I didn't wake you."

"Oh, no. I'm always up at this hour." She walked back to the kitchen, cradling the phone, to fetch her juice.

"I'm sorry to call so early, but I've got to talk to someone. I don't have anyone else to tell. At least not in Madison."

"That's all right, Sandra. You can tell me anything." Immediately she felt guilty; yes, Sandra could tell her anything and then she'd go and tell the world.

"I don't know how to say this. So I'll just be blunt." She paused for some seconds as Cissy waited for her to continue. "I'm going to file for divorce from Vance." Her voice, which had quavered briefly with this statement, now became resolute: "I'm not even going to go through the tenure process. We all know I'd never get it anyway and, with all the pressure from Vance, it's already been turned into a sham. I'm going to try to finish the semester's teaching, resign, then leave."

The information overwhelmed Cissy. "But this is so sudden."

"I've thought about it. It might be sudden. But, for all our differences, I don't want to drag Vance down with me. I'm going to make a quick, clean break. Now."

"Maybe you should talk this out with someone impartial."

"No. I've decided." Sandra's voice gained firmness.

"Well, I'm glad to listen any time." Cissy feared there could come a point when Sandra told her more than she felt comfortable knowing.

"Thanks for listening, Cissy. I suppose I should go. I teach in less than an hour."

"I'll see you at school. Any time you want to talk..."

"Uh-huh." The voice was again faint, dejected. "Thanks. Good-bye, Cissy." The phone went dead.

This was too much information to process. All she could think was that Vance was already dragged down with Sandra.

Evan came out of the bathroom, a towel around his waist and remnants of shaving cream dotting his face. "Were you talking to me or yourself?"

"It was Sandra." She realized that this was Rickover's teaching hour, undoubtedly the only time Sandra felt safe to call. "And you won't believe what she just told me."

"By now I'd believe anything."

# 34

When the SS Lamprey docked for the day at Ocho Ríos, Juan was eager to disembark and see a piece of Jamaica.

"You go," Pepper grunted from the bed. He'd been out several hours later than Juan. Gene and Glen had introduced him to a horde of San Franciscans and New Yorkers, all rich, sophisticated, and into leather.

"I thought this vacation was to restore your spirits, not to hibernate." Juan tried to speak nonjudgmentally, not to let his irritation show. He and Pepper had barely spent time together on what was supposed to be a "romantic" cruise.

"Don't worry, I won't." Pepper seemed oblivious under the sheets.

Juan went off on his own and returned a few hours later, having searched futilely for an up-to-date newspaper and fended off locals trying to sell him dope.

Although he'd left Madison at less than a pound above his desired weight, he debated faking an illness to the ship's physician, just for a chance to get on a scale, if they even had one. He concluded that the complications might outweigh the benefits, and wished he'd brought along his own. He could be gaining a half pound per day; one could never be too careful.

He went to sunbathe and read on the deck and looked out over the afternoon pool games. After reclining, his stomach tightly sucked in, he removed his shirt. The first game consisted of stuffing ping pong balls into bathing trunks. Bored, Juan decided to have a Bloody Mary. As no waiters were in sight, he ambled down to the poolside bar, shirt back on and buttoned, Marguerite Yourcenar's *Memoirs of Hadrian* in hand. He took the drink back to a poolside table. A group of drag queens called the Texas Chainsaw Cheerleaders screamed in favor of both competing teams.

In the next game each team had to coerce as many people as possible to join them in the pool. The first group convinced a dozen or so buddies to jump in. Juan sipped his Bloody Mary, paying scant attention, emotionally bruised by Pepper, and distracted from his reading. The second team of ten jumped in, promptly removed their suits and twirled them in the air. The crowd immediately edged toward the pool get a better look.

"Juan!" He heard his name called. His eyes circled the vicinity, then landed on the pool and Edwin.

"Come on, jump in for us!" He saw Edwin's glistening torso bobbing up and down out of the water. Since they'd made eye contact, he couldn't ignore him, so he left his drink and book on the table and edged toward the pool.

"Thirty seconds to go!" the recreation director yelled.

Everyone else was jumping in; Juan felt silly standing stalwart by the edge. Edwin swiped playfully at his feet.

What the hell? He stepped out of his thongs, removed his shirt and, clad in baggy black trunks, eased into the pool. It wasn't deep; his feet touched bottom easily. Edwin came up to him and gave him a wet hug. The hug prolonged itself, as people splashed on all sides. His peripheral vision instinctively checked the area for signs of Pepper, then he let himself be kissed, then kissed back.

Edwin's legs grabbed his below the water, and Juan went under.

❧

Rough seas all the way to Nassau left a mass of passengers seasick and insomniac, though Juan was bothered by neither. Pepper, always coming in late, slept as though in a coma, in spite of the buffeting waves.

Edwin joined Juan for afternoon conversation and drinks on the upper deck. Here Juan felt most comfortable, as he didn't have to eat. That Edwin's stomach was slightly bigger than his own diminished his uneasiness a little. At dinner he'd carefully measured his intake, neither under- nor overeating.

After Nassau, the final night featured the captain's reception, followed by a formal dinner and the masquerade ball. Juan and Pepper struggled into their tuxes.

"I've got a surprise for you tonight," Pepper announced.

"You're going to bed when I am?" With their differing sleep schedules, they hadn't — at least Juan hadn't — had sex all week.

"I'm going to be part of a group costume."

"Oh." He could guess the group and didn't care to hear the details.

"So after dinner I'll be dressing in Gene and Glen's cabin. I don't mean to leave you out, but you don't have the leather for the costume." Pepper's mental health had clearly rebounded.

"You know I don't like to dress up anyway."

"Then you won't mind."

"Of course not."

At the masquerade, first prize for the winners of each category was a weekend in Key West; the grand prize winner of all would receive $1000, plus other gifts.

"Celebrity look-alikes" was followed by drag, then leather. Next came the general category, in which Edwin appeared in a

G-string under an elaborately constructed spider web, to much applause. The final category was group costumes.

Five pansies — the flower — danced in a circle around an explicitly phallic May pole. Next came "Boys by Day, Daddies by Night." Pepper, Gene, Glen, and two others moved stiffly to center stage, showing blue jeans and white T-shirts to the crowd. Then they turned around: The blue jeans and T-shirts had been cut in half. They only wore leather harnesses above black work boots and white socks. The crowd roared with laughter and applauded. Whether planned or spur-of-the-moment theatrics, the five of them bent over and mooned the audience. They won first prize in the category.

Pepper's behavior infuriated Juan. It was bad enough that he'd practically deserted him for the entire week; now he'd taken off his clothes and displayed his backside for everyone to see.

The contest concluded, he went straight up to the elaborate midnight buffet. A gigantic chocolate chimpanzee sported a banana for a penis. Watermelons wore intricately carved indigenous faces, with fruits and vegetables sticking out of the rinds as hair. Tropical fruits were stacked together and decorated as birds. The tables went on and on.

Juan loaded one plate after another and ate gluttonously, barely refrained from chomping on the chimp's penis. He felt unnoticed among the frills of the oversized costumes, and the night's darkness facilitated his anonymous eating. Gorging himself on his fifth or sixth plate, he saw Edwin, still costumed, and waved. He didn't want to confront him now and hurried off to his cabin.

Not surprisingly, Pepper wasn't there. He went right to the bathroom, half-savoring traces of his feast, half-sick to his stomach, and vomited it all up. The ship was noisy enough he didn't even bother to turn the shower on.

Rapping knuckles rattled the door gently. He washed out his mouth and flushed the toilet. The knocking persisted. He finally deemed himself sufficiently presentable to open it.

"Was that wave of yours upstairs my only good-bye?" Edwin, still spidery, looked sexier than usual.

"Oh, I was about to come back out and look for you." Frankly, Juan hadn't thought about it.

"I wasn't sure. Want to go somewhere and have a drink?"

"Why not?" Soda water sounded like a good antidote to his

little episode.

They took their drinks to the upper deck, heard the revelry below, sat in silence under a sky half-clouded, half-starry. Finally, the seas had calmed.

"Quite a feast they have down there," Edwin commented.

Juan didn't know if it was a casual opener or not. "Sure is. Never saw anything like it." He sipped his soda, hoping to feel a return to normalcy after his binge.

"The crowd certainly loved Pepper and company."

"You weren't bad either." Edwin leaned back in his deck chair; he'd won second prize in his category. "Hot costume."

"Thanks."

The atmosphere should have been comfortable, but... "I don't know why we're up here," Juan blurted out.

"Because you're a very nice gentleman. At least that's why I'm up here."

"Thanks." More silence. "You might have guessed I have an eating problem. So now you know, in case you were wondering." He felt safe telling Edwin, knowing he wouldn't see him again.

"That's not why I wanted to see you now. I mean, if you ever want to talk about it, I'll be glad to listen."

"Maybe another time."

"Right. It's after midnight now, we dock at six a.m., and have to be through customs by eight."

"Yeah." Mixed emotions battled in Juan's mind. Even if Edwin knew why he was there, Juan wasn't sure why he himself was. He only knew he didn't want to have a cheap seduction, never to see Edwin again. But he knew he wanted — needed? — something.

"I'd like to see you again, you know." Edwin combed his blond mustache with his index fingers. "If you're ever free to get away."

"Cab drivers don't exactly lead lives of luxury."

"I meant in regard to Pepper."

"Oh." Juan had rather mistaken his meaning.

"You could come to New Orleans and be my guest. Mardi Gras is coming up soon. Like everyone else in New Orleans, I have other friends coming to stay, but they come and go on their own. There's space for you in my bed. It could be a great time."

"Pepper did just win a weekend in Key West," Juan thought

aloud, and wondered if Edwin meant the "great time" would be Mardi Gras, in Edwin's bed, or both. "I'd like to see you again..." But he had to let Edwin down politely. "There's just no way I can afford it."

"I'll send you the ticket. You know that doctors are filthy rich." Edwin laughed the necessary laugh at his remark, and Juan pretended amusement.

But if Pepper was going off to Key West, why couldn't he go to Mardi Gras? "I'd like that. I'd just have to arrange to take off work for..."

"A long weekend. Three or four days. Five, if you could swing it."

"Maybe I could." He thought of Pepper, cavorting in Key West, working off his winter depression. Perhaps Juan could work off his romantic depression. "Maybe I will. But I can't promise."

"It'd be great if you could."

He polished off his soda. Edwin patted the deck chair for him to lie down beside him. Juan complied. It felt easy and natural and, finally, he relaxed.

Edwin caressed Juan's chest. Juan closed, then opened his eyes to the stars in the sky, punctuation marks to his trip. Among them he thought he could discern a constellation in the form of an astronomical question mark. This was the perfect romantic setting he had envisioned happening with Pepper, but, he realized, he didn't mind it happening with Edwin. They hadn't had sex, they'd barely touched, and it seemed like the beginning of an old-fashioned romance, Juan's kind.

# 35

Irv had had enough. Roz refused to put on a stitch and Rhoda, he swore, hadn't removed her mink except to bathe. Dayne, who now considered it fun to play naked, had removed his clothes at a neighbor boy's house, causing an irate complaint and unsavory allegations from the parents.

Already stripped to his boxers, Irv peeled them off and put them in his briefcase. He began to descend the stairs, briefcase in hand, almost hoping Roz and Rhoda would be too caught up in their recriminations to take notice of him. He had to resist the temptation to dart back up the stairs.

"Irv?" Roz's voice came from the kitchen.

"Yes?" He had reached the study. His own ploy might be

dangerous, but this was a last resort.

"Don't you think it's better to target the twenty-second ward first?"

"Sounds good." Right now he'd agree with almost anything, and Roz's campaign needed help. This morning he'd found her and Rhoda discussing it, two breasts and a mink's head and tail sparring over the table. Rhoda's idea of campaigning was to collar adolescents in the street, ask them if they were registered voters and, if not, lecture them on their civic duty and Roz's brilliant qualifications. Half the time they turned out to be no more than sixteen. Roz's campaign strategy sessions with her manager, Dave, often turned into damage control regarding Rhoda.

This was the moment: either face them or run. He'd gone this far... He appeared in the kitchen doorway, forcing himself to leave behind his briefcase.

He leaned on the door jamb — an over-the-hill *Cosmopolitan* centerfold — until Rhoda finally saw him and screamed.

Roz's eyes immediately followed. "Irv!" Consternation filled the syllable.

"I can't believe this!" Rhoda shot awkward glances around the kitchen, her glance trying to alight anywhere except below Irv's waist.

"Irv, why now of all times...?"

"First you, now him!" Rhoda berated Roz.

"I should think we can all coexist in peace," Roz said. "Just take off that mink, then keep removing clothes, and we'll all be equal."

Oh God. Irv hadn't counted on this.

"If you think I'm going to do that, you're more meshugge than I thought!"

"Do as you wish, Mother. You always do."

"Just like you." Rhoda gave a flourish of her index finger at Roz.

"Mother, keep your hand out of my face!"

"Rosamond!" The tone was clearly a warning, the two women seemingly prepared to ignore him.

Dayne appeared on the scene, naked as the moment he was born. "Daddy's naked too. Daddy and me take baths together."

"Mommy and Dayne do too. All the time." Roz actually tried to one-up him.

"The next thing you know, you'll all want me to join you

naked in the Jacuzzi." Rhoda now glanced at Irv's feet, then his head. "But you can just count me out!"

"No one's asking you to, Mother."

"This is enough! Here, take my mink!" She had it by the tail, circling it in the air like a lasso, as she surveyed all three of them. "You'd rather kill your own mother than let her wear her fur!" Now she hurled the mink at Roz's face. "There, it's yours. Which means you have to put your clothes back on!" She gave a victorious snort at Roz.

Heaven be praised, thought Irv.

Rhoda looked at him, eyes going back and forth, but now peeking at his crotch, then jerking her gaze up to his face. "I suppose we have you to thank for this, Irv. I always knew Roz needed a husband who would keep her in line. No easy task, as you know."

"Mother!" Roz bellowed. "That remark was totally uncalled for!"

"Please don't get started." Irv directed his words to both women. "Roz, let's just put our clothes back on."

"Dayne, come here, please," Rhoda said gently. The boy walked up to his grandmother and she bent over and stared at his tiny genitals. "How's my little schmendrick?"

"Mother, what are you saying?"

"It's Yiddish for 'child.' I'm using it affectionately."

"Yes, and it also means 'penis' or 'prick'."

"Don't give Yiddish lessons to me, Roz. Yes, I was looking at the boy's... you know, schmendrick... And it doesn't match his father's."

"What the hell? He won't even be four until April. And why the hell should it?"

"Just look," Rhoda explained, and turned Dayne around like a courtroom exhibit. "The boy's is so dark. I thought it came from his father. But Irv's is so... white."

"I'm putting my pants on," Irv said, sensing danger.

"Stay right there!" Rhoda had never before ordered Irv around; he obeyed.

"Why is it, I've often wondered, that Dayne doesn't seem to resemble either of you too much? His complexion, his eyes, everything matches the boy downstairs."

"His name is Juan, Mother, and he's not a boy."

"If he weren't... you know..."

"Gay?"

"Yes, if he weren't... I'd swear..." Then she looked contritely at Irv. "Oh, I'm sorry, Irv. Roz too. I've just always wondered. You have to admit..."

At that moment, a knock came from the downstairs door and a second later Juan burst in. "Oh," he said, as though surveying escapees from a sanatorium. He'd seen Roz's nudity, but hadn't seen him, Irv, in the all-together since some naked encounter sessions in the commune — almost twenty years ago. Irv covered himself with his hands.

"Roz, everyone, I had something to show you, but I think I'd better come back later." He whirled around and began to scurry to the door.

"Wait right there, young man!" Rhoda ordered.

Juan turned around, befuddled.

"Would you mind coming over here and... dropping your pants?" Rhoda asked, oozing a sudden grandmotherly sweetness.

"Mother, this is too much!"

"Hey, look, people. If you want to be naked up here, go ahead and do your own thing. But if this has turned from a clothing-optional zone to mandatory nudism, I'm out of here. But take a look at this." He put down a newspaper on the floor, steering clear of them as if they were diseased, and backed off. "I think you'll be interested in the front page, lower right hand corner." With that, he closed the door behind him, and escaped down the stairs.

"What the hell can this be?" Roz got up, marched over and retrieved the newspaper from the floor.

"I took off my mink, so, Roz, put your clothes on before you read that."

"They're all upstairs. And I'm not going to try to cover myself with that!" She pointed to the mink, which Dayne was now propelling around the floor as though it were a wind-up toy. Irv himself had slipped into shorts during their argument.

Roz stared wide-mouthed at the newspaper. "Your goddamned foul piece of fur! It's on the front page of this paper! And worse, they say it's me. Look, I was standing behind you. They cut out your head, moved mine over, and put it on top of your body. It looks like I'm wearing the fucking mink! I knew Maddie Son was up to something! Now we'll sue for sure. I might as well give up. The election's over!"

Roz placed the paper on the kitchen table, and she, Rhoda

and Irv gathered around. Irving barked in the background. Dayne tried to get a view too, his chin barely reaching the table. The paper was *Outrage!*, one of several underground Madison newspapers of no particular political bent or worth, except to stir up trouble.

In the lower right hand corner Irv saw a waist-up shot of Rhoda, indeed with Roz's head on top of her mink-clad neck. Someone had done a quite adequate job of touching up the photo.

The headline blared "New Fashion Trend In Sixth District?" The three adults all read the story underneath:

*The bare-breasted women last summer at B. B. Clarke Beach were making a political statement rather than a fashion one. But we wonder what Roz Goldwomyn, Labor Farm candidate for thes sixth district council race, has up her sleeve. It's apparent what Goldwomyn has around her neck, but is it a fashion statement or a political one? Is Goldwomyn really a closet fur lover? That would make for a very interesting election in the sixth district hotbed. Goldwomyn is a confirmed nudist, but has yet to appear in public with her pants down, although* Outrages!*'s spies say she has appeared topless in the Labor Farm office.*

*It's still unclear if other candidates will follow Goldwomyn's untrendy lead, though it is a well known fact that sixth district incumbent R. John Claypool has often been caught with his (political) pants down.*

"If that's not libel, I don't know what is!" Roz lunged for her cigarettes.

"Give me one too." Rhoda grabbed one and lit up. "I'm the one who's been libeled!"

"They got Claypool too," Irv said.

"This is an outrage!" said Rhoda.

That's the idea, thought Irv.

"If you hadn't been wearing that damned fur, this would never have happened!"

"If you'd put some clothes on, I wouldn't have been wearing my mink."

"Don't go blaming it on me. You're the one who opened the damned door!"

"This is the last straw. I'm leaving! I've had nothing but tsuris here lately!"

Irv looked at Roz for a translation: "Trouble. And you've given me much more than I've ever given you, Mother!"

"See what your nudity led to, Roz!" Rhoda got up and began to head upstairs to her bedroom.

"We'll sue now!"

"I'm sure you have a case, but why dignify this tabloid journalism with the attention? We can force them to print a retraction easy enough. A threatening letter on my stationery should do it. After this stunt, Maddie Son is out of the race, as if she weren't before."

"It's not just that. They claim I've been topless at Labor Farm."

"As, I believe, I myself observed one day."

"Who could have told? Certainly not Beth or... Veronica?"

"I don't know. The article does say *Outrage!* has its spies. But, as for me, let me go put my blue jeans back on." Irv left Roz, sputtering, fuming, blowing smoke, and dashed past Rhoda, who'd stopped near the bottom of the stairs. His ploy had been more successful than imagined. Not only had he gotten Roz to put her clothes back on, but Rhoda to leave.

And with luck, she'd forget that Dayne bore any resemblance to Juan.

# 36

Beth voted in the primary, then passed out campaign leaflets to passersby on her way to school: Roz shaking hands with citizenry of color and staring solicitously into the eyes of the physically challenged; Roz behind a desk at one of her many volunteer jobs (all duly noted below), doing manual labor at another; Roz posing with Irv and Dayne. At the bus stop, she distributed one to an elderly man and another to a pair of women she recognized from the lesbian community.

The first woman eyed the literature skeptically. "Why should we vote for her? Look at the nuclear family." The tone was more apropos for "nuclear meltdown." "I'm not voting at all."

"We don't even have a lesbian to vote for in the district. Maybe we should put in a protest vote for Maddie Son," said her partner.

"But you know that Maddie Son was behind that *Outrage!* article," Beth protested.

"Since Roz broke up with Erva Mae, who no doubt did treat her like shit, Roz has tried to gain 'respectability' under the guise of heterosexuality."

Beth didn't know what to say or who Erva Mae was — an

ex from Roz's mysterious lesbian past?

"There's not even a politically correct candidate to vote for in the sixth district this year."

"Goldwomyn is a fur lover as well as an exhibitionist. We have it on good word."

Beth managed to defend her on the "fur lover" score before the bus came, ending the conversation. The *Outrage!* article had been very unfortunate, and a retraction wouldn't appear until next month, after the primary. Beth had wondered how they'd known of the topless incident at Labor Farm until she remembered she'd told a friend or two —maybe three— about it. If Roz claimed that she was the leak, she could claim reasonable innocence, since *Outrage!* boasted it had spies. Hell, it might be true.

Her bandage now removed, she arrived at the Museum Studies office at eight o'clock sharp and, now in possession of keys, let herself in a few minutes before Wilhelmina's entrance. Rickover, apparently preoccupied, had ignored her and her "YIKES DYKES!" button lately, and his office hours had lost their usual ramrod rigidity.

By nine o'clock, Ginger Carter marched in haughtily — like some sort of African queen who treated everyone else as her indentured servants — and deposited a load of work on her desk. "Do you sleep in that button or what?"

The comment rankled Beth. "I've got as much right to wear this as you do to wear a 'Black Power' button."

"Spare me, please, and do your work. This is academia, not politics." She strutted off, dressed like a cover girl for *Ebony*, in designer clothes probably assembled by women in China or Central America earning twenty cents an hour.

She finished Ginger's work, toying with the idea of stapling her pages in the wrong order, but then thought better of it. Back in the office, she placed them in her mail box. Cissy was standing nearby, sifting through her own mail.

"Oh, hi Beth."

"Hi, Cissy. Hey, you're votin' for Roz today, aren't you?"

"Well, yes," Cissy whispered, as if it were an embarrassing secret.

"You used to be her neighbor, right?"

"Yes. Why?"

"You ever see her naked?"

"What?" Cissy's face registered immediate shock.

"First that fur stuff they said about her in *Outrage!*, and now some people are saying she's an exhibitionist." The fur photo had been damning, but Beth knew that that part had been a hoax. "I'm her campaign treasurer, you know. Some people have been givin' me a hard time about her."

"I've known Roz since she first lived with Irv. She once helped me out in a time of great distress."

"That's good to hear."

"Since we're talking, and no one else is here, I might as well tell you this now." Wilhelmina had left on one of her frequent breaks. "Professor Carter, I mean, Ginger, has been complaining about your, uhm, button. She is, you know, associate chair."

"Yeah, she's told me a trillion times."

"She says she's received various complaints from faculty and students about it and, since I know you, she's asked me to ask you to take the button off."

She imagined that Cissy was putting it as politely as possible and didn't agree with Ginger. She restrained herself from going on an anti-discrimination tirade, reluctantly removed it, went over to her backpack, and stuck it on. "She can't complain about that."

"I suppose she can't."

"Or this." Beth took her "GOLDWOMYN FOR COUNCIL" button off her backpack and clasped it to her blouse.

"Believe me, Ginger's not interested in non-academic politics. We're rather overloaded just on academic ones. I think Roz's button is safe."

"Thank God something is around here."

At that moment, Rickover stormed in, glaring accusingly. "Where's Wilhelmina? Who's running this office?"

"I guess I am," Beth said, irked by him and emboldened enough to say almost anything.

"Stop gossiping with the faculty and get to work! Or you'll be out of a job." His door slammed shut.

"From what I hear, he might too," Beth said.

Cissy went as pale as Snow White. "Who on earth told you that?"

❦

On her way home from classes to catch the bus, Beth saw Maddie Son and Dane County as she headed to Library Mall. They were distributing campaign literature; Beth took a leaflet.

"Are you sure you're three hundred feet from the polling place? Otherwise you're in violation of the law." Maddie was just past the fountain, covered for the winter, in the middle of the quadrangle. Beth calculated the distance to Memorial Union and figured they were probably illegal.

"What does it matter? This isn't even my district."

This truth made her sure that Maddie Son was demented. If she was going to break a law, she might as well do it where it might do her some good.

"Yeah, no one'll vote for you there."

"Why don't you come to my victory party tonight at Ho Chi Minh's? I hear your candidate isn't even having one."

"How do you know? And how do you know who my candidate is?" Beth saw she had a Goldwomyn button on her jacket as well as her blouse. "Oops."

"We have our spies. We know who you are, Beth Yarmulkelinsky."

Beth was mildly amazed, didn't know how Maddie knew her or her name, but corrected the pronunciation, possibly an intentional anti-semitic slur. Meanwhile, her husband had strayed nearer to the Union, now in clear violation. "No one can win tonight, you fool. The top two vote-getters necessarily go into the general election."

"I'll be among them. You might as well come to where the fun is."

"Fuck off. And go retrieve Dane County." She spoke as if referring to a dog. "You're both in violation."

"Why don't you stick your tongue up your ass?" Maddie then spat at her.

"How dare you? You goddamned bitch!"

"Oh, yeah? Then why don't you stick it up your lesbian cunt?"

"You can be disciplined, arrested, for calling me names like that. Hey, someone, call the campus cops!"

Beth saw that a small group had formed around them. "Hey, you heard her! She called me a 'lesbian cunt.' Somebody stay and be my witness."

The next thing she knew, she and Maddie Son were engaged in a shoving match. Maddie Son's nails scratched her; Beth rebounded by grabbing her turban and pulling. On the second yank, off it came, unleashing a mass of hair dyed white.

"This is goddamned bodily assault."

"You assaulted me first, verbally!"

"Beth, I'm your witness." She looked over her shoulder and, to her relief, saw Merkin, a member of Yikes Dykes! Then she felt Maddie pull on her short hair.

*"That's* bodily assault! You're out of your fucking mind."

"First time you're right. I'm the ultimate mind-fuck!"

"Beth, keep away from her!" said Merkin. "She's dangerous. But her husband ran off like a scared rabbit."

Maddie seemed unaffected by his absence. "I don't need a man to protect me against you two."

"Neither do we," retorted Merkin.

"Oh yeah?" Totally unprovoked, Maddie lunged at Merkin, entangling her in a hair-pulling match. Beth jumped back into the fray.

The next thing she saw was a campus cop on the scene. "Break it up, women."

"She started it," screamed Maddie.

"I've got witnesses to the contrary." Beth craned her neck and saw that the original witnesses had vanished. Then she noticed that a man with a camcorder was videotaping it all. Maddie spat at the campus cop, who grabbed her by the arm.

"Police brutality!" she screamed and spat again.

This time the cop slapped handcuffs on her. The camcorder moved toward them. Maddie said, "Good job, Dane."

Beth realized that Dane County had taped it all.

"All three of you had better come to security with me," said the cop.

"I'm filing a discrimination complaint first. She called me a 'lesbian cunt.' That's in violation of the speech code."

"We're going to security first and sort this all out. Then you can do whatever you want."

❧

The incident merited a brief mention on the local evening news, as Beth watched it at home with Verla. She'd sustained only a scratch in the incident. Maddie simply had wanted media coverage and had gotten it, even if Dane County hadn't found any takers to broadcast his film. All Beth knew was that she was going to file a harassment complaint against Maddie tomorrow.

"Put her out of your mind," said Verla.

"I can't, I'm so ticked off. I can't believe she duped me like that. She knew who I was from the start and planned the provocation."

"Beth, darling, it's not your fault." Verla reached out to stroke her hair.

Beth tried to get through to Roz, without success. A news spot on TV gave election results, but only for the mayor's race, in which the incumbent was pulling off a landslide.

Finally at ten came the contested council races. "In the volatile sixth district," said the newscaster, "with one hundred percent of the vote in, the results are..." The numbers flashed on the screen, as the newscaster read them: "Claypool, the incumbent, 649. Goldwomyn, 575. Son, 79."

"Roz won!"

"Not yet," Beth said. "Now all she has to do is get Maddie Son's votes and she can beat Claypool! I'll try to call her again and congratulate her." She dialed the number, got the answering machine again and hung up without leaving a message.

"We might as well go to bed," said Verla. "You need to relax after a day like today." Beth went off first to the newly repaired bathroom.

As she walked back into the bedroom the phone rang. Verla picked it up in the kitchen. "Beth, it's Roz."

Beth trotted over. "Roz, congratulations. I knew you'd make it."

"Thanks. We trusted Maddie Son wouldn't." The voice was oddly distant, none too chipper for someone who'd just survived an election. "Beth, I saw the six o'clock news."

Oh, no, Beth thought. "She provoked it. She's a 'media whore,' like you told me. She's..."

"Beth," Roz interrupted. "They identified you as my treasurer. Now that the hardball with Claypool starts, I can't have this type of publicity."

"It won't happen again, I promise. Maddie Son's out of the race."

"Beth, I'm sorry, but I'm not going to need your services..."

"What do you mean? Maddie Son started it all. Just like she did with your mother. What would you do, fire her too?"

"We got rid of my mother. At least for the time being."

"And you're doing the same thing to me? After I took your mother off your hands, helped you with damage control, and promoted you to the whole lesbian community! I don't believe this!" Now Beth's blood was boiling.

"I'm afraid we have to, Beth. The election's at stake. I hope you understand. It's for the sake of the party."

"Then just see if I'll file your February campaign expenses report."

"Beth, you wouldn't."

"Wanna bet?"

# 37

Cissy and Evan lay in bed, his arm cradling her neck. He'd taken her to Ovens of Brittany for dinner, and afterward, they'd made love as the phone rang beside them, letting the answering machine, sound turned down, pick it up. On the fourth call, Cissy said, "Maybe it's an emergency," and grabbed the receiver before the machine took the call. "Hello," she panted.

"Cissy. It's about time you answered."

"This is at least the fourth call," she said, uncertain whether to admonish Ginger for the late hour or to be worried. "Evan and I were... sleeping."

"I thought you'd want to know this. I waited until my Workaholics Anonymous meeting was over, but then I couldn't stand to wait any longer."

"Know what?"

"Know who's teaching Sandra's Intro class."

"I've got to give my lecture tomorrow, Ginger." It was entitled "Preservation of Pottery Vessels at Tres Zapotes," where she'd had been on a grant in Mexico last summer. "This couldn't have waited?"

"Vance. Vance is teaching it."

"You called just to tell me this at eleven at night?"

"Not only that. Museum Display Techniques. Vance is teaching it. Selected Topics. Vance is teaching it. Sandra's resigned."

"Resigned??" She must have had a serious breakdown. And Vance's magnanimity was startling, if not suspicious. He apparently didn't know that Sandra planned to divorce him. "When did you find this out?"

"This morning."

"And you couldn't have told me earlier or waited until tomorrow?"

"I forgot earlier. I thought you'd want to know today. Always better sooner than later, isn't it?"

"Only if you mean sooner in the day."

❧

At the last minute, Cissy decided to call her tenure talk a "work in progress."

"After all, it's just a talk," Evan had told her that morning over breakfast. "It's not a finished, published article."

Cissy knew he was right, but had to protest a little: "But, as far as I know, no one in the department has ever called their tenure talk a 'work in progress'."

"But, hey, no one's ever called it a 'work of plagiarism' either. Maybe you'll get some feedback that will be helpful for turning it into a first-rate, publishable article."

After all, the departmental faculty had always specialized in telling each other what they did wrong or could do better, hadn't they? "But, no, I don't want them to tell me a list of things that might be improved on. It's not as if I'm a grad student."

"But you're not supposed to be giving a published paper. Until it's published, in theory it can always be improved on."

"Are you driving me in or should I take the bus?"

"Oh, let's splurge and call a cab. My treat."

"Why don't we go all the way and rent a limo?" She didn't mean to sound sarcastic, but suspected she did.

"Oh, that's what I've planned for our trip home this afternoon."

❧

Her lecture finished, Cissy awaited questions. She'd stumbled over some of the English — the Spanish and indigenous words she'd spat out perfectly, as if anyone would know the difference. On one hand, she feared she'd get no questions, which might look bad. On the other, she dreaded what some of them might ask.

"Certainly, someone has a question for Cissy," Rickover, today a rare model of civility, said for the second time. Sandra was not present, but Davidine had come especially to hear her lecture. She wished Blake were here; he'd help her out. Most of the M.F.A. students were present, duly taking notes, as if the content were going to appear on their next exam. She was sure most of them had only the dimmest notion of what she'd been talking about.

"Did you say Tres Zapotes was in Guatemala?" asked one of them, confirming her suspicion.

"No. Mexico. Southern Mexico. The state of Veracruz. Southern Veracruz."

"Doesn't the place name mean 'three shoes'?" asked another.

"No. That's *zapatos.*" That much Spanish Cissy knew. "*Zapote* is a sapodilla tree."

"What's the weather like there in the summer?" It was Davidine, smiling brightly, hands clasped on her lap, and probably truly curious.

"Oh, it's hot. Hot and humid. Even the nights hardly cool off. It's not exactly a vacation site, not of the usual variety."

An awkward silence followed; Cissy wondered if she was supposed to ad lib or make a joke. Rickover, again amazingly calling her "Cissy" and not "Pankhurst," asked for questions once more.

"When was Tres Zapotes last occupied before the Spaniards came?" asked Nick.

Had she omitted to mention this? At least it was a minimally relevant question. "Approximately 1000 A.D. Though there's evidence of another occupation, short-lived, and undatable, some time before the Spanish conquest."

Everyone looked around at each other and smiled, as if Cissy had just pulled out an amazingly obscure fact, or perhaps congratulating themselves that, among them, they'd managed to come up with one semi-intelligent question.

Surely, they had to ask her something more: the preservation of the figurines as opposed to the pottery vessels; the middle Tres Zapotes phase versus the ancient one; the difference between the Olmec and the Mayan calendars in establishing dates; anything general about the Olmec culture, or even the Mayan one. She was even willing to field a question about the theft of artifacts across the border and into private hands in the United States and Europe or the looting of them by locals who knew — or didn't know — their value.

Cissy waited patiently as the audience did nothing but smile, probably as eager to go home as was she.

"Well, that wraps it up, I guess," said Rickover. "Thanks, Cissy, for enlightening us all this afternoon."

It was, she suddenly realized, over. Over and out of her hands. Then a terrible thought occurred to her: They were simply being polite, by nodding and smiling, pretending they and she knew everything, and then they were all going to go vote against her.

❦

Cissy gazed out the seventh-floor room picture window overlooking Memorial Union and, in the background, Lake Mendota, still frozen. Today's was the first departmental meeting since her lecture. Afterwards, the executive committee would convene to vote on her tenure.

She and Evan sat to Rickover's left; Rutledge and Rothschild, and Nick to his right. Ginger, as secretary, sat at the end of the table where he stood. Among the small group, Sandra's absence, compounded by Blake's, was conspicuous. At that moment, Cissy was blaming herself for the fact that they had played in the snow, that Blake had died, that a tenure vote in her favor had succumbed with him.

"Today's agenda, that is the departmental committee's, is very short," Rickover began in an allusion to the executive committee's agenda, which, with Cissy's tenure vote, might well be longer.

"You all have your tentative teaching schedule for next semester, but there's the immediate matter of covering Sandra's classes this semester. As you know, I've been teaching all three of them."

They'd all voiced their fears that Rickover would try to assign them her classes. Even in cases of hardship, no one would be thrilled to teach someone else's classes for an extended period of time. Many would refuse, if they could, to do it for a single day.

Murmurings turned to rumblings and verged on thunder before Rickover managed to outshout his department: "I only think it fair to distribute them among you. Can we have some order, please!"

An eerie calm took over, momentarily.

Rickover seemed pleased with himself and began to dole out death sentences: "I've assigned her Intro class to Pankhurst, who has lots of experience teaching it; Museum Display Techniques to Schultz, our curator; and Selected Topics to Ginger. We all have to do our part." Of course the assignments had gone to the three lowest left on the totem pole, the rest being full professors.

"This is outrageous!" Evan raised his voice "My class limit

is always three. And no one else should have an overload either."

"I believe your letters of appointment state that the chair will determine your teaching schedules."

"Yeah, in consultation with us, and we haven't been consulted!" said Ginger.

Rickover started to respond, but the whole faculty shouted him down, Bob Rothschild finally winning out. "This is rather irregular, Vance."

"Have you consulted the dean about this? He wouldn't approve these teaching loads."

"You shouldn't be giving Cissy that gigantic Intro class in her tenure year," Rothschild said.

"She'll have tenure soon enough," Rickover barked unthinkingly, then corrected himself: "*If* she passes the departmental vote, then the divisional committee." It seemed to Cissy that she couldn't challenge this excessive teaching load now. "For your information," Rickover went on during a lull in the complaints, "the dean has approved this emergency measure. I'd think you might want to step in and help a colleague in need." Which colleague, Cissy wondered, Sandra or Vance? "If the untenured among you want to keep your jobs..." Now he eyed Cissy. "I suggest you cooperate."

"What's happened, exactly, to Sandra?" Ginger piped up. For once, her curiosity was legitimate. "We all have the right to know some details." Cissy knew that in private Ginger would have said "the dirt."

"It's a private matter," Rickover said stuffily, and seemed to contemplate his next move. "But since you're all involved in this, I suppose I can tell you." He paused, probably the better to rehearse his lies, Cissy imagined.

"As the pressure of the tenure process was getting to her, she slowly started to crack up. You all saw her freeze during the questions after her lecture. She never recuperated from it. She taught her classes as long as she could, and now I've taken them over, *temporarily.*" Rickover folded his arms across his chest, as if the matter were settled.

"But where is she, Vance?" Rothschild asked.

"She's committed herself voluntarily."

"As opposed to 'committed herself involuntarily'?" Evan cracked.

"What'd you do, lock her up?" Ginger stared up at him. At

least she didn't add "in the attic?" or "again." Cissy had never before seen Ginger, a devious model of academic decorum, let her curiosity so obviously get the best of her in public.

Rickover's narrowed eyes almost met in the middle, as he silently mouthed "How dare you!" The whole department likely had the sufficient lip-reading skills to decipher the three syllables. "This has been hard enough on us."

"Fine. We sympathize, Vance," said Rutledge. This was likely to be as much sympathy as he was going to get.

"But where exactly is she?" Cissy found herself asking.

"I consider it a private matter."

"We might want to visit her." Cissy surprised herself by pursuing this.

"She certainly hasn't been asking for you, Pankhurst. In any case, she's not allowed visitors. She needs rest, privacy, and professional care."

"Vance, I don't see how you, how we, can do this." Ginger now spoke with polite restraint. After all, she was one of the targeted three. She'd been too riveted to the proceedings to take any minutes, as far as Cissy could discern. "In any case, I taught Selected Topics in the fall and I don't think I should teach it again so soon."

"It's a quite different topic."

"Indeed it is," Ginger agreed. "One that's much closer to Nick's area than mine."

All eyes fell on Nick, who'd been silent up until now, and remained mute.

"I don't think the dean would approve of the recent happenings in the department," Ginger went on, and Cissy began to panic. What she'd said could be taken as a clear allusion to Sandra's lecture.

"Can we stop this nonsense!?" Rickover looked to where his allies sat, obviously hoping for help.

"I think you ought to produce Sandra and let us hear what she has to say about this," Ginger continued sparring.

"As I said, she's locked up."

"Do you have something to hide by keeping her from us?" Ginger stood up defiantly, almost gnashing her teeth as she spoke.

"What the hell are you implying?" Rickover turned to his side and faced her. Their noses were no more than a foot apart.

Cissy's nerves were falling apart. Blake had died, she'd lost a vote, Vance had written Sandra's lecture, they'd told Ginger, Ginger was now about to accuse Rickover, and she began to see her academic career crumble in front of her.

"I'm sorry. Nothing," Ginger said in a low voice, sat back down, and smoothed her indigo dress. "I think, Vance, that before assigning Sandra's classes, you should ask for volunteers to teach them." She looked up at him, now batting her eyelashes, extracted a handkerchief from her cleavage, and dabbed at it, as if perfuming herself.

Rickover sat back down, at least feigning cooperation. "All right, volunteers first. Anyone for Selected Topics?"

"I'll do it, Vance," said Nick. "I've never done it and it's only a two-credit course."

"Fine. Nick will teach Selected Topics." Cissy imagined that Ginger's threat had gotten her just what she wanted: off the hook. "Next: Museum Display Techniques. Volunteers?" Rickover looked slowly around the room, first at Rutledge and Rothschild, then a longer glance at Evan and Cissy herself. Finally, a cursory view of Ginger's bust. Ginger, everyone knew, wasn't going to volunteer in a millennium.

"Fine," Rickover said. "I'll keep teaching it myself."

This shocked Cissy; Ginger's threat or allusion had obviously scared him.

"But I'm *not* going to keep teaching the Intro class. Do we have a volunteer?" His gaze rested on each of them except Nick, and finally landed on Cissy, his eyes boring meaningfully into hers. How could she not acquiesce? All of them except Evan were going to vote on her tenure in a few minutes. It might well be the only way to save her career.

"I'll do it," she said, not too lamely, she hoped.

"Fine. The matter's take care of. Thank you all for being so cooperative." Cissy couldn't tell if he was being sarcastic or not. "Anything else? That's the whole agenda. Motion to adjourn the departmental committee?"

The motion made and the vote having passed, she and Evan, the two untenured among the bunch, got up to go.

"My tenure vote couldn't have come up on a worse day," she wailed to Evan in the hall. "With my luck, I won't pass the vote, and I'll still be stuck with the Intro class."

She cursed Amelia's Christmas party, mourned Blake, worried about Sandra, hated Rickover, distrusted Ginger, and thought of all her years of wasted work.

# 38

Edwin picked Juan up at the New Orleans International Airport. In the baggage claim area, a voice announced, "You must have your claim ticket to exit, as this is a high crime area. Welcome to New Orleans."

Their vacations coincided — almost. Pepper, still distraught for reasons unknown, had flown to Key West a day before Juan flew to New Orleans. He'd taken four days off from work for the trip.

Edwin's house in the French Quarter sat on a narrow, deep lot. It was on "lower" Bourbon Street, the gay part of the Quarter, safely distant from the throngs of straight tourists at the other end.

"Mardi Gras weekend." Edwin smiled broadly, with a touch of... romance. Or lust? "You'll have a complete New Orleans experience."

"Great."

"But it won't be complete unless you get mugged."

Juan had thought he was going to say "laid," although he always thought of sex as "making love." "It's not that unsafe here, is it?"

Edwin chuckled like the all-knowing, seasoned veteran he probably was. "Sometimes it's a combat zone, but with all the tourists this weekend, I don't think you'll be mugged in the middle of the mobs."

To Juan, the Quarter had a mixture of European and Caribbean flavors. Magnolia trees kept leaves year-round. Dampness filled the air, though it was nothing compared to the summer humidity, Edwin told him. The city was draped in gold, green and purple —the Mardi Gras colors. Estimates were that up to a million people had descended on the city, which was clearly a madhouse.

"We won't leave the Quarter. Traffic and parking are impossible. But there's enough to see right here. Twenty gay bars in walking distance and all the major parades come near. Want to go out tonight?"

"Can I rest up? It's all sort of overwhelming." Juan envisioned a romantic night, without the constraints of a cruise ship, small cabins and Pepper.

"Anything's fine with me."

After a nightcap, they retired to the bedroom and Juan, knowing that Pepper would be doing the same, made love. Or rather, tried to make love. After the cruise, he and Pepper had come to an uneasy truce, agreeing that they needed time "to be with other people" — left open to each one's interpretation — and to reevaluate their relationship. Pepper was sorry for more or less deserting Juan on the cruise; Juan feigned regret for letting Edwin "romance" him.

In the morning, Edwin pounced on him with unexpected passion. Again Juan couldn't respond.

"I think I'll take my morning swim," said Edwin. "Come on out and we'll have a poolside breakfast."

When Juan followed him a little later, Edwin was swimming nude in the pool. Roz swimming nude in the lake, Edwin in his pool. Irv, Dayne and Roz nude upstairs. He couldn't seem to get away from it. What was wrong with people keeping their clothes on? Didn't people have any modesty? And didn't clothes serve the useful purpose of hiding imperfect, overweight bodies like his own?

"What's back there?" Juan pointed at a narrow building against the back wall of the property.

"The slave quarters. I rent them out to a couple of gay guys. No problem. Everyone who wants to swims nude."

The idea that others — Edwin's tenants or Mardi Gras guests — might appear made Juan even more modest. "I'll keep my trunks on, if you don't mind."

After breakfast they toured the Quarter. From the edge of upper Bourbon Street, full of night clubs with expensive drinks and strip joints, Juan observed the masses. Men on balconies screamed "Show your tits!" Women complied and received gifts of beads. Almost everyone wore them, some sporting dozens of strands. Roz ought to visit here, he thought; she'd fit right in.

"You have to 'earn' your beads," explained Edwin. "That's what those women are doing. Now you'll have your chance in the gay area."

In the gay area, the Bourbon Pub balcony overflowed with men who screamed "Show your dick!" Many did, and caught their beads. The whole scene felt more than a little alien to Juan. They went a block down to Lafitte's, where the scene repeated itself. "I'm too old to do this."

"You're still a Mardi Gras virgin," Edwin countered. "What

color do you want?"

"What color what?"

"Beads, of course."

"Oh, whatever." Juan tried to sound animated.

A few minutes later, Edwin returned from the Mardi Gras Hut, four strands of beads in his hands. He put a black and white one around Juan's neck, draped the other two around his own. Juan was not about to drop his pants to garner more. Voyeurism was strange enough, but exhibitionism? Edwin seemed disappointed by his lack of daring.

That night they went on a bar tour and crammed their way into a leather bar, carrying their own drinks in go-cups, as Edwin had warned that service inside would be nearly impossible.

Juan was as shocked as if a thousand volts of electricity had jolted him. He knew he wasn't in Madison any more. From what he could see in the dark, the activity started with nipples and went downward from there. He looked at the floor: An appparent slave was requesting permission to lick his boots. It was all a little too much. He had to scream at Edwin over the music: "Mind if we get out of here?"

"Just showing you the sights."

Juan concluded he'd seen enough "sights" to last him a lifetime.

❦

Monday was either a business day or day of rest for locals and  Edwin had taken the day off. His clinic was out of the Quarter and Juan didn't feel like visiting an Eating Disorders Clinic anyway. Tactfully, Edwin didn't bring Juan's problem up. Juan ate normally, even relaxed, though be began to wonder, what the hell he was doing here? They hadn't made love, Edwin didn't seem to mind, and Juan couldn't figure out his own or Edwin's intentions.

That night they went to a parade. The crowd jostled each other for the throws from the floats: beads, doubloons, and engraved plastic cups. It all had a distinct Third World aura, reminding Juan of Cuba. Edwin jumped and caught all he could, passing on the loot to Juan.

"Don't kid yourself. People will step on an old lady's hands to scoop up this stuff."

They retired right after the parade, the better to rise early Mardi Gras day, when they went to a breakfast where the alcohol flowed freely. By noon they had toured ten blocks and two bars, and worked their way through the crowd to get a peek of the Bourbon Street Awards —not on Bourbon Street— for the gay costume contest. Edwin again wore his spider outfit and had decked out Juan as a pirate. He watched as a profusion of feathers, The Drag Queen Emergency Repair Squad, and septuplets dressed as Whistler's Mother — complete with chairs — paraded across the stage among hundreds of others.

After two open houses, where they rested, ate, drank coffee and used the facilities, they trooped back out. The sun was descending; unlike the cruise, which at least had had possibilities, this was not at all romantic. Juan had a sudden urge to be with Pepper.

Edwin led them to a country western bar, which could, he mentioned, "get wild." He pushed their way into the bar, said, "Have at it," and moved on.

Momentarily stunned by Edwin's desertion, Juan restrained his impulse to flee the bar, if not the city, but instead struggled toward the back.

Fat Tuesday, was, after all, the day when anything went, to let it all hang out. Juan had come to New Orleans for some sort of romance — he'd thought — and in lieu of it encountered only an orgy.

Letting it all hang out was exactly what many of the customers were doing when Juan reached the back, almost pitch-black. He took off his eye patch, but it made little difference. Hands groped him everywhere. What with the crush of humanity, it was difficult not to have sex on the premises.

"Here, put this on." Someone put a condom in his hand. It took him a second to realize what was happening until the man, in a deft motion, undid Juan's fly and bent over.

"Thanks, but no thanks." He doubted the guy could even hear him. "I'm sure someone else will oblige."

A few seconds later he saw that someone else was. Unable to avoid the crush of humanity and lacking an escape, he positioned himself on top of a stack of cases of beer bottles. Beside him, someone flashed a lighter to observe the happenings, flashed it again. He looked over to see Edwin splayed against the wall, two guys on their knees, blocking the view of where Edwin's pouch was — or had been.

Juan fought his way out of the bar and, not without effort, reached the door unmolested. At least Edwin had given him house keys. Thank God he was flying home tomorrow. Yes, flying home, to Madison and, he trusted, to Pepper.

# 39

The election loomed less than two weeks away. A retraction had been printed in *Outrage!* Claypool had received the *State Journal's* endorsement, but Roz felt triumphant that she had actually gotten the *Cap Times'*, which opined that the sixth district needed "new blood" and Roz had it.

Tonight she'd accepted an invitation for candidates from the Isthmus to attend a forum of the Ten Percent Society and the Yikes Dykes! Of the six districts on the Isthmus, five were contested elections. She wondered how many of the candidates would show.

Seth met her at Memorial Union, site of the forum, to offer moral support.

"Irv's seemed a little distant lately," she told him, as they sneaked cigarettes outside the meeting room.

"Don't worry. It's hard on spouses."

"What about it being hard on the candidate?" She blew a smoke ring into the air and watched it dissolve.

"Better watch it. Two more weeks and this campus will be smoke-free," chided one of two females heading in.

"Shit." There were no ashtrays and Roz ground it out on the floor.

"You'll do fine. Irv has your best intentions at heart, but I'm here for you." Seth clasped her shoulder and held on. Was she actually shaking? In any case, his firm, but gentle touch relaxed her.

Seconds later Claypool strode past her into the room. "Shit."

"Roz. Good evening."

"John. Same to you."

Claypool, liberal Democrat that he was, had the support of some gay and lesbian Democrats. But most of the city's radical queers lived in her district, and she had to show them she hadn't abandoned their cause. Beth, she'd realized, could be an asset there. Just like Rhoda, Beth had simply been in the wrong place at the wrong time. Roz detached her herself from Seth's arm and walked in, leaving him to sit in the back. He was going to offer her a post-debate analysis and offer tips for honing her skills.

Only four candidates had shown up, the other two from the largely student-populated eighth district. At a previous

neighborhood forum, she and Claypool had agreed on everything except the convention center. He mouthed her positions
on health care, housing, and day-care centers; she repeated his
on traffic concerns, in which she still couldn't get interested,
no matter how much Dave lectured her. She'd been tempted
to dump Dave and replace him with Seth as her manager.

Lesbian and gay student leaders stood side by side and
addressed the audience of about sixty. "This isn't going to be a
formal debate. We'll just let you ask questions of candidates
and all who want to can respond."

The first question involved health benefits for gay and lesbian partners of city workers. Madison now had a domestic
partners ordinance, but about all you could do after register-
ing was get a couple's membership at the YM- or YWCA. The
eighth district candidates both favored this — how could they
not in front of the partisan group? Claypool did likewise; Roz
was able to get in the last word:

"It's every alternative family's right to health care. Not only
for lesbian and gay partners and unmarried heterosexuals, but
for their children," she said, going a step further than the others. "Whatever it costs." She knew this was unlikely to be imple-
mented, so she might as well go out on a limb: "And it should
happen now. Lots of people don't know how many lesbian and
gay couples here in Madison have children of their own."

On the next question about city AIDS funding, Roz spoke
first. The other candidates echoed her position, almost verbatim, unable to elaborate or give a stronger AIDS-positive response. She could see that this forum was going to be a bore;
only if some right-winger were present, would there be any
controversy. Questions followed about lesbian and gay bashing, kicking ROTC off campus, a gay/lesbian studies major at
the University, and treatment of those who were HIV-positive
and incarcerated.

"What about a multilingual, multicultural police force?" The
candidates looked at each other; Roz motioned that she'd field
the question, thinking maybe she could score a point, and stood
up to speak: "I've met with the Chief of Police." This was a
white lie; she'd met him socially, but had never met "with"
him. "He's all in favor of multiculturalism and he and I whole-
heartedly support recruitment of lesbians and gays. And..."
Here she was going for a laugh, now knowing that many elections came down to personality as much as experience. "...I

think, as some of you may know, if lesbians are considered multicultural, Madison already has quite a multicultural police force."

The expected laughs came, even scattered applause.

"What about lesbians of color? Don't you think it's time Madison went in that direction?"

Roz couldn't spot a lesbian of color in the entire room. "I'd certainly support it. I know the Police Chief does too."

"What would you actually do?" the same questioner pursued.

Roz swallowed her exasperation. What was she supposed to do? Go into a lesbian bar, round them up, and trot them down to the Chief of Police? "I'd do what I can. Talk with the Chief again, talk with lesbians of color in the community." Adroitly, she turned to the other candidates on stage: "Any of you care to add anything?" No one cared to, or was able. Relieved, she sat back down.

"I have a question for Roz Goldwomyn," said a woman in the back.

"The others are free to reply also."

"Oh, I don't think they'll be able to."

"Go ahead."

Roz beamed, since, obviously, someone deemed her the only candidate knowledgeable enough to handle whatever was coming. Although it wasn't necessary, she again stood up to answer the question. She might even get down off the stage, the better to make more personal contact with the crowd.

"Some say you've forsaken the lesbian and gay movement. Some of us have been here long enough to remember when you were supposedly a lesbian." The woman now wielded Roz's campaign literature in the air. "Now I see that you have a husband and child. Would you care to comment? Are you or are you not one of us?"

Jesus Christ. She thought she'd finished coming out as a straight person five years ago.

"Yes, I was a lesbian. Yes, I did get married. My child, if it's of interest to you, was alternatively conceived." That, she hoped, might pacify some of them. "Spiritually, yes, I'm still one of you." She looked to her side, saw Claypool managing to hold back a smirk. Had he put someone up to this?

"In all fairness," the male moderator interjected, "I think it would be of interest to know if any of the other candidates present are lesbian- or gay-identified." A trio of no's followed, though of course — the sons of bitches — they were all with them "spiritually." Her answer had been ripped off again.

"One more question," said the same woman in back. "Again for Roz Goldwomyn. What about your radical tactics of the old days? Wasn't it you who sprayed the UW sidewalks with 'Pro-lifers Eat Caviar'? What about a sit-in at a reputedly anti-lesbian movie, which, I believe, resulted in your arrest?"

"Yes, I did both those."

"So you have a criminal record?"

"I was arrested at the sit-in, but never convicted. And, for your information," she added, to boost her ground, now that they were on the topic, "I was the one who dressed as a cow, labeled its quarters, and made it to the stage of the Miss University of Wisconsin Pageant. Which was cancelled in subsequent years." Scattered applause. She omitted that she was also arrested for this.

"So you admit to all this."

"Yes."

"So you committed the criminal act of spray-painting the sidewalks and were never apprehended for it?"

Roz didn't like the phrasing of the hostile question, but could only say yes again.

"So we have an unapprehended criminal, once a lesbian who later supposedly became straight, and we're supposed to vote for her for city council?"

"You're badgering the candidate."

"Hey, I'd do those same things," said a young woman in front. "Except breed with a man," she tacked on quickly, causing laughter all around. Roz was about to add that she hadn't "bred" with a man, but the same hostile woman went on:

"We've not only read, but seen the photographic evidence that you're against humane treatment of animals."

"Those are unfounded allegations and totally untrue."

"And the picture in *Outrage!?*"

"Just this week they printed a retraction." She wished she'd brought it with her. "It was my mother wearing that fur. My mother, from New York. I can't help..."

"Sounds like some cheap publicity trick to me."

"If that was 'publicity,' it was the most unfortunate kind. I have grounds to sue Maddie Son."

"Do you support women's rights to sunbathe topless?"

"I most certainly do."

"I don't know that that's in the best interests of the community, Roz," said Claypool. The eighth-district candidates agreed, and Roz was glad to hear the crowd's lesbian sector — the majority in attendance — boo them.

"If you don't get your way," said a man next to the hostile questioner, "I've heard you're going to propose a city ordinance for equal treatment of both sexes, requiring men to always wear shirts in public."

"Not true."

"How can we be sure?"

"That's bullshit." The word was out before Roz knew it; no one seemed to mind.

"Utter nonsense," Claypool seconded, either to rescue her, or to be the voice of more diplomatic language.

"I think that's enough questions of this nature, all directed at the same candidate," the female moderator said.

"Hold Goldwomyn accountable!" screamed the woman in back.

Roz got a good look at her before she ran from the room. Unless she was mistaken, it was Melissa Marker, the current lover of Erva Mae, Roz's ex. She noticed that the man who'd posed the shirts-for-males question followed quickly on her heels. She should have known that even after all these years Erva Mae would still bear her ill will. But she hadn't expected her to try to sabotage her campaign.

Fuming, she sat back down. "Don't let one nasty lesbian get you down," Claypool whispered and put his hand on hers, a supposed gesture of comfort.

"Keep your paw off me, you old fart," she barked back, then realized the audience, now laughing, had heard.

Perhaps it was the best thing she'd said all evening. Maybe she would emerge tonight with her credibility intact.

Claypool glared at her, obviously having taken offense: "You want war, Goldwomyn? You'll get it."

# 40

Ginger wished she had gone somewhere for Spring Break. Melvin had left on a business trip to Dallas and she had the house to herself. She liked a certain amount of time alone, but didn't know what to do with this much. The first day of vacation she'd finished her latest article mailed it off to *The Small Museum Review*. She'd be damned if she was going to go to a Narcotics Anonymous meeting just to get out of the house. In any case, she'd only gone lately for pretense, so that Melvin would know she was regularly attending. She wondered if her departmental colleagues really believed that she was attending Workaholics Anonymous meetings.

Since Amelia's party she'd been tempted, but had so far resisted whenever she could, largely due to Melvin's presence. She kept thinking back to the party, knowing she should have followed her therapist's advice: "Don't be around people who are doing drugs. Under any circumstance." She didn't even like marijuana and hadn't been tempted by it; it was simply the fact that they were getting high and she wasn't. And look what had happened to Blake. But, no, that was a freak accident, she told herself, though she'd had to distance herself emotionally from it. Coke had never killed her, never would. She'd had relapses ever since last summer, and had kept it under control, so what was she worrying about? But Melvin was still going to be away for four more days...

A visit to her parents in New Jersey almost sounded good and she cursed herself again for spending the break in Madison. The temperature was sub-normal and felt sub-zero. The sky formed a bleak grey canopy above the snow-covered ground. She could have gone to a conference in Hattiesburg; even that almost appealed now. Or to the one in Washington, D.C., where Rickover had gone. But his was a face she didn't care to see, and no one at either convention could do her career particular good. Maybe she should have gone to southern California, like Cissy, basking in the glow of her unanimous tenure vote from the department. There had to be nice resorts in Palm Springs and other exotic warm places she'd never visited. But here she was...

She made a pact with herself for the day: If she got through to Sid today and he had any she'd buy a gram and only one gram. If she didn't get through to him, she'd give up the idea. One gram couldn't hurt; it wouldn't even last her a day. She was living in hell, was lonely and deserved a little boost. Although she trusted it would pass some day, she knew she was suffering from the "shit-I-got-tenure-and-now-I'm-stuck-here" syndrome. As was her habit, she'd perused the NMA Job List, even more seriously than usual, looking for a lucrative position at Berkeley or Stanford, or an attractive one in any place with a better climate, which should be almost anywhere. But her field was small and the number of positions minuscule — almost nonexistent for tenured faculty. If she had to stay in Madison permanently, she was damned if she wasn't going to be the next departmental chair now that, one way or another, they were going to get rid of Rickover.

By early evening she got through to Sid. His Brooklyn accent irritated her and she envied his beautiful house in Maple Bluff. Business executive that he was, he had to be earning at least one hundred thousand a year, in addition to his income on the side.

"Surprised to hear from you again. I wondered if you got busted — though I didn't read about in the newspapers — went clean, or what."

"I have *not* been busted," she countered firmly, "and it hasn't been *that long.*" She then stated her request in code.

"Only one?"

"Yes, just one, if you've got it. This is a one-time thing."

"You're always doing one-time things. You know I don't like to deal with shit that small."

"Sid, I was one of your best c..." She stopped herself from saying "customers," a telephonic taboo. "...best people for years!"

"I suppose for you, I can scrape one up." She took this as a compliment, that he could scrape it up for *her,* as opposed to others.

"Perfect. When can I get it?"

"How about ten tonight?"

"Sure." She'd hoped it would be earlier, but she'd make do.

Ginger held off until noon the next day, then decided it was time to do a few lines. She took the excessive powder and rubbed it on her gums, liking the feel of instant anesthesia. She was not, she swore, going to shoot it up.

Zooming around the house, she started talking to herself. Coke made her talkative and she didn't need an interlocutor. After she finished a few minutes of rapid-fire babbling, her mind zeroed in on one subject: Sandra.

"Who really cares about Sandra? But we've got to find her so we can nail Rickover. There's an easy way to crack this case open, and Sandra is the key. Finally, Sandra will be good for something!"

She settled down enough to call all the local hospitals — no easy task — but none would admit to harboring a Sandra Rickover. Plus, if she were in a psych unit, they'd never tell you anyway. On a roll, even if unsuccessful, she called the Alumni Office at the University of Michigan, Sandra's alma mater, pretended to be a cousin, and tried to get a home address, hopefully her parents'. The only address she got was Sandra's in Madison. If her maiden name hadn't been Schmidt, it would have been easier to track her parents down in a Detroit phone book, which she could get at the Reference Room at Memorial Library.

After snorting another line, she attempted to call Melvin at his hotel, and then re-called all the area hospitals, asking for Sandra under her maiden name. It was dark by the time she finished.

Four thin lines later, she decided to take a spin in the car. She zipped out of the driveway and headed west. Before she knew it, she was going down Regent Street toward Midvale and realized that Rickover's house was only a block away. She took a quick right, then a left. She stopped the car across the street and parked it.

The house was unassuming and dark. The driveway showed, not surprisingly, no evidence of recent traffic. She walked around the sidewalk to the back of the house and stared upward. There was a light on in the tiny attic window above the second floor.

It couldn't be true, could it? A shiver, generated more by the circumstance than the cold, rattled her body. She stepped into the snow, just short of turning into slush, the better to see the window. Only a faint light, nothing more. If only she had a pebble or something to toss...

She tramped back to her car, took out her purse. There was nothing tossable in it but a tube of lipstick. She grabbed it and retraced her steps to the back of the house. Aiming at the attic window, she launched it into the sky and it missed. Trudging through the snow, walking in circles, she finally found it again. Gloveless, she retrieved it, tried again, and missed twice more, making a game of seeing how quickly she could find it in the snow. The fourth time she nicked the small pane of glass.

She stood and waited, but nothing happened. At the back

of the lot stood a border of leafless bushes. Fences separated
the backyard from the neighbors'; at least she hadn't been seen.
Perhaps leaving the attic light on was Rickover's notion of
guarding against burglars; she remembered that the house had
been burglarized last summer. After a couple of minutes, beginning to feel bone-chilled, she started to walk away.

Then she heard a shattering of glass. She gave a start and
began to lope back. Was she only imagining she heard the faint,
dismal voice?: "Hello? Hello? Is anyone there?"

She galloped on as fast as she could through the snow, which
had now soaked her feet. "Sandra?" No answer. "Sandra? It's
Ginger." She peered up at the small, dimly illuminated window.

"Ginger, It's me!" Now she could make out the face that
went with the voice. "Vance has me locked in! Call the police!"

"I'll help you, I'll help you, Sandra. I'll get you out!" Ginger
and her adrenaline took off, as if a sprinter in a marathon, and
she ran toward the front of the house. It seemed that Sandra
screamed one last thing, but there was no worry, she was on
her way.

"Idiot," she yelled at herself at the front door. Of course it
was locked and Sandra couldn't open it from inside if she was
locked in the attic. Although Ginger had keys to every private
office in the department, she had yet to acquire them to the
faculty's houses. Foiled, she gave the door a swift kick with
her boot, then another, shaking the door, and an alarm promptly
went off.

"Motherfucker!" Rickover had installed a security system.
A siren wailed and wailed. She dashed down the sidewalk,
fleeing the scene. At least the security people should come and
find Sandra. She sped away in her car, zigzagging down the
snowy side street.

At least she had liberated Sandra, and, more importantly,
had begun Vance's ruin.

# 41

Spring Break had come and gone, and with it a week of
Beth's income. She hadn't known until the last minute
that her services as a student worker wouldn't be needed during the break. As Wilhelmina had explained, "No faculty to
bother you, no work for you to do."

"What about summer?" Beth inquired on her return. Her

appointment was for the semester only, but it didn't hurt to ask.

"Well, as you know," Wilhelmina began, fussing with a ring on her finger, "the department's in somewhat of a state of turmoil this semester, with Professor Abell's death and Mrs. Rickover's resignation."

"You're tellin' me."

"We do offer one course in the summer, to be taught by Professor Rutledge, so some help might be needed. But we'd have to go through the usual channels to get you, or anyone."

Beth wondered if she'd have to be enrolled in summer school to get the job. Probably. "This department's been in a state of turmoil for years, from what I know."

Wilhelmina's curious gaze didn't discourage her from continuing.

"I know the old chair raped Cissy. Word got around campus about how they fired him for it."

"Professor Isaacson did *not* rape her and was not fired for it. He retired. I myself was there that day in the service room, and it was a case of fourth-degree sexual assault. I'm not excusing it — quite the contrary — but it was not rape. You shouldn't go around repeating information like that, whether you think you're sure of it or not. I don't think Professor Pankhurst would appreciate having it spread around."

"S'pose you're right." Beth chided herself, not wanting to contribute to Cissy's post-rape trauma, even if it was five years ago. "I took her Intro course once. Got an A in it."

"You did?"

"Yeah, kept me from flunkin' out my first year. I was real proud of myself. Then I found out that because of the rape, I mean the assault, she flipped out and gave an A to everyone in the whole class."

"Professor Pankhurst did not give an A to everyone in that class."

"Oh, yeah? Well, almost everyone, then. I was lucky to be averagin' a C or a D, and I got an A." Beth wondered fleetingly about her grades in her current courses: Death and Dying was turning out OK; in AIDS and Ethics, she had yet to receive a grade. "How do you think that course got so popular? Word of those A's spread like herpes all over campus."

"The Intro course was *always* popular, even before Professor Pankhurst taught it."

"Whatever you say. But it sure had a rise in popularity after Cissy freaked out. I suppose she can do what she wants, now that she's got tenure."

"Professor Pankhurst doesn't have tenure yet."

"You mean they changed their minds and are firin' her? I thought the department voted in her favor."

Wilhelmina surveyed the undone work in the office, shook her head hopelessly, then explained: "They did, but it's only the first step. Now the divisional committee, made up of members elected from all the departments in Fine Arts, has to vote on her tenure." Beth hadn't known about this. "That's the hurdle to get past. Of course, we all hope she gets it."

"Yeah, otherwise, you're gonna not have any department left, the way they're droppin' around here."

Wilhelmina stared into the video monitor of her computer. "I have a lot to type. And I think I hear Professor Rickover coming."

From what Beth had seen, Wilhelmina's typing speed was almost as slow as her own. Not only that, she'd heard faculty complaints about the administrative secretary's questionable mastery of WordPerfect.

"Morning, ladies," Rickover boomed, then looked at Beth and lowered his voice: "Referring to you, I use the term loosely. *Very* loosely."

"You mean 'women,' anyway," she shot back, uncertain if he heard, as he swung his door shut.

Now she couldn't insult him further and, in any case, saw that tears were forming in her eyes, threatening to cascade down her cheeks. She'd never imagined that a job on campus could subject her to so much humiliation.

For Beth and Verla, "celebrate" was a code word for sex. That night they planned to celebrate Verla's new job as a part-time teacher in the county schools, where she was replacing someone who had resigned mid-semester. Full-time teaching jobs in Madison were nearly impossible to come by; part-time ones, even in music, hard enough.

Maybe they'd make it, after all. With her job in Museum Studies and the money earned as Roz's campaign treasurer, her situation didn't look so bad. Granted, she'd only get one or two more small checks, whether or not Roz won. The election was coming up soon and Rhoda was returning for it. Maybe Roz would hire her again to take care of Rhoda. On second thought, maybe not.

"So I'll just have to shuffle my private students' hours around," Verla said, and Beth realized she hadn't been listening. "Even if I end up losing one or two, I'll still be much better off. Though we'll have to see what summer brings."

"Cheers." Beth, then Verla, hoisted token glasses of club soda, a prelude, she knew, to sex. Two cats hovered around the kitchen table as if it were feeding time, Brooklyn letting out an exceedingly high-pitched meow.

"Cheers," Verla repeated, and guzzled her soda in one gulp, an obvious holdover from the days when she'd guzzle anything in a single gulp.

"Get the hell away, kitties," Beth admonished, anxious herself about summer, wanting to put it out of her mind and to enjoy an evening of sexual abandon. Verla had fewer than usual private students in summer, and Beth herself might have no job at all. She might as well worry about it right now; she didn't want thoughts about money — or lack thereof — racing through her mind while they occupied the bedroom.

"We just have time to eat, then go to ACT UP," Verla said.

"ACT UP?"

"There's a meeting to plan a protest outside the Department of Corrections because of the way they're treating HIV-positive inmates."

"Oh." Beth had forgotten.

"You did plan to go, didn't you?"

"Yeah, I just thought we were going to..."

"We'll do that later," Verla said, picking up on her meaning. Beth brightened, almost seeing lust written across Verla's forehead. "I've got a surprise for you." She stopped, leaving Beth hanging. "For us," she clarified. This seemed to be all the clarification Beth was going to get.

"Great. Let's go now." The better to get home sooner, she thought, savoring the night to come.

Beth sat alone in the Museum Studies office, thinking of last night's surprise. It had been a dildo, not at all erotic, and the evening had proved a disaster. Wilhelmina had called her this morning, ill, and asked if Beth could come in for the whole day.

She'd have to miss her Death and Dying class, she'd been up late with Verla, upset and unable to sleep, but at least she'd earn extra money today. Maybe being in the office would help to take her mind off the dildo, which had made her wonder if Verla wished Beth had a penis. She felt unsettled; last night it had been so late that they hadn't even discussed their botched attempt at sex.

She put her "YIKES DYKES!" button back on her blouse and spruced up the front of her desk with a large ACT UP poster. Evan came in with his morning coffee and sat down to chat, as he often did with Wilhelmina or whomever was available. "Whomever" excluded Rickover.

"Willy's out today." Beth sensed she could get away with informality. She secretly enjoyed the power of being the lone secretary for the day, the fact that the faculty would be solely dependent on her.

"Nice poster."

"Yeah, I think so. Hey, let's go for a coffee refill?"

"Mine could use freshening."

They went to the service room, Beth eyeing it eerily as the scene of Cissy's assault, and refilled their cups. When they returned to the departmental office, Ginger stood at Wilhelmina's telephone. "Just call back tomorrow," she shrieked into the receiver. "I don't know, the secretary isn't here, and I'm sure the chair doesn't know." Then she hung up, turned around and scowled at Evan and Beth. "What do you think this is, a café?"

"Hey, easy, Ging. Wilhelmina's sick today. The office staff has the right to have breaks."

"Give *me* a break." Ginger's tone sounded as nasty as Rickover's. "Faculty shouldn't have to be doing secretarial work."

"Then why'd you answer the phone? They would've called back if it was important."

"Yeah," Beth backed him up.

"You!" Ginger pointed. "I thought you've been told to take that button off."

"Maybe I have. I forgot today."

"Now you've been reminded."

"It doesn't hurt a thing, Ging."

"I may take it off today, but next month, for 'Out & About' — you probably wouldn't know that's Lesbian and Gay Pride on campus — I think I'll have to wear it."

"Like hell you will, if you're even still working here. I'm practically acting chair. I could have you fired."

"Ginger, you're loaded this morning."

"I most certainly am not."

Ginger Carter a drunk? This was a new development. But, no, she didn't act like a drunk. Maybe she was a speed freak.

"How dare you? In front of her!"

"Better than in front of anyone else."

At that moment, Rickover walked in. "What's all the ruckus?"

"These two were having a kaffeeklatsch while some of us are trying to get some work done."

"You, shrimp. As I've already said, off with the button. And down with that poster."

"Come on, Vance," Evan said.

"I happen to agree with Vance," said Ginger.

"You think this is Fag Week or Dyke Week on campus, or what?"

"You've violated the speech code. Again," Beth said. She'd tried to file a complaint against Maddie Son, but found out that non-students were not subject to it, though faculty were.

"Stop calling it a 'speech code,' because it isn't. And if you can wear a button that says 'dyke,' I can certainly use the word."

"For all you know," Evan said, "I'm bisexual, and the word 'fag' offends me. You just might have multiple complaints on your hands, Vance."

"You're as fucking crazy as she is!" bellowed Ginger.

"You still can't call me a shrimp just because I'm four-foot-nine. I can file a complaint against you just for that!" Rickover was the most odious man she'd ever known.

"Why don't you all get the hell out of here and leave me in peace?" Rickover yelled. Beth had never seen him quite like this; he seemed at the breaking point.

"You can't send me home. I'm scheduled to work eight hours, I need the money, and I intend to get paid for all eight."

"We can't close the office, Vance. Wouldn't look too good to the dean," Evan said.

"You two go back to your offices." He indicated Evan and Ginger. "And you stay glued to that seat and answer the phone! Screen my calls as usual."

"You want a secretary today, I'm leaving this button on. And

I think you should apologize."

Rickover hesitated a second, eyed his faculty hopefully, as if awaiting support. He got none.

"I'll have you fired if it's the last thing I do!"

Rickover stormed into his office and Ginger marched away, leaving her alone with Evan.

"Though I hope not for your sake, it may well be the final thing he does," Evan whispered to her.

# 42

Pepper sat alone in Amelia's study, engrossed in reading a select part of her chapter on the "commune years":

*In August, 1972, we were joined by seventeen-year-old Pepper Isaacson, who had more than a glint of revolutionary chutzpa in his dark eyes, a refugee from what he called his 'fascist' parents' house. A glint of another sort, noticed by more than one of us, seemed to appear whenever he saw Juan Bellefleur...*

"Amelia?" Pepper called.

"Coming."

A minute later she glided in. "I bet I know what you've been reading."

"You can get by saying I called my parents 'fascists'." If this superfluous part mentioning all the commune members is ever published, he thought. "But what about this 'glint' in my eyes for Juan? I didn't even know I was gay then!"

"Well..." Amelia pondered, head down and hands clasped together. "Now don't take offense, but... We all talked back then, everybody about everybody. And even though maybe you didn't know it then, we all suspected you might be gay. Mainly because of the way you always looked at Juan."

All of them in the commune? He couldn't or didn't want to believe this for a minute. "Amelia, was it — was I — that obvious?"

"Obvious, no. But the way you looked at Juan, or *didn't* look at him... We all suspected something was there."

"Amelia, I think you misspelled 'chutzpah'."

"I guessed. It's not in my dictionary."

"I'll call Juan. He'll know. He still even runs his one-man organization, SPELL." Amelia threw him a puzzled glance, and Pepper elucidated: "'Society for the Preservation of the English Language and Lexicon.' Mainly he sends out 'citations' for misspellings in advertising and asks the offending businesses to send a donation. A few do. Very few."

He reached Juan at home and could hear him exhaling smoke into the phone. A few seconds later he informed Amelia, "The first spelling begins with CH and ends with H."

"Then we'll use that one."

Pepper changed the spelling, then said, "I think I'll leave this paragraph for tomorrow." He exited the document, then added, meaningfully, "In case you want to rewrite it tonight."

"That's the first time you've mentioned Juan in a while," Amelia said, as Pepper made a back-up disk of the day's work. "I hope you and Juan are going to keep living together."

The remark gave him a start. "Have I implied otherwise?"

"No, but I know you, Pepper, and I know Juan. I was thinking about these separate trips you took. Excuse me if I my question was out of place."

"No, it wasn't." The disk backed-up, Pepper took it the out of the computer and put it in the disk container. "I just needed to get away. Juan did too. I'd wanted to visit San Francisco and, after Key West, it seemed like the right time, since Juan was still in New Orleans." Pepper had accompanied Gene and Glen directly from Key West.

"You have to watch out for your health." He imagined she was referring to the bad cold he'd caught in one place or the other and, like his parents, held the not-always-remote fear that he could be HIV-positive.

He couldn't tell Amelia — or Juan — the whole truth of his vacation, not to mention the months preceding it. He hadn't had sex on the cruise, nor in Key West. In San Francisco he'd gone to leather bars in search of... Blake? A facsimile of him? He'd known he had to get Blake — or something — out of his system. He'd had a safe one-night stand, sexually but not emotionally satisfying, with only a dim replica of Blake. Perhaps he was losing his capacity to have sex for sex's sake. Maybe this was good, he thought.

"Tell me, Pepper, do gay men still have so much sex these days?"

Amelia's questions always amazed him, but shouldn't have, knowing her as he did. "Hmmm.... Probably not. No, they probably do. Anyway, they do it safer. With a condom. Or they have phone sex or computer sex." He realized he could tell her ten times more than she wanted to know. Then again, he feared she might well want to know it all.

"And if you — how should I say it? — step out again, you'll have safer sex, won't you?"

"Yes, Mother." He was convinced she was clairvoyant.

"I mean, I assume if you're gay and you go to San Francisco, one of the objects is to get laid, right?"

The question apparently required an answer. "You never give up, do you?"

"If I don't ask, how will I know? Just because I'm almost seventy-six, doesn't mean I'm not interested in the outside world."

"Yes. One object usually is to get laid. Today, safely."

If she could ask him, he could ask her, he thought, recalling her observation about the "glint" in his eyes for Juan. "And what about you?"

"Oh, since Ned, and it's been almost twenty-one years, there's been the gardener. A physician. A university dean. All widowed or divorced. Now I always insist they wear a condom. You insist now too."

❧

Juan attended a "Men Stopping Rape" meeting with Irv. Anything was a welcome respite from Roz and her campaign, he'd told Juan. Unaware of his eating disorder, he'd also commented casually that Juan was "looking good," that he seemed to have "gained a few pounds."

Traumatized by the remark, he'd gone home, weighed himself and, indeed, he'd gained two pounds. He'd done sit-ups, fifty at a time, until he'd lost count; hours later, his body still ached. Perhaps he should confide in Irv, Roz, or Pepper, as the problem was not going away, he showed no signs of getting better, and he'd told no one about it. He deposited a "Rape-Free World" pamphlet on the breakfast bar.

When Pepper got home, he picked it up, inquisitive, and skimmed it. "Juan, we have to talk."

Juan feared he knew what Pepper meant, had dreaded the moment and decided to be flippant.

"Sure. So how *do* we achieve a rape-free world? It might be a little difficult to stop among the male prison population."

"OK. Let's assume you and I are the male prison population." Pepper was evidently playing along.

"OK," Juan went along. "Did you get raped in a cell of some dark leather bar in Key West or San Francisco?"

Pepper gazed back down at the "Rape-Free World" pamphlet. "No, but I had contact. Only once. And you?" He raised his eyes to meet Juan's.

"A failed attempt — two, to be totally truthful — at sex."

"I take it we're not talking about rape."

"Right. I shouldn't have used the word anyway." Juan now took the pamphlet in one hand and shook an ultra-light out of its pack with the other.

"Give me one of those too." Juan knew he didn't mean the pamphlet. "Just kidding. You can put your eyeballs back in their sockets."

Juan lit up, inhaled deeply, then stubbed the cigarette out.

"Did you like it?" Pepper asked. "The sex?"

"Sex was not had. I said 'failed attempt.' There was nothing to like. I told you how repulsed I was by Mardi Gras and by Edwin's behavior. What about you?"

"Didn't like it as much as I'd hoped. But — since we're being totally truthful — I might want to try it again some day."

"Well, I don't want to. Edwin's nothing but a slut." This was perhaps an overstatement; it *had* been Mardi Gras day. "I didn't get into it."

"I didn't that much either." Pepper continued looking at Juan as if they should have more to say, then asked, "Juan, don't you want to say anything else?"

So the conversation had struck a sour note already. Here they were discussing had-been and would-be infidelities, even if they'd been more-or-less agreed on. Juan didn't like it one bit; it was about as appealing as gestalt group therapy. Everything had been Pepper's doing: the cruise, the separate trips, this conversation. Juan decided he just might have to have a little snack afterward.

"So, we've each spent a little time on our own, like we agreed to." Pepper leaned back on the sofa, ostensibly relaxed, which unnerved Juan. Relaxing was the last thing he could possibly do right now. "Have we reevaluated our relationship?" Pepper asked. The question was definitely not rhetorical.

Juan plucked the half-smoked cigarette from the ashtray, straightened it out, and lit it, stalling for time. "Not together."

"Shall we?"

"Let's." A late November swim in Lake Monona sounded just as appealing.

Pepper jumped right in: "Well, sex with others wasn't quite

what we'd hoped, right?"

Juan nodded slowly. Not that he'd hoped so much for sex as for... he wasn't sure what. Romance? Revenge?

"So that means we should work on strengthening our relationship and improving our sex life together, right?"

"Sex life? What's wrong with our sex life?"

"Frequency," Pepper answered. "Or maybe I should say, infrequency."

"Oh." The next thing he knew, Pepper would be calling him "frigid," or the male counterpart thereof.

"There's no reason two men can't still have satisfying sex together after five years."

This time Juan agreed, then blurted out the only question on his mind: "Does this mean we're staying together?"

"What do you think, *cabrón?*" It was the one Spanish vulgarity Pepper had picked up from Juan and occasionally used.

Juan let his tensed facial muscles relax into a full smile. "Well, I'd hoped so."

"So had I. I just needed a taste of freedom again."

"Do you mean once every five years?" Juan hoped that Pepper meant no more than this. "I suppose a little freedom every five years isn't necessarily bad." He trusted he could accommodate a once-per-lustrum infidelity into his definition of monogamy. He probably could have counted Gil's —his ex's— by the hour, and casually wondered how he was doing in Chicago.

"But I had more than a little taste of freedom." Pepper's voice began to quaver.

"I expected you did." Juan knew that among the cruise, Key West and San Francisco, Pepper must have seized more than one of his multiple opportunities for contact. "I accept that you did, but please spare me the lurid details."

Pepper had seemed poised to speak, but now his mouth clamped shut.

"Come on. I didn't mean that you shouldn't tell me what you need to tell me." Juan trusted he could maintain his cool. "Besides the details, which you're not going to tell me, this is the time we're putting things out in the open," Juan found himself saying, their roles having done a curious reversal. "So go ahead. Open up."

Pepper opened up his tear ducts, not at all what Juan expected. He cried at length, in raw, noisy sobs. What could be so serious? Finally Juan went over and steadied Pepper with his arm. "I won't be angry. No matter what."

"Oh, I wouldn't bet on that," Pepper managed through sniffles. Then he stood up, stared out at the lake, away from Juan, and spoke in an oddly distant voice: "I'm still in love..."

"That's good to hear."

"...with a dead man."

Juan took this in silently, stepped back and leaned on the door to the outside. "Dead man?" he said to himself. Pepper hadn't been in love with his good friend Rick, who had died last year, had he?

Then it hit him: Amelia's memorial service, Pepper's strange reaction, his depression since then. Pepper had just said "in love." Fine. Well, less than fine, provided that they hadn't had sex. "You mean...?"

Pepper nodded quickly, hung his head, and turned away. Then more tears came. Whom they were for, Juan didn't know.

# 43

"Labor Farm Office," the voice snapped.

Juan hesitated a second. "Roz?"

"Juan? Yeah, it's me. I don't usually take personal calls at the office."

Juan tended to believe Irv's suspicion: that Roz's moves from one office to another throughout the day, even during her campaign, were, in part, to facilitate the difficulty of tracking her down, should anyone need to reach her. "Roz, you're a volunteer. Can't you do what you want?"

"Please, Juan, don't tell me that Dayne has fled from Rhoda, now he's with you, and you can't stay with him today. Just march him right back up there, find out or don't find out what the problem is, and I'm sure the two of them can coexist for a few hours."

Juan decided to toy with her. "As a matter of fact, I can't." He let her ponder that, then added, "But Pepper and Irv can. Rhoda's out campaigning for you, door to door. I didn't know she was coming back before the election."

"Campaigning door to door!" Roz let out an extended groan.

"In any case, that's not why I called. *I've* got to talk to you today."

"Today?"

"Today. It's urgent." He gave "urgent" the appropriate, ominous tone. "If you possibly can..."

"Well, Seth *is* here with me..."

She finally consented to a late afternoon time, only after Juan insisted it was important and convinced her that the Baltic States Liberation Committee could survive a meeting without her. She had to pass by Womynspace, where she had an errand and would be replenishing her campaign literature and, since she'd be on campus, said she'd see him at the Rathskeller in Memorial Union. "By that time of day I'll be able to use a beer."

"But we can't buy beers there. Neither of us is a registered student and, as far as I know, neither of us bought lifetime memberships to the Union upon graduating."

"I'll get a student worker from Womynspace to come over with me."

"Roz, this has to be a private conversation. Plus, I don't think Womynspace will appreciate your dragging their student workers away to buy us beers."

"Don't worry already. We'll make do."

At the appointed time, Juan arrived at the Rathskeller, modeled after a 1930s German beer drinking hall — large, open and, by late afternoon, raucous. German proverbs, which Juan couldn't decipher, adorned the walls along with murals. He sat in the circular back part, where a row of windows looked out on the Union Terrace and, behind it, Lake Mendota, which had just begun its spring thaw.

Roz arrived fifteen minutes late, smiling, with a pitcher of beer and two cups in her hand. "Don't lecture me on being late. It took me fifteen minutes to find someone to buy us this beer — which I see you didn't bother to do — and then she had to wait in line to get it. Nothing like the good old days. Straight from the classroom to the bar. The unofficial 'University Extension.' Not to mentioning running out for a beer — or a toke — during a class break."

"Ah, the truth comes out. Now we know why you didn't finish, or rather, start your dissertation."

"Fuck off, Juan, and give me a light."

They lit up cigarettes and sipped their beers, when a man approached them. Juan looked up at him: a nerdy, bespectacled, middle-aged graduate student.

"You know, the Union — the entire campus — is smoke-free as of today. Please put those out. Some of us are physically impaired by cigarette smoke."

Roz stood up, anger boiling, and Juan hoped she wouldn't make a spectacle. He hid his own cigarette under the table.

"If you wouldn't walk around sniffing out cigarettes, then you wouldn't get so physically impaired, would you? What are you, a student?"

"Yes." The man stepped back, clearly incensed by Roz, who went right on:

"I recommend you finish your dissertation, or whatever the hell you're working on, get the hell out of here and Madison, and go somewhere else and found your own smoke-free university."

At the next table several students applauded. Roz daringly took a drag on her cigarette right in front of him as he furiously waved away smoke.

"You can be reported and fined for this. Put that out now!"

"*You* beat it, motherfucker," said one of the nearby students who had applauded.

The man skittered away, to report them, or to recover.

"Fine performance, Roz." Juan helped her sit back down. "I just hope no one recognized you. The election is only three days away. Maybe you should have run on a pro-smoking platform."

"Glad you weren't my campaign strategist, Juan-boy."

"Twenty-six percent of the adult population smokes."

"And tell me this, is that a majority? A majority to vote me into office?"

"No, but smokers are the most poorly organized group around. Someone's got to stand up for them."

"I just did," Roz said righteously. "As well as took important time away from my campaign to come here and see you."

"Hell, Madison being Madison, they'll probably end up banning smoking, next in restaurants, then in bars, then outside, then everywhere except in your own house, and only if you own it. Hell, they'll probably end up outlawing it altogether." Juan saw Roz stub out her cigarette on the floor.

"We could quit, you know."

"I'll quit after you do." Juan had no doubt he'd turn into a balloon if he stopped. He needed to have something in his mouth besides food, and cigarettes fit the bill much better than gum, toothpicks or fingernails.

"Then you've got a long wait."

"I don't know if smoking in public is a good idea for an elected official. You know, as we've just seen, how politically incorrect it is to smoke these days. Especially in Madison."

"I don't smoke in public."

"The Union should be considered a public place, I'd think. You won't dare smoke, for example, around your constituents."

Roz grimaced, took a quick look around her and lit up another one. "They're not my constituents yet. Even though the election's in three days, I won't be sworn in for three weeks."

"I still say smokers should have some public official to represent them."

"That public official," Roz said, expelling smoke, "would never be publicly elected. So, what's up, Juan? I take it you didn't call me over here to talk about smoking."

"Hey, can we wait a minute? How about we relax? You can still relax, can't you?"

"Of course I can relax. But I take it you can appreciate that for me the next seventy-two hours are crucial. As you said, the Baltic States Independence Committee can live without me. At least for today." Just as well, she missed his implication.

Juan knew he had to take the first step. He tried out the sound of different words to himself: "I'm a binge eater." Well, he certainly was. "A compulsive over-eater." Not exactly inaccurate. "An anorexic?" He'd been an undiagnosed one for many years, no doubt about that; now he was at the other end of the spectrum: "A bulimic." No denying that. "Bulimarexic?" He'd heard the term, wasn't sure exactly what it was, but it might well describe him. "An eating-disordered person." Probably the most politically correct term, but it sounded awful. "A dieter with strange habits." He liked this one best, sounding, as it did, the least threatening.

Though Irv was his best friend, Roz was a woman and this was a "woman's disease," wasn't it? She'd understand, wouldn't she? He had to talk to someone now. Since Pepper's revelation about him and Blake, Juan's life seemed reduced to bingeing and purging. He didn't want to talk to Pepper about it, didn't know if he could talk to Pepper about anything, and definitely didn't want Pepper to catch him at it.

"Well, are we relaxing?"

"Roz, this is serious. It's not easy to talk about."

"It's not about Dayne, is it? He's not putting a strain on your relationship with Pepper, is he? Irv, as you know, has had this ridiculous notion that he's not getting enough attention. Although I've had serious doubts about having Rhoda here at times, caring for Dayne *is* one good reason to have her here."

Juan omitted mentioning that there were also a dozen good reasons not to have Rhoda here.

"No, Roz, it's not about Dayne at all. It's about me. Get a grip. Drink some more beer and relax, OK? I need to talk to someone rational, sane, and whom I can confide in. If you think you just might be able to live up to that for a few minutes."

He saw Roz repress a snarl before pouring herself a second beer. "I'm relaxing, OK? I thought I might need this to steady myself for this 'important' revelation you have to make. I'm still waiting." She gulped beer, took in too much and almost choked.

"Right. If I don't hurry up, you could be drunk before I begin."

"Don't worry, I'm here for you, Juan." She reached across the table and grabbed his free hand, as if it were a matter of life or death, his hand her only anchor in a world about to self-destruct.

Juan extricated his hand and examined the indentations from Roz's nails in his skin. "This is hard to talk about. I've never told anyone before."

"Oh, no. You're not going to pull a repeat on me and come out as a straight person?"

Juan let himself laugh, unsure if she was kidding. "Jesus Christ, Roz. Are you out of your mind? No, I'm not going to do what you did to me five years ago."

"That's good to hear. I mean, straight people, I don't have anything against them. I mean, I am one, though I still have a little lesbian piece in my soul. Emotional piece, not sexual, mind you. I just couldn't stand it if you were straight and white, a member of the ruling class. But you're half Cuban and a fag, so you're not in danger."

Tempted to pop a tranquilizer into her beer, which evidently wasn't doing the job, he refrained from adding that Irv did qualify as a member of the ruling class and that Roz, as his spouse, was also a member, or at least, an appendage.

"I think you know, up to a point, what this is like," he said, a flicker of how to begin dawning on him. "First, you don't know a name for it and think you're the only one in the world. Then you learn a clinical name, and later realize you're not the only one in the world. Finally you've got to tell someone."

He seemed to have Roz's rapt attention, then she blurted

out, "Well, you're already a fag, so you can't come out again. And I trust you're not going to tell me any horseshit about 'refinding' your virginity."

"Shut up and let me talk. And, by the way," he joked, "now that you're no longer a dyke, I don't know if you're permitted to call me a fag." She looked at him pleadingly, as if he were stripping her of a precious possession. "Hey, I was only kidding."

"All right, you've got this condition, similar to being gay, but you're not gay. I mean you're gay, but you're not coming out to me. So, what next?"

"The analogies with homosexuality end there. If you're gay, you don't seek a cure. I need a cure." Now Roz appeared totally baffled. "I can't talk about it with Pepper. I have to do something before he catches me. It could be embarrassing."

"I suppose being caught with your pants off can. I never would have pegged you as a sexual compulsive. I don't want to stereotype gay men, but I always thought there was something strange about your rare case of monogamy. I knew there had to be something..."

"Roz, lots of gay men are monogamous, or these days even celibate. Lately, I haven't even been totally monogamous, and believe me, Pepper certainly hasn't, though I'll tell you about that another time. It's exacerbated my problem, but I'm *not* a sexual compulsive."

"You're not?" Roz seemed deflated. "Well, what the hell are you then? Don't tell me you're becoming a transsexual."

"No, Roz, no," he said firmly. "And you might watch your language. The correct term today is 'transgendered person.' I am not," he lowered his voice, "a transgendered person, transvestite, hermaphrodite, or any other such thing you're imagining. Got it?"

His emphasis seemed to have a temporary calming effect on her. Then she erupted: "Well, you're the one who called me over here on this extremely busy day to tell me something's wrong with you, so what the hell is it?"

She was right. He had to come out with it, now: "I'm, uh, I guess the best word is, bulimic."

"That's all?" she scoffed.

It was if if he'd just come out to his best friend and she'd said, "Yeah, you and twenty-five million others."

# 44

Cissy lay in bed, nuzzled up to Evan, slipping in and out of dreams. She was late to catch a plane flight to the divisional committee deciding on her tenure, Evan was reprimanding her for it, and Ginger was saying, "Go for the gold, Cis." Then Rickover appeared and said, "No hard feelings, Pankhurst, but they've closed the department down. We're all out of jobs..."

A jangling telephone put an end to her nightmare. She picked it up, realized she had the receiver upside down, then righted it. "Hello?"

"Cissy? It's Sandra."

"Sandra, where are you!?"

"I've escaped! I'm at my parents' house in Michigan."

"You 'escaped' from the hospital? Vance told us you were there voluntarily."

"I was. But I was released and when Vance went away for Spring Break and locked me in the attic..."

The attic? So the stories really had been true?

"Then after Ginger called the police, I mean the security people, who broke in and got me out..."

"What? Wait, Sandra. Back up. Ginger broke in?" Suddenly, Evan sat upright in bed and stuck his head next to Cissy's, trying to listen in.

"I'm sure Vance became afraid I'd break down and tell someone about my lecture and, don't freak out, I'm sure he suspected I told you. So when he went to the conference in D.C., he shut me in the attic. I mean with food, TV, and all, no telephone, of course. He had a bathroom built in there years ago. And I had my Valium, bottles and bottles of it. I was in a such a tranquilizer haze, it didn't even occur to me I *could* get out. But when Ginger came and started throwing things at the attic window, I woke up and finally got my head clear. I decided to leave. I gathered some things and tried to call you..."

"Evan and I went to California for Spring Break. My mother broke her arm, I went to visit..."

"I finally made my way to a Battered Women's Shelter. I spent some time there, got my head more together, and flew to Detroit. Now Vance has been calling, trying to track me down. I'm getting out of here, but I can't tell you where."

Evan tapped Cissy on the shoulder. "Can you hold a second? Evan wants to tell me something."

Instead he snatched the receiver from her: "Look, Sandra. You've got to help us. If you'd just let Vance know that you'll substantiate what you told Cissy about the lecture..."

Cissy moved up to listen, almost shivering in the cold air outside their haven of blankets, but heard only dead silence. Then Sandra said, "I don't care what happens to him anymore. But my whereabouts have to be kept secret. You can call me here. Here's the number."

Cissy untangled herself from Evan and found a pen and envelope on the nightstand. Sandra recited the number and Evan jotted it down.

"I'll give you a password. Let's say, 'bamboozle'."

"Bamboozle?"

Cissy stole the phone back. "Without a password, my parents won't necessarily know it's you and not someone else Vance has put up to calling. This way, my parents can give you the phone number where I'll be, if you need it."

Evan reclaimed the receiver. "Sandra, can you put everything in writing and mail it to us at home? You have our address, don't you?"

"No, Evan," Cissy whispered. "Give it to her. She never gets it right."

Evan recited their address and Sandra went into silent deliberation. "I don't see why not. He's made my life hell. I was prepared to let him get off. But after all this harassment, he's got it coming. Just one stipulation: I won't go back to Madison."

Cissy jerked the phone away from Evan. "You won't have to, Sandra. We guarantee it." Now he laid his head on her chest, overhearing.

"Then everything's set. Send it to us as soon as you can."

"Uh-huh." Sandra's voice faded. "I mean, I will." The connection sounded as though she were calling from Mozambique or Madagascar. "Thanks so much, Sandra. We just hope you make it through all this. It's been awful for you, I'm sure." Teaching Sandra's Intro class was also awful enough for herself.

"You're right about that. But things will get better. Don't worry, all right?"

Cissy had enough worries of her own. "You just take care."

"Well, bamboozle, then."

"Bamboozle."

&#10087;

Cissy faced the Intro class of some 350 students and looked out at the sea of faces, ranging from defiantly bored to inert. As the bell had just sounded, no one was snoozing yet, as far as she could see. Then a latecomer grabbed her attention by rollerblading into class and crashing into a back-row seat. Cissy next looked down from the faces to the T-shirts. FUCK YOU and SHIT HAPPENS greeted her from the front row. Further back, BUTTON YOUR FLY and its counterpart, UNBUTTON MY FLY, revealed themselves. In the fourth row, a boy's shirt read MOTHER. Cissy feared she knew what was on the back. Where were the usual T-shirts like SHOPAHOLIC or JEWISH PRINCESS, the ones advertising rock bands and local bars, and those disparaging the surrounding Big Ten universities? Were these your typical freshmen? She hadn't been in a freshman class for three years. Had she missed something? She realized she had to get tenure, wanted to teach M.F.A. students or, at least, advanced undergraduates, not just undergrads dutifully — or not so dutifully — filling requirements. If she didn't get tenure, this is what she'd be stuck with. Or worse, no students at all. She enjoyed teaching, stimulating young minds, directing students along a path of self-fulfillment. But looking out at this group, she felt she was in the middle of a nightmare, just as she'd been when Vance had told her a few hours ago that the department had closed down. Maybe the department would close down. But this was reality and that was fantasy, right?

"Hey, you gonna take attendance?"

"Yeah, if you're not, I'm leavin'."

"You sick or something?"

"Today, she's as spaced out as the last one we had."

"We heard she went crazy and they locked her up."

"But at least this one is better-looking."

"Yeah, better-looking than that ugly bastard who was in here for a couple weeks."

"Why don't you all shut up?" A young woman in the back of the room had stood, startling her classmates and Cissy, her bellowing voice belying her petite size. "If you all shut up, maybe she can begin. Personally, I came here to learn something!"

"Yes." Cissy's mind jolted into academic gear. "Today you're going to learn something. We'll do something interesting. It's not on the syllabus, but it's a topic dear to me. We're going to learn a bit about Mexico, the Mayans in particular, the ruins they left behind, how they've been preserved in the natural setting and how others have been preserved in museums, and how some have even been stolen from their setting and are now in private hands. When we're finished with this, I'll bring in slides. To start with." Cissy's voice became more and more forceful. "We're going to throw out this syllabus. We'll even eliminate a few quizzes, maybe all of them. We're going to learn and we're going to have fun! Does everyone understand?"

Scattered applause broke out in the back of the room and slowly spread toward the front.

Cissy thanked God and the female student in the back. She felt saved, the class was saved, and she'd get through this nightmare of a semester. A nightmare that went far beyond the sterile walls of the lecture hall.

There was no return address. Cissy tore the letter open, praying that Sandra's resolve hadn't weakened. She found a short personal note that began, "I'm doing this my own way." Cissy feared what might be Sandra's "own way." It could be sending the letter via Africa, to throw Vance off with the postmark. Worriedly, she read on:

> Here you have two original copies, in my own handwriting, and I've also sent one to Ginger and to Bob Rothschild. Show one to Vance only if you must. Put at least one in a safety deposit box. The letter should be strong enough to have the desired outcome.
> Regards,
> Sandra

Cissy studied the originals, indeed in Sandra's handwriting, addressed to the Dean of Fine Arts. They looked terribly unofficial; Sandra's penmanship seemed to have been stunted back in the fourth grade. But the inimitable scrawl should erase any doubts of their authenticity:

> I am writing this of my own free will so that the truth be known regarding what occurred in the Department of Museum Studies in

*January, 1991, when I gave my "tenure lecture."*

*The entire lecture was written by my husband, Vance R. Rickover, Chair of the Department of Museum Studies. I gave this lecture only under coercion and threats from my husband. It was for this reason that I withdrew from the tenure process and resigned from my position.*

*It is also true that my husband attempted to isolate me from all other members of the department to insure my silence. As I have escaped from my marriage and fear possible recriminations from him, this letter bears no return address or any way of contacting me.*

*This letter is for the sole use of the administration of the University of Wisconsin-Madison and the faculty of the Department of Museum Studies. I have purposely written this letter by hand so that the veracity of its authorship can be confirmed.*

> *Sincerely,*
> *Sandra S. Rickover*

Cissy marveled at the letter. Sandra seemed to have covered the important bases: coercion by Vance, fear of Vance, and authentication of its author.

It was a Saturday, the day she'd normally take a nice refreshing jog or, when it got too cold, go swimming at SERF. Today she expected the telephone to start ringing as soon as Ginger and Bob Rothschild got their mail. That, she suspected, would only be the beginning of a weekend departmental meeting by conference call, and she thought of plotting a brief escape. Now that she'd told "the world" the truth of Sandra's lecture, she wondered if she'd be up to dealing with the consequences.

# 45

Roz planned to devote election day to rest. Irv was hosting a victory party at their house, beginning when the polls closed. Claypool had waged no real war, but no longer mouthed her positions; rather he attacked and distorted them. Maddie Son and Dane County had been the likely vandals of a portion of both candidates' yard signs. Rhoda had insisted that the party required a larger, public venue, but was out-voted, and had settled for taking care of catering details.

After getting up fom her nap, Roz dressed, walked into the hall and saw Dayne coming up the stairs, apparently to take his.

"Today's Mommy's big day."

"Yep. 'Lection."

"We're going to celebrate tonight."

"Dance?"

"Well, dancing isn't the main event, but... Why don't we dance? Mommy and Dayne?"

"I'm tired, Mom."

"Don't worry. I'll dance *you*." She scooped him up, no easy load, and carried him back into her bedroom. As Dayne watched, she found her favorite Janis Joplin CD, put in on and picked him back up. A few seconds later, she was whirling him around the room to the strains of "Me and Bobby McGee." She let herself be caught up in the music, banishing thoughts of all but Janis and Dayne. Tiring before the song ended, she put him down, listened to the rest of it, then put him to bed in his own room.

Mildly exhausted, yet relaxed, she went downstairs to face the world. In the kitchen Rhoda was talking to the caterers on the telephone. She walked into the living room and, to her horror, saw that Rhoda had plastered it with green banners, the Labor Farm color. The room appeared as though it were decked out for an out-of-control St. Patrick's Day brawl.

"Everything's set, darling." Rhoda put the phone down and walked toward her. "Have you noticed how much easier it is to live in harmony when you're dressed?"

"Whatever you say, Mother." Any feeling of relaxation began to evaporate. She planned to revert to nudism the second Rhoda left.

"'Low turn-out predicted.'" Rhoda waved the *Wisconsin State Journal,* from which she'd been reading. "We'll just have to get the vote out ourselves."

"Mother, you're not going out into the streets to harass people." She wondered how many votes she'd already lost by Rhoda's tactics.

"I'll just go vote myself, then."

"You can't vote here." Roz took a slug of coffee as she perused the Metro section of the newspaper.

"I don't know why not. I'm registered."

"Mother! How could you? What lies did you tell them? You vote in New York, not here."

"We both know what's required to register. No one asked me if I intended to stay here. And at that time, my plans were quite uncertain."

"I can't believe you perjured yourself."

"I most certainly didn't perjure myself, Rosamond. I'm sure my registration in New York was automatically canceled when I registered here. When I vote back there, they'll notify them to cancel the one here."

Roz shook her head in despair and wondered about the legality of it. She guessed it seemed logical enough. A vote was a vote, but... "I know your intentions are good. I guess it's all right, as long as I don't win by just one vote."

"I'll go with you to the fire station to vote as soon as you're ready."

"Mother, you will not. Vote if you want to, but you're not going into the polling place with me! And remember, you can't pass out any campaign literature within 300 feet of a polling place."

"Do I embarrass you, Roz?"

The truth was that her behavior did. "No, Mother. It just wouldn't look right."

"All right. But who said I was going to vote for you anyway?"

Stunned, Roz pierced her mother's eyes.

After a second, Rhoda's face cracked into a smile. "You can't take a joke, Roz. You never could. You know your mother loves you."

People began to gather at the house at the eight-o'clock poll-closing hour. Final results would be on the ten-o'clock news, or might even be known earlier.

Pepper and Juan had come up for the evening. Labor Farm people milled about, probably disdaining the sumptuousness of her house, a fact not helped by Rhoda's lavish spread of food and champagne. Roz had had to send Irv out on a last-minute run for cases of Point and Leinenkugel and, what the hell, even some Garten Brau, Madison's own new yuppie beer. Beth came with her lover, part of a small —very small—lesbian contingent of friends and supporters. By nine, the group perhaps numbered fifty or sixty.

They had the radio turned on, which by nine-fifteen brought the first results. Soglin, the incumbent mayor, was again leading by a landslide. Then began the council races. After three districts, they got to the sixth:

"With approximately half the numbers in, Roz Goldwomyn is leading the incumbent John Claypool, by a total of 313 to 297 in a hotly contested race."

Whoops of congratulations went up, though everyone knew they were premature. Irv squeezed her gently.

Roz tried to keep up her strength and enthusiasm. Campaigning — especially the odious door-to-door variety — had worn her down. She would have preferred to have no victory party at all. The volts of political electricity she'd been working on the past months had slowly run out.

The phone rang; it was her vote-watcher, who had gone to the City/County Building, where the votes were actually counted and the first results known. "It's 410 to 405, Claypool ahead. I think with the twenty-fourth ward to go."

Roz passed the information on to Irv, but they didn't announce it to the room. If she had to be losing, she wished it were a certainty, not so damned close.

When he called back again in fifteen minutes, she pounced on the phone. "Roz, you won't believe this."

"Believe what? You mean, did I win?" A brief pause. "Or did I lose?"

"Neither. They just updated the numbers. A 482-482 tie."

"Jesus Christ." She realized those around her had heard her exclamation. "Thanks, Lon."

Her supporters looked on expectantly. "Claypool, 482. Goldwomyn, 482," she announced, wondering about her mother's vote.

"And it ain't over!" Beth yelled.

"You'll pull ahead, just wait!"

She needed to escape, at least briefly. On the third try, she found an unoccupied bathroom, went in and smoked a cigarette as she sat on the closed toilet seat. A knock came on the door.

"Just a second!" She could get no peace anywhere, not even on the toilet.

When she came out, she found Seth in the hallway.

"Sorry I couldn't vote for you."

"Why the hell not? My mother did." Roz let herself laugh, then fall into Seth's outstretched arms. Had he not caught her, she could have ended up on the floor. This was what she needed: physical comfort, which she hadn't had much of in a long time. She wished she could close her eyes, stay just like she was, and let it be over.

"Roz, you've actually tied him. It's going to be close. Do you know which ward hasn't been counted?"

"The twenty-fourth. I think."

"Then you'll make it, Roz!" He leaned over and kissed her briefly, pulled back and beamed at her.

"Have I ever met this nice Jewish boy before?" Rhoda was coming down the hall toward them; Roz trusted she hadn't seen Seth's kiss.

"Don't make assumptions about people's ethnicity, Mother. And Seth is not a boy!"

"Seth Rubinstein. Pleased to finally meet you, Mrs. Goldmann."

"I told you so, Roz."

"Let's go back to the living room." Roz was anxious to end the awkward three-way encounter.

The ten-o'clock news, the moment of reckoning, approached. If she were in the upstairs bathroom, she could at least snack on some Xanax. "Come on. Let's go hear the good news!" She forced herself to fake a smile for Seth and Rhoda. He tried to lead her by the arm, but she shook him off, lest Rhoda jump to some ludicrous conclusion, and marched on ahead.

Rhoda immediately took over, commanding Juan and Pepper to bring down the upstairs television. That, coupled with their own two on the first floor, made for enough to tune into all three local networks at once. Another, perhaps unfortunate sign of the household's conspicuous consumption.

When the clock struck ten, everyone quieted and all three televisions blared simultaneously.

Mayoral results came first, with no surprises. The CBS affiliate went straight to the city council races, beginning with the "hotly contested" sixth district, and reported the 482-482 tie they'd already known, as if it were the breaking news of the night. NBC went to School Board elections, where the politically correct Labor Farm incumbent had been upset. Hearing this, Roz's supporters seemed struck dumb. A disturbing sign: The School Board was a city-wide election and this meant Madison was moving further to the right. At least Roz hadn't gotten snagged in the fray prohibiting religious celebrations in schools, like the poor incumbent, who'd supported it and now lost. Perhaps she still had a chance.

Then came ABC. The room fell silent. The newscaster began with the council races, numerically. Roz couldn't even focus on the winners or losers. Irv stood behind her, more or less propping her up, Seth at one side and Rhoda on the other. Someone had deposited another can of beer in her hand. As they announced the fourth district, the phone rang.

"Let it ring!" Roz ordered. She'd face the news in person, along with all her supporters.

"In the sixth district, with one hundred percent of the votes counted, R. John Claypool, the incumbent, has squeaked by, the final tally being 612 for Claypool and 607 for Rosamond Goldwomyn, the Labor Farm challenger."

Moans of sympathy mixed with cries for recounts. Roz knew that voting machines usually didn't make mistakes and had little hope in a recount. It was over. Too soon, the crowd quieted back down. She had to say something.

"Thank you so much for all your support. It's been wonderful." It had been hell. "We'll try again in two years." Like hell, I will. "Thank you all again." Now, get out of my house.

She stared at the group sadly, then began to hurry toward the stairs.

"I'm sorry, Roz." Irv grabbed her arm, while Seth muttered more condolences.

"I'm going upstairs," she said sternly. The word "recount" still bounced off the living room walls. Didn't they understand? It was *over*.

"Can't you wait a little?" Irv whispered.

"No. In any case, you're the host."

Rhoda cornered her next. "I'm truly sorry, darling. I did everything I could. Before I left the voting booth, I jammed your remaining literature under the lever with your name."

"Thanks, Mom," she said automatically, wondering if she'd really heard what she'd heard.

"You'll win next time. If you'd just learn to be a little less abrasive, you might have gotten those five votes."

These words she heard with certainty and they slapped her in the face. "Like mother, like daughter," she replied, and began to hurtle up the stairs. She heard Rhoda puffing behind her and forced herself to stop. She didn't want her mother to have a heart attack on the stairs at her "victory" party.

"What, Mother?"

"You have no sense of humor, Roz. I was kidding. You certainly didn't inherit your father's humor or mine."

"I'm sorry." She was indeed glad not to have "inherited" *their* humor. "But your timing was off."

Rhoda embraced her and they almost toppled off the two stairs they were occupying. "Don't you know how proud I am of my daughter? I was just trying to help." She trailed off into Yiddish endearments and Roz found that she herself had begun to cry.

"Thanks, Mother. I love you. But I'm going upstairs. Good night."

She looked up and saw that Dayne had been observing them. He'd been put to bed before the party.

"Mommy lost," she said softly, and Dayne too began to cry.

"Quiet, Dayne. People will hear you." And think it's me, she thought. Dayne only cried harder.

She scooped him up, took him into her bedroom and locked the door. She lay down on the bed, cuddled him, and joined along in his crocodile tears, as relieved as she was disappointed.

# 46

Rothschild agreed to call Nick and John Rutledge and request an eight-o'clock meeting on Tuesday morning, when Vance would be in class, without adding that others would be there.

Cissy felt in high spirits and dressed accordingly, "archeologically," someone was bound to say: a long brightly colored Tehuana skirt, ruffled top, and various pieces of indigenous jewelry garnered on her trips to Mexico. When she and Evan arrived, everyone but Rutledge and Nick was waiting in Rothschild's office.

"They will come, won't they?" Cissy asked anxiously. She sat down, her jewelry jangling, and took in the double-window view: to the west, Chadbourne Hall; to the south, the Communications building, an architectural monstrosity that rivaled FAB.

"I told them it was about an important personnel matter that we should discuss before we talked to Vance. I'm sure they assumed it referred to you," Rothschild explained. Cissy felt a pang of nerves and wondered how many other secret personnel meetings had taken place with her as the agenda *in absentia.* "Don't worry. They'll be here."

A minute later Rutledge slipped in silently, with no knock, his apparent custom with Rothschild. His eyes bulged as he observed the departmental crew. He regained his composure, quipping, "I thought departmental meetings were always at three-thirty."

"Only when Vance is present," said Evan.

A half-minute later, Nick knocked on the door, and Evan, the closest one to it, pulled it open.

For the first time ever Cissy saw Nick's jaw drop. "What the hell is this about?" he blurted out.

"Come in, Nick, if you can lower your voice. I'll make this short, but it's not sweet," Rothschild began, ominous. "Read this letter and you'll understand why, as friends of Vance, you and John were the last two to know." He offered them each a copy of the letter.

Rutledge read and reread it, then shook his head, mystified. "Do you all believe this? What do you propose to do?"

"I can't believe this! We all know that Sandra cracked up!" Cissy had recently concluded that Nick's bluster shielded a parched intellect.

"You wrote — or began to write — Sandra's tenure narrative," Rothschild said to Rutledge. "We assume you don't want to be connected with Vance's..."

"Deceit," Evan finished for him and flashed Cissy his fluoride smile.

Nick appeared shaken, his bluster crumbling. "Isn't this a little... premature?"

"We've known about it for some time. Finally we located Sandra and convinced her to put it in writing," Ginger said, taking credit for it all. She had taken to referring to herself as Sandra's "liberator," once Cissy had pried a confession of the Spring Break events out of her. "Vance should consider himself lucky she's not pressing charges."

"Friends and colleagues may help you advance your career," Rothschild said pointedly to Nick, "but when they do things like this, I'd think you'd no longer want to be associated with them."

"We're going to talk to Vance, show him the letter, and tell him we'll go to the dean with our information if he doesn't resign, effective at the end of the semester, rather than *now*," Ginger said.

"I suggest we all go down to his office when he's back from

class and present this to him."

"We're doing him a favor by not exposing him."

"Today?" Rutledge gasped, and his toupee executed an involuntary jig.

"And ruin the man's career?" Nick squared his jaw, arms crossed over his chest, as though he could serve as sentry and blockade Vance's door.

"I'd say we're giving him the chance to escape gracefully, his career intact, to continue somewhere else," said Evan. "And may God have pity on *that* department."

"The sooner we finish this ugly little affair, the better," Rothschild said. "You certainly can't condone what he did, certainly don't want to be implicated in Sandra's bogus tenure process."

Rutledge seemed to reach a quick decision: "Of course, you're right. But don't you think we ought to consult with someone else first?"

"We'll only 'consult' with someone, namely the dean, if he doesn't cooperate. This way we're making it easy on him," said Evan.

All eyes came to focus on Nick. Cissy swore she could see the muscles rippling under his shirt. Slowly, his smirk gave way. "I don't see..." he began. Brows furrowed, eyebrows arched and mouths frowned, all daring him.

"If you think we must," he said quietly. "I take it I'm a minority of one."

No one disagreed.

"Besides," said Evan, "we're all here now and when do we all want to get up so early again?"

"Next year at Amelia's Christmas party?" Ginger said, an attempted joke that fell flat.

"Amelia's parties are over," Cissy said, wishing Blake were there.

"And so is Vance's," Evan added.

By eight thirty-six they heard him barrel down the hall, keys clanking. Once he was inside the main office, Ginger headed them down the hall in a loose formation, Rutledge and Nick tagging behind, whispering to each other. As they straggled in by ones and twos, Wilhelmina and Beth eyed them with ever greater astonishment, but didn't ask questions. Rothschild tapped on Rickover's door.

"Yeah?" came a snarl from inside.

Rothschild led them into the office and they stood around his desk.

Rickover affected a bluster akin to Nick's: "What do you all want? A ten-percent salary hike? Then you'd better look for jobs elsewhere. Here's the job list!" He shoved it at Cissy; she didn't want to be here. Vance, though he couldn't vote, formed part of the divisional committee that was considering her tenure.

"Read this, Vance." Rutledge handed him the letter. "I've lost trust in you. I'm shocked — no, personally offended — that you would have implicated me in this..."

"Deceit," Evan finished again.

"And, by the way, we have several other original copies."

Rickover read in silence. "And?" he said, defiant. "Do you actually believe this?"

"Shall we see the dean or shall you? We've been in contact with Sandra and can be again if you don't cooperate," said Ginger. "You can resign effective the end of the semester. In exchange for that, we'll keep this covered up."

"I have lawyers!" Vance shot back.

"So do we," Rothschild said, his voice cool, yet menacing. As a group, they didn't, Cissy knew, but she supposed that among them they may well have had a dozen.

"Any more idle threats, Vance?" Ginger said, and Cissy saw him now fidgeting and sweating. She wondered if the others enjoyed his humiliation or pitied him.

"No one has to see the dean," he said in a low voice, as though seeing the light. Or having a trick up his sleeve?

"Here, you can have the job list back," said Evan. "You could be needing it."

"Now if you'll just leave me alone for the rest of the day... Make that the rest of the week." He got up to open the door, which met with banged heads. "What the hell do you two think you're doing?" he barked, now his usual self.

Wilhelmina and Beth scurried back to their desks.

"You," he growled, and pointed at Beth, "are fired."

"You can't fire me. Besides, I'm filing a complaint against you for calling me a 'lesbian shrimp'."

Cissy stifled a laugh. She hadn't remembered his using the two words togther, but had little doubt that he had.

"Go ahead. A lot of good it'll do you!"

"Can we keep some decorum here, Professor Rickover?" said Wilhelmina.

"Decorum? What room do you have to talk, Miss Ear-to-the-Door? I ought to fire you too. This office has been incompetently run since the day I arrived here. Excuse me, since the day *you* arrived here."

"Vance, leave her alone," Rothschild ordered. "Anything anyone in this department has done pales in comparison to you."

Now Rickover directed hateful eyes at his accusers, then glanced at Nick uncertainly, as if Nick could save him. Nick looked at him pityingly, shook his head in helplessness, then turned away.

"Besides," Wilhelmina said, "you can't fire me. Not only do I have seniority, the equivalent of tenure, but I'm a member of the union and hard to get rid of."

"So there!" Beth sneered at him. Rickover threw her a baleful gaze and hurried out of the office.

"You're sure dressed up today," Beth said to Cissy, as though unfazed by the morning's events. "What you gonna do with all those bracelets? Show off artifacts in class?"

# 47

Juan weighed himself: 133.2 pounds. Even after Irv's remark, the ounces had come piling back on, despite his efforts. He knew that if he didn't keep bingeing and purging, he'd continue to mushroom.

He'd heard of a bulimic woman who lowered her weight by donating blood. Juan began to ponder the idea. After another HIV test, assuming it was negative, he could donate. Perhaps if he did it regularly...

No, no one wanted gay men's blood, unless they'd been celibate since 1977, or forever. And he himself, with his New Orleans escapade... Not that he and Edwin had really done anything. Maybe he should have another HIV test... And only God knew what Pepper had done with Blake, besides fall in love. Juan hadn't wanted to know details, and Pepper wasn't giving them, except to say that they'd used condoms. That, Juan concluded, meant they'd actually been fucking. No one, or no one he knew, used condoms for oral sex. Or did they?

Since Eric had died, he had no one to keep him informed of what gay men actually did, except for his own personal informant — or non-informant — who lived right with him. Maybe he could think up a new strategy to lose weight... Maybe if he'd been as thin as Blake, who was some ten years older, Pepper wouldn't have... But even if he were ten or fifteen pounds thinner, he wouldn't resemble Blake. Only one in a million men had those looks.

"See if you can find it in yourself to forgive me," Pepper had asked him. "It wasn't planned. I didn't do it on purpose. I don't mean to say I wasn't interested in him. It all just happened."

Juan had turned his back on him, looked at himself in the mirror, and in it saw Pepper in the distance, wringing his hands.

"I'll need time to think," Juan had answered. One couldn't always control one's emotions, could they? "I suppose I can forgive you for your feelings. But for sneaking off with Blake in the first place, that's another matter." It seemed his destiny to meet up with faithless lovers.

"Whatever you do, don't start comparing me with Gil."

Maybe he should just jump off their Lake Monona pier and swim away and let everything fade with him, Juan now thought, reflecting back on the conversation and the unsettled outcome. What was the lake's temperature in early April? Cold enough to die of hypothermia? Hmmm. Maybe that's what Pepper deserved: two lovers dead from hypothermia.

But what about the ozone layer? And the Persian Gulf? Antigay violence was on the rise. No AIDS cure was in sight, government funding insufficient. Republicans had occupied the White House for over ten years. Even locally, things were dim: Roz had lost, the city's "red" mayor of the seventies had turned mainstream in the nineties, Madison's liberal congressman had been defeated by a Republican last fall.

Two of his pet projects, Wiscaragua —the symbolic Wisconsin-Nicaragua sisterhood — and The YUDs — Young Urban Dropouts— were no longer. SPELL was still alive, but the language was going to hell and no one but Juan and William Safire seemed to care.

More importantly: What about Dayne? Juan was a father. Of course, Dayne had Irv too. But Irv was older, he could have a heart attack tomorrow and be gone, leaving Dayne with only Roz. That was a scary prospect.

No, there was no way Juan could leave the planet, at least not right now. He couldn't even leave Madison.

It was too much to deal with. He went into the kitchen, grabbed an unopened bag of potato chips, and began scouring the cupboards.

❧

He was sitting on the kitchen floor in a daze, his stomach aching, in too much discomfort even to get up and go vomit. The evidence littered the floor and counters; there were too many opened bags, jars and other containers to count and Juan couldn't be bothered to put them away. With his tongue, he flicked a few flecks of sugar out of his mustache, reeling a few of them in, as others fell to the floor.

What the hell did it matter anyway? He could grow to whatever size he wanted and it shouldn't matter. Pepper was in love with a dead man. Pepper was a necrophiliac. That was it. A necrophiliac. He wondered if in San Francisco Pepper had visited the grave, if there was one. He bet that he had. Maybe he'd ask him.

In the open refrigerator, he saw a tall narrow jar of olives stuffed with anchovies that he'd missed. He contemplated them a while, then crawled over on his hands and knees. Sustaining himself with one hand, he grabbed the jar with the other, opened it, sat up and began eating. One by one he savored them, then drank the juice from the jar when he finished. He tossed the jar over the counter onto the living room carpet and waited to hear if anything broke.

A few seconds later he heard the noise of the jar being set down on the glass coffee table. He forced himself to stand up, looked over the counter, and saw no one. Laboriously, he walked around to the living room. There lay Pepper on the sofa.

"How long have you been here?"

"Long enough. I finished work at Amelia's and came home early. You looked busy, so I didn't interrupt."

"How dare you...!"

"You'd better be careful. Karen Carpenter died of one or the other. It could happen to you."

Juan snapped back to reality, lucid enough to take offense at the Karen Carpenter comparison. "Whatever irregularities there are to my eating habits, they don't compare with hers. I saw the TV movie."

"That's a low admission."

"I was interested in the topic." Juan fumed to himself. "It was educational. I saw what could happen should things get out of control."

"And of course that would never happen to you. Nothing happened in the kitchen this afternoon."

Obviously, Pepper had seen the mess, and Juan, caught up as he was, hadn't noticed a thing. His Pink Floyd T-shirt bore ketchup stains, he saw. He knew he must look ridiculous. Instinctively, he wiped at his face with his hand and came up with traces of mayonnaise and mustard. The food gone, he rubbed his face again and felt stubble. He probably hadn't shaved in two days, not that it mattered.

"Why don't you mind your own fucking business!"

"I was, or was trying to." Pepper was still calmly reclining on the sofa.

There was no reason to hide in the bathroom now, nor to clean himself, or the kitchen, up. Pepper had seen everything. "Well, why don't you try a little fucking harder?"

At this, Pepper jumped up off the sofa, his features bearing down on Juan, who imagined him as a stern orthodox rabbi, minus the yarmulke and sidelocks. "I know one way to do that: to leave. Amelia has, as you know, more than one spare room."

"I can forgive you for falling in love with Blake, but..."

"But what?"

"But... I don't know." Juan truly was confused; he didn't want Pepper to go, didn't want him to stay, not right here, not right now.

"This, I think, is all more about you and eating than it is about me and Blake."

That did it. "Oh, so you shift the problem to me. This is all my fault because..."

"That — Blake — is over. This..." Pepper gesticulated at Juan, then at the kitchen. "...evidently isn't. If you can't forgive me, I think I'll just have to wait until or if you can. Meanwhile, I think you should get help. You need to figure out if your primary relationship is going to be with food or with a person!"

Juan stammered, stuttered, didn't know what to say.

"I'm going to pack a few things. I'll be at Amelia's. You know the number."

Juan decided to storm off to the bathroom.

"This," Pepper said, before he could close the door, survey-ing the post-binge disaster of the kitchen, "is too much." An-noyingly, he kept his cool, not even raising his voice.

"Be sure to take some condoms!" Juan was about to stop, but sputtered on: "Condoms! Are... Are you sure you and... Blake... and whoever else... always used condoms? We're in the middle of a goddamned AIDS crisis! Who knows what you exposed yourself to, exposed me to! Who knows...?" He was about to go on but, seeing Pepper about to walk out on him, Juan made a point of slamming the bathroom door shut first.

❧

Pepper got into his Sunbird and drove. He passed Schenk's Corners and found himself on Atwood Avenue, heading the opposite direction from Amelia's. As he reached Olbrich Gar-dens, he pulled into the parking lot and let the motor idle, and his mind wander. He remembered that this was the route he used to take to Blake's condo.

What had he and Blake had together? To call it a fling cheap-ened it. If it was a passing affair, it was only passing because of Blake's death. Had they continued it, they, or at least he, would have been headed for... hell. Or heaven. Yes, he determined, it would have been nothing in between, and the fact that he didn't know, could never know, bothered him as much as anything else.

Abruptly, he shifted the car back into first, and turned back onto Atwood. He'd had five years of happy domesticity with Juan and had threatened it all by his actions — a wonderful interlude that might well have prolonged itself into something more, might have changed his stagnant life. Speeding down Willy Street, he braked at the light at Baldwin and he saw that his gas gauge read perilously low. At the gas station up ahead, he pumped five dollars' worth into the tank, went inside and found himself grabbing a pack of cigarettes before he paid. Back on Willy Street, he lit one, the second ever in his life, and thought of Blake, who had smoked so... sexily. There had to be some-thing to cigarettes, sexy or otherwise. Maybe they were meant for times like this. Trying to derive satisfaction, he inhaled more deeply, coughed and put it out. The street took him up the in-cline on East Wilson, he veered onto what became West Wilson and, two turns later, found himself in front of the Bull Dog. He parked, stuck the cigarettes in his jacket pocket, but didn't go in.

A light rain spat down on him; the temperature, he calculated, hovered in the forties. He walked to the back of the parking lot and stopped to cup his hands around another cigarette and lit it. He cut over and began to walk down the railroad tracks. A bearded guy in tight jeans cruised him, but he looked away and inhaled once more. Then he threw the pack of cigarettes to the ground, concluding there was nothing appealing, much less sexy, about them. He tried to concentrate on Juan and what was happening between them.

He continued down the tracks, cutting over from one to another, heading west. Why couldn't his and Juan's troubles just be over? He'd had outside sex, not unsafe, but how could Juan be expected to know for sure? Maybe Juan did have a point. Could the resolution of it all be as simple as their both going to have HIV tests and, presuming the results were negative, continue as they had before?

The raindrops, he noticed, were becoming fatter, and he sped up his pace, aimless. Then, to his left, he spotted a small, dilapidated concrete building, windows and doors open. He began to make his way over to it. No, the effects of the recent past were still being felt, he concluded, and if he and Juan continued as a couple, they'd have to clean up some messy details. The problem was Juan's bulimia, a disease as serious as... drug addiction, and Juan was using food as a drug. That's what he couldn't live with.

Pepper peered inside the building, dimly illuminated from the outside by pole lights in the vicinity. He was able to discern wine bottles, empty food containers, a diaper and other paraphernalia inside. The diaper made him shudder. He stepped in out of the rain.

He struck a match to verify the shack was unoccupied. The dirt floor was dry enough and he crouched down, picked up and straightened out a cigarette butt, then lit it. Maybe this is was he needed to do: sit alone and think in some ramshackle hut and watch the rain. What would his life be like without Juan? He could make do, couldn't he? He didn't need his parents or Amelia. But Juan...?

He turned away from the window, shivering slightly, and inhaled the butt down to the filter.

"Hey!" Came a voice behind him and he jumped up. A

middle-aged woman, carrying a backpack and a bedroll tied in plastic, stepped inside. "Think it's safe in here tonight? Cops been on the move, runnin' people out." She approached him, staring through the dim light, and he struck another match. "You never been here before," she stated, with disappointment or disgust. "What the hell are you doin' here?"

"I have no idea."

# 48

Beth arrived at work promptly at eight o'clock. Although Rickover was in class, she wouldn't put it past him to post spies by the door to check on her punctuality. Wilhelmina, already behind her desk, looked up and said a timid "Good morning."

She took off her coat, wondering what Wilhelmina would think of the latest politics attached to her blouse: "U.S. OUT OF MY UTERUS!"

"Came in early today, huh, Willy?"

Wilhelmina seemed taken aback at the nickname, but said nothing about it or the button. She took several seconds before speaking, as if to compose herself or think out her words: "Since Professor Rickover's a little displeased with both of us, I figured..."

"Like, 'We better tow the line'? Well, I'm towin' it. As much as I can."

"You'd better look at the memo on your desk."

"What?" Beth turned around, saw a piece of paper placed squarely in the middle. Approaching it, she saw that it was typed on departmental letterhead and looked official. She picked it up and speed-read:

*April 15, 1991*
*TO: Beth Yarmolinsky*
*FROM: Vance R. Rickover, Chair*
*RE: Your Employment*
*Your employment as student worker in the Department of Museum Studies is hereby terminated, effective today, for reasons of gross incompetence and insubordination.*

"That son of a bitch! How could he?"

"He must have dropped it off before he went to teach at seven forty-five. I'm sorry. He also left a message to the same effect for me."

"You mean he canned you too? Sorry, Willy. You've been here forever. Must be the pits, a woman of your age havin' to look for a new job."

"No, Beth. He didn't fire *me*. What I meant was, he left a note on my desk telling me he was dismissing you."

"Lemme see!" Beth loped over to Wilhelmina's desk and stole away the note, which read: "Ms. Wiggins: The shrimp is gone. Effective today."

"It took me a minute to realize what he meant."

"Now I got it in writing." She stashed the note in her pocket. "There must be something I can do." She paced the office, clenching her fists. Her job didn't fall under the auspices of MULO, the student labor union. Maybe filing a speech-code complaint was all she could do, what she should have already done, even if Rickover was on his way out.

"I'm afraid you work at the pleasure of the department, and the department —or rather, Professor Rickover— is displeased. I'm sorry," Wilhelmina repeated. "It's been..." Beth waited for her to finish with "nice," "educational," even "real."

Instead, she said "eventful."

"There was nothing I could do. When Professor Rickover makes up his mind... And now it's almost the end of the semester and I'm without a student worker again."

"You ask me, I think they oughta fire Rickover and Ginger from their teachin' and let them do it. It'd serve 'em right." Wilhelmina didn't deign to respond to this, so Beth went on, "I better get paid for today. At least for my four hours."

"I take care of the paperwork. I'll make sure you get credit for your all your hours, including today's."

"Hell, I should sue. Cissy and Evan would take up my cause."

"Whatever you do, please leave me out of this. I've got to hold on to my own job."

"Don't worry, Willy, I won't. I'm outta here now. Not gonna hang around to see that ugly bastard's face at eight thirty-six."

"I wouldn't either, if I were you."

She didn't think she'd hang around for her AIDS and Ethics class either. It was a warm April day. She wandered aimlessly through Library Mall, where dogs ran and frisbees flew.

The evangelist preachers would soon be stationed on the Mall to harass students about their "evil ways." Signs advertising the upcoming "Out & About" series dotted kiosks.

Beth saw herself impoverished again. She had to graduate, was tired of going part-time. A brief pang of remorse for skipping her afternoon class followed, but soon vanished. Today would have to be a "mental health" day.

"Beth!" She heard her name called behind her. The voice sounded like Maddie Son's. She turned around and saw her old roommate, Lou Lautermilk.

"Lou! What are you doin' on campus?" Beth hadn't seen her in some time, probably not since Lou had finished her Master's Degree in Psych. "Hey, kid, you look like you've dropped forty pounds!"

"Yes, I've lost weight. And what do you mean, 'Why am I on campus?' I told you I was going to work toward my Ph.D." Beth remembered, dimly. "With only a Master's, you certainly don't just go out and hang up a shingle and establish yourself as a psychologist."

"Whatever you say. I'm still goin' part-time, tryin' to work part-time." In light of Lou's success, she decided to omit telling her of this morning's firing. "Everything's a little rough. But at least I'm still with Verla."

"That's great! And speaking of spouses, I might as well tell you. I'm engaged, Beth! His name's Ben, he's defending his dissertation in psychology in two weeks, and guess what?"

"You're gonna open up shop together as shrinks? I don't know, Lou. What?"

"He's Jewish and I'm converting."

"Now, that's wild!" Lou, a Jew? Lou, the naive, Wisconsin farm girl who'd been her freshman roommate? She realized Lou had changed dramatically over time, while she herself had stagnated, unreconstructed. "Well, congratulations."

"Thanks, Beth. I'm so happy. You and I have to get together. I mean it. You know I don't issue idle invitations."

Beth knew. Whatever Lou said, Lou did. She could make a date for three years from Wednesday, and she'd show up.

"Yeah, sure, let's do. Call me, I'm in the book." If my phone's not disconnected soon. She'd had enough of Lou's happiness, wanted to get away. "See ya, kiddo."

She saw Lou wince at her old nickname for her. "I'll call

you, Beth. I've got to teach a class now. Great seeing you."
    "Yeah."

                              ❧

    She ambled up State Street toward the Capitol, veered right
on Frances. At the corner of University Avenue, she found herself next to the 602 Club, which she'd heard had been Madison's
first gay bar. Inside, she ordered a glass of burgundy, bought a
pack of Camel Lights from behind the bar.
    A pleasant sensation of recklessness overtook her, drinking
as she was on a weekday morning when others were in class
or at work. A few customers came in, making her no longer the
sole customer. She'd seen that the bar sported an interesting
clientele, a mix of graduate students and non-students, off-beat
locals, and older men playing cards. She ordered a second burgundy, toyed with the idea of asking if they needed a bartender,
but wasn't up to the inquiry.
    The encounter with Lou had depressed her more than she'd
realized. Lou, who'd had little or nothing together when they
were freshmen, had matured, had earned two degrees while
she herself had done... what? Worked at a restaurant, would
be lucky to graduate with one degree, and that wouldn't be for
a couple more years. At least Beth had a partner, even if she
couldn't marry her, but Lou was outdoing her here too. She'd
have the heterosexual sanction of marriage, and she was marrying a Jew, at that. Verla was Beth's only consolation.
    Three burgundies later, she tottered out, knowing she
shouldn't have spent so much money. She took a circuitous
route east. The temperature had warmed up even more; the
sun had made a bold appearance and the clouds had scattered.
    Still in no particular hurry, she bypassed the Capitol and, a
few blocks later, turned off Willy Street, to Jenifer, then to
Spaight. She saw B. B. Clarke Beach at the foot of a steep hill
and scampered down it.
    After taking off her jacket, she sat down to bask in the sun.
A woman with two children was at the opposite end of the
beach, otherwise deserted. She rolled her blouse off her shoulders, leaned back and closed her eyes. The day was a pleasant
blur. She wondered at what time Verla would get home.
    In the distance she heard rap music, to which she'd taken
an odd liking. The music came nearer. She opened her eyes,
saw that two men had sat down nearby with a boombox. They

pulled cans out of a sack and began to drink. Behind them, the woman dragged her children up the hill and away.

She closed her eyes again, let the sun envelop her shoulders and face. Then came a voice: "Hey, there. Want a beer?"

Beth looked up, initially alarmed. The taller of the two men hovered almost right above her, proffering a can. Why not?, she thought, and accepted. At least it wasn't a Miller product, but she probably would have taken it, no matter. "Sure. Thanks."

"Funky day."

"Yeah," she said, popping it open. Foam sprayed her hand. She took a sip: lukewarm. Well, she couldn't be choosy. If she was going to drink, she might as well drink free or cheaply.

"Good way to pass the day," he said. He seemed sober, though she was in no position to judge anyone's sobriety.

"Yeah. Got fired from my job this morning." She was glad to have a stranger to talk with, one who might empathize.

"Bummer."

"Yeah, a real drag. Second or third job I lost this year."

"Too bad."

"I decided to forget the day and enjoy the sun."

"Hey, Ray, man!" It was the shorter guy, who'd been deserted by his companion. "Why don't you all come on back over here?"

"Come on over?" said Ray, motioning to Beth. She reached for and retrieved her jacket and backpack, then walked over with Ray. "Sit yourself down."

Beth plunked herself on top of her jacket, backpack on one side, beer in her hand. "Nice sun," she said.

"That's what me and Bryant thought. Didn't expect to find no one here today."

"I wouldn't be, except I got fired from my job this morning."

"Where?"

"The big, fat fuckin' U. 'U' as in university," she replied, glad to spew some venom.

"Good place to skim some trim, though," the short one — Bryant? — said.

Skim some trim?, she thought to herself, never having heard the expression. It sounded vaguely criminal. "Yeah," she agreed, comradely, feeling criminal herself.

"Have another beer?" asked Bryant, keeper of the six-pack.

She was holding an empty can, felt good, and had the after
noon in front of her. But... "That's OK, thanks. You guys only
got a six-pack. Don't wanna drink up all your beer."

"Oh, we got more than a six-pack." Bryant shoved a Bud at
her.

"OK. Thanks." She took a drink, let the breeze hit her face,
and lay back down. Relaxation suffused her whole body. She
stared up into the sun's early spring rays, then closed her eyes.

They sat briefly in silence, Beth opening her eyes and drinking intermittently.

"You like to show skin, don'tcha?"

She looked up, unsure who had spoken.

"You was showin' your shoulders back there, wasn't ya?"
It was Ray. A small alarm went off in her head. She took a
healthy swig of beer.

"You think this is a nude beach?"

It *was* the beach where three women had bared their breasts
last summer in a "tit-in," which had resulted in an equal rights
to be topless controversy. Doubting that they knew of that, she
ignored the remark and looked toward her belongings, making to stand up.

"Hey, no reason to move. 'Less you wanna move over there
by those trees and uncover all you want."

Combating tipsiness, she tried to assess the situation. "I don't
think so. I better drink up and go." Or not drink up and just
go. She glanced down at her jacket and backpack. The buttons
on her jacket were face-down; Bryant and Ray must have noticed the one on her blouse.

"Goin' already?" said Ray. "I thought we was just enjoyin'
us our beers here. No reason to go."

"I'm sorry. I think I better." She stood up.

"Hey, you think these beers are free?" Ray stood up, menacing.

Beth grabbed for her backpack and jacket and set the can
down.

"Why you think we came over here? You, half-topless, on
the beach."

"Thanks for the beers, but I'm outta here." She began walking swiftly up the hill and heard Bryant's voice behind her.
"We smelled pussy from way up there. You down here advertising it. And your ut'rus too!"

So they had seen her button. Beth stopped in her tracks,

now at a safe enough distance. "Don't you have anything better to do than harass women?" She scrambled up the top of the hill, possessions in hand.

"Listen to that bitch."

Turning onto the sidewalk, she saw both men standing and laughing. This was no laughing matter. Livid, she ran toward Jenifer Street, saw a bus approaching and flagged it down urgently.

It stopped for her and she dug in her pocket for change. "This isn't a legitimate stop, you know," said the driver.

"This is an emergency. I coulda been raped back there. Hey, which bus is this?"

It was the Monona, the one that would take her as close as she could get to her house. She found the door unlocked, Verla at home and realized she'd lost total track of the time.

"Beth, is something wrong?"

"More than one thing, I'm afraid. Rickover fired me, I had a few drinks, stupidly, I admit. Passed by B. B. Clarke and two guys harassed me. I coulda been raped."

"Oh, no! My poor Beth." Verla held out her arms to her and Beth fell into them. She recounted the day's events in all their lurid detail.

"Positively awful," Verla concluded. "Well, you know that 'Out & About' starts Friday and goes on for two weeks. A few empowerment workshops sound like just what you need."

"Yeah, I shoulda karate-chopped those assholes."

"That's not exactly what I was thinking, though it might have taught them a lesson. Here, look at the program."

"Just kiss me first, please."

# 49

"Roz, it'll be OK." Seth patted her on the back, gave her a brotherly squeeze of the shoulder, as they sat on the sofa in Roz's living room.

"One fucking vote," Roz more or less bawled. "I told them I didn't want a recount. It would have been much easier to lose by five."

"Hey, I know." Seth prodded her to look straight into his eyes. They were dark soulful eyes. "But look how close you came. How fucking close. It's a goddamned shame." With his last sentence, Seth gestured theatrically, stood up, then sat down closer to her.

"Seth, can you reach me my cigarettes?"

"Get one and light one for you is what I'll do." Mission accomplished within seconds, he handed one to Roz and inched nearer to her.

Roz took the cigarette, inhaled, and smoke got in her eyes, triggering tears, which she finally let flow.

"It'll be OK." He patted her on the back, and squeezed her more closely.

"At least I didn't win by my mother's one vote," she said, trying to lighten the atmosphere. "Or I could look at it this way: I lost by two votes, since hers shouldn't have counted."

"No. Rhoda was residing here, her vote was legitimate. You just lost by one miserable, little vote."

"I think she really wanted me to win."

"Of course she did. We all did."

"It's Irv who doesn't care, is probably secretly glad I lost." Her words came out with unexpected vehemence. Irv was at his office, doing nothing as usual, and had offered only a modicum of consolation.

"Well, as I told you from the start, I had the same problem with Sunny, more or less. These things are difficult."

"If Irv had gotten out there and gotten me one more vote..." Roz's tears had now subsided, a tiny pique taking their place.

Now on the edge of the sofa cushion, she turned toward Seth and looked him in the eyes. She felt — how could she describe it? — a magnetic pull toward him, a simple human need.

They fell the remaining inches toward each other, embracing tightly, and Roz's lips found their way to Seth's.

Roz knew that she needed to talk to God and had made the arrangements.

She'd driven west to Middleton Beach Road and now sat in Emma Leiverman's den, not in her basement office where she usually saw clients. To Roz's relief, the den sported a variety of ashtrays, which resembled African tribal carvings. They both struck a match to different varieties of Camels.

"Roz, we should both stop smoking. It took emphysema to get Howard to stop. I'm telling you this as a friend, not as a therapist. I'm planning to quit May first. But you didn't come here for me to lecture you."

"Oh, maybe I did. I don't know." Roz took a quick puff, with less gusto than usual. She'd known Emma, a long-time peace guru, since the late sixties.

They finished both their cigarettes and social preliminaries, and Roz decided to let it all out: "I feel so... empty. All at once, the election is over and I've lost. Dave insisted on a recount and the result was even worse...

"I'm disappointed, but I can handle that. My mother was here for about three months, drove me crazy, but, strangely, I miss her now." Roz judged Emma a few years younger than Rhoda.

"I don't know what's worse." Roz deliberated how to continue as Emma smiled, silent incitement for her to go on. "There's Dayne. He's only three. No, he just turned four. I always thought I wanted a child, but... I have a hard time relating sometimes. Kids and their noise get on my nerves. Worse yet, Dayne's bonded more with his biological father, Juan, than he has with Irv.

"I know Irv feels left out. Juan's taken to Dayne, and Dayne's taken to Juan, though of course Dayne doesn't know the truth, yet. Dayne even calls Juan 'Daddy' sometimes. We started out letting him think he had two fathers, which he does, but then Irv began to feel hurt, I'm sure, though he never said so. But when Dayne's only three, I mean four, how can you start suddenly telling him that Juan's been demoted from 'father' to 'uncle'?"

African carvings on the walls stared down at her threateningly. She trusted the basement had a more inviting decorative motif. At least from there, one could look out at the peaceful shore of Lake Mendota.

"Then there's our sex life." She was glad Emma was a straight woman, as opposed to lesbian Gods she'd talked to in the past. "The first few years it was fine, but the real problem just happened recently. Part of it was all the pressure of the election. We've only had sex three or four times that I can remember in the last six months. It's not that I don't want him, it's... At times I've thought he just doesn't find me attractive. I don't know if you ever breastfed, Emma, but it makes firm little tits go straight to hell.

"Then there's my nudism. One practical thing to say for it: It makes for lots fewer clothes to schlep downstairs to the washing machine." She stopped and laughed, waiting for Emma to join in, but Emma only smiled thinly. Roz wished it were only a social visit, was uncertain how to proceed.

Emma finally broke their mute standoff. "Roz, you've gone this far. Unless you want to wait until another session to go on..."

"No, I've gone this far." Roz paused again and blew out tiny ripples of breath. "I let things get a little out of control with my breast exercises." She craved another cigarette, but refrained. "My lesbianism started out political, you know, it was just the thing to do, to be with other independent women and prove we didn't need men. But it wasn't the real me. But back to the point. One morning I went to the Labor Farm office and took my top off to do my exercises, not that you have to take your top off, but I like to do them in front of the mirror and watch for progress. I knew that two lesbian volunteers were going to come in. Well, they did and I left my top off. Then, unexpectedly, Irv came in too. Oy, was it embarrassing.

"I guess I wanted to prove to myself that women still find me attractive. I don't know if they did, probably not. I'm not even bisexual. I think."

She stopped and let the tears begin to flow.

"No, I don't think I'm bisexual," she managed to repeat through tears, an all too common phenomenon recently. "The real problem, if it's a problem, is... there's another man." She glanced up, waiting to see shock on Emma's face, but it registered nothing. "There's another man and I want him. He's married too. The other day, in the living room, if it hadn't been for Dayne's appearance, I'm sure we would have..."

❧

"I thought one of these days, now that the election's over, things might normalize." Irv said. "God forbid, if she'd won." He sat in a wooden lawn chair in Seth's backyard.

"Your personal is getting in the way of your political, I'd say. The council needed another good Labor Farm voice."

Seth, sporting his eternal pony tail, sat in a matching chair — probably handmade — opposite Irv. The April sun bore down on them, giving the appearance of an early summer day.

"Seth, I agree. But I'm here to talk to you as an old friend, who's got a wife who has problems, which means I have problems. Can we forget the election for a minute?"

"Sure, man. Toke?" In shorts, Seth stretched out his hairy legs and looked up at the sun.

Irv was tempted, but said, "No, thanks." Seth admitted — or bragged? — that he spent every weekend stoned, that it was the best condition in which to do house and yard work. Irv considered this a nothing but a rationalization for being stoned hours on end.

"Roz is getting worse. I thought things would improve after the election. She almost totally neglects Dayne, as if she was the one who..." Irv caught himself in time, opting not to tell Seth he was not the natural father. "I can say this to you, if I can say it to anyone: You know I'm not a sex maniac or anything. But we haven't had sex but once since Roz announced her candidacy. I'm sure —I think I'm sure— there's no one else involved. But I really don't know what to think."

"Sunny and I, we still do it everyday. Twice or three times on weekends."

Just what Irv didn't need to hear. He looked around the yard and saw Sunny pottering in the distance.

"You're missing out, man."

"Seth, I'd settle for twice, no, once a week."

"You're sure there's no one else involved? Maybe a woman?"

Seth held the joint under his nostrils, drew smoke in, then expelled it. "Bisexuality's really in these days, you know."

Another thing Irv didn't need to hear. He let his eyes roam over the idyllic setting. Both the front and back yards were native Wisconsin prairie gardens. The garden shed had a sod roof that Sunny was planting in flowers. Irv wished he'd bought a farm in the country, instead of the Queen Anne house Roz had fallen in love with.

"I can't know for sure. I don't think she has time to be involved with anyone else."

"I don't know, Irv. Men who want to find time." Irv wondered if Seth was speaking from experience. "I'm sure if a woman wants to, she can find the time, too."

Irv thought of all the hours Roz spent volunteering, of how he often couldn't locate her; of how she thought her breasts were unattractive since breastfeeding Dayne; of the dubious breast exercises, or at least their dubious results. Maybe, in ways he hadn't thought of, he had ignored her. Maybe Roz *was* seeking approval from outside the bosom of the family.

"But no," Seth went on. "I think you're right. Roz has neither the time nor the inclination to have an affair."

Irv was glad to hear this, though he knew that Seth couldn't know this any better than he. At that moment Sunny came toward them, a plastic tub in her arms. "Seth, the door, please."

Seth seemed not to hear, or was slow on the uptake. Irv jumped up and opened the door to the back porch for her. He looked inquisitively at the tub's contents, water.

"Rain water for washing clothes." He swore Sunny's smile was permanent, the result of month-long drug trips twenty years ago, or of constant sex. "Much easier than melting the snow on top the wood stove in winter."

They were undoubtedly the most politically correct family on Madison's west side, though they'd have some competition on the east.

"I suppose so." He watched her shapely backside, and wondering what it would have been like to marry Sunny. He ambled back out and sat down next to Seth, who was finishing off the joint. "She's a good woman, Irv."

One who does all the work, Irv suspected. Roz, in comparison... Even if she wasn't having an affair, he didn't know what to think, nor had he for months.

Roz returned from Emma's and found Irv gone. As Juan was taking care of Dayne, she decided to go back out, just to walk around and think. She walked for a few blocks, up to the purple house on Jenifer Street, and turned back. One of Claypool's signs still resided in a nearby window, she saw as she made her way back to Orton Park. She admired the burr oak they'd saved, and realized that someone had to keep last fall's protest going in case the city forestry crew tried to chainsaw it again, which they probably would. She lay down in the grass briefly, then got back up, wandered over to the gazebo and sat on its steps. Being outdoors felt good, but she wanted to be farther away than here, from where she could even see her own house.

All at once a man in brief shorts, tank top and dark sunglasses came jogging right up to her, and flopped down in the grass near her feet.

She let her gaze fall on him; his attire left little to the imagination. The muscled arms and defined chest were quite appealing. If Irv exercised like this... She wondered what Seth looked like, shirtless. But, no. This man seemed younger than both of them, apparently in his thirties. He also looked vaguely familiar. Her eyes kept falling involuntarily on his body and she saw that he'd opened his and they met hers.

He leapt up and clapped his hands, then did a few short jumps, as though shaking off sweat. She couldn't deny finding him attractive.

"Nice day in the park, hey?" he said, short-winded, still moving around.

"Yeah, it is. Especially for April."

"Come here often?"

"I live here on the park." She almost pointed out the house, but stopped herself.

"I just like to crash here after my five-mile run." Now he started stretching, touching his toes, and doing other contortions that she'd seen joggers do. She looked over instinctively to her house, as though, if Irv were watching, he could sense her interest, innocent as it was.

"You look like you could use some cheering up."

Did it show that much and was this true concern? It couldn't possibly be a come-on, could it?

"Oh, maybe I could. I just needed to get away, outside, Just being in the sun is good after this long, dreary winter."

"Sure is." The man smacked his thighs, as if slapping a horse to giddap, winked at her and jogged away.

Longingly, Roz watched him disappear into the distance.

Hmmm, he mused, jogging homeward. Fucking a politician. Or a would-have-been one. He'd recognized her from the newspaper, but she hadn't seemed to recognize him. If she were a little younger or a major babe, perhaps... The fantasy of taking her right there in the park had been appealing, and it wouldn't have been the first time. Still, a fuck was a fuck, he always felt like one after exercising, and sometimes he'd take whomever he could get. He'd fucked everything female fuckable that he'd been able to in his two years in Madison. A librarian, cashiers, secretaries; girls in the neighborhood, girls met in parks and at beaches, waitresses who'd served him at restaurants. His students, others' students, a colleague's wife, and even a colleague herself when they'd done coke once. If Evan hadn't moved in with Cissy, he would have had her too, he was sure, and reproached himself for not having been quicker to make a move. He didn't want to screw up relations with his landlord anyway by fucking his wife. But if she were receptive, she certainly wouldn't tell her husband. He'd caught her eyeing his chest, ogling his entire body, if he wasn't mistaken. Anyone who said many women weren't discreet crotch-watchers hadn't been watching many women. He extracted his apartment key from his sock, let himself into his first-floor apartment, and wondered idly if Cissy was home alone upstairs.

# 50

The clock in the main office struck eight fifty-nine. Cissy saw Wilhelmina staring into her video monitor, not typing, but trying, it seemed, to ignore that all was not normal. She suddenly wished Beth were there to break the tension. No one spoke.

Rickover had requested a nine o'clock meeting in his office with the faculty. Cissy speculated what he might try to pull. They hadn't heard from Sandra again; Cissy wondered how she was doing, and scolded herself for not calling her.

At the dot of nine, Rickover flung his door open and, with a brusque gesture, motioned them into his inner sanctum. Ginger and Nick took seats across from his desk, the rest at a small conference table behind. Rickover appeared to do a quick body count. "I see you're all here."

Yes, all six of us, Cissy thought. Blake had died, Sandra resigned, and Cissy envisioned herself departing, as it were, on Rickover's coattails, heading toward some reliquary in the sky that held ex-professors in her field.

"Have you thought over our offer?" Evan jumped in as Rickover mulled over his next words. "Offer" was an understatement.

"Matter of fact, I have." Belligerence oozed into the tone.

"And?"

Cissy was glad she wasn't seated under Rickover's nose. He reminded her of a particularly intimidating eleventh-grade chemistry teacher she'd had. Both men looked like explosions had blown up in their face.

"I'll accept it on one condition. Otherwise, you'll all be in for some legal wrangling." Rickover stopped, as though enjoying leaving them in momentary suspense or cowed by his power. Cissy didn't yet trust that it was for the last time. "You all promise not to say one word about the reason for my resignation to the dean, to any other faculty, staff, students, or any person connected to this campus, or to any colleague in our field, whether associated with a university or a museum, in this country as well as abroad."

"Do you want us to put it in writing? We could sign an oath," Evan said.

Rickover actually seemed to deliberate for a second before Evan's ploy dawned on him. "Go to hell, Schultz." Evan laughed in his face.

Everyone was more than willing to comply, the talk of lawyers having apparently been idle. Cissy couldn't help but derive secret satisfaction from his poor job prospects at this late date in the academic year. It was hard for her to summon up more than a smidgen of pity.

"All right. Agreed. And if I ever trace a leak back to any one of you, I'll sabotage your fucking career. Now, get out of my office!"

"You can't sabotage mine, Vance," Rothschild said. "I'm retiring, getting out of this climatic hellhole, and moving to Florida."

❧

A few days later, Cissy opened the wooden paneled doors to the faculty mailboxes. She snatched a sealed envelope out of hers and took it back to her office.

It contained the ballot for acting departmental chair for the coming year and bore Ginger's and Nick's names. The accompanying notice instructed them to return their ballot to Rothschild or Rutledge, who made up the election committee, within two weeks.

Predictably, Cissy heard Ginger's heels making a march toward her door. "That goddamned two-timing son of a bitch!" she said in a barely restrained whisper, and shut the door.

"I take it you mean Vance." Cissy hoped for innocence.

"Who the hell do you think I mean?"

"Nick?" she squeaked, still pretending to have no idea.

"Who else?" Ginger thrust the ballot at her and threw herself onto the cushioned chair next to Cissy's desk.

"Who is he two-timing?"

"You know what I mean. The nerve, not to tell me! Why

didn't you tell me, Cis?" Ginger wore an evergreen dress and had wedged a bulbous jade pendant, or the best-looking imitation Cissy had ever seen, into her cleavage.

"It was only a rumor." This was true.

"And what, may I ask, is wrong with spreading a perfectly good rumor?" If the question required an answer, Cissy didn't give one. "Well, we'll just see." Ginger gritted her teeth, ripped the top page off of Cissy's memo pad, grabbed a pen off her desk and began writing.

Evan's secret knock came at the door and he slipped in. "Thought I might find you two here."

"Motherfucker," Ginger mumbled, scribbling furiously.

"Hell of a way to greet me."

Ginger barely looked up. "Not you. That drugged-up asshole who thinks he's God's gift to women."

Cissy didn't doubt the latter part, agreed perfectly with the "asshole" remark, but didn't think Ginger had room to talk in the drug department. Her main fear was that Rickover, from some location unknown, would still try to manipulate the department through Nick.

"'Drugged-up'? What do you mean?" Cissy asked.

"Believe me, he uses."

"How would you know?" Evan asked. "Ever use together, or what?"

Ginger gave an offended snort. "I won't dignify that with a response. But believe me, I know."

Cissy didn't doubt that she might. Besides academic secrets, Ginger routinely ferreted out everyone's vices, past skeletons and, of course, sexual indiscretions.

"But Ging," Evan reasoned, "wouldn't it actually look better to defeat an opponent rather than to win by default, with no opposition?"

She pondered this logic only briefly. "No, I don't care how I win!"

Cissy feared — no, knew — that she was serious.

"In any case, I've got it wrapped up." She dangled her tally sheet between thumb and forefinger. "There are seven votes. I have three absolutely guaranteed: the two of yours plus mine. Nick has one, for himself. Certainly John or Bob, most likely both, will vote for me. So it's over. And it doesn't even matter if Vance votes for Nick."

"See. You didn't have to get so worked up." Cissy hoped to

pacify her, but doubted Ginger's calculations.

"That's not the point. Nick doing this behind my back! We'll just see who gets the highest merit increases when I'm on the committee that decides his. I know how to reward my friends..." She reeled the two of them in with an ingratiating glance, as if tempting dumb animals with sugar cubes. "...and to screw my enemies."

"Come on, Ginger, Nick isn't exactly an enemy. We all worked together to get rid of Vance," Cissy said, and observed Evan as if he were a savage stud, shaking his blond mane. Thank God she'd convinced him to take the styling gel out of his hair.

"If he wasn't an enemy before, he is now."

"There's one little drawback I'm sure you've thought of, Ging," Evan said. "Nick's a full professor. You know the dean prefers chairs to be full, not associate professors."

"The dean doesn't vote."

"But the dean has to approve the departmental vote."
Ginger ignored the comment. "I think I'll go campaign now." Cissy imagined her plastering posters all over the fifth-floor walls. "I'll get either Bob's or John's vote and it'll be over."

"Better get both of them to be sure," Evan said.

"Of course. Do you think I'm a fool? You never know who you can trust in this department."

Cissy wondered if she referred to the two of them. Their votes for her were by no means guaranteed.

"You've got that right," said Evan.

"Don't I know." Ginger stood up, admired her pendant, and marched out purposefully.

❦

Cissy took refuge in Evan's office and checked her wristwatch. The divisional committee, composed of nine tenured faculty, would be convening two floors above them in a matter of minutes to vote on her tenure.

"I can imagine it now: 'Rickover's Revenge'." Unfortunately, he still formed part of the committee. "He gets to call me after the vote and say, 'Pankhurst, you flunked.'"

"Nonsense. The departmental vote was unanimous."

"Only because Vance, as chair, couldn't vote. I'm truly afraid he's going to try some last-minute stunt."

"Ginger's out taking bets. Three-to-two odds in your favor."

"If that's meant to be humor, I don't appreciate it." She lacked the nerve to ask if this was really true, felt like having a breakdown, but didn't want to have it here in FAB.

Evan stood up and shoveled papers into his backpack. Cissy held her briefcase, thinking if she didn't pass the vote, maybe she'd just never come back, and let the department flounder for the rest of the semester. Concern for her students would indeed be the only reason to finish.

"Don't think that way. I know that look on your face," Evan said, smiling his best, confident, manly, yet gentle. "You're going to pass. Everybody says so."

"'Everybody' is not the committee. We all know that Streckenbach from Art History is a stickler for publications and, even though I've got my book, mine still aren't excessive."

"Just because he's got it in for Museum Studies doesn't mean he'll vote against you. After today, the rest is just pro forma."

Cissy knew, but could only concentrate on today. "You can't blame me for worrying until I know the results. Look, I'm almost trembling already."

"I know how to keep you occupied." Evan encircled her in his arms and she let him kiss her. She felt his hand on her blouse, aiming for...

"Ev, we can't do this in here." She wanted affection, but... Evan's divorce would be final by summer; she wondered what, if anything, it would mean for their relationship.

Evan disentangled himself from her. "We'll go home, smoke a joint and have a few hours of ecstasy. When we're finished, it'll be over and you'll find out. It'll all be pain-free."

"Let's go. This building gives me the creeps today. Always has."

They arrived home and Evan wasted no time in lighting a joint. Cissy had changed into jeans and a sweatshirt, come back to the living room, and sat down beside him. As they smoked it, she noticed that the light on her answering machine was flashing.

"Look!" She got up and rewound the tape. It was long enough to contain a real message rather than a hang-up. She pushed the "play" button and a voice began:

"Pankhurst. Rickover here. The vote was in your favor."

Her heart leapt, she fixed ecstatic eyes on Evan, then heard him add, "Five to four. The dean will certainly have fun deciding what to do with you now." End of message.

"Five to four! So I guess this is what three-to-two odds in my favor meant."

"I can't believe it!" Evan left the joint smoldering in an ashtray and began pacing the living room. "That bastard Rickover!"

Cissy wondered if he'd somehow sabotaged the committee. She'd expected Streckenbach and probably one other to vote against her, and had convinced herself that a seven-to-two vote wasn't bad, would indeed suffice to gain the dean's approval. But five to four... The badly split vote meant professional homicide, she was sure. Rickover had been right. She should have followed his suggestion, faced the firing squad last fall and spared herself all these months of pain.

"When the dean doesn't give it to me, I'll fight it. I'll appeal it. I even talked to Irv last fall about representing me if I need a lawyer."

"C'mon, Cissy. It won't come to that." She didn't know if he meant it, or was simply trying to console her. "We could call Ginger for confirmation of the vote. It could just be a dirty trick of Rickover's."

Passing over his suggestion, she slammed her fist into the wall and the plaster started to crumble. "Just like my career," she said.

"No. Just like Rickover's face."

She examined the new indentations in her knuckles. "Oh, I think someone's already done that to it."

# 51

Beth smelled the air, sniffing for traces of smoke from yesterday's fire, which still raged on. Central Storage and Warehouse was burning on the east side, the flames fed by melting butter and cheese. Nearby streets were rivers of lard; she pictured city blocks turned into a gigantic soufflé flambé.

Verla gave her a hurry-up look. "If you're that interested, you can bike out to see it later." Last night they'd been able to see flames three hundred feet high from their backyard.

On the bus they read the day's schedule of "Out & About's" lesbian and gay workshops to be held in Memorial Union. They were on their way to first one of the day, oddly if appropriately titled "Lesbian Sex in the Morning."

Sex at almost any time of the day sounded good to Beth, as long as Verla kept dildoes out of it. "What's this gonna be? A safe-sex demo or what?"

"I doubt it," Verla answered. Beth thought she looked particularly stunning, her blonde hair pulled back and just long enough to bounce off her shoulders. Her tight white "DYKE PRIDE" T-shirt accentuated her breasts and nipples. She took secret pleasure in being the lover of the most attractive lesbian around, and saw the two of them as the envy of all others. She herself had worn a regulation blue work shirt.

By the starting time, the workshop had garnered nine attendees, including the facilitator.

"Good morning, everyone. My name's Twyla." The facilitator then had them introduce themselves. "I suppose some of you may be wondering exactly what this is going to be all about."

"Sex, we hope."

"Ah, yes. You're right about that. And to plunge right in, let's start off by thinking of what are our associations with nighttime sex." She paused, awaiting answers.

"Romance and candlelight."

"Very true. Anyone else?"

"Unbridled passion," said Beth. "Anything goes."

"Thank you for sharing that. What else?"

"Personally I prefer it at night," said a woman Beth recognized. "Because, and I know this is going to sound looks-ist, but I can be looks-ist about my own body. I like it at night in the dark because I don't have to see myself naked."

Various murmurs of agreement and dissent went up.

"Anything more?" asked Twyla.

No one responded immediately. Before the interval became embarrassing, a woman next to them spoke: "About the first comment, 'Romance and candlelight,' let's think a little bit about the heterosexual symbolism of it. Man romances woman with dinner by candlelight, probably with wine. Then what happens?" She stopped; apparently the question required some dumb answer.

"Well, if it's a man, I suppose you have sex," said a woman who had yet to speak. "Just like if it's two women, you both might choose to have sex."

"Perhaps the key word here is 'choose'," said the woman who'd asked the question. "Does a woman have free choice with a heterosexual man who can dominate her if he wants? I associate it all with seduction by and submission to the patriarchy."

"Thank you, Jane," purred Twyla, glowing like a light bulb whose wattage was too bright for the early morning hour. "Has anyone else ever thought of it that way?"

"I never have, but it makes sense," came a timid voice.

"Well, I haven't," said the companion of the woman who didn't like to look at her body. "What is this really supposed to be about? To tell us dykes that if we have sex at night we're aping the patriarchy?"

No one said anything; there was no such thing as a good lesbian workshop without a little tension.

The woman continued: "Oh, now I get it. Lesbian sex at night is politically incorrect."

"It's something to think about," said Jane. Beth wondered if Jane was Twyla's lover, had helped plan the workshop or was planted in the audience.

"Yeah? Well, I think I have better things to think about. This is all a bunch of bull, if you ask me."

A silence again ensued after the hostile comment.

"There are other workshops to attend if you'd like." Twyla strained, with little success, for a modicum of courtesy.

The woman cast her eyes at her partner, who nodded. "Well, I think we will. So now we can't have sex at night!?"

"This is just an exploration of the topic."

"I think this is classist. What about working class dykes? That's what Sammy and me are. If we can't have sex at night, that means we never get to have it but maybe once a month. She works Monday through Friday. I don't usually have weekends off, like students or others of you do. Today's probably the first day in six weeks we're both off during the day and we saved it to come to these workshops. What do you say to that? You're gonna deny me my sex life because I'm oppressing myself by doing it at night?" No one responded; Sammy and her lover got up. "Well, it seems I gotcha all there. Excuse us."

The two marched toward the door, and Twyla mumbled some token thanks for their "contribution." "Of course, I didn't expect us all to agree," she continued. "This is just supposed to be an interchange of ideas, a way to open our minds to non-patriarchal, non-heterosexist thought. How do others feel?"

"I got nothing against sex in general," said Beth, "but some of us aren't exactly that chipper in the morning."

"Perhaps we've got to break down old stereotypes, norms and habits, and form new ones," said Verla. Beth suddenly wondered what was wrong with their current habits.

"Now that sounds sensible," said Jane.

"But what are some of us gonna do? Set the alarm for six-a.m. sex before class?"

"Yeah!" Beth agreed. Verla looked at her skeptically.

"We should all appreciate our bodies and not be afraid to look at them at any time of day. Or night."

"Lots of it comes down to questions of practicality."

"But we don't want to imitate the patriarchy."

"It may be hard, but perhaps all of us need to be thinking about how to be more chipper in the morning, as the woman over there said. I have the same problem."

"Frankly," Verla began, "I have many urges and bodily needs. I think the more time we all make to satisfy them, the better." That Verla even spoke up shocked Beth; that she was implying that the two of them might have a problem in front of other women angered her. The failed dildo experiment came back warily to her mind.

"That sounds very healthy," cooed Twyla. "Now what are some strategies we could enact to accomplish this?"

"I suppose we could stay up all night," said Beth. "Then when the sun comes up, we could go at it."

"Beth," Verla chided.

"Well, that's a little far out for some of us. But, as someone said, it's a question of practicality."

"If sex at night is supposed to be bad, we could, you know, just 'take back the night'."

"That's interesting. But how?"

"Oh, we've already got the night. Liz and I feel safe. I don't see what's wrong with it."

"What about single lesbians like me? Most of my chances to meet women are at night."

"You don't have to become intimate the same night that you meet."

"I'd say that's a rather personal choice."

"Sue and I have actually dealt with it. Not only does she not like sex in the morning, the only time she likes it is before dinner. So we tried non-monogamy."

"You mean you did."

"All right. I did. Now the whole room knows. You were monogamous and I was a wanton slut."

"I think we'd better stay out of certain realms of our intimate relationships."

"'Slut' is offensive to lesbians. That term's best applied to gay men or straight women."

"Hey, let's not bash them."

"They bash us verbally all the time."

"We're getting rather off the topic."

"Not totally," said Verla. "I don't see why, if your partner has less sexual energy or more time constraints than you, that non-monogamy couldn't be possible."

Beth couldn't believe what she was hearing. "Oh, you mean like a 'fuckbuddy'?"

"I suppose, sort of. Though that's another gay male term."

"I don't find it offensive."

"Or fucksister," said Verla aloud, but as if to herself, savoring it. "I like it."

"It doesn't sound so good to me," Beth said, looking her right in her baby-blue eyes.

"Now, let me emphasize again, let's not personalize this excessively. I realize there are couples here, but there are also singles."

"I think two couples, that makes four of the seven of us, are already on the topic, and four out of seven is a majority."

"I didn't come here for singles bashing. I happen to be single by choice."

Beth restrained herself from responding, knowing personally three women who had dumped the speaker.

"This is not really what the workshop was intended for," said Twyla, looking worriedly about the small conference room.

"So you wanna have a fucksister?" Beth faced Verla. "And you announce it in public? I can't fucking believe this."

"Perhaps a little restraint is in order."

"Are you gonna answer me?" Beth repeated.

"Hypothetically, it's an idea," Verla evaded.

"And you haven't been thinking about putting it into practice?"

"Please. Can we keep...?"

"Tell me you haven't."

"All right. I have. I thought here in a group might be a safer place to bring it up, in context with other women's experiences and ideas."

"Guess what? You thought wrong. What makes the day safe? I myself almost got raped the other afternoon in broad daylight!"

"Beth..."

"And before she tells you, I'd been drinking. So does that make it my fault?"

"I'm sorry. Of course it doesn't. Though I hope you reported it," said Twyla. "But we're way off the topic now."

"Isn't this supposed to be open-ended? It goes where it goes."

"Yeah, I see where it went. You wanna fuck somebody else and you announce it here in a group," Beth said.

"I'm sorry. I made a mistake."

"You sure as hell did." Beth stood up. She didn't deserve this simply because she hadn't liked experimenting with a dildo. In any case, she was sure that dildoes for dykes had to be politically incorrect. If a dildo wasn't "aping the patriarchy," what was?

"Might I suggest you two go to the Non-Monogamy Workshop in the afternoon?"

"Beth, don't leave in a huff. I'm sorry."

"Well, be sorry later. It's still morning. Maybe you can find your own little fucksister right here! Or, better yet, in the afternoon Slut Workshop!"

Out in the hall, she stared numbly at the photos and paintings lining the wall, in amazement of what she'd just said, and heard Verla say. She picked a smudged cigarette butt up off the floor and lit it up in Abe Lincoln's glass-encased face.

# 52

Roz sat in her Acura Legend in the hotel parking lot on the far-east side. She couldn't quite believe it had sunk to this: a Howard Johnson's. After they established that neither her house nor his would work, leaving them with no other options, she'd agreed, stipulating that it had to be a some place classy. But the Mansion Hill Inn, downtown and too close, was out of the question, and the suburbs had no class. She craned her neck and looked up at the brand new Howard Johnson's. If they had to do it in a hotel, couldn't they at least have a romantic setting? Door County, with its New England charm, occurred to her. Hell, even Milwaukee, with its grand old hotels, would do.

Roz ventured through the lot once more in her Acura and this time saw Seth's beat-up car parked, in of all places, next to a Dumpster. Why on earth had he parked there? Was he trying to hide?

She knew that she simply had to walk through the lobby and up to Seth's room, speaking to no one. And this part of Madison was a different world; she certainly wouldn't see anyone she knew.

Forcibly ridding herself of the irritation at the Dumpster, Roz pulled the Acura as close as possible to the hotel's entrance. *She* did not have to hide. She looked down at the nervous gooseflesh on her arms, then realized she had the air conditioning on, quite unnecessarily. As the motor idled, she switched it off. She knew that, if she wanted, she could be out of the parking lot in thirty seconds flat and zooming back down East Washington Avenue toward home. For the fifth time, she went through her "I've come this far" argument. But she *had* gotten Seth to agree not to be upset if she changed her mind. He'd merely requested that she call him at the room and tell him, if she did. There was probably a pay phone right in the lobby. She bet that Seth had probably figured she wouldn't even show up.

Well, she'd show him. In the flesh, in person, there she could be, in two minutes, at his door and fall into his arms. She knew she needed an escape and this, she'd told Seth, was what she wanted, having banished, at that moment, the word "infidelity" from her mind.

Roz turned off the motor, got out, and marched purposefully toward the hotel.

It was a pleasant early May day. It was also, she remembered, Seth's birthday.

❧

Irv looked at the note Roz had written him. She'd be back, she'd assured him, but she "didn't know exactly when." She had "to sort things out." She left no indication if the sorting-out process would be a matter of hours or days. Irv knew she thought herself unsuited to motherhood. Would she also judge herself unsuited to marriage?

Before his thoughts ran totally away, he took the note downstairs to show to Juan. "What do you make of it?"

"It's pretty clear, isn't it?"

Irv reread, aiming for between the lines. "On the surface, sure. She's left. She just doesn't say for where or how long."

Juan took the note back. "I think she just needs to leave for a while to get her head together. Like Pepper," he added sourly, and Irv thought perhaps he shouldn't have broached the topic with him. The two households, it seemed, were simultaneously falling apart.

"And there's no one thing you can pinpoint that triggered this?"

"No, not one specific thing." Irv considered enumerating — the election, their marriage, their sex life, Dayne — but refrained from reciting the litany, which Juan well knew.

"I don't suppose it would do any good to call Rhoda. Or her sister out in Oregon or Washington." He inched toward the door. "I've got to drive in about fifteen minutes."

Irv suspected he'd been working all the extra hours possible since Pepper had left. Indeed, Juan had hardly seemed upset about it. Maybe he should follow Juan's example. Roz had only been gone a matter of hours, and might be back in a few more.

"She did take her car. But I don't think she'd go back to Rhoda."

"Right. Roz is unpredictable," Irv said, a tiny fissure in his voice, "but if there's one thing we can be sure of, she wouldn't run home crying to Rhoda."

He realized that this was indeed the only certainty he had about Roz. She would come back, eventually. And then she might leave him. Juan and Dayne might be the only real family he had.

❧

Roz sped north on I-90, got off at an Eau Claire exit, and headed north. After her second visit to Emma, she had agreed that Roz's problems were not catastrophic and that Roz, if determined, could solve them herself. The sign of a good therapist, she concluded, not out to get your money by stringing you along. Emma had approved her plan — except for the part about not telling Irv in person — and now she was off and almost there. Emma, of course, hadn't known that Seth was another part of her plan.

An hour after her exit from I-90, she was following the directions dictated to her by telephone. She found herself on a gravel road, a few minutes later spotted a sign that said "WWWL" and turned into the lane. She tried to remember what the acronym stood for. "L" was for Land, and two of the "W's" for Wisconsin Womyn. After reading about it in the alternative press, she'd finally gotten through, and the owner had replied that they weren't officially open, but that Roz could stay free for a week by working for her room and board. When she replied that she'd gladly pay instead, Hester had countered that, no, they were working hard to be open by June first, and that they could only accommodate her if she agreed to work. Roz consented readily enough, and Hester added that there would be time for relaxation. About two miles down the lane, Roz came to the locked gate and through late-leafing trees saw a cement-brick building on the horizon. As instructed, she gave the secret honk of her horn, twice to make sure she was heard. Within five minutes someone came to open.

"Roz Goldwomyn?"

"That's me."

"Welcome to WWWL." It sounded like a radio station's call letters.

"Right. You're..."

"I'm Hester. I'll take the padlock off and you can drive in."

Roz drove in, then Hester closed the gate, and jumped in the car with her. "I hope you bought a heavier jacket. It's still pretty cold up here at night. And we don't have central heat yet, you know."

"Oh." Roz hadn't known. "I brought a wool sweater." It had been a warm spring in Madison; she wondered how much cooler it might be up here.

"At least now we have indoor plumbing."

"That's great," said Roz, thanking God, the womyn, and anyone else who had a part in it.

"If you ever want to make us a donation to us..." Hester was evidently apprising or appraising the forty-thousand-dollar car.

Roz nodded, paying little heed, and parked. Hester showed her to her cabin, down a hill past the lodge. It contained a single bed, toilet, sink, and wood stove. Period.

"Why don't you wash up if you want? Sorry it's only a cold-water sink. Rest a few minutes if you feel the need, and go on up to the lodge, meet the womyn and get a work assignment.

There's still a few good hours we can all put in today."

After the long drive, Roz felt like a long nap. Though still the same day, it seemed like eons since she'd gone to Seth's hotel room, told him she couldn't go through with it, and before he could protest, left.

"What are the work choices or assignments?"

"There's always wood chopping and carpentry. Or if you want to go in for the lighter stuff, there's cooking and childcare. Take your pick today."

"Excuse this dumb question. What does WWWL stand for? I can't seem to remember what one of the W's stands for."

"Wisconsin Womyn Working the Land. What else?"

Roz swore she saw a malicious gleam in Hester's eyes.

Determined to make a good impression, Roz herded herself up to the lodge within fifteen minutes. A "Chem-Free" sign on the door greeted her. Underneath, someone had added "Smoking and Drinking in Cabins Only. P.S. No Smoking in Bed Either." She felt her pack of Camels and the lighter in her pocket and walked in. The lodge was large, barely furnished, and silent. Perhaps she would donate them a little money; they obviously could use it. She heard a faint noise from what had to be the kitchen and approached it. A short blonde woman, muscled and roughly her own age, stood scrubbing pots over a large steel sink.

"Hello," she said timidly. "Hester told me to come up here to choose my work assignment."

"Oh, you're the woman from Madison." She took her hands out of the water. A flannel shirt served as a rag for drying them. "Dew here."

Do what? "Excuse me?"

"I'm Dew. Short for Dewdrop."

"Oh. Nice name," Roz said automatically. "I'm Roz."

"When I got free of my husband, I changed it from Dolores. That means 'pain and suffering' in Spanish, I found out. And I'd had enough of that. But today I've got to watch out for those three." She pointed out a window, where a trio of young girls was attempting to build a tepee out of sticks. "They belong to Helaine and Randa. Went and conceived them themselves. With outside help, of course. Only God... excuse me, I have to learn to say 'Goddess,' I'm new at all this. Only She knows why. But they did and there they are.

"They could use looking after today, if you're up to it. Helaine and Randa are building a garden shed, even though we can't plant many vegetables for another month, and Hester is chopping wood for the stoves. Unless you have a strong urge to chop wood — now I know I shouldn't judge by appearances, but you don't look that strong to me — I'd appreciate it if you could look after those kids. God knows what they'll get into. Randa herself told me they only have girls. Sorry, I mean 'pre-womyn.' They said if they found out they were going to have a boy, they'd abort the fetus. I really can't believe that and certainly hope it's not true. I raised a half-dozen myself, and the girl was the only one that hasn't turned out OK."

"I have a boy myself," Roz ventured, "also alternatively conceived." She immediately realized she needn't have mentioned the mode of conception.

"Nothing wrong with it, if that's what you wanna do. Me, I had no choice. I was pregnant and married — in that order — at seventeen. Five kids before I was twenty-five. Took one more before I learned about contraception. One died, run over by the milkman's truck. The day those kids were grown, I left them and Ed. I'd waited twenty years, figured I'd done my duty to my nuclear family." She pronounced it "nucular." "The kitchen is still what I do best, so I'm the cook whenever I want. I don't mind. At least I'm not cooking for Ed. We rotate duties, so any time I don't want to cook, I can do something else."

Dew went back to the sink, attacked another pot. Roz moved in closer to converse over the running water. "I had to get away," she said, careful how much to reveal. Perhaps Dew's predicament wasn't that different from her own. "I knew of this place, called, and Hester said I could come."

"Glad you did. We can use the company." Dew abandoned her scouring.

Neither the long or short form of her name seemed appropriate; to Roz, she seemed more like a Dolores. But at least she was empowering herself, and evidently had a ways to go.

"Randa and Helaine, they're a couple, and don't much socialize with the rest of us. And there's only five of us, including you, plus the kids. Even though it says 'womyn,' you know, plural, the woman in question is Hester. She owns this place and she lets you know it."

"I see." Roz was glad to learn the inside stories on the others, yet had a sudden urge to get away from Dew. After all, she'd come here to be alone, get naked, and think things out. She could, however, have done without toddlers on the Land. "Why don't I go out and play with the children?" Maybe she'd find it easier being with girls than a boy. She refused to use the term "pre-womyn."

"They always need watching. Their names are Sesame, Saffron, and Sage." At least she hadn't finished with "Rosemary and Thyme." "They'll tell you who's who."

"Great. I'll go outside then. Nice to met you, Dew."

"Same here."

"Will anyone mind if I take my top off?"

"Might be a nip cool, but if you want to, it's fine by me."

"OK." Roz skittered out the kitchen door into the wide, wonderful Land.

The sun shone; the temperature hovered near sixty, just warm enough to doff her top. With a slight trepidation foreign to her, she did so and walked over to the children, not exactly toddlers. The youngest was perhaps three or four, the oldest maybe ten or eleven.

"Hi, there. My name's Roz. What's yours?" she said to the oldest.

"Randa's got bigger tits than you do."

"So does Helaine," said the middle child. "Helaine's my Mom. Randa's Sage's Mom."

"What's your name?"

"Sesame," she said proudly.

Roz tried to order the names in her head: Sage was the oldest, Sesame in the middle, leaving Saffron as the youngest. So she thought.

"I see you've built a tepee. How constructive. It's good to learn skills at an early age."

"We're gonna burn it down!" screamed Saffron.

"We are not!" Sage protested.

"We did yesterday. I think it's fun," said Sesame.

"The wood might make good kindling, if you save it," Roz suggested.

"What's kin'ling?" asked Saffron.

"Oh, shut up, barf-bag."

"We told Saffron she was gonna be yesterday's sacrifice in

the tepee, but soon as we tied her down, she barfed," said Sage. "But we do need a sacrifice for today." She studied her companions and as if searching out a suitable offering.

"Why don't you lay down under the tepee, what's-your-name? We won't burn you." The child eyed Roz as if a vulture contemplating carrion.

"Oh, I don't think that's a good idea," Roz said lightly. She feared that the child might not be joking.

"Oh, come on. It'll be fun," she said as though daring a peer to some delicious deviltry.

"I don't think your mothers would want you to."

"Let's get her!" In a second Sesame and Sage were pulling her by the arms. Sage punched her in the jaw, and Roz fell to the ground, dizzy. Sage sat on her stomach and Sesame straddled her legs.

"Let me up," Roz ordered, trying to stave off panic.

"That's good," Sesame screamed. "Go see what she's got in her pocket and we promise we won't tie you up any more, Saff."

Roz saw the youngest child approaching them in compliance, realized the error of taking off her top, with its now-dangerous contents in reach of the children.

"Oh, look! A lighter, and cigarettes too! I can smoke tonight!" Sage squealed in forbidden pleasure.

"I'm sure your mothers would disapprove. Now you girls let me up or I'll have to tell them."

"And we'll tell them you called us 'girls'."

Roz began to be fearful, waved her arms, hoping Dew would appear by the window. From her position on the ground she couldn't even see the lodge. "Goddamn it, let me up." She heaved, pushed and swatted, all to no avail.

"We'll tell our mothers you sweared too."

"And hit us!"

"Listen, you little brats...!" Now Roz struggled with all her forces. "Dew! Help, help! Anyone!"

"Quick, Saff, be a good sister and sit on her face."

"Dew! Dew! Help!" Roz screamed, as Saffron's bottom came squarely down on her nose and mouth. She figured as a last resort —not far off— she could bite her if she had to.

# 53

"Call him, Pepper. He's ill," Amelia said as they sat in her study, the day's work completed.

"Why bother? I'm sure he's screening his calls. He's never once picked up the phone and hasn't returned my messages."

"You can't stay here forever."

Amelia's tone was neither sweet nor harsh, but Pepper took it as a reminder that he was beginning to overstay his welcome or, even if he wasn't, a strong suggestion that he should return to Juan.

"Oh, sending me back to the homeless shelter, huh?" he joked. Indeed, he'd spent his first night there, talking to the homeless woman until she'd fallen asleep. Then, to his amazement, he'd fallen asleep. He'd arrived at Amelia's at six the next morning.

"You have a home to go to and someone who very much loves you and needs you right now. It's a disease. He has no control over it. If it were any other disease, you wouldn't desert your partner at the very time he needed you most, would you?"

"No, I guess not." They'd had variations of the same conversation several times before, though this time the words sank fully in, the end of a long trickle of reason, firmly resisted up until now.

"Then, call him. No, don't call him. Go back home. I never would have imagined you'd want to stay here so long."

"I like your company. I like not having to walk on egg shells, being able to say whatever I want, without worrying about your reaction. Unlike at home. You don't know what it's like to live with a bulimic, not to mention it's a terrible waste of food..."

"You've told me what it's like to live with a bulimic."

"I've had other issues to settle. To stay or not stay in Madison. Believe me, I've considered leaving, considered staying in Madison without Juan. But what would be the point? And finally, here, I've been able to grieve for Blake." He'd told Amelia the full truth of his involvement. "I couldn't function as a whole person in a relationship as long as I was in love with someone else, dead or alive."

"Do you think you're finally a whole person again?"

"I guess I am."

"Well, since you're not moving to San Francisco and you're

not going to stay here forever, why don't you go home tonight after dinner? I'll start making it soon."

"All right. I'll go, but on one condition. You have to let me make dinner."

❦

Juan got up to leave the ACT UP meeting, unsure if he was glad or disappointed that Pepper hadn't been there. One prisoner — or was it two? — hadn't received proper care, had died at Waupun of AIDS-related complications; the governor was not enacting his HIV Advisory Council's recommendations; demos were being planned for summer and fall. The meeting had rather bored Juan, but it had taken his mind off Pepper.

"Hey. How ya doin'?"

He cast his eyes down to the speaker and recognized Beth Yarmolinsky.

"I was Roz's treasurer," she reminded him. He knew this, and remembered hearing Roz complain about her more than once during the campaign.

"Sure, I remember you."

They went down the stairs and out into the street. The May evening called for jackets. A few blocks away, the illuminated Capitol towered above them.

"Bummer about Roz losin' the election."

Juan nodded in polite agreement, not about to voice his own or Irv's thoughts on the matter.

"How is she these days? Haven't seen her in a while."

"Oh, she's... gone on a sort of post-election escape." None of them knew where she was and Irv was growing more frantic by the day. At least Juan knew — for better or worse — where Pepper had gone.

"Me, that's what I need, an escape. Hey, mind if I have one of those? I quit, but whenever someone lights up around me I get the urge." Juan extended his ultra-lights and cupped the lighter around her cigarette. "Thanks. You've probably seen me with Verla. She was at Roz's party too. She was the one who took me to my first ACT UP meeting."

"Long blonde hair?"

"Yeah, that's her, or was her. Haven't been sleepin' together lately. She dropped a major bomb on me in one of the women's workshops at 'Out & About.' Just 'cause I don't get into dildoes, now she wants to sleep with half the dykes in Madison. She's probably screwin' up a storm right now. She hardly ever used to miss an ACT UP meeting. I guess for her *fucking* has become more important than *fighting AIDS*."

"Too bad you're not getting along," Juan offered, feeling obliged to respond.

"What are these cigarettes?"

"Hey, don't worry. They're not a Philip Morris brand."

"I meant the taste. Sorry, but these cowboy killers of yours got none."

"Want a ride home?" Juan asked, having borrowed Irv's pickup for the evening. "You live on the near-east side, right?"

"Where else is there?"

"Then I'll drive you."

"I was gonna take a bus. Not safe to walk in the daytime, let alone at night. Almost got raped in broad daylight a few weeks ago."

Juan was still focusing on the word "rape" when she asked, "You and your boyfriend into dildoes?"

"Uh, we're not sleeping together at the moment either."

"Personally, I don't see how we need 'em," she said, obviously embroiled in her own domestic drama and oblivious to all else. "I mean, what's wrong with our natural parts? 'Course, you guys don't have the same problems in that area, do you? I mean, I'm not talking about small penises or anything..." She stopped, sighed and stared in awe at her surroundings, as though she'd landed in Patagonia or ancient Egypt. "Sorry. Guess I got off track."

Juan guided her around the corner, sensed hurt behind all her conversational bluster. If she usually wore her heart on her sleeve, it had now slid from the cuff to her fingertips.

"You know, I'm thinkin'. With Verla out screwin' away, what'd be the best revenge?"

Juan looked at her blankly, no idea what she could have in mind. "Sleeping with another woman?" he said before realizing the stupidity of his answer. But in his condition, with Pepper gone, he could be excused. He wondered if Pepper had slept with another man since he'd left.

"Close. I was thinkin' of sleeping with a man. That way she can't compete. I figure, hell, she wants to play with dildoes, why not go for the real thing? I mean, I never did slept with a guy before, don't know what it'd be like. Did you guys ever have sex with a woman?"

"Not Pepper and I at the same time," he evaded. "Here, get in." He opened the passenger door, let her hop in.

"Maybe you should drop me off at the Cardinal instead, where there are some men."

"Are you sure that's really what you want to do?" Juan fastened his seatbelt, then pulled out into traffic and began to skirt the Capitol Square. "Doing it on the spur of the moment, for revenge? If you did it, what would you do, take him home and parade him in front of her?" Maybe that's what he should do to get Pepper to come home. Or maybe not. And, he realized, he couldn't do it, as Pepper was *not* at home.

"Hey, why not?"

Juan added two more cents: "Is that what you really want? To have sex with some horny straight guy who probably wouldn't even care about you or want to wear a condom? Not to mention, you might not even like it."

From East Doty Street he turned onto King, then East Wilson; the Cardinal stood across the street. Juan stopped the truck in a bus stop zone. "You really don't want to do this, do you?" he said, taken aback by his adamancy.

Uncertain silence. "No!" she finally wailed, and sobs started to come. "I just want Verla back. Out of the arms of another woman. That's all I want." The sobs now bordered on hysterical and he put a hand on Beth's shoulder.

"I think you could stand some cheering up or a chance to let it out. Do you want to go somewhere for a drink? I could use some cheering up too." Maybe the two of them could actually commiserate.

"Let's go, then. Anywhere but Ho Chi's."

"Fine." Juan stepped on the gas, seeing in the rearview mirror a bus rounding the corner. "Where to?"

"How about the Bull Dog? Always wanted to go there. I don't feel like seein' any women." Her tears began to ebb.

Juan stifled a groan; the Bull Dog was the last place he wanted to go.

❧

Women populated the Bull Dog occasionally and he hoped, for his own sake, that Beth wouldn't be the only one there. The large U-shaped bar tonight held perhaps twenty people, every single one of them male, except Beth. None of the males was Pepper.

"This is it?" She sounded incredulous or disappointed.

"I'll get us drinks. What would you like?"

"Oh, a burgundy." She followed him up to the edge of the bar and he ordered for them both. "I always thought this place would be good and wild. Whips, chains, slings, you know."

"This is about it." Juan gestured toward pictures of leathermen on the walls, not about to inform her of the existence of the back bar.

"Is it true there's a back *room* here?"

"Yeah. But it's a *bar*. And no one talks back there. I thought you wanted to talk." He was not going to take her to the back bar under any circumstances.

"I never saw two guys do it before."

"Believe me, no one 'does it' in the back bar. You're in Madison, not Chicago, New York, New Orleans or San Francisco."

"That's not what I heard."

"Perhaps you had a bad informant. Here." He handed a glass of burgundy to her and picked up his own vodka and tonic. Behind the bar he saw a few snacks, but was not going to gorge himself in public. Bars. he realized, were a good place to avoid food.

Beth took a sip, opened her mouth as though to speak, but nothing came out.

Juan himself was debating what to say when the glass almost fell from her hand and she broke into tears again. Nervously, he glanced at her, then around the bar, to see who was watching. He let his hand graze her shoulder. The bartender stared at them, clearly displeased. It was bad enough that he'd brought a woman into the usually all-male domain, but now she was making a scene. "It'll be all right."

"No, it won't!" Beth managed through tears. A drop of burgundy rolled down her chin. "Verla doesn't want me! Nobody wants me! I can't even keep a job. I'll never graduate. I don't even have a reason to live!" All of this she more or less announced to the whole bar, successfully combating the music.

"It can't be that bad."

"It can too, and it is!" She had yet to lower her voice or to stem the tide of her tears.

"You maybe should go to the ladies' room." When she didn't move, he took her by the elbow. "After you pull yourself together in there, everything will be all right." As soon as he said this, he knew it was a moronic comment.

She let herself be led away from the bar, her noisy sobs still not diminishing. He couldn't remember where the ladies' room was. In fact, he began to doubt that the Bull Dog even had one.

Juan had slowly cleared the house of all tempting food. Gone were the potato chips, tortilla chips, salsa, popcorn, peanuts, cashews, cheese, olives — in short, anything to tempt his salt tooth. All except a small bag of Fritos he had hidden away sealed inside two Ziploc bags now floating on top the water in the toilet tank. He'd put it there just to prove he could resist one little temptation, or for an emergency, in case he couldn't.

He'd had to resort to buying frozen broccoli, since the garden space no longer permitted cultivation of such space-consuming vegetables. A front yard garden would be aesthetically incorrect on this posh block, posher than Willy Street's best, though Irv would probably agree to it if Juan asked him. Before tonight's ACT UP meeting, he'd thawed and heated two packages of the broccoli, then salted, peppered, and smeared a dollop of fat-free margarine on it. It was an adequately sized, healthy meal, but the fat-free margarine, not surprisingly, had refused to melt. The broccoli had not been satisfying. He was neither hungry nor full; he simply wanted to eat something tastier.

He now wandered around, restless, tried to put Beth's scene out of his mind, tried to concentrate on SPELL. He'd all but given up on it; no one could spell correctly, in English or Spanish or probably any other written language.

Determined not to succumb to the Fritos, he opened the refrigerator to view the contents: fat-free cottage cheese, a withered kosher pickle, a rotting apple, leftover rice. None of it appealed. He sat down on the floor and opened the vegetable crisper, pawed through the contents, and settled on a bag of snow peas. He put one in his mouth and chewed. Not bad. He set about consuming the bag's contents, one pod at a time, remaining on the floor in front of the open refrigerator.

He heard the bedroom door open, and his heart leapt, but he continued, methodically, to eat the peas.

"What are you doing, Juan?" Pepper spoke in a controlled voice.

"I'm eating snow peas."

"Are you sure you're all right?"

"I'm fine," he said, and went back to the peas.

"Can I take you into the bedroom?"

"I don't want to have sex now. I'm eating snow peas."

"I didn't mean for sex. To talk. In the living room. Wherever. You're very ill."

"I suppose I am, but I want to finish eating my peas."

"I came back because I was convinced we could talk rationally about this, and whatever else you think we might need to."

Juan looked up sluggishly at him, as he munched away, then swallowed. "OK. Now I can talk. You missed the ACT UP meeting tonight. Afterward I ran into Beth, Roz's treasurer, whose lover's left her. She wanted to go to the Bull Dog for a drink, so, reluctantly I took her, but she fell apart, made a big scene, and when I finally found the women's bathroom, she locked herself in for forty-five minutes, irritating patrons interested in inhabiting those premises for purposes, I presume, of sex or drugs. They complained to the staff, one of whom beat on the door and had to call the manager to get her to come out. Finally she did, I dropped her off at home, and came back here."

"Sorry to hear all that. I'm sure that's just what you didn't need. But I meant I wanted to talk about us, you, or even me."

"Did you come back only to talk, to get more stuff, or are you staying?" Juan asked, having filled his mouth again. The peas were quite edible, the bag perhaps now two-thirds gone.

"That depends on you. You *know* you have to get help."

"I'm not going to therapy, though I'll seek help privately if my insurance covers it. And I'm eating, *not bingeing*, right now, if you'll excuse me."

"Did you eat dinner?"

"I did, but it wasn't satisfying. If you've come to stay, I'll get help, OK? I mean, I can probably even stop this by myself."

The heels of Pepper's boots moved firmly away, back to the bedroom or bathroom, as Juan continued to eat the snow peas until the bag was empty. He remained on the floor, staring blankly into the refrigerator.

Finally, he struggled to stand up, closed the refrigerator door and figured he'd better go find Pepper before he left again. He admitted that his eating disorder was what this had been all about. The question remained: Could he admit it to Pepper?

# 54

It was Roz's sixth day on the Land and she was determined to stick it out for all seven.

Today she and Dew were relegated to the kitchen and childcare. She knew they'd have their hands full.

The better to keep a watch on the kids, they decided to have them help in the kitchen. Saffron, the least dangerous and, in the kitchen, the most useless of the three, was allowed to watch. Sesame was to wash the morning dishes, and Sage to peel potatoes, which had been grown on the Land, kept in a cellar from last year's harvest. Before she'd finished peeling the first one, she announced, "I'm gonna make French fries."

Dew cast her a stern glance: "Those potatoes are for tonight's stew."

"Yuck!" said Saffron.

"Randa lets us make French fries," said Sage.

"I'm sure she does," said Dew, obviously in possession of better parenting skills than Roz. "But not on the Land."

"And what's more, they're greasy and unhealthy," Roz put in, as much to counter the kid as anything. Since they had no fresh fruit or vegetables, meals usually consisted of potato-based stews and an ample amount of Wisconsin cheese. No wonder Helaine and Randa were "womyn of size," heavily into the Fat Liberation Movement.

"I don't care. I'm gonna make French fries," Sage repeated, and threw her potato into the sink. Her aim was on target, splattering suds and water onto Sesame's face and sprinkling Roz's arm.

"Sage, that was totally uncalled for." Dew bent down to retrieve the potato, now soggy if not mashed. "If you do that again, I'm going to have to tell your mothers."

"Go ahead."

"They won't believe you!" said Sesame, drying herself off.

"Yeah," Saffron seconded.

"They told us that you..." Sage motioned toward Roz. "...are anti-social and a poor role model."

Roz fumed silently, wondering if the child was indeed telling the truth.

After the first day, she'd put her top back on, having found no pleasure in nudism, what with the children ridiculing her breasts and their mothers ogling them, alternately with disdain and a vague lust, as if she might do for a cheap, desperate roll in the hay. After she'd bitten Saffron's backside and Dew had rescued her, it was hard to tell if Hester, Helaine and Randa were more displeased with Roz or the children. Only Dew's testimony had saved her and the three womyn had finally decided that the three pre-womyn be sentenced to one day's "hard labor," to consist of picking up brush in a remote corner of the Land and separating it from suitable wood to be dried for kindling. Roz had herself received a sharp rebuke for not leaving her lighter and cigarettes in her cabin. She wondered why the older two children weren't attending school. If their behavior here served as an indication, they'd no doubt been expelled. "Relaxation" was unplanned, if not nonexistent. By the time they'd finished the evening meal, Roz had little energy left except to go to bed. It was like a miniature Womyn's Music Festival, without the music or workshops.

"I'm sure they didn't say Roz was a poor role model," Dew countered.

"Did too! And they said your food sucked!"

Now Dew appeared dumbstruck, perhaps even wounded. "If it weren't for me, you girls wouldn't be eating!"

"She called us 'girls'!" Sesame screamed with glee. Roz saw that Saffron now appeared to be bathing herself in the sink. Sage had balled up potatoes in both fists.

"I'm sorry. I mean 'pre-womyn'," said Dew.

"No she doesn't!" Roz exploded. "She means goddamned misbehaved brats from hell!"

"You can't call us that!"

"Sage, give me those potatoes! Now!" Roz bellowed. Sage promptly threw one, nicking Roz in the hip. She aimed the other at Dew's backside and hit her squarely. Sesame romped around the room, squealing merrily. From the sink, Saffron flung soap suds in all directions.

Roz lunged at Sage, grabbed her and, as the child squirmed, began slapping her behind.

"Roz is right!" yelled Dew. "You're all the worst little monsters I ever saw in my life!" She began to chase Sesame around the kitchen; Roz continued to swat at Sage as the child kicked her.

"What's going on here?" They turned to the door, fell silent, as they saw Helaine, backed up by Randa.

"I'm sorry," said Dew, composing herself. "But your children are out of control."

"We'll see who's out of control."

In silence the womyn and children ate lunch, consisting of yesterday's leftovers. Afterward, Hester, Helaine and Randa held their own version of court. The self-appointed judges heard Roz's, then Dew's corroborating version of events; next, all three children, the older two lying outrageously, were permitted to have the last word. The judges stepped into the kitchen to confer and left the accused parties on opposite sides of a long, institutional dining table. After a few minutes, they reappeared to announce their verdict.

"This is all unfortunate," Hester began. "While we believe you and Roz, we also think that the children's words, perhaps a little exaggerated, have some merit." This angered Roz, but didn't astonish her.

"Roz, you and the children just don't get along. They incite you, I'm aware, but you make the mistake of inciting them back. Then we have warfare on our hands. We've never had that with any of the other womyn, even Dew. Counting the children, there are only eight of us here and, in any case, the idea is not for us to avoid each other. So Roz, I'm sticking by my promise to let you stay the whole week, but I do think you should leave tomorrow. Dew, will you just try to do your best? Sage, Sesame, and Saffron, you'll be supervised by one of your mothers this afternoon and be responsible for the evening meal. And, if it's not done right, you'll do it every morning, noon and night until it is. Roz and Dew, you can have the afternoon off."

The children smiled smugly at Roz. She felt like taking a willow switch to the three of them, as well as to their mothers' ample behinds.

"They're always like that. Their kids can do no wrong. And Hester always supports them," Dew said, as they roamed to one of the far reaches of the nearly flat Land, rocky in places, clumped with trees in others.

Dayne seemed tame and easy in comparison; Roz was beginning to miss him. The day was bright, but it had yet to revive her spirits. "I was going to leave tomorrow anyway." She felt like a pariah, cast out to the elements. "How can you put up with it all?"

"Oh, I've gotten used to it. I'm just striving to be strong and independent and I ended up here. There are no expenses and I don't have many skills to support myself. Sure, I could get a job as a cook, but I don't want to do that the rest of my life, even if it's what I usually do here. I guess I'm growing little by little, and will learn to do other things, and get back eventually to the regular world. They say there's a strong, supportive community in the Twin Cities."

"You'd probably like it there."

"Yeah," Dew said, scratching her back and tilting her blonde head toward the luscious sun. Roz followed her example. "Hey, wanna take off our tops?"

"Sure." The idea sounded good to Roz. She might as well spend one hassle-free afternoon bared to the sun.

Dew pulled her T-shirt over her head, unhooked her bra, and let it fall away. Large, firm breasts were released to the sun and air. Roz took off her own T-shirt, looked at her own breasts —neither large nor firm— and put it down on a rock.

"Good idea." Dew placed her clothing next to Roz's.

"Let's lie down? I don't think it's damp anymore."

Roz touched the ground, stretched out, and Dew lay down beside her.

"Oh, this is what I've longed for," Dew purred. "Freedom and good company and sun. The winters up here are pretty rough."

"I can imagine." Roz almost flinched at Dew's words; She hadn't imagined that they spent the whole winter here.

"It gets a little lonely, but other womyn'll be coming for the summer. I made one good friend last summer, but I'm afraid she won't be coming back."

"Too bad."

"Yeah," Dew said longingly.

Reality intruded on Roz's idyll. Tomorrow she'd be back in Madison, back to Dayne and Irv. Compared to the scene at the lodge, it sounded like paradise, but Roz knew it would be a grind of its own, far removed from the pastoral surroundings of the moment.

Dew rolled over on her side, as if pondering the tiny mounds that constituted Roz's breasts. After a second, she perched her chin on an elbow and faced Roz. "This is so relaxing."

"Especially after the kangaroo court up there," Roz said, as Dew spoke simultaneously, something about "being with womyn." Roz could appreciate the desire for all-female cama-raderie.

"Roz, can I touch you?"

"Pardon?" Had she heard right?

"Oh, I'm sorry," Dew said meekly. "I asked if it would be all right if... I touched you."

Oh God, thought Roz. She'd clearly misread all the signals. She considered the idea for a few quick seconds, but no. The setting was right, Dew was attractive and pleasant, but no. If she'd ever thought she had any lingering lesbian desire, she was wrong. And even if she did, it would be wrong to hurt a woman like Dew.

She forced herself to meet her eyes. Dew still looked at her, hopefully or helplessly.

"I'm sorry. It wouldn't be right. I have to leave tomorrow. Not that it..." She was struggling for words and the right ones didn't seem to exist. "Not that it... couldn't be 'right,' but I'm afraid..." Her final words, "to hurt you," dissolved.

"Oh, that's all right." Dew sounded more comforting for Roz's sake than stung by the rejection. "I was afraid the first time too."

Roz didn't bother to counter her, and Dew went on: "Some day you'll find the right woman."

"And some day you will too. I'm sure of it." She squeezed Dew's hand, trying to impart strength. A tear on Roz's cheek glistened in the sun.

# 55

"Models, beauty queens, actresses, Karen Carpenter, I don't know. And now, here I am living with someone who has it. His doctor wouldn't even believe him and Juan doesn't know where to turn."

"Bummer," Evan said.

"Cissy never... did she? Don't get me wrong, she's just got that svelte, sort of tall, thin, could-have-been-a-model look to her."

"Cissy? I don't know her whole past. But she exercises, eats healthy, but I can't imagine..."

Pepper stared at "Alexa," the statue with a spiral whisk for her head and saw-toothed rotary disks for a body that graced the little park at Jenifer and Willy streets where they were sitting. "Alexa" herself seemed to suffer from some eating disorder, and appeared daunting and phantasmal by night. Pepper imagined her as Juan's body underneath his flesh — nothing but bones — and the thought made him squeamish. Perhaps getting stoned hadn't been such a good idea.

"Hey, man? You still with me?" Evan jarred him out of his reverie.

"Ah, just a little out of it. I don't know what to do about Juan. He's got to get help. I don't know if I can go on living with him like this." In frustration, he kicked one of the feet of the wrought iron bench on which he and Evan had perched themselves. "It's like, he admits there's a problem, but he doesn't *do* anything about it."

"Must be hard," Evan said, distant, as though preoccupied by worries of his own.

"Hey, is something wrong? Is there something you want to talk about? I didn't mean to get heavy about Juan's bulimia. I just needed to talk about it to someone. What's up with you?"

"Nothing new," Evan said, failing to keep weariness at bay. "Just Todd. Suspended again. Set a library book on fire and put it through the return slot. The librarian got scared, pulled the fire alarm, and sent the whole school out into a driving rainstorm."

"Too bad."

"And Geo... I mean, the carpenter finished building the tree house I started for the kids. And Danielle — she's only six years old, seven next month — went in the tree house with three boys from the first grade. It's not what you think, at least I don't think they did any... exploration. I rather wish they had, instead of making a fire. Anne saw flames and called the fire department. Burned a hole in the floor and scorched the roof. At least no one was hurt."

"Whoa!" Pepper found himself saying. "That's wild! Two kids, two fires." He realized after the fact that this perhaps was not the best response. "I mean, I'm sorry about it all..."

"Yeah, it's like I've got a recessive pyromaniac gene in my blood and passed it on to both of them," Evan said in disgust.

"A pyromaniac gene. Interesting concept."

"It's not a concept, it's reality, and it sucks. There's no way Cissy..."

"Cissy, what?"

"Never mind. Sorry about Juan's bulimia. I think we should both go get stoned."

"I already am."

"Then let me join you."

"Be my guest. I've got some with me."

Evan scuffed his heels on the bricks and pointed. "Weird fucking statue, don't you think?"

"No weirder than the neighborhood."

"And no weirder than our lives right now."

"Remember, you can be Ginger's associate chair," Evan joked the next day. Ginger had gone so far as to tempt Cissy with this to make sure she got her vote. But unless she got tenure, the point was moot.

"Sure. I'm certain she offered it to Nick too if he'd drop out of the race."

"This is a tough one, Cissy. If we vote for her and she wins, she could make our lives hell."

"And," Cissy completed, "if we don't vote for her and she figures it out, she'll make our lives hell whether she wins or not."

"All we can do is hope she can't figure out how we voted."

"I'm afraid you're right."

Cissy hoped that no one abstained, which could cause a tie. The dean was capable of putting the depleted department into receivership and bringing an outside chair in to manage them. On second thought, maybe that was exactly what they needed. The department had not one suitable candidate for chair, except maybe Evan, who, not officially tenured, remained ineligible.

Museum Studies was without a doubt the most notorious department in the College of Fine Arts. A fact that would not help when the dean considered her tenure. What good could a unanimous vote in her favor by a group of lunatics and liars possibly do?

When Evan appeared at her office door, she was grading a final paper that, miraculously, had arrived ten days early. Now it hinted at plagiarism.

Cissy kissed marijuana breath. "I smell that you've prepared for the meeting." In the past he'd popped a Valium or, when he still drank, taken a coffee mug of Canadian Club to meetings. Now he simply smoked a joint beforehand outside on Muir Knoll. Since the university had become smoke-free, Rickover had been sniffing out secret cigarette smokers puffing behind their closed doors throughout the whole building.

"Look. Ev, do you think this paper was plagiarized? This student couldn't have written this, but I don't know where he could have gotten it from."

Evan gazed at the paper, and Cissy faced the hallway. A gangly young man appeared, looking lost and wearing a T-shirt that read "Nobody Knows I'm a Lesbian," then walked on. Cissy glanced back at Evan, still studying the paper, and realized the folly of having him pin down plagiarism in a course he didn't teach, from a student he didn't know, and when he was stoned.

A tap came at the door and Ginger breezed in. Cissy and Evan both did a double take. It was eighty degrees and she'd worn a red velvet dress embroidered in gold. All she lacked was a tiara. She was probably waiting to put it on when she assumed the departmental throne.

"Don't say anything. I know I've overdone it. This is what can happen when you do six lines in the morning before you get dressed for work." She looked down at her attire, mournfully eyed her cleavage, for once not set off by a pendant. "I forgot my necklace!" she bawled, as though this were her main distress.

Cissy didn't know whether to laugh or cry, tried to refrain from both. Ginger could certainly be pathetic, in her own unique, obnoxious way.

"It'll be all right, Ging." Evan spoke as if she were woebegone and needed comfort.

"Of course it will." Her mood swung back to the familiar. "I've got the election won, by at least five to two. And if Vance votes for me, six to one."

Cissy knew this spelled trouble.

Rickover convened the meeting, the last of his tenure. As secretary, Ginger sat beside him, in front of a new lap-top computer, the successor to the typewriter Rickover had once demanded when he was secretary, more efficiently to record the minutes. Cissy imagined that next year — if by chance she got tenure — she herself would be railroaded into the unwanted job.

"Let's get through with this," Rickover began, and had everyone read over the minutes Ginger had taken at the last meeting. They dispatched with routine business, then did a final perusal of next fall's scant course offerings. The dean had demanded budget cuts and since the department didn't have the staff to cover its usual advanced courses, all was working out adequately, in its own perverse academic way. They had to give her tenure, Cissy thought, otherwise there'd be no one to teach anything, what with Rothschild's retirement, Rickover's and Sandra's resignations, Blake's death, and a dean who had not yet authorized fall replacements. Perhaps the dean was behind it all, eliminating the faculty one by one, with Cissy as the next victim, before he closed down the whole department. She again remembered the dream in which Rickover had announced as much to her.

She heard Rickover call for a motion to end the "open" departmental committee and another to go into "closed" session.

"All right. First and only item in closed session is the result of the vote for next year's acting chair. I trust professors Rothschild and Rutledge have brought the ballots."

"We have," Rothschild said, clearly bored. "Do you want us to read the votes one by one, or just give you the totals?"

"Totals will do."

Ginger turned her head to one side, as though to affect a casual pose. Then suddenly she turned, eyes bugged, as if ready to leap into a flying assault to steal or alter the result, if not in her favor.

"The result of the vote for acting chair, academic year 1991-1992, for the Department of Museum Studies...," Rothschild prefaced. Cissy enjoyed the suspense as little as Ginger. "Certified and verified," he went on, now sarcastically, toying with them, his last act before retirement, "by Professor Rutledge and myself are as follows..." He paused, and Ginger let out an irritated pant, audible to all. Cissy stole a glance at Nick, cool as ice.

"Are you sure you want the vote tally?" Rutledge interrupted. "It's simpler just to announce who won."

"I want numbers!" Ginger screamed, as though demanding blood.

"Fine," said Rothschild. "Nick Wren, six. Ginger Carter, one."

A stunned, momentary silence followed as eyes flitted cautiously around the room, afraid to catch Ginger's. Then she stood up, defiant. "Let me see that! Six to one! Impossible!" She rushed over to the two of them, grabbed the ballots from Rothschild's hands. She went through them one by one and threw them on the floor.

Cissy knew what they all knew: Ginger's only vote was her own. She tried to avoid panicking, now that Ginger had discovered her and Evan's "disloyalty." Only with reservations had they voted for Nick in such a no-win situation.

"I'll sue the lot of you. You can't deny a black woman a promotion because of her gender and race. Don't you tell me I haven't been discriminated against! This is the absolute last straw! I ought to leave this department and leave all of you with four or five classes to teach next fall, you traitorous sons of bitches!" Now she cast homicidal eyes at Evan and Cissy, then slowly turned them on everyone else. "We'll just see who has the last word! I'll see all you motherfuckers in court!"

"You're quite out of order, not to mention control," Rickover said coolly, under the circumstances. "And you won't see me in court either, if you ever see anyone." It seemed that Rickover had actually enjoyed the spectacle.

Ginger got up, evidently ready to give the door a theatrical slam, when she wobbled on one heel, tipped over and fell flat on her derrière. Cissy smothered a smile as barely restrained laughter came from everywhere. For some seconds she didn't move; Cissy began to wonder if she was injured. She and Evan got up and went over to her, others following.

"Don't one of you lay a fucking hand on me," she snarled, coming to life.

"I don't think Ginger took any minutes today."

"Hardly necessary," said Evan. "I don't think this is a meeting anyone's likely to forget."

# 56

*Why I Want to Die*
Beth Yarmolinsky
Sociology 473
Death and Dying
Professor Anderson

*On April 15, I was unjustly fired from my job as a student worker in the Department of Museum Studies. The Chair verbally abused me, constantly demeaned and insulted me, as did the Associate Chair. In the end he fired me because of my politics. Professors in positions of power sure can be jerks. (If you're Chair of your department or anything, sorry, I'm sure you're the exception.)*

*Later that day I was harassed by two men while at a public beach. They became verbally abusive and wanted to rape me. By the great majority of men, women are viewed as sex objects. (I'm sure you're one of the exceptions and would never sleep with your students.)*

*Last fall I led a boycott of Ho Chi Minh's Bar and Restaurant. The boycott was successful, but I lost my job over it. Then I had a series of humiliating jobs that emotionally damaged me. During the course of my work I was bitten by a rabid cat and ended up spending a week in University Hospital and had to have a series of painful rabies shots. I've lost about 10% of the use of two of my right hand fingers, ruining my dream of a career as a concert pianist. On the other job, as treasurer for a candidate for city council, an opposing candidate verbally abused and physically attacked me, with the result that my employer, the candidate, tried to fire me over the bad publicity. Now I have no job.*

*I'll never graduate from the University. I've been going part-time for so many years. I can only go on so long.*

*Women, especially lesbian women, will never have an equal place in this world.*

*My partner, whom I rescued five years ago from alcoholism, a religious cult and the closet (for which she ought to thank me), announced in a workshop in front of a large group of women that she wants to sleep with someone else. Since then we have not reconciled and sleep separately. I have had to conclude that she is an ungrateful, egocentric bitch. She goes about her routine like nothing has happened. Either she loves me or she doesn't. I have had to conclude that it's the latter. She has torn my heart apart and I don't think it can ever be repaired. My only refuge from all this is alcohol (only a little, which can be fun for a while, but you can only be high for so long and then reality will slap you with its big, brutal hand).*

*I have been slapped around enough.*

*The books I have read in this course, and surprisingly during this turbulent semester I have read all of them, have made me realize that dying is not only natural, but it's not nearly as bad as it's cracked up to be. I'm ready and my death should be a fitting end to this course.*

*P.S. Pass me if you want to. I guess it really doesn't matter.*

### I Can't Cope
### Beth Yarmolinsky
### AIDS and Ethics
### Social Work 413
### Professor Jansen

*Last fall, my partner and I became heavily involved in ACT UP. It led to me leading a boycott of the bar/restaurant where I worked because they supported Miller Beer and Philip Morris cigarettes. (I'm sure you know about Jesse Helms and the boycott, even though I never got a chance to talk about it in class.) Anyway, the boycott was successful but I lost my job. So you see, through ACT UP and the boycott, I was doing ethical things about AIDS, even if it didn't show in class.*

*During this semester, two ACT UP members have died. (Well, maybe three, but I didn't know them all.) I can't cope. If I get involved more, I will simply make more friends and acquaintances who will die an early death from AIDS related complications. Then I won't be able to cope again. I know this is a defeatist attitude, but I am defeated.*

*Dying an AIDS death is more noble than the one I will choose, though I believe that suicide, for an AIDS patient, any patient with a terminal illness, or anyone else who decides they want to end their own life, is an ethically justifiable decision and I will die "A Death of My Own."*

*For additional reasons why I can't cope, please contact Professor Anderson, Sociology 473 (Death and Dying) and see what I wrote for that class. Sorry this paper is so short, but I already spilled my guts in that one.*

Beth put the two papers through the spellchecker, printed them up, took the bus to campus and delivered them. Never had she turned her final papers in so early; classes had ended, but the papers were not due for several more days.

Verla had gotten up early to teach and left a note saying that she had plans for the evening and would be home late. Well, fine. Fuck her. Or let someone else fuck her. Or let her fuck herself. Better yet, let her be doomed to a totally fuckless life.

Verla's upcoming absence made today the right day.

Beth again debated the idea of sleeping with a man — this time not just for revenge. It was still something she thought she might like to do just once for the experience of it. The Pub had guys ogling you out the window at all times of day, and that was only one of several places.

At the Credit Union she stopped and took out her meager savings, not bothering to close the account, but simply leaving the minimum balance. She walked up State Street and surveyed the guys behind The Pub's plate-glass window. Ugly, she concluded, now not really wanting to risk the chance of being humiliated by another member of the patriarchy. She'd simply have to die a heterosexual virgin.

She decided to walk all the way home. State Street seemed lackluster: no bag ladies, no punkers, not even a hot lesbian cop — only kids on rollerblades. She entered the Capitol one last time and went up to the platform of the dome to say good-bye to Madison. When she stepped outside, thunderclouds were rolling in from the west.

It all seemed quite appropriate. To die on a Monday in May in the rain. She hadn't even left the Isthmus — let alone Madison — in... Was it months or maybe years?

She looked over the Isthmus, first to the northwest, at unappealing church steeples. Then to the west, at State Street, which, oddly, almost seemed to zigzag. And to the northeast, at big old Lake Mendota. She circled over to the north: smokestacks spewing and more steeples. The glass bank and an ugly office building blocked the view of her own neighborhood. She'd seen enough.

She walked down King Street — good-bye Café Europa, good-bye Majestic Theatre. East Wilson Street — good-bye Cardinal Bar. Willy Street — good-bye El Charro. She jaywalked across the street to Machinery Row and the Fauerbach Condominiums and was almost run down by two speeding bicyclists, who had veered out of their half of the path. Hell, it might not have been a bad way to go, but she didn't really want to have her death on anyone else's conscience. Composure regained, she continued her final sentimental walk down Willy Street and, by the time she reached Ingersoll, it was indeed raining. She looked at Cissy and Evan's house, rounded the corner to where she and Lou had once lived, then went over to Orton Park for a final visit to the Gay Liberation statue. Shit, they'd already taken it down and sent it on to New York.

You win some, you lose some.

Back on Willy Street, she went into the neighborhood liquor store to choose her poisons. Her scant savings got her two bottles of cheap burgundy, one of vodka, and —what the hell?— a Drambuie. She might as well go out with at least a shred of style. She asked for a pack of Marlboro Lights before catching herself. "Camel Lights," she corrected, then paid. Schlepping her purchases in a backpack flung over her shoulder, she crossed the street, bade adieu to the Co-op, walked down to Ho Chi Minh's and spat at its door. Five blocks later she was drenched and at home.

After changing into dry clothes, she opened the burgundy, poured herself a tumbler, and sat down in the kitchen. She thought about a will, knew something about writing a holographic one from her AIDS and Ethics class. Having pulled out a sheet of paper, she began to compose: "To Verla McSurely, I hereby bequeath the balance of my savings account at the UW Credit Union." There, that ought to serve her right. Five dollars, it was all she was worth, on a good day. "The rest of my worldly possessions," she proceeded to enumerate the important ones, "I leave to persons with AIDS." Then she added, after signing it and dating it, "P.S. If Verla McSurely fails to take good care of my six cats, she shall be disiniherited."

She finished off her burgundy, poured another and lit a Camel. What else to take care of? She contemplated the idea of an obituary. Having gone this far, she might as well leave the world in orderly fashion. While thinking, she finished off the second tumbler, and poured more in. The alternative newspapers didn't regularly print obituaries unless you were a big-name activist, so *The Cap Times* and *State Journal* would just have to do. At least you could write whatever you wanted in their paid obituaries. She began to write:

*Beth Yarmolinsky, age 23, died Monday, May 13, 1991, at her home in Madison, of a drug overdose, caused by a broken heart. She was born August 18, 1967, in Skokie, Illinois, moved to Madison in*

*1985, and was pursuing a major in Social Work at UW at the time of her death. She was manager of the once politically correct Ho Chi Minh's for almost three years. She was active in ACT UP of Madison, Yikes Dykes!, and various lesbian/gay organizations. She is survived and will be sadly missed by her six cats: Brooklyn, Skokie, Wilmette (Willy), Lady, Miami (Mammy), and Jenifer. Donations in her name may be made to ACT UP of Madison or Yikes Dykes!*

She stared at what she had written, not displeased. The words began to blur slightly. She thought of adding something about funeral arrangements or a memorial service, but dismissed the notion. If anybody wanted to organize one, let them. Getting up from the table, pleasantly woozy, she sought out an envelope on her desk, inserted the obituary and her remaining cash in it. She went back and got her will, sealed it, looked up the address of the newspaper and copied it on the envelope. Unable to find a twenty-nine-cent stamp, she fumbled through her desk, coming up with various small denominations totaling twenty-eight, and plastered them on. There, she'd taken care of her business in this world as well as she could.

Now it was time to get more serious. She poured a glass of vodka on the rocks and guzzled it, then decided to enjoy a coffee cup — they had no snifters — of Drambuie. Carrying it around the house, she found Jenny, Willy and Skokie, and petted them good-bye, determined to remain unsentimental. In the kitchen she opened a can of salmon — certainly unhealthy but reserved for special occasions — for the cats. The noise produced the three cats she'd just taken leave of, plus Mammy and Lady. She petted them, but they ignored her, eager for this unexpected afternoon feeding.

"Damned cats," she muttered. "Brooklyn! Brookie! Here, kitty, kitty!" Whether it was the smell of the food or her owner's voice that brought her, Brooklyn came wandering in. Beth grabbed her up and broke into tears. Did she know what she was doing?

Yes, she might be drunk, but she'd planned it out and she knew.

She carried Brooklyn into the kitchen, wiping tears from her face. Brooklyn wanted to be let down. All right. She couldn't blame the cat for wanting to eat, for not knowing this was the real good-bye. She tried to assure herself that Verla would take good care of them after her passing.

Finishing the Drambuie, she took another a tumbler of vodka to the bathroom. In the cabinet, she first found a bottle of Tylenol, then some Codeine and other prescription painkillers, and collected them all in the Tylenol bottle.

She put down the vodka and the Tylenol to lock the front, then the back door. Forcing herself to finish the vodka, she poured another, drank it, then switched back to wine. Her head ached, but some of the painkillers ought to cure that soon enough. She pulled out a large container of yogurt from the refrigerator and stirred the pills in. Forcing herself not to look back at the cats, she lit a Camel, took her burgundy and the yogurt to the bedroom, and closed the door. She polished off her drink and extinguished the cigarette.

The digital alarm clock read four fifty-five. She lay down on the bed and hugged a pillow. With luck she'd go out in a pleasant blur. She stared at the yogurt, squinted to read the fine print and forced herself to sit up in front of it.

# 57

"I've never known anyone else who had to meet person-ally with the dean about their own tenure. He wants to see me in person to let me down easily," Cissy said at the bus stop.

"Not necessarily." Though Evan knew it very well might be true. He watched the East Towne bus approach, stop and load on a dozen passengers. They were waiting for the Lansing or Lakeview, both of which would leave them a block from their house.

He didn't know whether to placate her or be frank, so he stated the obvious: "It's a fifty-fifty chance. But since the divisional committee tipped the scales on your side, let's go with sixty-forty, in your favor."

"No more odds please. I feel like a horse in a race."

Evan bit his tongue; he was just trying to help. "Don't worry, I mean, I know you're going to worry." He couldn't seem to come up with the right words, and tried again: "What I mean is, I'll be there for you no matter what the outcome."

"If I have to leave after next year..." Those denied tenure could leave immediately, or remain one more year, giving them time to find another job or to appeal the denial. "...how would we ever get jobs in the same place?" Her tone was tinged with despair, her words more of a bleat than a question.

Evan put his hand on her shoulder and stared over to Paul's Book Store, glad to hear what she'd implied: that she viewed their relationship potentially as permanent as he did. "We don't have to worry about that yet. Maybe we never will. I'm not going to let your tenure decision separate us." If she didn't get tenure, he didn't know what they'd do. He wanted to be custodial parent of his children, didn't want to leave Madison, but nor did he want Cissy to leave. It was a dilemma he'd have to keep to himself for the moment. For better or worse, it would be clarified soon.

"Here comes the bus." She moved away with no heed for him, as if making her own journey through life and he chose to follow her, he was welcome.

Classes had ended and Cissy held a final office hour during exam week. Errant students from the Intro class streamed in and she didn't mind that they took up more than a whole hour, thus taking her mind off her appointment with the dean. Tomorrow she'd probably have a more testy meeting with the student who had plagiarized, now that she'd tracked down the source. Predisposed to be generous to a student who had been absent for months due to medical reasons, she told him that if he did the museum tours on his own and passed the quiz on them, they'd just pretend he hadn't missed twenty-two classes. After taking this extra time with him, she hoped he'd at least pass the final. She hoped the dean would "pass" her too.

Finally free of students, she went to Evan's office, where they ate their packed lunches. No one had seen Ginger since the departmental meeting, but her final grades had been left in her mail box and Cissy trusted she was safe from an interruption by her now. At one twenty-five, Evan squeezed and kissed her, then off she went, heading bravely up the two flights of stairs to Dean Luedy's office. The seventh floor sported plush, pale green carpet.

"You must be Professor Pankhurst," the receptionist said, and led her to the dean's door. It was the same office where she'd first met Davidine Phipps six years ago.

Dean Luedy, a tall red-haired man, walked briskly over to her, extended his hand and bade her sit down at a small table by the window. He took a chair a few feet away from her. They were close enough to have held hands; she felt like gripping his, or anything, for moral support. It seemed that their talk was to be informal. Or was this proximity the personal style he favored to fire faculty gently?

Cissy didn't think she was quaking outwardly, but realized she was nibbling on a fingernail.

The dean leaned back, pensive, in apparent debate how to begin. Now Cissy knew that the news would be bad. "Quite a year Museum Studies has had."

"Indeed. Professor Abell's death was tragic."

"What a pity to lose such a great man. Bob Rothschild is irreplaceable too."

"Of course he is." She said exactly what she thought expected of her. "Thirty-five years of experience in the field..."

"So you elected Nick Wren as acting chair." The dean looked out the large window and Cissy's gaze followed his. "What do you think of him?"

The question surprised her, and she surely couldn't tell the dean the truth. "I voted for him. I think he can administer the department." This didn't mean she'd like the way he'd administer it.

"Cut from the same cloth as Rickover. Then there's Rickover himself. Quite a sudden, unexpected resignation, wouldn't you say?"

"Well, yes." If the dean meant to relax her by departmental chit-chat, it wasn't working. She wished he'd get to the business at hand. As a matter of fact, she realized for the first time, he hadn't told her that the business at hand was indeed her tenure.

"It's a pity when family problems intrude like this. Sandra's breakdown, if you can call it that, then Vance's resignation. I suppose it shouldn't have been so unexpected. Although it's hard on your department, I admire his family loyalty."

So that was what Rickover had told the dean?

"Even though he's going to Detroit to be with her, I still don't understand why he couldn't have taken a year's leave instead of resigning. I tried to insist, but he was adamant, saying it was time for both of them to make a change. I trust *he's* not leaving the profession too. Beyond going to Detroit, he's been quite silent about his intentions."

"Yes, it's too bad..." Cissy conjured up the most positive statement she could make about him: "...to lose a scholarly mind like his."

"And it's all leaving Museum Studies very understaffed. That's four losses in one year. I was beginning to have major doubts about all of you down on the fifth floor. In fact, I still have a few. Your own department cut its budget more than I had. But Nick Wren came up to talk with me and and we're undertaking a national search, admittedly late, for two full-time lecturers next year."

Thank God, Cissy thought, and wondered why she hadn't heard this news. It might mean she wouldn't have to teach the Intro class again; more than three hundred exams awaited her this weekend, and she had no student grader to help.

"Though having an understaffed department is definitely not a reason to grant someone tenure in a department, especially one with declining enrollments."

Cissy didn't like the sound of this. She sat parallel to the dean, staring out at a piece of the State Historical Society, a piece of Memorial Union, Lake Mendota supplying a bluish background.

He turned to face her and she swiveled in her chair to meet his gaze.

"Of course you have a seventh year here in any case. So it's not like we'd be losing you too."

So it was over and she was out, she thought numbly. Right now she didn't even feel like fighting it.

"And I certainly don't want it to happen. A five-to-four vote is very shaky, you know. No one in Fine Arts has ever received tenure with a divisional committee vote like that."

That, Cissy knew. She wished he'd just get it over with and dismiss her — from his office, from her job — before she fell apart.

"But I think there are mitigating circumstances. I don't think Vance, with all his stress, has been in his right mind since Sandra's breakdown or Professor Abell's death. With your publications, I really don't understand why Vance didn't do a better job of supporting you on the divisional committee. His support there could have easily swayed two more votes in your favor. Actually — I'll say this only now that he's leaving — I've had doubts about some of Vance's non-scholarly dealings from time to time. The fact that he gave you almost no support, I could take to be to your credit.

"Your department has been all but decimated. Dean Phipps,

Isaacson, Rothschild, Rickover, Blake Abell, all luminaries in their own way and in their own right."

Yes, yes, get to the point.

"May you be one of the department's future stars. I'm sending my recommendation on its way, ultimately to the Board of Regents, and your tenure is as good as automatic. Congratulations, Miss Pankhurst."

Cissy didn't know whether to let herself faint or to hug him, but spat out a "thank you."

"It's always nice to chat with the younger members of a department. I'll try to make it more of a practice in the future." The dean stood up and Cissy did the same, wobbling from relief.

"May I assume you'll stay, that you haven't scouted out a better offer?"

"Oh, I'm staying!" She jumped off the floor and somehow managed to land in the dean's arms.

# SUMMER, 1991

# 58

Summer in Madison meant bike rides, and Pepper had suggested one. Juan didn't add that, in Madison, fall, winter and spring also meant bike rides, even if the winter ones tended toward the utilitarian. Paoli was their destination, a common one for Madisonians, out of town, yet nearby. Juan considered how to back out of their outing. He felt tired; his bike's tires needed air. Hell, they needed replacing. But if he went, he'd burn off some calories. He'd been eating normally, even exercising, helping himself, as he told Pepper, to be "cured." He was sure Pepper didn't appreciate how difficult this was.

"You can borrow Roz's bike," Pepper said.

"Roz might be needing it today," he said automatically. For some reason he felt out of sorts, if not feisty.

"Roz is still in New York."

"Oh, I'd forgotten." He hadn't forgotten at all. She'd returned from the women's Land and, to everyone's shock, had flown to New York to visit Rhoda. At least they all knew where she was this time.

An hour later Juan and Pepper were riding single file, south of Madison. They had to be back by mid-afternoon, as Pepper had invited his parents for dinner. They passed farms and barns, still in the city limits of suburban Fitchburg, and Juan liked the rural feel. As the road was devoid of cars, he sped up, passing Pepper in a spurt of energy, to show off. Just because he was riding a woman's bike didn't mean he couldn't go faster.

His legs ached by the time they reached Paoli. It wasn't much of a town and had the aspect of having once been larger. They parked by the Wisconsin Artisan Gallery, went inside and idly perused the merchandise; then stopped at the Cheese Cottage, which sold food and post cards. It was a quaint little yellow brick building, and had once been the scales for the mill, the clerk told them. Pepper bought a bag of cheese curds, which were just salty enough to tempt Juan.

"Let's go rest in the park," Pepper said.

"I'll join you in a minute."

As soon as Pepper was out of sight, Juan bought six packages of cheese curds, then inserted them in his backpack.

Not knowing how the cheese would weather the trip back, he decided to eat a bag now. Two bags later, he found Pepper flopped down in the grass of the park, a block away, near a tiny gazebo.

"It's all clouded over," Pepper observed.

"The ride back won't be so hot then."

"It was hardly 'hot' on the way down."

A group of bikers, one of many, pedaled past them, speeding past a carload of elderly tourists. Pepper cradled his head in a bent arm, as though to snooze.

"Hey, we could go on down to New Glarus," Juan said, though he had little interest in the imitation Swiss village or its shops that sold rich pastries. Such a trip would, however, postpone the return home and the dreaded dinner with Sumner and Vonda.

Pepper sat up as if to ascertain that he'd heard right. "That's a schlep. Twelve more miles, and hills. And don't forget, we'd have to bike all the way back."

"It was just an idea."

"I know what you're thinking." Juan hated it when Pepper "knew" what he was thinking, especially when he was right. "You want to get more exercise, and biking is more pleasant than sit-ups."

"Not what I was thinking. In any case, you mean 'less unpleasant'."

"You don't want to become an exercise bulimic," Pepper went on. "Look at you, you're so thin."

"You've certainly been reading up on the topic."

"Hey, I'm living with you, so I have to know something. You want me to be ignorant?"

The truth was that Juan did, that Pepper's remarks irritated him, but he didn't respond to the last one. "I'm only 'thin,' as you put it, through great effort. You want me to grow a gut? You could take me down to the Bull Dog and show me off for one of their 'Bears' Nights' or whatever they call it. A prize catch. Five-feet-eight and one hundred seventy-five fat-laden pounds."

"Your pounds aren't due to fat. They could give you an exam with calipers to find out your ratio of muscle to fat. You'd be surprised how much of it is muscle."

Juan didn't like this idea at all. "You know, one can burn off two hundred calories through vigorous sex."

Pepper threw him an interested gaze. "As a matter of fact, I didn't get that far in my readings yet. Why, do you want to burn off those calories when we get home?"

"You never know."

"Maybe we should get going. Those clouds to the west are beginning to look a little dark."

❧

"Juan, can you get some cilantro from the Co-op?" Pepper had already begun preparing the chicken, the entrée he planned to serve with cream and cilantro.

"Sure." He felt eager to get out of the house again. "Anything else?"

"Just cilantro, I think."

On the way out, Juan parked Roz's bike in the garage and made the four-block walk to the Willy Street Co-op, which, enlarged and modernized, was beginning to resemble a miniature Woodman's. He purchased the cilantro along with two bags of blue corn chips. After exiting, he decided to rest his aching legs at the picnic table by the side of the building, next to the bike racks. In ten minutes he had consumed both bags. He deposited them, empty, in a trash can, went back into the store for another bag, and headed back.

Pepper was chopping vegetables for a salad. "Here, I'll chop this too," he said, as Juan handed him the bag of cilantro.

"Just don't put it in the salad. A little of that goes a long way and it doesn't taste good in salad." Neither did anything else, thought Juan, except nice salty cheese, croutons or bacon bits. He'd decidedly OD'd on vegetables in the past few weeks. "I'm going to shower, OK?"

He took his backpack with him, turned on the water and

ate the rest of of the cheese curds before stepping into the shower. As he was drying off, he remembered the bag of Fritos floating in the toilet tank. He removed the lid, wondered if they'd be soggy. Indeed, the Ziploc bag had held up. He ripped it open; the chips were as dry as the Sahara, and gone within a minute. He wiped the crumbs off his face, rinsed his mouth with mouthwash and circled his waist with a towel.

He lay down on the bed, wished he could doze, wished he didn't have to endure this dinner. They hadn't invited Sumner and Vonda for dinner in almost a year, and Pepper had determined it was time to repeat the invitation.

He must have slept. Pepper walked in, waking him, and he saw that it was six-fifteen.

"There's still time to burn off those two hundred calories before dinner. They're not due for a while yet."

"Whatever," Juan said listlessly, thoughts of burning off calories long gone. *Only* two hundred calories, *only* if it was *very* vigorous sex. Maybe it would relax him before dinner. But how could he even eat dinner? He felt quite full from all the cheese curds and the chips.

A minute later, Pepper was naked under chaps. Five minutes later, he'd convinced Juan to whip him gently with a belt. Not more than two minutes later, Juan turned and saw Dayne standing in the bedroom doorway.

Sumner and Vonda arrived at five after seven. Not only had Juan not got back into "sex" after the interruption by Dayne, he was traumatized by it. A four-year-old, not only seeing his father with a naked man, but in the midst of Pepper's kinky perversity. Though he hadn't told him so, he blamed it on Pepper, as well as on Roz, whose absences were straining everyone's patience and, evidently, Irv's attention to Dayne.

By seven-thirty, they were all seated at the small table, which held four cozily.

"Congratulations, Mom." Pepper raised a glass of ice water, and the rest of them followed. The dinner was technically to celebrate the acceptance for publication of Vonda's latest romance novel.

"Thank you. What a nice dinner."

"Very good," said Sumner. "You cooked it all by yourself?"

"It's not from Kentucky Fried Chicken. So, Mom, I take it

you left the lesbians out of your novel?"

"Oh, that's not the one that was accepted. It was the one before that. But I have left in a lesbian angle in the new one. It's really quite simple. Margo is attracted to Dominic, Dominic is attracted to Candace, and Candace is attracted to Margo. Candace is willing to let Dominic have Margo, knowing that he'll treat her badly, and hoping that Margo will take solace in her arms in the aftermath."

"Sounds complicated to me," Sumner said with a yawn. "You tell them the plot when you've refused to tell me for months."

"You criticize, Sumner, when I'm not asking for constructive criticism."

"Mom, you're treading on dangerous territory with lesbians."

"Don't worry, no one knows if Candace is really a lesbian. Even I don't know for sure. And in any case, I don't get graphic."

Juan had been listening to the conversation in silence. He'd already finished his chicken and salad, and now had piled his baked potato high with sour cream and chives, gooey melted butter below.

"*Your* appetite has certainly picked up," said Vonda.

"Oh, my appetite's fine," Juan said casually. Pepper eyed him with wariness. Dayne weighed on his mind so heavily that he wasn't even thinking about what he was eating. "More water, anyone? Pepper, you left the pitcher in the refrigerator. I'll get it."

He got the pitcher, and a handful of olives, which went promptly into his mouth before he returned. He set the pitcher down and said, "I think I'll have another piece of chicken." Vonda would never accuse him of undereating again.

"It's really quite delicious, Pepper," she said. "Do you always do the cooking?"

"Not always."

"No, he's not always the wife," Juan said, and saw Pepper flash him a hint of alarm. "The chicken is truly delicious, Pepper." He scooped out extra sour cream, burying the chicken under it.

"Juan, you don't want to overeat," Pepper said meaningfully. "You know what happens when you do."

"I don't want to eat more than my portion. Has everyone

had enough?" Sumner and Vonda asserted that they had.

"*I'll* have the rest of the salad, then," Pepper said.

"And I'll bring dessert," Juan said.

"We don't have any."

"Yes, we do." Juan got up and returned with the last bag of chips from the Co-op that he'd left outside by the back door.

"He doesn't always eat like this, does he?" he heard Vonda whispering as he returned.

"Oh, more often than you think," Juan answered for Pepper.

He grabbed a plastic bowl out of the cupboard, dumped the chips in, and set it on the table, as though it were a centerpiece or a second entrée. "Chips, anyone?"

Out of politeness or awkwardness, Sumner grabbed a handful. "Blue corn chips?" said Vonda. "I think I'll try one." She tried exactly one. How anyone could eat only *one* of any kind of chip, Juan had no idea.

"I'll pass." Pepper left the bowl beside him.

"Then pass them to *me*," Juan said and, reluctantly, Pepper handed him the bowl.

Juan began slowly, two chips at a time, four, then six. He glanced up at the others, who were trying to pretend that all was normal.

"Hey, I eat like this all the time at home," Juan blurted out, as the others were evidently at a loss for words. "Don't I, Pepper?" Juan didn't know why he was saying this; he only knew that he'd lost control when Dayne had appeared, was losing control again and wanted to take it back.

"I've caught him at it before," said Pepper.

"And this time no one has to 'catch' me." Juan spoke through a mouthful of chips.

"Could you have some sort of latent eating disorder?" Vonda asked. "I thought only..."

"Oh, no." Juan stood up, grabbing the last fistful of chips, crunching them in his hands. Crumbs fell onto the table and floor. "Men can have eating disorders too. Usually athletes, dancers, models or gay men, or combinations thereof." He shoveled in the last of them, and tried to smile. "And I'm one of them." He began to turn toward the bathroom, but, no, it was too close. He had to flee, so he ran outside.

He lay stomach-down on the pier, his stomach now rumbling, even aching, and he realized he'd reached the point of no return. If he didn't make himself vomit, it would happen anyway, sooner than later. By now he'd trained himself merely to contract his stomach muscles to trigger the desired reaction and, on the second try, the food started to come up, disgustingly. It almost would have been better to force himself to keep it down. But, no, he thought of the fat that would accumulate. Inert, he remained lying on the pier and even considered washing his mouth out with lake water, but opted for the outside hose. Belatedly, he let himself wonder if they'd all watched him from the picture window, but assumed they had. Never had he subjected himself to such public embarrassment and, today, he didn't even feel any post-purge relief.

He'd certainly never vomited into the lake before and vowed never to do that again. In the lake, or anywhere.

# 59

I rv was reading *Isthmus* when Dayne walked by, a question on his face. "Is something wrong, Dayne?"

"Uncle Pepper's bad."

"What?"

"Uncle Juan's spanking Uncle Pepper."

Irv didn't know what Juan and Pepper were into, but quickly put the scene together, more or less.

"Who told you you could go downstairs?"

Dayne hesitated. "Nobody."

"If you go downstairs again without asking, it'll be Daddy, and maybe Uncle Juan and Uncle Pepper, all spanking you. Understand?" Irv wondered if he should have made this violent, if idle threat. He and Roz were firmly against any corporal punishment.

"Mommy lets me go downstairs."

And Mommy would also let him live downstairs. "Mommy isn't here now. And I'm sure she always tells you to knock first."

"When's Mommy coming back?"

At least this time he could answer the question. "Wednesday night. In three days. We'll go meet Mommy's plane at the airport."

"I wanna sleep in your bed tonight. I miss Mommy."

Irv did too. As no one else had been in his bed for so long, he consented.

"Maybe you should see Dr. Kafka while you're still here," Rhoda said.

Roz looked around the apartment she'd grown up in and wondered how she'd ever stood it: the dark curtains, velvet everywhere, the heavy mahogany furniture, the lack of ventilation and sun. If she stayed here long enough, she'd indeed be seeing Dr. Kafka. For treatment of claustrophobia and sun deprivation.

"Roz, did you hear me?"

"You know we have psychiatrists in Madison too. If I ever need one."

"Dr. Kafka did worlds of good for Susan."

"Yeah." Roz had her doubts about that. That her sister was still one of the Rajneeshee out in Oregon, although Bagwhan had long departed, was proof to Roz that Susan was still more messed up than Roz had ever been. Susan, whose name was no longer Susan, had found so many levels of inner peace that she must resemble the living dead.

"At least you had a son, Roz."

"Mother." Rhoda lit a cigarette. She'd told Roz that Roz could smoke in the apartment only as long as she didn't complain about *her* smoking. Roz had had to agree. "We've already been through that before. You have one grandchild, and I don't think you should expect any more."

Although there was no wood chopping, nor potato stews, infernal brats, or lost lesbians soliciting her affections in Madison, life there still hadn't looked like the paradise Roz had imagined; she hadn't been quite ready to stay at home yet.

"Susan still could." Rhoda blew smoke, then Roz lit up and blew smoke back at her. "You know, sons are so much easier to raise than daughters."

Roz knew the remark referred to herself and her sister, though what did Rhoda know about raising sons? But after her experience at WWWL, Roz was not about to disagree.

Rhoda leaned back, inhaled and closed her eyes for a second. "And what does Irv think of your coming here? It's not always a good idea to leave your husband alone for long."

"Irv is *not* the type of man who's going to jump into another woman's arms just because I'm gone for two weeks. You know Irv, and you should know better than that."

"I was thinking of the *downstairs* influence."

Now Roz let out a lengthy sigh of exasperation, watched

the embers of her cigarette burn, then stubbed the dregs out furiously. "Pepper and Juan love to take care of Dayne. We consider ourselves lucky they're there to help out."

"That's not what I meant." Rhoda's cigarette ashes spilled onto her lap. "I meant, you know..."

Now Roz had an inkling that she did know what Rhoda was hinting at. "Are you suggesting that because Juan and Pepper are gay, that Irv might...?"

Rhoda beamed, and gave Roz one of her "I-told-you-so" looks. "Not that your father was ever unfaithful, much less ever had...*faygeleh* tendencies." At least Rhoda could pronounce the word in one language, even if it was Yiddish and the word derogatory. "But in Madison — now don't contradict me, because I've seen it — everyone seems to have a... phase. Either they're attracted to Madison because of it or maybe Madison does it to you. You yourself have been a prime example. So you never know, even about Irv."

Roz shook her head at Rhoda, at the ridiculousness of it all. "Thank God you were never a social worker, much less a marriage counselor, and stuck to something safe like real estate."

"Are you implying...?"

"I'm only implying that I know what's best for my marriage." At least now she thought she did, though the last nine months had been a different matter. "And I thought it would be good to come here and talk things over with you."

Roz stopped, not knowing if she really meant what she'd said, and watched Rhoda smile grandly at being taken into her confidence. At this point, it seemed she had to go on. After all, Rhoda and her father had had a seemingly happy marriage for thirty-five years.

"I've got nothing on my hands but time." Rhoda reached to grab another cigarette, but stopped herself.

"Mother, I really do want you to be around a long time. If you'd smoke less, I mean, smoke not at all... I know, I have no room to talk. But I don't have a heart condition either."

"Well, smoking these could give you one," Rhoda shot back, then got up and grabbed her own and Roz's cigarettes. She took them into the kitchen and Roz heard water running.

"There. They're gone, doused, in the trash," Rhoda announced from the kitchen doorway, and came back in to sit down. "Now we can do something together. Stop smoking. Mother and daughter."

"Fine." Roz trusted she had at least one more pack in her luggage and that Rhoda probably had one of her own hidden somewhere.

"Now let's talk about your marriage."

Now Roz was stuck, to talk about her marriage, of all things, and even worse, stuck without cigarettes.

"My marriage is fine. Irv's a wonderful person. I'm the problem." She figured that at least the last two statements were true.

"What *is* your problem, Roz?

"Good question, Mother. I can tell you one thing that will please you: My lesbian 'phase,' as you put it, is definitely over. It has been. I've had the chance, but I didn't want to. I wouldn't think of being unfaithful to Irv." This was true; she no longer would. "As to Dayne, I guess there is no problem. I got obsessed with the election and ignored him a litle. He's growing up to be a nice, healthy, thoughtful child." This, Roz hoped, would prove true.

"It sounds like you have no problem then."

"Maybe I haven't." Could that actually be the case?

"I think you should go home then and satisfy Irv."

Roz managed not to be irritated by the suggestion, knew that her mother's thinking followed the Orthodoxy with which she'd been raised, mandating marital relations — the husband's duty, if she remembered correctly — at least once a week.

"I suppose I should go," Roz said as much to herself as to Rhoda.

"While we're talking openly, I'm going to mention my will. Don't look so panicked, Roz. I just might be around for a while. But when I'm not, you'll be amply provided for. And Susan too, if we can keep track of her, and if her religion will let her accept the inheritance, which I'm trying to stipulate she can't give to them. Though that may not stand up in court, it might scare her back to her senses. If any case, you should know I've set up a trust in Dayne's name for his education. You'll be able to send him to Brandeis, Tufts, Columbia, Harvard, wherever. And I'm going to start giving you a large annual stipend now. That way you won't have such awful inheritance taxes, and believe me, I'm saving money for myself too, in case I have to go into a nursing home or something."

"Nonsense, Mother. You'll come to Madison and stay with us."

Rhoda's eyes did somersaults and, to Roz's amazement, she

didn't contradict her.

Yes, Roz thought. She'd better leave soon, very soon, before she made further dangerous statements. As she sat, half-stupefied, she realized that Rhoda stood behind her, hugging her, and then gave her a peck on her cheek. "Rhoda Goldmann loves her daughter. I do. Now, I've just got to find my other one and straighten her out."

# 60

Beth sat at home, alone, and stared at the cheap bottle of burgundy. She didn't think she'd ever touch the stuff again. After her trip to the Emergency Room — courtesy of Professor Jansen, who'd read her paper and become frantic — then to detox, and several subsequent visits to a psychiatrist, she'd been strongly advised against drinking, and so far she hadn't wanted to. She hadn't even taken the pills, but the alcohol had certainly incapacitated her, worse than her worst drunk freshman year. She'd missed the beginning of the season of her softball league, but thought it was probably just as well; all they ever did was go out and get drunk after the games anyway.

The worst part of it all was that Verla had left, rather precipitously. A job interview up north, she'd claimed, plus a visit to her parents. Beth wondered if she dared to call Verla's parents and why the hell had she gone there. No, she decided, she couldn't call *them* to get to Verla, but she needed to talk to someone. She could call suicide prevention and chat them up, as she'd done before, but they didn't really like you tying up the phone, unless you were seriously contemplating the act. University Hospitals had a shrink on call that she could contact, but all they usually did was ask you about your medications and urge you to get in touch with your regular shrink. Instead, she decided to call Lou. After her first call, during which she'd related the particulars of what she'd done, Lou had said to call any time. Twelve-thirty a.m. was "any time," wasn't it?

"Hello," a *man's* voice answered.

"Oops. Guess I got the wrong number. Sorry."

"Wait a second. Who are you calling for?"

"Lou Lautermilk."

"Just a second. She's right here."

So Lou was sleeping with her fiancé before she was married? This was very interesting. Lou, who five years ago, wouldn't have known sex if she'd...

"Hello?" The voice sounded grumpy, not at all like Lou.

"Lou? It's Beth. Sorry if I woke you, but you did say to call any time. Sorry it's late. So you're sleeping with... what's his name? Ben, right?

"Right, it's Ben. And no," Lou's voice lowered to a whisper, "we are *not* sleeping together. Yet."

"Oh. He answered the phone, passed it right over to you, and I figured you two were in the sack, 'specially since you sounded sorta groggy, like I'd woken you up."

"We're studying together on the sofa. Ben was sitting closest to the phone, so he picked it up. I figured it was a wrong number, since no one ever calls for me at this hour."

"OK, I'll let you go back to studying, no problem."

"Wait a minute, Beth. Unless you've called to interrogate me about sleeping with Ben, I'm glad to talk for a few minutes."

"What are you both studying for? Classes aren't in session."

"Beth, I'm getting my Ph.D. There are exams to take that aren't part of your classes. You can study twelve months a year and not be studying enough."

Obviously, Lou was still the same, her own hopelessly prudent and studious self. "OK, sorry. I'll get to the point. Verla left after I talked to you last, went up north for a job interview and to see her parents, of all things. Left the first day she could get away from the county schools. And she hasn't even called me! And these are the Jesus-freak born-again parents who disowned her! She hasn't seen 'em in years."

"Perhaps she's escaping. Your would-be attempt traumatized her. The family unit is very strong, no matter how much you try to deny it. Plus, you just said she hadn't seen them in ages."

"All I did was get real drunk and write an obituary."

"You planned to do much more than that."

Beth should have known she couldn't white-lie her way past Lou. "OK, I did, but I still don't understand. Verla's family said she could only come back home if she gave up her 'sinful ways' and me. So she's gone up there, and now maybe they're trying to brainwash her, do lesbian-deprogrammin' or somethin' to her. Maybe we, or I, oughta go rescue her before it's too late."

Lou paused before responding. "Do you mean like the time you tried to 'rescue' me from the religious cult you thought was the Ku Klux Klan?" The voice reeked of skepticism.

"OK. I s'pose not. But what am I gonna do?"

"I don't think there's anything you can do about Verla right now. But after she's been a lesbian for five years, and active in the community, I don't see how it's remotely possible that she's going to 'change' in a week's visit home."

"Guess you're right. But she went up there for a job interview. She... she could be leavin' me."

"Beth, you don't know. Even if she ended up taking a job up there, she might want you to go along."

Beth had voiced her worst fear: that Verla would abandon her. After a few seconds of silence on both ends, she said, "Thanks, Lou. I guess that's all I got to say. Sorry to bother you at this time of night."

"Don't worry, Beth. Call me any time."

"Can I meet Ben some day soon?"

"Of course. Whenever you're up to it."

"The family unit is very strong, no matter how much you try to deny it." Lou's words reverberated in her head the next afternoon. Beth was sure that her family was the exception. She'd called her mother in Miami, told her of her financial difficulties, and she'd sent a check for a thousand dollars. Ditto for Steve — her father — in Wilmette. The only "strength" in her family unit seemed to be money. She'd been loath to accept it, but saw no other way out of her immediate cash predicament. Both of her parents had remarried, were busy with their own new families, and she felt... left out.

She needed a parental figure to talk to. She thought of Roz, who was practically old enough to be her mother. But Roz was so messed up, couldn't even keep her clothes on in public and still couldn't figure out if she was a dyke. No, no way was she going to call Roz. Emily? Emily was probably was a good person to talk to, but after the Ho Chi Minh's boycott, she was the avowed enemy. If it hadn't been for Emily, she'd still have her job and have money.

Then it hit her. Why not call Rhoda? Rhoda was Jewish, as close to her mother's age as Roz's, and Rhoda must have been put through all kinds of hell rearing Roz.

Beth waited until after early evening, when the rates were cheaper. She called information and got the number, not wanting to ask Roz for it. With mild trepidation, she dialed, then waited through three rings, until she heard the familiar voice, "This is Rhoda Goldmann." Rhoda sounded like the answering machine, but the machine, this wasn't.

"Mrs. Goldmann. Rhoda. This is Beth Yarmolinsky in Madison. I was Roz's treasurer. Then we met a bunch more times, remember?"

"Of course I remember, Beth. How are you, darling?"

"Oh, I'm fine," Beth said, not knowing how to start.

"Don't tell me that you're calling to say that Roz has gone off again and done some meshuggeneh stunt. She was just here last week and I thought she'd straightened out her life."

"No, Rhoda. It's not her, it's me. I've got the problem. Can't talk to my own mother, all she's good for is sendin' me checks. So I didn't know who else to call, and I thought..."

"Of course you can talk to me," Rhoda said in her familiar nasal twang. "I've been mother to two daughters, who've turned out... as well as they could."

"Now, Rhoda, don't be shocked, but..." Beth went on to relate in a nutshell the gist of what had happened, then said that her Verla had left her. If Rhoda couldn't deal with lesbianism, Beth would just have to find someone else to talk to. Or, who could say, Rhoda might have forgotten or construed it as a case of "romantic friendship."

"At least you've got the sense to call. Roz, at your age, never told me a thing, lived with a bunch of hippies in a commune, that's probably when she started this nudism phase, now that I think of it. She never had anyone sensible to guide her, and look at her this last year. I guess you've seen. Not that she hasn't finally come to her senses, but it took her until she was in her forties. If she'd sought advice from me back then, I'm sure she would have got her life together much quicker. Now what's the problem between you and your mother?"

"Rhoda, that'd take more time than we've both got, but... she's distant. I was a JD sorta kid, you know. Juvenile Delinquent. Not really, but that's what she thought. Her only child, and I don't think she liked me much."

"All parents love their children, even if they go through periods of not liking them or what they do."

"Oh, you don't know Nick."

"I thought you were talking about your mother."

"I am. Nicole. Everybody calls her Nick. And now she's got a new husband with big bucks, lives in Miami, all they seem to do is play golf or jai alai, take cruises, and I don't know what else. All of his relatives are down there and she sorta forgets about me."

"I'm sure she doesn't really forget. So, she's married again. She's enjoying her new happiness. After Roz's father died, I never remarried. I kept on in my business and tried to watch out for my daughters, who'd moved everywhere on the continent. A mother's job is never easy, you know."

"I guess not." Beth fantasized what it would be like to be a mother.

"I'm sure your mother really loves you, darling. But just like you isolated yourself from her when you were younger, going off and getting into trouble and not wanting anything to do with her, now that she's in her new marriage, she's probably taking time off from the rest of the world too."

"And you think she thinks about me, really loves me?" A dumb question. How could Rhoda possibly know?

"I'm not your own mother, but, the family, even today, well... I suppose it takes some families a few decades to come together. Roz and I never really did until this year. You know, she's invited me to come live with her."

This Beth didn't know. Something strange must have happened between the two of them for Roz to make such an outrageous invitation.

"And I'm actually considering it at least part of the year, starting with another visit this summer. Just don't seek any advice from Roz. She'd probably tell you something ridiculous about loving women or the joys of nudity and how you should get this Verla friend of yours to come sleep with you or go naked to one of these women's festivals in the backwoods."

To hear these words relieved Beth; Rhoda had evidently forgotten, or perhaps, never understood about her and Verla.

"But I think you should give me your phone number, and I'll call you when I'm back out in Madison in a few weeks. I can see Dayne, and you and I can talk some more, and form a nice little relationship, something that Roz should have done with her mother twenty years ago. It's never been easy to teach her anything, but maybe she can even learn from your and my example. After all, she's going to need all the good examples she can get if she's going to raise a son properly and, frankly, I think she's got a lot to learn. Not that you don't too. And you know you'll need to do that before even thinking of having children. Now, Beth, do you have a boyfriend?"

# 61

Evan's divorce would be final in two weeks. Anne was going to marry George six months later, as soon as the law allowed. She wanted to remain the custodial parent, but Evan wasn't ready to give up. The original custody agreement allowed him to have the kids for two months this summer, every other weekend during the school year, and half the major holidays. When he first moved in with Cissy, he'd thought it was all he could reasonably ask for. But things were different now, were going to change radically — he hoped — soon.

"I want to fight. At least negotiate," he told Mark, in his law office. "Look at all the trouble the kids have been in the past year, living with Anne and... the carpenter. If Cissy and I get married..."

"You don't *have* to be married to Cissy to be custodial parent. You're living with her, just like Anne is living with... the carpenter."

"But it could only help if I were, if I bought a larger house, couldn't it?"

"Of course. But it won't be easy for you. Marrying Cissy is no magic remedy. Your basic problem is, you're the father, not the mother, and the courts..."

"I know, I know." Evan waved his words away, fearing that winning custody would be tantamount to crawling out of an abyss.

A few minutes later, he left the office, wondered how much the consultation had just cost him, how and when to broach the topic with Cissy. But what topic exactly? Having Todd and Danielle live with them for two months or... the other?

When Cissy returned from her conference in Nashville, he waved a letter at her from the Chancellor.

Cissy ripped it open. "She says the Board of Regents has approved my tenure!" she exclaimed, as though amazed.

"I told you it was all *pro forma* now."

"I know. It was just hard to believe it until I had the letter in my hand."

"What's that other paper in your hand?"

"Faculty Document 475," she read. "Dated or passed August 31, 1981. Four causes for which my employment can be terminated: retirement, just cause, financial emergency, voluntary resignation. What constitutes financial emergency? And this 'just cause' is a little vague, to say the least."

"Cissy, you've got tenure. You're *not* going to worry about financial emergency. I think something like blowing up FAB might constitute 'just cause'."

"All right. I'll shut up about it and not worry."

How could he bring the children up now? As soon as one burden was removed, here he was about to lay down another. He took Cissy into his arms, kissed her neck, hair, ear and cheek, then landed his lips on hers.

The telephone rang. What could it be now? They kissed through the first ring. By the end of the second, Cissy pulled away.

"I'll get it," Evan said, just in case it was his lawyer; he didn't want to have an awkward conversation in front of Cissy, or let her hear Mark's message. He snatched the receiver out of its cradle just before the answering machine could intercept the call.

"Hello?"

"Evan? It's Ginger."

"Ginger?" He saw Cissy's face register perplexity. They'd had no contact with her since the last faculty meeting. "I thought you were in New Jersey, or Europe." Ginger regularly deserted Madison for the summer, visiting her parents, then going on to Italy or France.

"I could have been, but I'm not. I'm at White Oaks."

"White what?"

"Oaks. It's a treatment center on the far west side of the city. I'm here for chemical dependency." Ginger's coke use clicked immediately to his mind. "Personally, I call it Poison Oaks, the inmates' nickname for the place. Ev, I want to ask you and Cissy a favor. I know I don't deserve it, but... Can you come visit me? I've been here two weeks. I'm now allowed visitors during visiting hours, three times a week, but Melvin is on a business trip —what's new?— and can't come this weekend. Visiting hours are from two to five on Sunday. And I don't have any

friends..." She stretched "friends" into three syllables and began to sniffle. "...to visit me. Are you free then?"

"Sure we are. We'll gladly come." He saw Cissy's face turn
from perplexed to alarmed. "Now just tell me exactly how to
find you."

Summer was predictably unpredictable in Madison, but it
was a sunny day, a passable replica of the season that would
begin officially in one week. On the far-west edge of the beltline,
Evan exited where Ginger had told him to. Some two miles
later, amidst a new sprawl of exurbia she hadn't known existed, Cissy saw the sign that read: "White Oaks: A Private Psy-
chiatric Hospital." Minutes later they were in the lobby and
gave the receptionist Ginger's name. She made a phone call,
issued them visitors' cards, and pointed them toward the chemical dependency unit.

They stepped outside through the back door of the lobby.
The hospital looked like a small campus, with separate buildings and recreational areas that spanned a large green yard.
Cissy looked up at the trees and wondered if indeed they were
white oaks. As an undergraduate, she'd had to struggle to earn
a C in a botany course on tree identification.

Ginger stepped out of the building and came toward them.
"Cissy! Evan! Thanks for coming!" Not generally prone to dis-
plays of physical affection, she hugged them both. "It's so good
to see familiar faces. Where would you like to go? We can sit at
one of the picnic tables under the awning, head inside, or just
walk around."

Cissy had no preference. "Whatever, Ging," Evan said.

"Oh, let's sit at the picnic table." Ginger led the way to the
table, flanked by two lounge chairs and a large standing ashtray. Cissy noticed that she was carrying a large rag doll. "Excuse how I look today. I didn't bring enough clothes when I
came here, and Melvin can't bring me any until Wednesday.
I've got a few catalogues, so I ordered some by Federal Ex-
press." She wore pants and a simple blouse, no cleavage or
pendants exposed.

As they sat down, Ginger's doll fell to the cement.
"Motherfucker," she said, and leaned down to retrieve it. When
she had the doll back in her hands, she brushed it off, and said,
"I'm sorry, Ginger. I didn't mean that. You're not a

motherfucker. You deserve credit for trying to be a good, honorable and honest person."

Uncomprehending, Cissy watched from the other side of the table. "Oh, this. I mean, 'Ginger.' Ginger's my doll. I'm supposed to pretend she's myself and take good care of her, just like I should of myself. And my inner child is also in there somewhere and I'm supposed to be getting in touch with it. If I haven't killed it. But I'm not supposed to be thinking that way."

Cissy imagined the thought of Ginger's inner child: frightening. She had no idea what to say. Nor, by his puzzled face, did Evan.

"Lots of strange stuff goes on here. Don't pay it any mind."

Cissy indeed considered the whole situation strange and was trying to think of a conversational opener, when Ginger spoke:

"I'm sorry I've behaved so awfully to you both the last year, for that matter, even to the whole department. Well, almost all of them. I know I deserve a 'Razzie' for my performance at the last departmental meeting."

Cissy wasn't going to dispute this.

"Anyway, I slowly began to relapse last fall. All those Workaholics Anonymous meetings I said I was going to, those were NA --Narcotics Anonymous-- meetings. I still went to them, high as a kite sometimes. I'd spend fifty dollars, snort it all up, no big deal, I thought. Then as the year got more intense, so did I. Melvin was gone a lot, and I'd use every day he was gone, and even some days when he was here. Then I started shooting it up."

"Excuse me, Ginger, but how do you *shoot up* cocaine?" Cissy's drug experience and knowledge came to a halting screech with marijuana.

"Oh, easy. You melt down the powder, add a little water, put it into a syringe, and inject. Thank God I used clean needles. Anyway, I was so coked up the day of the last  meeting, you wouldn't believe it. Then, when I found out I'd lost — I mean, who was going to vote for me anyway? — I really went over the deep end, and I don't mean at the meeting. A week later, I'd spent my entire savings and," she said, sobbing, "Melvin's and my joint account, both bled dry. At least I didn't touch his account, or he might never have had me back. Not that he has yet. We still have to go through 'Family Week' together. That'll be toward the end of my incarceration." Cissy threw her a faintly shocked glance. "I mean 'stay.' I'm here voluntarily."

As Ginger was now clutching her doll to her chest, rather sniffling a lullaby to it, Cissy got up, went over, and put her hand on her shoulder. "It'll be all right." Her words sounded to her like the dumbest in the world, though perhaps saying the dumbest thing was occasionally appropriate.

Ginger's fingers reached up and grabbed hers. "Thanks, Cis." Now standing behind her, Evan put his arm around Cissy's waist.

"You don't have to tell us all this, Ginger," she said. They both sat back down when Ginger's sobs subsided.

"Oh, but I need to. I have to apologize to everyone I've wronged. I manipulated the two of you and the whole department this past year."

"You weren't the only manipulator," said Evan. "Whatever you want to tell us, fine."

"The week after the vote was hell for me. So I stayed constantly high. Then Melvin came home, and stayed four whole days. I couldn't wait for him to leave. His background's very conservative: His father's a Baptist minister. He knew I had a problem once before, could deal with the fact that I was recovering, but wouldn't have dealt well with the fact that I was using at home. I hid the joint account checkbook and the unpaid bills. I used up all my money and all the coke I could get, so I got a loan from the Credit Union. As soon as he was gone, I was at it again. A few days later, that money was gone. So I pawned some of my jewlery, didn't give it a second thought. Then one night I needed a fix bad. I was almost penniless. I grabbed one of the paintings — you know, my impressionist ones — off the living room wall and went to my dealer's house in Maple Bluff. He was out of coke, but I gave him the painting, and I followed him to a crack house somewhere outside the city. We smoked crack until there was no more. The next morning I wondered how I'd driven myself home, then I noticed the missing painting and remembered what I'd done. That's when I decided I had to go to treatment, before Melvin caught me, I spent all his money, or sold all my jewelry and paintings. I'm still trying to get my painting back from S... my dealer in Maple Bluff, but he's taken an unfortunate liking to it. He thinks it gives his living room the class it's always needed."

"I'm sorry, Ging."

"You don't have to be. I am. Can you imagine if I'd stayed on coke and been departmental chair?"

Cissy began to envision the ghastly circumstance and held back a shudder. "Truly, Ginger, I don't think I want to imagine that." It suddenly made Nick, for all his faults, look good.

"Neither do I." Ginger laughed feebly. "With luck I'll be out of here by July first. Of course I can check myself out any time. Though at almost a thousand dollars a day, if they don't think I'm ready to be released by then, I may have to check myself out. The insurance only covers so much. No way can I go to Europe this year. Melvin wouldn't trust me, I'm not sure I'd trust myself, and there's no money. I think I'd better work at putting my life back together."

"You can do whatever it takes."

"We know you can, Ging."

"I suppose so." Ginger appeared suddenly weary and stroked her doll. "Tell me what's been happening to you."

"I went to the Nashville conference and, as I assume you know, I got tenure!"

"Oh, I knew you would." Ginger almost seemed to brush it off as if the whole harrowing process had been a mere formality.

"And I...," Evan began, "Oh, I'll tell you news when there is news."

Cissy had wonder what he was implying by this.

"I just wanted to see you, tell you how sorry I was for all of this. I hope I can be back to normal to teach in the fall. And be a better colleague and friend. Of course, I'd like to see you before then."

"If you want to, we'll be here. Hell, we might even buy a house."

Cissy threw him a look of astonishment. Was this the "news" that wasn't yet news?

"Hell, we could." He threw a sheepish glance at Cissy. "We've talked about it before, even if it's been a while."

Cissy's mind whirred. She was barely aware that Ginger was leaning over the table to hug her again. Or to congratulate her? On what? Tenure? Possible homeownership? The doll dropped to the table and Ginger cut off the hug. "There, there, Ginger, you'll be fine."

Cissy and Evan stood up, as Ginger seemed ready to call a

polite end to the visit.

"It's nice out here today. Can you believe there are almost twenty of us in the CD Unit — chemical dependency — and I'm the only one who doesn't smoke cigarettes?" Now Ginger got up too. "Over there is the sexual compulsives building, that's the sexual trauma unit." Her voice seemed oddly detached. "And that's the Eating Disorders Unit."

They walked in silence back up to the lobby. "Thanks for coming. Oh, and one last thing. I don't care who knows what I've been through, with two exceptions. The dean and Rickover. Promise me you won't tell them."

"We won't, Ging. We're having the dean to dinner tonight and we won't tell him."

It seemed to take her a second to realize that he was joking. "By the way, where's Rickover these days?"

"Not to worry. He's in Africa." The continent was one of his areas of "expertise."

"Good, I hope the son of a bitch stays there!"

Cissy had to agree, was glad to see some shred — but no more — of Ginger's old self.

She and Evan went through the lobby and out its front door. She turned her neck around for a final look. Ginger was visible through two panes of glass, bending the doll's arm to wave, and mouthing "Bye-bye."

"Bye-bye," Cissy mouthed back.

# 62

Ben was actually handsome, and not even a nerd. Beth had been sure that Lou's fiancé would be ugly or nerdy or both. He was the type of young man Beth's mother probably would have wanted her to marry. After a dubious Italian dinner at the Monastery, for which Ben paid, he dropped Lou and Beth off on John Nolen Drive by Lake Monona.

"If I'd eaten any more, I would've plotzed," Beth said.

"I always ate all I wanted and I never plotzed," Lou said, astonishing Beth that she knew the meaning of the word.

"Right, Lou. You just ballooned for a few years." Lou directed her an odd look, which Beth tried to deflect.

"That memorial's here somewhere."

"Whose memorial again?"

"Otis Redding's."

"I'm sure I never heard of him," Lou stated with finality.

"Even though you're becoming a Jew and a shrink, you're still out of it, Kiddo." Beth didn't know quite where to look, and headed them in the opposite direction, determined to find it, now that Ben had told her about it over dinner.

"I'm not becoming a 'shrink,' Beth. I'm getting my doctorate in psychology. There's a big difference."

"Shrinks, psychs, I've seen 'em all. They're all the same to me. Hey, here it is!" Beth pointed, and hurried up to the memorial, Lou lagging behind. It was a simple circular bench, in memory of Otis Redding, whose plane had crashed in Lake Monona in 1967. "Don't tell me you never heard of 'Sittin' on the Dock of the Bay'," she said to Lou as she caught up.

"Sing it for me."

Beth groaned at the request. She couldn't sing one note on key and wasn't sure she knew how the lyrics began. She hummed it as best she could. "Huh, Kiddo? Now you recognize it, don't you?"

"Well...," Lou demurred. "Maybe if I heard the actual recording, I would."

"I give up. I'll find it and play it for you some time."

She hadn't come to talk about this anyway. "Let's sit."

"Are you sure this memorial is for sitting?" Lou asked.

"Lou, It's a *bench*! What the hell else is it gonna be for?" Beth plunked herself down and watched Lou lower herself doubtfully, as if she were about to sit on her grandmother's grave.

Beth pulled out of her pocket the note that Verla had sent with the July rent check, two weeks early. "Listen to this, Lou!" She began to read:

*Beth. Here's my half of the July rent, plus a check made out to you, which should cover the utilities. When I'm back, it will have to be decided what to do with the apartment in August when the lease expires. Have the landdykes been over lately? Verla.*

"Can you believe it? That's all she wrote. What do you make of it?"

"She's fulfilling her financial obligations."

"I know that, Kiddo." Beth looked out on the calm lake, then to the west, where the sun was just setting, the sky purple and pink. A few pedestrians milled about in the park behind them. "What about the rest?" She thrust the letter under Lou's eyes, as though she might find something else written in invisible ink.

"There's not much else. Beth. It's a bit... impersonal, to say the least."

"I know. I think she's leavin' me." Beth had dealt with this possibility in theory, but now it seemed to be happening.

"Well... You almost left not only her, but me, your parents, your cats and the whole world!"

Beth leaned back and gripped the bench with her hands, momentarily stunned by Lou's vehemence.

"Did you or did you not?" Lou pressed.

"I didn't *do* it. I didn't even take the pills. I got the attention I wanted. I hurt everyone. I'm sorry." She recited the words in a purposely bored monotone.

"Do you mean one word you've just said?" Lou asked, now sounding more like a confrontational therapist than a friend.

"I said 'em and I mean 'em," she said, not knowing what she meant.

"You don't sound like you mean it. I know you're depressed, but you can't go on like this forever."

"'I'm just a-sittin' on the dock of the bay, wastin' my li-i-i-ife." She didn't mind that she sounded atrociously off-key.

"The bay is over there." Lou pointed behind them. "And this isn't a dock. But you're right about one thing, Beth. Right now you're wasting your life. You've got to do something!"

Lou's words almost jolted her off the bench. She didn't know that Lou had had it in her. Obviously, she was no longer the timid, naive Wisconsin farm girl.

Verla was resting at the edge of the large garden space, having finished weeding between the many rows of beans. The sun came and went, and the breeze had a light chill to it, causing gooseflesh on her arms. At the moment, she had no energy to move.

"Surprise!" She felt a hand go down the back of her T-shirt and turned around.

"Sage! You scared me. And, besides, you shouldn't go putting your hands under anyone's clothes. At least not without their permission."

"But I'm a lesbian!" Sage affirmed, for at least the third time.

Verla knew that Helaine and Randa had sheltered their daughters to the extent that they'd almost never seen a man in their life. But it wasn't Verla's place to dissuade Sage from this notion of her sexual orientation.

"Lesbians don't go around putting their hands where they don't belong."

"Nobody but Ses and Saff'll let me touch 'em. And I don't wanna touch *them!*" She wrinkled up her nose and made a face, as though touching her sisters were like rubbing poison ivy. "They're probably gonna be boylovers anyway!" She said 'boylovers' with the same scorn with which her mothers used the term.

"When you're the right age, I'm sure there will be another young woman who'll let you touch her." She'd thought of adding "or young man," but was not going to have Helaine or Randa accuse her of trying to 'pervert' their daughter.

"But I'm almost twelve."

"Listen, Sage. I never touched another woman like that until I was twenty. Your time will come."

"You're no fun," Sage huffed at her, and ran off.

After dinner the women — about fifteen of them, plus five children — had a songfest, then retired to their cabins, exhausted by nine o'clock. Alone in hers, Verla had just begun to doze off when the sheet was pulled off of her and hands were aiming for her panties.

"Sage! Get off me!" When Sage didn't move, Verla yanked her up by the hair. "This is totally inappropriate! I've had enough. Get out of here right now!" Sage stared her down as Verla covered her breasts with a pillow. "Stop looking at my breasts and get out of here!" She stared Sage down until she reluctantly obeyed.

"Shit-for-face!" Sage screamed as soon as she was out of the cabin, then disappeared.

Verla had had enough. Four attempts at molestation were four too many. She put her clothes on and set out to find Helaine and Randa's cabin. One of the two largest, it was easy to find. She knocked tentatively at the door.

"This is private time," came a stern voice.

"This is an emergency."

A minute later Randa stuck her head out the door. Verla couldn't remember which of the women was which child's mother. "I'm sorry to bother you. I know it's private time. But

Sage was just in my bed trying to molest me. It also happened
this afternoon. I assume you're aware she thinks she's a lesbian."

"She *is* a lesbian," Randa affirmed.

"That may be, but you can't let her go around molesting
the women on the Land."

"Molesting the women!" Randa scoffed, and Helaine
opened the door behind her. "How can an eleven-year-old
molest a woman in her twenties? The issue is all about power,
and you have all the power over her. You must have enticed
her."

"We ought to charge you with child molestation!"

"You women from Madison are all troublemakers. The last
one that was up here this spring, we had to kick her out."

"Now I've heard enough!" Verla yelled back, now
emboldened, or better yet, empowered. "I'm leaving!"

"Good riddance, Velma!"

"I'm Verla, goddamn it! Not Velma, Viva, Velva, Velveeta
or anything else! Got it?"

She stalked back to her cabin, gathered her belongings, toss-
ing clothes wildly into her backpack. But she was not going to
leave quite yet, and not in disgrace. They'd remember who
she was *and* get her name right.

If Sage had tried it with her, she'd probably tried it with
other women. She went back outside and wended her way
through the trees until she saw a cabin with a light on. She
knocked at its door, hoping she wasn't interrupting something
intimate.

"It's unlocked!" answered a raucous voice.

Verla stepped in and saw four women, two of them smoking cigarettes, playing cards on the floor. At least a dozen beer
cans littered the cabin.

"Wanna join in?"

"Sorry to interrupt your game, but I need to ask you all
something. I just had to get Sage out of my bed, as she was
bent on trying to have sex with me, and when I went to tell
Helaine and Randa, they had the nerve to accuse me of child
molestation! I wondered if..."

"She follows me into the communal restroom all the time.
And tries to open the stall door on me."

"I can top that. She sat in my lap tonight at songfest, pinched
me everywhere and said she'd tell her mothers that I pinched

*her,* if I said a word."

"She always asks to sleep in my room," said a woman named Dew. "She told me if I didn't let her, she'd burn my cabin down!"

# 63

"What do you mean, 'bad'?" Roz asked, flicking ashes onto the sidewalk as they sat at a table outside Café Europa. She'd met Irv at his King Street office this morning, they'd gone to the Farmers Market, and now sat drinking coffee.

"I deduce they're into a little S and M. It seems Juan was spanking or whipping Pepper when Dayne walked in on them. I gave him a strong lecture about their privacy."

At least Dayne had never walked in on them having sex, not that they'd had it lately, except after her return from the Land. Today she'd taken the initiative to plan a relaxed, perhaps romantic day for the two of them, which, she hoped would culminate in a nice romantic evening. Dayne was in Juan and Pepper's care only for today; she and Irv would take full care of him the rest of the week.

"You know, I went to a therapist," she ventured. She had to unburden herself to some extent, knew they had to talk, and didn't know how much to reveal.

"Oh?" She saw that Irv had finished his coffee already.

"Just twice and I let it all spill out, even my topless morning at Labor Farm. Emma gave me the confidence that I could begin to solve my own problems. She agreed that going to the Land would be good for me. I went, hated it, and it was."

"Please just don't do something like that again without telling me."

"I'll never do it again." Go to the Land or fail to tell him if she left town. "I'm really sorry about that." She tilted her head, puckered her lips, leaned toward Irv and closed her eyes. In mid-kiss, she was jostled by a bag of Farmers Market produce that had hit her chair. She looked up annoyed at the unwary pedestrian who went ambling down the street, nonchalantly swinging her bag of goods. Roz saw small waves in her coffee cup, then, behind her, a duck attempting to cross the street, waddling, stray, a not infrequent sight on the narrow stretch of land between the lakes.

She banished her irritation at the pedestrian, minor com-

pared to the dogs, strollers and wagons she'd endured among
the throng that descended on the Farmers Market every Saturday morning. Noon was her preferred time to go, when the
masses had thinned out and prices were sometimes reduced.

"I thought I could be an activist and a mother at once." Irv
at her side, she spoke facing the statue of a Norwegian soldier,
the Capitol behind him. "I mean I was, but not a very good one
on either front. I didn't realize that I had to cut back on my
activism. I was being selfish, depending on you and 'the boys'
to take care of Dayne more than you should have had to." She
took the last swig of her coffee, now lukewarm.

"But we all wanted to."

A breeze hit her face. She wished he'd simply let her apologize. "I know, but I should have done more. And I should say
something about that day at Labor Farm. I suppose I did it to
see if women still might find me attractive. Now don't freak
out, but on the Land I had the opportunity to be sexual. But I
didn't want to be, couldn't. I've got you and that's all I want."
She took a final drag on her cigarette, ground the butt out and
flung it into a trash bin. Briefly, she once more debated telling
Irv about Seth, but she'd already had that debate with herself.
"That's about all I can say." It was true; she feared she couldn't
tell him now about Seth, even though nothing had happened,
without a major rocking of her marital boat. Perhaps she'd tell
him in five years, or maybe after Seth's death.

"You've said enough. I believe you."

Hearing these words, she immediately felt stabs of guilt,
but silence was better, and could even be golden, right? "Those
monster children on the Land make Dayne seem like perfec-
tion," she said, wanting to steer the conversation elsewhere.

"Now Juan and Pepper won't have to adopt him."

"What?" She tried to distinguish the real meaning behind
Irv's poker face.

"Just kidding."

She didn't appreciate the joke. "I'll try to be a better mother.
And daughter to my own mother."

Irv didn't pick up on this, or kept silent if he did, and she
didn't yet think it a good idea to mention that Rhoda would
soon be visiting. "We'll be one big, happy family," he said.

Both of them had used that line before, always in the sixties, commune sense. "Better, one little happy family. I'm convinced, after what I saw at the Land, that no one should have

more than one child."

"We don't have to worry about that."

"Right, we don't." Roz turned her next words over in her mind, then she admitted it aloud: "I'm almost glad, in a way, I lost the election."

She tried to discern Irv's reaction to her statement, but the poker face had now turned to stone. Obviously, there was no way he was going to respond to this.

"But I only meant this time. Two years from now Dayne will be in school, I'll have more time, and I'm sure I can beat Claypool! Now let's take the arugola home, I'll make a nice salad with it later, and we can hang the impatiens baskets in the atrium."

The next morning Roz sat topless in the dining room, coffee, cigarette and Dayne at her side. He had announced his intention to become an artist and was completing a crayon drawing every fifteen minutes. So far he'd drawn a tree, the lake and a starry night sky. He pushed a new one in front of her.

"Hills," she said admiringly. "How nice. But in Wisconsin hills are usually green, not pink."

"No." Dayne took the paper away, shaking his head maddeningly. "Mommy."

"What? Me?" Then, not so slowly, it dawned on her. He'd used one of the new flesh-toned crayons and had rendered his version of her breasts. At least he hadn't drawn Daddy's penis.

"Mommy toplest."

It made her think of "Mommy Dearest." "Top-less, Dayne, not top-lest."

He repeated, rhyming it with "acropolis."

"Just don't show this drawing to your friends. This is a home drawing, all right? You can show Daddy, or Uncle Juan or Uncle Pepper, but no one else. You go draw some more if you want, because Mommy has to write a letter."

"I can write a letter," Dayne announced. Slowly, he constructed an awkward "A," followed by a backward "B," and a perfect "C" on the back side of the breasts drawing.

"Very good. Now let Mommy write."

She'd only written "Dear Dew" before the interruption and

forced herself to continue, motivated by her some vague, perhaps irrational guilt, but wanting to reach out to help a somewhat lost soul.

She looked at what she'd written, offering introductions to the lesbian-feminist community, and wondered what lesbians were still speaking to her. Hmmm. At least there were Beth and Viva. Or was it Verva? She decided she'd finish the letter later, and debated putting pen to paper again, this time to give Seth a piece of her mind. But no, that could end up being incriminating evidence.

"Look what I drawed, Mommy." Dayne tugged on her elbow.

"Drew, Dayne, drew." Juan didn't need to have the monopoly on grammar correction. She took the paper and stared at it. It appeared to be two men, holding hands, a good sign that he viewed this as natural. But a long squiggly line protruded from one of the stick figure's hands. "What's that? A snake?"

"Don't be dumb. Uncle Juan doesn't like snakes. It's a belt. He spanks Uncle Pepper." At least he'd stopped calling Juan "Daddy," for good, she hoped.

"Yes, I see Dayne, but that's... that's private, like my breasts. You can't show this to your friends. Just to the four of us who live here." She could see it now, her son the artist, the future pornographer...

"Five."

"Right, darling. Five."

"Nobody spanks me. Why does Uncle Juan spank Uncle Pepper?"

Oh God, she thought. Already? "That's a grown-up question. A very grown-up question. I'll tell you next year." Or the year after, or maybe by the turn of the millennium.

# 64

Beth was shocked when Emily called her at home. "I wondered if you'd talk with me. I have a proposal to make. Ho Chi Minh's may have to close its doors by fall unless something is done. "

"If it's about money, I don't need a job." Beth was definitely going to play hard to get, assuming that it was she that Emily wanted. "You see, I just got this big inheritance." Of course, the money from her parents was not an "inheritance," two thousand dollars hardly qualified as a "big" sum, and she doubted if Verla would be coming back to share expenses, or their bed.

"Well, then, what I'll tell you right now is that it has to do with AIDS. Will you talk to me?"

AIDS? Had one of the scabs who had taken their jobs become ill and now Emily had to deal with it and didn't know how? She supposed she could do it for the Movement, for the sake of the PWA, maybe even for the sake of humankind. "OK. Sure, I'll meet with you, but not at Ho Chi's."

"Thanks, Beth. How about down the block at the Willy Bear?" That was still safely politically correct. "Say, five o'clock Wednesday. Is that a good time for you?"

"Just a sec. Let me check my calendar." Of course, Beth had no calendar and, if she did, it would have been empty except for her therapy appointments. She put the receiver down, meandered over to rub Brooklyn's tummy, and took her time heading back to the phone. "I'm afraid I'm busy then. Can it wait till Thursday?"

"It's important, but sure. Thursday, at five, at the Willy Bear?"

"Yeah, that'll work." With luck, she'd be working too.

With or without Verla, she'd have to be, and soon.

"How could you possibly think I'd go back to live with my parents?" Verla asked. It was Wednesday morning, Verla had arrived back late the night before, when Beth was already in bed, and had slept on the sofa. "You know me better than that."

"What else was I gonna think?"

"For all I knew, you'd never want to see me again, and I found out about this position near the Rapids. Since I only have a part-time job here, I decided to check it out, but I realized I don't want to work up there. I called my parents from my hotel. They wanted to see me, so I went over. Believe me, we didn't talk about 'it' or you. They were embarrassed that I wasn't staying with them and they almost pleaded with me to. I decided it was safe enough, so I spent a week there."

They sat on the back porch, overlooking the garden plot that should have been flourishing. Beth had put in only six tomato plants, which she should have been talking to, monitoring their energy fields and spurting their growth. Instead they were now parched, and the morning sun beat down on them. Beth saw the tail of a cat protruding from under a vine that covered the garden fence and separated them from the adjoining property.

"But they must've hassled you about religion. They didn't go rebaptize you in a river or somewhere to cleanse you of your 'evil ways'?"

Verla laughed gently, perhaps nervously, at Beth's comments. "Sure, they talked about religion. And I talked about my higher power. I just didn't tell them that I found her through AA, and that she was a big lesbian earth goddess who encourages all the women of the world to love each other carnally."

"And that she crushes beer cans between her breasts."

"In your version. My goddess is sober."

"I suppose mine is too." Beth still hadn't touched a drop, nor wanted to. "But you said only a week? Where were you the rest of the time?" She knew she was beginning to tread on dangerous personal territory, as they had yet to talk about their relationship. Verla could have spent the remainder of the time in the arms of some woman in Wausau, for all she knew.

"After my parents' house, I went to take some time off at some Womyn's Land north of Eau Claire."

Beth immediately felt a little envious and threatened by this "Womyn's Land," but was resolved not to show it. "You mean, like a Womyn's Music Festival? That's great. I didn't know they had one in Wisconsin."

"No, not a music festival. Frankly, this was more like a lesbian labor camp. But in the end it was healthy for me, working hard, being back in touch with nature, my spirituality and all these strong, empowered women."

"Hey, maybe that's what I should do."

"Oh, no, Beth. I don't think you'd like it. Two of the women have these three children, all named after spices. The oldest one decided she's a lesbian, tried to molest me, and when I told her mothers, they accused *me* of child molestation. They said women from Madison were troublemakers, and the last one from here had been kicked out. And guess who it was?"

"I haven't the faintest."

"It was Roz!"

"Roz?" Thinking about it, Beth wasn't that surprised. Indeed, this served as further evidence that Roz was still a lesbian, bisexual, or infinitely confused, and had tried to pull a big hoax over the sixth district in her council campaign.

"She must have gone up there after losing the election. Anyway, I didn't back down about that molestation nonsense. I quizzed almost every woman on the Land and found out the kid had tried something with more than half of them. So I stayed on and Sage was sent to spend the rest of the summer with an aunt, uncle, and her cousins. Boys. At least I did some good."

"Sounds like a concentration camp. Oops, shouldn't use that term. But tell me more." Beth realized the necessity of keeping the conversation light this morning, even if she really didn't prefer to.

❦

Beth and Emily sat in one of the wooden booths of the Willy Bear's ample patio, trees spreading above them, tree droppings of various sorts scattered over the benches and table. Although the waitperson had wiped them away, more had fallen.

"We didn't mean to alienate the lesbian, gay and bisexual community, Beth." Emily sipped at her beer, her red hair glowing in a piece of the late afternoon sun. "It was one of those things... We felt backed into a corner. But let me get to my point..."

Beth was about to ask "Who's sick?" or "Did your whole staff quit?" Instead she contained herself, playing with the straw in her tonic water, which she suddnely wished were wine, or even beer.

"We want your business back and we want you back. Just let me finish." She took a fortifying swig of her beer. "We're prepared to do the following, and I should tell you Miller beer will remain on the premises. We'll donate three percent of all Ho Chi's net profits to local AIDS organizations. We'll host a benefit a week if there's interest, for any AIDS or pro-gay cause."

"Sounds good, but I myself ain't the gay, lesbian and bisexual community."

"But you have contact with ACT UP and... What's the women's organization called?"

"Yikes Dykes!"

"Yes, Yikes Dykes! There's also the United, the Ten Percent Society..."

"Yeah, and a few more." Beth scanned the patio for other clientele and realized that there were probably at least two members of every organization inhabiting the Willy Bear's very correct premises, and the place wasn't even officially gay.

"If you could be our emissary, at least to the two groups you're connected with, that would be a start. As to you, if you're interested, Ron and I are prepared to give you your old job back with a salary, as opposed to an hourly wage. We'd need a commitment of, let's say, forty hours a week this summer and would let you decrease your hours, with no salary cut, when classes begin. The groups I mentioned would have to endorse ending the boycott. If they do, we'll pay for the ads announcing it in *The Insurgent* and *Isthmus*. And, you have to be aware, even if the boycott is ended, this might not even work. There. That's the gist of it. Is there anything more I'm missing or you'd like to ask for?"

"Flexible hours," Beth said, to say something, "and some time, I mean just a little time, to think." She was going to add "profit sharing" too, but thought better of it, as she was going to get a salary. *If* this all worked out.

"You'll think about it and get back to me?" Emily stood up and pulled out a bill. "Here's a five, which should cover my beer, your drink and tip. Sorry to drink, propose and run, but Ron is staffing the place alone right now and I've got to hurry back."

"No problem, Emily. I'll be in touch."

"Thanks, Beth, just for listening to me."

"Yeah, thanks."

Beth sat for a second, pondering the proposal and the five dollar bill, figuring there'd be a buck left over after the tip. The first of many desperately needed dollars of a proposal that sounded very good. Now she had her work cut out for her, to convince Madison's opinionated communities that Ho Chi Minh's heart and pocketbook were in the right place.

She got up and began to hike up the sloping patio, when she saw two Yikes Dykes! she knew.

"Hey! Mind if I join you?"

She figured she might as well start now.

Verla spent the following morning on the telephone, contacting her private students and making up new lesson schedules. Beth felt almost like a stranger in her own home, and decided to make her own appointments. The two Yikes Dykes! had sounded agreeable enough to Emily's proposal and Beth convinced them to hold a summer potluck, even if many of their members were gone. When Verla finished her calls, she dialed Sol from ACT UP, explaining that, as she'd been the one to propose the boycott, she thought it was her place to help end it. He agreed that it was a good idea to discuss it at their meeting next week.

That evening after dinner, she and Verla again sat on the back porch. Beth knew that the moment to talk had come. Verla evidently planned to stay in Madison, but would she stay with her?

"I know what I did was horrible, announcing that like I did in the workshop," Verla said out of the blue. "But we weren't communicating. You were having one catastrophe after another. It was all I could do to get you through each one. You didn't seem to have any energy for lovemaking. I thought you didn't want me, didn't want to experiment with anything I wanted. That's why I brought it up when and how I did. I didn't think I could talk to you alone and I had to do something." Verla spoke almost as though reciting a prepared speech.

Beth contemplated this explanation, saw Lady swish his tail on top of the compost pile. Verla's words made a reasonable amount of sense. "Well, did you do it?"

"Do it?"

"Do *it*."

"Oh, that 'it.' No, but I'll tell you the details." Beth was unsure that she wanted to hear, supposed she'd have to endure some unpleasant truths, and Verla went on:

"Terry, the woman I met at the workshop, was in a relationship a little like ours, with a partner she wasn't having sex with and who wouldn't consider anything but monogamy. So we set up a dinner date to discuss how it would impact on our respective relationships, and we'd go from there. Well, she got cold feet, called me at school, left a message and canceled. Normally, I would've been home by four that day, but I had a private student. I got here some time after you left behind all those liquor bottles, which told me something was wrong, then your obituary, which confirmed it. Only later did I see that you'd mixed all those pills together. I just hoped you hadn't taken any of them."

"You're forgiven for the workshop and this Terry woman, even if your timing at the workshop could've been better."

"Your will and obituary were none too nice to me."

"I was crazy, angry, and drunk when I wrote them. I'm

sorry."

"I trust you've been getting help."

"Help, shmelp. Therapy, shmerapy, Shrink, shmrink? That one really doesn't work. Yeah, you name it, I been gettin' it."

"I'm glad. If we've gotten through... this, we can get through lots of things, don't you think?"

This was it? Verla's words absolutely startled her, coming quick and easy as they did.

"I don't know." Having been up for a good argument or at least a lengthy discussion, Beth unexpectedly found herself playing devil's advocate. "We're a mixed marriage, you realize." Verla looked at her wide-eyed. "Well, to start with, Jew, Gentile. Non-alcoholic, alcoholic. Urban, rural. Sorta butch, sorta femme. Monogamous, polygamous."

"Wait a minute." Verla's tone was a clear indication that something was amiss. "I haven't been anything but monogamous. Or perhaps celibate is a better word, applied to the last couple months."

"You haven't?" If this was true, it was a shock. "Then that makes two of us. Wanna put an end to it?"

Verla faced her as if she'd been slapped.

"Sorry. I guess my hormones got the best of me. I didn't necessarily mean right now or anything." Beth wondered what she'd said "wrong."

Several beats passed before Verla spoke: "No offense, but I don't think you're much of a butch, and I don't think you think you are either."

Skokie appeared from around the corner, tail in the air and purring, and several others appeared, as if heeding the call of the can opener. Beth nuzzled the cat's neck, then pushed it away. "Listen, kitties. We got major issues to work on in this house if the six of you are gonna have a happy home again. So you cats stay outside! We need privacy. Lots of privacy! Just don't go wanderin' over to the landdykes with your tags on. Or off!"

"Beth, the problem's not them, it's us."

"Just tryin' to inject a little humor," she whispered, somewhat deflated, and the cats, as if sensing the sudden change in mood, or perhaps just engaging in routine feline behavior, strayed away.

# 65

"The city council tabled the ordinance to prohibit topless sunbathing at city beaches." Topless as usual, Roz sat with Juan on the pier behind the house.

"Meaning, it's tolerated, at least this year." Juan, in blue jean cut-offs, dangled his feet above the water, toes occasionally skimming the murky surface.

"Who cares? This is private property."

"Technically, yes. But look how many other piers are visible."

"So? My neighbors can hardly choose to gawk at me and then call the cops. Unless, that is, you and I create a public disturbance. In any case, my breasts aren't big enough to create a public disturbance." She eyed him, as he stuck his big toe in the water, making no effort to disagree with her. He at least might have told her that her breasts were firm, or not that small. "Juan, have I gained weight?"

The question seemed to take him off guard. "That sounds like something I'd ask you. The bathroom scales can tell you better than I can."

"I'll take off my shorts and you can get a better look." She wore cut-offs almost identical to his.

"I thought that was illegal."

"Fuck the law. And, no, it's not illegal, Mr. Smarty-Pants. This is private property."

"A fine councilperson you'd have made."

"Nonsense. I know the laws."

"Regarding nudity, yes, I'll grant you that."

"Fuck off and answer me. Have I gained weight?"

"I don't know."

"What about you?" she snarled, turning the tables maliciously.

"What about me what?"

"We were talking about body size, if I remember."

"You were," he shot back.

"What about your eating disorder? I found out you never told Irv. And Pepper spent several weeks away from you because of it, didn't he? It doesn't sound like you're dealing with it too publicly."

"Oh, you think I should take out an ad in the paper? 'Juan

Bellefleur hereby announces to all interested parties that he is bulimic. For more information on Juan's disorder, call...' Anyway, I don't know that it has to be dealt with publicly."

"Juan, this is serious."

"I've only purged once in the last month."

"And quite publicly. Right into the lake, I heard. Must've been a charming sight. Now Dayne won't be able to play in the water all summer."

"Fuck off, Roz."

"So you've vomited only once in the last month and you pronounce yourself cured?"

"Maybe, maybe not."

"I went to a therapist, you know."

"Well, bully for you. I'm sure you sorely needed it."

"You just might too." She wondered what was the cause of his nastiness today. And he was the one who always accused her of being unfeeling or insensitive.

"OK, I might."

"You don't have any support, do you?"

"What about Pepper, Irv, and maybe even on a good day, you?"

"I mean professional support. Group support. Group therapy."

"Group therapy? Pardon me while I vomit." He stuck his finger in his mouth, leaned over the water and erupted into uncontrollable laughter.

"Not funny, Juan."

"*I* thought so." He sat up, stretched his legs out on the pier, the sun to his back.

"You're hopeless. But you just might consider getting help. All on your own, with no support, you could have a relapse."

"I hate that word."

"You hate every other word in the dictionary: relapse, empower, co-dependent."

"At least I've *seen* every other word in the dictionary, unlike you. And I dare you to name one more that I hate."

Roz tried to think of one, without success, and noticed that Juan seemed to be watching an ant crawl on the pier. Waves lapped at the shore behind them; in the distance she heard the quacking of ducks. "You need professional help for your bulimia."

"I can see you're back to normal. Boss me around, tell me

what to do with my life."

She barely registered his remarks. "Juan, there's something else." She'd wanted to tell him more directly, but he, she or both of them had gotten her off track.

"I had a reason to ask you if I've gained weight. I mean, I don't think I have. It's too early to tell." She heard her voice quiver, tried to steady it. "I missed a period and I feel just like I did when I was in the first trimester with Dayne: headaches, vertigo, appetite shifts. And feel like I have to go to the john all the time, and I do."

Juan started to fall backwards; she jerked him up before he tumbled head first into the lake. "Thanks. Are you implying what I think you are? I can't believe you ran off up north and let some guy knock you up! So that's what that whole thing was about? I take it you at least know who the father is. I hope he wore a condom. But I guess he didn't, or it broke. Thank God abortion is still available in Wisconsin. I can't fucking believe..."

"Juan, shut up! Or this time I'll push you in!" She turned around to face the house, hoping no one inside had heard. Again facing Juan, she saw that clouds had skimmed past the sun, and lowered her voice back to normal pitch: "There's only one possibility, if indeed I am."

"At least you know who it is."

"And so do you, but I haven't told him yet." Having glimpsed a mosquito nearby, she swatted at air. "Up north the place was swarming with lesbians. Remember, it was *Womyn's* Land. Not a man within miles."

"Do you mean... Irv? I thought that was permanent, irreversible?"

"So did we."

"Have you been to a doctor?"

"Not yet. But if I am... Two children? I came back content to be a mother to one, but..." She held out her hands, pleadingly, as if he could help. "Hell, I'm forty-two years old, Juan."

"If you'd had a severe eating disorder, it might have caused early menopause to set in and this wouldn't be happening."

"Thanks a lot. Why do I even confide in you?"

"Sorry. I was kidding. Go ahead."

"What's there to say? We never thought we had to practice birth control. And when I got back from the Land, Irv and I, well... It was the first time in months. If it happened, it happened that night."

"Are you two coming in?" Pepper appeared on the back porch. "It's almost ready!"

Tonight was her fifth anniversary, which Juan and Pepper also celebrated, since it was at her wedding reception that they'd met again.

"Yeah, we're coming!" she screamed, loudness drowning out her irritation.

"I hope you weren't saving this little surprise as some sort of sick anniversary present tonight at dinner."

"Juan, you're mean, nasty and sick yourself. Of course I wasn't."

Dinner was over, a superficial success. Roz expected that Irv counted on making love tonight. They'd only done it once since that fateful night and she knew she couldn't do it again without telling him. Maybe it *was* some sort of sick anniversary present. But it was unintentional, the timing not her fault.

Irv was three feet away, as she rinsed off dishes and he loaded them into the dishwasher. Juan and Pepper had taken Dayne downstairs. She didn't want to spring the news on Irv in bed.

"Why don't we go for a walk? Just over through the park. It could be romantic."

Irv gave her an amused stare. "You, who don't like to get wet, call rain 'romantic'?"

"It's just drizzling now." A dramatic midwestern thunderstorm had struck during dinner. "The two of us snuggling under one umbrella. I don't see why not."

"Fine with me."

Five minutes later they strolled into Orton Park, Irv holding a large red and white umbrella that was no longer necessary. "Let's walk over to the gazebo," she said.

"It should be dry under there."

"Maybe so. But that was quite a storm."

They reached the gazebo and walked up its wet steps. The railing she leaned on was wet, but she didn't mind it. She wanted to be any place except her bedroom. The storm had blown down a few branches, she saw.

"Let's check out the burr oak. I bet it weathered the storm fine." Last year's group had not quite yet mobilized this year;

chainings to it had been only sporadic.

"OK." They walked down the gazebo's slippery steps. "The moon's clouded over tonight."

"Big surprise. It's been raining." She didn't mean to sound sarcastic. "Irv, I have to talk to you."

"Any time, anything you want or need to say."

All she could think was that she truly didn't deserve Irv. She kept repeating to herself that what had happened — and she was sure it had — wasn't either one's fault.

"Irv, I have news. You might consider it good, you might consider it bad." Hidden from the street view, she now rested against the burr oak.

"There aren't any political offices open to run for, are there?"

She trusted he meant this as a joke. "No. The news I have I consider frightening." She thought she detected a trace of panic in his face, upon hearing "frightening."

"Go ahead. I can handle anything except Rhoda moving back in with us."

She saved comment on this remark for the future, but knew she had to tell him her news quickly. The poor man might be imagining she wanted to divorce him.

"I missed a period. Remember that night after I got back from the Land? If I am, and I'm almost sure I am... pregnant, it had to be that night."

"Do you mean...?"

"It would seem you're not sterile any more. If you ever really were. I don't know."

"I had tests done when I was marrried to Harriet. But that was at least fifteen years ago."

"Maybe it undid itself. You trust me, don't you, that it had to be you?"

"That..." Now she could see a broad grin on his face, as he had stepped aside into the faint glow of a streetlight. "...is the silliest thing I've ever heard you say. Of course I trust you."

"Come over here and hold me." She grasped the tree behind her with her hands, rubbing her head against it, as if she were about to make love to it, instead of Irv. "How do you feel about it, assuming I am... pregnant?" She herself would opt for striking *this* word from the dictionary.

"I'm ecstatic that I might be able to be a biological father." His arms were now over her shoulders and his hands, she presumed, were touching the bark. "But more important..." His mouth was only inches from hers. "How do you feel?"

"I haven't the foggiest idea." The truth was, she didn't. "Maybe I wasn't destined to be an activist, a political office holder or any such thing. If I have another child, I'll never get the chance to run for city council. Though, what does that matter? Maybe my fate is to be a typical Midwestern mother."

"Roz, I don't think you'll ever be that." He chuckled as he said it.

"Kiss me, Irv, kiss me."

He put his lips to hers. The bond — his lips, the burr oak, and the fetus in her belly — felt... primal. That was the word, primal.

# 66

"You've got some I can pick up?" Evan asked Pepper from the gas station pay phone where he was calling from Mount Horeb.

"Sure do. I made my rounds yesterday and today." Evan knew that the "rounds" meant to PWAs. "And I've got a whole ounce left for you."

"You'll be home in a half-hour or forty-five minutes?" He'd just finished visitation with the kids and tomorrow would pick them up and take them to Reilly's for a pancake breakfast, as he had no place to keep them for the night, short of renting a motel room.

"Juan's out driving, but I'll be here."

"I, for one, am ready for relaxation. See you within an hour."

"I'll be here and ready."

Evan took in the lake view from Pepper's living room window. This is what he'd like: a lakefront property on the east side of the Isthmus, though the prices probably skyrocketed on the lake side of the street.

"I've got to talk to Cissy when I get home. Stoned might not be the best way. Maybe I should put it off until tomorrow."

"You make it sound serious. I don't mean to pry, but is it anything you want to talk about?"

"Yes and no."

"Well, I'm going to light up some of my own. If you have the willpower to abstain, more power to you."

Pepper lit a pipe and Evan's resolve evaporated. "Yeah, pass the pipe, please."

They smoked the bowl in silence, Evan coughing when he'd taken in too much.

"Another?" Pepper asked, when Evan's coughing spell had subsided.

"Why not?" He didn't yet feel much effect from the first bowl.

Pepper, who had just inhaled, nodded his head and handed the pipe to Evan. After they'd each had three potent tokes, the bowl was empty.

"Now I think I'm more than buzzed."

"I think I'm mildly ripped." Pepper got up and turned on the ceiling fan.

"How's Juan doing?" Evan asked, putting off the subject that weighed on his mind.

"I gave him an ultimatum. He at least has to go to some sort of a support group."

"You remember the last time you and I and he got stoned together?"

Pepper seemed to ponder. "Afraid I do. Amelia's party, wasn't it?"

"Yeah. Cissy was sure she wouldn't get past the departmental level without Blake's vote. But she did, passed the divisional committee, barely, and now she's got tenure. And now Anne is remarrying and wants to be custodial parent of my kids. From skipping school and so many suspensions and God knows what else, now Todd has to repeat the sixth grade. And, about Danielle, Anne told me it's 'normal' for six-year-olds to set fires. But I want to be the custodial parent, and I don't have a chance in hell, unless I marry Cissy, and Todd may be hell no matter who raises him, but I think they couldn't help but get better parenting from me and Cissy." His thoughts had flowed naturally from one to the other to the next. He felt momentarily unburdened, as well as confused.

Pepper raised his eyes, incredulous, to Evan's. "With all that on your mind, I'd say you needed those two bowls."

"I think I did."

"Do you mean you were going to propose to Cissy tonight? Maybe then you shouldn't have smoked so much. The way you said it, it sounded like you want to marry her for her to be a mother to your kids."

Had it really sounded that way, or was it Pepper's own

stoned perception? Evan leaned back and became part of the sofa. Pepper gave him a silly, broad grin.

"You're higher than nine kites, aren't you?"

The grin continued and became an affirmative.

"I think Cissy and I could be perfectly happy together. It's just that I'm afraid Cissy hates kids."

"Cissy hates kids?" Pepper rolled his head, then his eyes, as though Evan had said Cissy hates men, marijuana or museums.

"We haven't talked about it. But I know that kids just aren't part of her world. Never have been. She had a repressed childhood." He realized the marijuana was making him talk a little crazy. "She's only met Todd and Danielle a few times, and she was polite, but distant. I could tell she didn't know how to relate to kids."

"Maybe you shouldn't spring it on her when you're stoned. I'm going to put on a CD, if I can get up." Pepper rocked back and forth in his chair, then bounced up. Only then did Evan remember it was a rocking chair.

"Yeah, I'm definitely postponing the conversation." Evan watched Pepper's chair rock by itself. "Don't even think I could get the words out right tonight." Classical music that he didn't recognize came on.

"Sounds like a good idea to me. Talk to her tomorrow."

Pepper was still kneeling by the CD player, fiddling with the buttons.

"Yeah. Maybe tomorrow. I don't want it to sound like I want to marry her because I want a mother for Todd and Danielle, because that's not the case. Everything's just all coinciding: her tenure, my divorce, the custody issue, our talk of buying a house together. I mean, maybe she even opposes marriage in principle, for all I know. Maybe she thinks I'm too old. Nick's about my age, and he looks ten years younger..."

"But from what I've heard and seen, Nick Wren acts like he has less maturity than an undergrad. I think the dope's making you paranoid or something." Pepper was now rocking again. Although stationary, Evan felt like he was rocking too.

"Yeah, maybe it is. I don't feel so well. I'd better go soon."

"Maybe you shouldn't drive. I'll walk with you."

"It's only four blocks. But, yeah, I think I am a little paranoid. If you want, you can walk with me." Evan thought of his own delinquent son, who was always in trouble, whom Cissy would hate. He felt as messed up as Todd probably was. Maybe he'd smoked too much marijuana in his life, maybe it had affected his sperm and he's passed it on to Todd.

Pepper stood up and stretched. "Hey, man. It'll be all right. I think you just have the jitters over proposing to Cissy."

Evan hadn't thought of it that way: "proposing to Cissy."

Cissy and Evan lay in bed Sunday morning. He had thrown on his robe, gone down and retrieved the newspaper, which was now in bed with them. Cissy had gotten up and returned with two cups of spearmint tea. She'd be spending the day alone, unless she changed her mind and consented to go with Evan and the kids to a pancake breakfast out at some tavern in the country. Maybe it wasn't such a bad idea.

Reading glasses perched on her nose, she went quickly through the news sections, then focused on an article about the upcoming Frank Lloyd Wright exhibit at the Madison Art Center. She finished the article, noticed that Evan had his head buried in the real estate section, and looked over at him with interest.

"One hundred and nine thousand. Lakeland Drive. Right across from the lake. See?" He pointed to the picture of the east-side house.

Was he serious? And, if so, how could they afford it? She snatched a page of the section away from him, slid her glasses back up her nose and began to read.

"Here. Two bedrooms, two-car garage. Ninety-nine thousand. Fox Avenue. Near-west side. What do you think?" She pointed to the house's blurry photo.

"I think we should buy a house together?"

It was what she'd had been waiting for months to hear, even if his statement had the intonation of a question. As to a ring on her finger, she didn't care at the moment. A jointly owned house would be a major step toward something.

"But how can we afford it?"

"Easier than you think. The market's hot, interest rates are low..."

"Keep going?"

"I've got job security, and so do you now. We can get a loan and a mortgage. Besides, Anne and the carpenter..." Did the fact that even now he refused to pronounce the man's name mean he still harbored unresolved anger over his broken-up marriage? "...are getting married, you might as well know, and that means I'll be getting money from the Mount Horeb farmette. Either Anne and I sell it, or the carpenter buys me out."

"Maybe it is feasible, financially." To hell with any unresolved anger Evan might have over Anne and the carpenter.

"Sure, it's feasible, if we want to. Here, look at another one. Evergreen Avenue." Of course it was the east side. "Three bedrooms. Only eighty-eight thousand."

"What's wrong with two bedrooms? We both don't need separate studies, do we?"

"I was thinking...." Evan was tentative, reached down under the sheet and patted his stomach, as if a sufficient amount of abdominal firmness were a prerequisite for house buying.

He appeared to have weathered his minor mid-life crisis. The styling gel was permanently and long gone. Last night he'd come home stoned as ever — a rarity — and had talked of getting a tattoo, in the pubic region, of all places. She'd attributed it to the marijuana, not to the crisis. "Go on."

"How would you feel if...?" Again he stopped. What was he going to thrust on her? "If I try to be custodial parent of the kids? When Anne remarries, I'd like more than joint custody. That's why three bedrooms. I know how you feel about kids."

"You do? That's interesting. I don't." Danielle was six or seven, if she remembered right, and Todd, twelve.

"You don't?"

"Not really. I always knew I wanted to get tenure first, then think about having children later. My own." But, at thirty-six, did she want to start her own family? She didn't think so, but wasn't at all sure. For one thing, although she had someone to make babies with, she didn't have a husband.

"We can think and talk about it, can't we?"

"Of course, we can." She reached over toward her tea, but stopped her hand in mid-reach, still taking it all in, not quite believing it.

Evan put down the real estate section and seemed deep in thought. She observed him with curiosity until he snapped out of it.

"One more thing. If I want to be the custodial parent, and Anne will sure as hell fight me with fire if I try, there's one little detail."

"Which is?"

"I'd maybe have a better chance of getting that custody if we were married."

A natural smile overtook Cissy's face. She fell onto Evan's chest, the real estate section between them, creased, smashed, then elbowed away, forgotten by their lovemaking.

# 67

"Hey, hey, ho, ho! AIDSphobia's got to go!" Juan and Pepper marched among some thirty other ACT UP members and "professional" demonstrators, picketing the Department of Corrections.

"DOC, you can't hide, we charge you with homicide!"

The thirty included six pallbearers of a coffin. A third prisoner, who'd committed some heinous crime, had died at the state correctional facility at Waupun, from lack of adequate medical care, and the governor still hadn't enacted his advisory council's recommendations. The heinous crimes of the prisoners weren't the question. Indeed, the heinous crime was, at this particular moment, that little or nothing was being done for those who were ill.

"Two, four, six, eight! All Tommy does is masturbate!"

Nearly a third of the demonstrators were women. Juan recognized Beth, who was walking hand in hand with Verla.

"Three, five, seven, nine! Prisoners don't have the time!"

"Here, can you take this?" A pallbearer walking in front of Juan handed him the coffin and relieved Juan of the placard he was carrying.

"What's this thing filled with, rocks?"

He received no answer, but determined that rocks it was.

On and on they circled the pavement — a legal picket, cops and DOC officials observing them. Juan felt the effects of the sun, heat and humidity. He hoped the die-in would begin soon; otherwise he might have his own personal one.

On the other side of the circle he saw Pepper marching, defiant, his fist in the air. Pepper went down on cue as the whistle blew. After placing the coffin in the middle of the sidewalk, Juan managed to fall to the pavement within touching distance of him. Still panting from exertion, he supposed that playing with Pepper's foot was frowned on under the circumstances.

The die-in ended and they resumed marching. This time

Juan managed to avoid pallbearer duties. Pepper grabbed his hand and the two held one sign jointly.

"Prisoners with AIDS under attack! What do we do? ACT UP! Fight back!"

Roz had had tests, Irv was going to, and she was indeed pregnant. The point of his tests was, for the moment, moot, trusting, as Juan now did, that Irv was the father. He wondered what the hell she was going to do with two kids.

It was Saturday and they were weathering the governor's Victory/Welcome Home Parade on the Square for the Desert Shield/Desert Storm troops. In his second demonstration of the week, he, along with Pepper, Irv, Dayne, Roz and Amelia, dressed in white and stood in silent protest along with several hundred others. They were a minority and often booed by beer-bellied, redneck, rural Wisconsinites, some of whom wore T-shirts sporting flags with such catchy slogans as "Try And Burn This One, ASSHOLE!"

What was their own private Madison coming to? Juan was secretly glad that the sixty flags draping the Square had been vandalized earlier in the week. And, he guessed, there were various others, who, like he, wouldn't admit it publicly.

"This parade charade constitutes nothing less than sacrilege!" he said. "What can we do?"

"ACT UP, fight back," Pepper said with a question mark.

"Remember all the times and places in the country where you wouldn't dare do something like this," said Amelia.

"Right. Amelia's been there," said Pepper.

"It's important just that we're here. That's all we can do today," said Irv.

"Oh, we're doing more." Roz spoke brightly and patted her stomach. "We're making an anti-war baby!"

Juan was, not unexpectedly, the only man in the group. After reciting a serenity prayer, they introduced themselves, and all welcomed him. The group of twelve sat in a semi-circle of chairs in a hospital meeting room. Three women spoke, two calling themselves "compulsive overeaters," one a "recovering bulimic," all talking about their "stuff," and everyone thanking them for "sharing." "Stuff" and "sharing" struck Juan as two more words best obliterated from the lexicon.

Last week his own doctor had in fact refused to refer him an eating disorders clinic, apparently never having met an adult male bulimic before. The refusal had angered him enough that he'd resolved to go to his first meeting of Overeaters Anonymous and to seek out a therapist too, moves that Pepper had not only applauded, but demanded.

Juan was asked if he wanted to say anything. "I'm still Juan," he reminded others of his name. "And I'm bulimic. And want to recover. I haven't binged and purged in over a month, but I'm here tonight since I finally admit that I don't have the situation under too much control and it's affected my, uh, relationship."

The women seemed to accept him well enough. He was eager for the chance to spill his whole story, but decided to wait until they knew him better, until he'd heard more of them talk.

At that moment, a large woman wearing large sunglasses came in and took what appeared to be her accustomed place in the group.

"Why don't you introduce yourself?" said Alice, the convener. "We have a newcomer this evening."

"I'm Erva Mae. A recovering..." Then she pulled her sunglasses off, seemed momentarily paralyzed, and her stare turned from benign to malignant. "And you're Juan Bellefleur!" she shrieked.

It was indeed Roz's spiteful ex-lover, whose new lover had attacked her verbally this year at the Ten Percent Society Forum for the council candidates.

"Erva Mae, no last names please."

"What the hell are you doing here?" She bore baleful eyes into Juan.

"The same thing as you," Alice said to her, impatient. "Recovering."

"If you're going to discuss women's issues, if I'm going to interfere with or impede discussion, I can leave, if you want."

"I want!" Erva Mae screamed. "This has always been a women's meeting!"

"Only in practice," said Alice. She then turned to Juan. "You are the first man we've had, at least since I've been here. But this is not designated a 'women only' meeting. The only criteria are that you have some sort of eating problem and want to recover. We don't discriminate on the basis of sex."

"I'd like to move that we take a vote to change the charter."

"Ah, shut your face, Erva Mae!" said the woman next to Juan. Then she squeezed his hand.

If anything, Erva Mae's presence firmed his resolve to stay in the group. Not that after his long journey to get this far, he needed any further motivation.

Juan and Pepper sat on the rocks at Picnic Point Sunday afternoon, watching sailboats and windsurfers. Cumulus clouds dotted the sky like continents, an Asia here, an Australia or Antarctica there, mushrooming or shrinking.

"I know I'll never be totally cured. Even if I stop the behavior forever, I'll still be recovering, but I still feel good about the meeting. I guess I could go to a different one if I wanted. I suppose I could go to a different meeting every night of the week if I needed. Maybe I could even start a men's group. There's got to be a couple other guys out there."

"It only takes two to tango."

"What?"

"It only takes two to have a meeting. You know, you can be awfully dense sometimes." The wind blew Pepper's dark hair, which he'd begun to let grow. "Go to as many meetings as you need."

"Yeah, I'll have to see."

Before three o'clock the wind began to whip up and a sudden, fierce rain descended on them. They hurried back to the car, soaked, and saw that the western sky had turned black. The wind was worse than the rain, and both were increasing ominously. They jumped into Pepper's Sunbird, Juan on the driver's side, and sped away, the road leading them by the lakeshore.

Tornado sirens sounded. Pepper turned on the radio. Through the crackling static, they heard, "Winds moving at fifty-to-fifty-five miles per hour, headed toward downtown Madison, and increasing in speed. Unconfirmed sightings of funnel clouds in Middleton. It is time to take shelter. Go to your basement. If you do not have one, take shelter in the innermost part of your house. If you're driving..." A thunderclap struck nearby, drowning out the words.

"Should we jump in a ditch?"

"Let's see if we can make it a little farther." Rain lashed off the lake horizontally, in sheets; the wind almost buffeted a Volkswagen in front of them. The windshield wipers barely kept up, visibility was near zero. "Looks like we're going to miss Cissy and Evan's party."

"I've never seen a storm in Madison this bad," said Juan.

"You know what they say: a tornado can never strike the Isthmus, since it's protected by the lakes."

"You can call that one a myth."

Juan eased the Sunbird to a stop at Observatory Drive and Charter Street and heard noise nearby — not a tornado siren. He lowered his window a slice; rain came in from the north. "Pepper, open yours a crack."

Pepper did and they heard... bells. The carillonneur, his tower to the left, was giving his Sunday concert in the middle of a potentially killer storm. "Sounds like Satie's 'Gymnopédie'." Juan was always astonished by Pepper's ability to recognize classical music, especially now, when its strains could be barely heard over the storm.

"And look." Pepper pointed to the right. There was a music-loving — or demented — audience of three under the ledge of the Commerce Building. "They could be dead meat."

"You and I too."

"Turn into the Bascom Hill lot."

Juan did as told. Branches large and small were snapping off all around them.

"I love you if we both die," Juan pledged, and quickly kissed Pepper.

"One day we will, I do too, but let's get out of here!"

"Where to?"

"Muir Knoll's closest."

"OK, let's make a dash for it."

They jumped out of the parked car and crossed the street, Juan using his hands as blinders at the side of his face. Drenched, they ran over to the grassy knoll with larch pines.

"Here!" Pepper motioned to a slab of rock that resembled a horizontal tombstone. They threw themselves down behind it and grasped each other in a hug, as the carillon bells tolled blithely away.

# 68

Cissy and Evan stood facing Beth. From her perspective behind the bar, they looked like a hip, blond, married couple, perhaps two-middle aged California surfers, minus their tans. Then she noticed two children accompanying them.

"Hey, how are you guys? Here to celebrate firin' Rickover?" Beth knew that a party had been planned, but didn't know the occasion.

"He wasn't exactly fired...," Cissy began, but Evan cut her off with, "We read that the boycott's over and decided to plan our party here."

"Great to see ya. Ho Chi's got their politics back together and I helped end the boycott. Got my old job back."

Beth hadn't really wanted to see this neighborhood institution disappear, didn't want to be supported by Verla, once her two-thousand dollars ran out, and knew that a job would give her... something that was lacking. So here she was, manager again. Although Miller and Philip Morris products tainted the premises, the lesbian/gay groups that had endorsed the boycott had unendorsed it, with Beth as go-between, plus personal appearances by Emily and Ron before the more unwaveringly correct organizations.

"Better to work here than Museum Studies, No Rickover to answer to here."

"Nor is there anywhere else," said Cissy.

"You hired a hit man or somethin'?"

"No," Evan said. "He's just in Africa, probably terrorizing the native peoples."

"So what *is* the occasion?"

"To celebrate Cissy's tenure."

"Great! I thought maybe Rickover fired you, like he did me. What can I get for you?"

"Two mineral waters and two lemonades for the kids," said Cissy. "It seems as though you expected the entire department to be wiped out."

"Well, in a way, it almost was, wasn't it?"

"Go ahead and get us the waters," said Evan. "But there are also eight bottles of champagne behind the bar."

"Evan?"

"For the guests."

"Here's your waters." Beth set them on the bar in front of them. "On the house, from me. Let me get to the regulars over there, and I'll be back to pop the corks whenever you're ready."

Cissy noticed Irv had trimmed his beard and observed with more than usual interest the well-behaved child at Roz's side. She trusted that Todd and Danielle would behave just as well.

"So you won't be needing my services," Irv said.

"No, I'm afraid, I mean I'm glad, I won't. It's official now." She had been concerned enough to ask Nick — not without hesitancy — what might constitute "just cause." His verbatim answer had been, "Maybe snorting coke and screwing your students on Bascom Hill. Maybe not."

Irv congratulated her, and Cissy said, "This isn't one-hundred-percent definite, but we might not be renewing the lease in August. You see, Evan and I are looking to buy a house and with Evan's children staying in the apartment..."

"Congratulations, again. Take the time you need, give me an idea of when the flat will be free, and I'll put up a sign."

"And I'm pregnant," said Roz, silent at his side until now. "And my obstetrician says to expect twins! Due in February. If it can wait that long at my age. In any case, my mother is here again, and will be, off and on, to help. I'll surely need all the help I can get."

"Well, congratulations too," Cissy said, somewhat astounded at the news. Roz had to be five or six years older than she was, so if she really wanted to have her own child...

At that moment she turned around, saw that Wilhelmina had arrived and behind her — Cissy did a double take — burst in Sandra. "Surprise!" she screamed giddily.

Cissy moved up to embrace her. "But how...?"

"Vance isn't contesting the divorce. So while he's gone, I came back to get my possessions and to sign the papers. He's put the house on the market. I reached Wilhelmina..."

"And I decided to bring along a surprise guest," Wilhelmina completed.

"Here, sit down, both of you. Or do you want something to eat or drink?" It was a cash bar, except for the champagne; she and Evan had supplied hors d'oeuvres from Ho Chi Minh's owners, who had branched out into catering during the long boycott.

"You succeeded in surprising us," said Evan, before either of them could answer. "And thanks for the letters about Vance."

"Oh, that." Sandra seemed almost to have forgotten or shrugged it off. "I'm in Texas now," she said, before Cissy could ask. "After leaving Detroit, I stopped in Kentucky to see a friend, and ended up volunteering at a battered women's shelter there, since the one in Madison helped me so much. And now, I'm going to help them set one up serving some of the southern border towns. I'm even learning Spanish. Screw academia. Sorry, Cissy. I know it's worked out for you, but if I hadn't met Vance, I never even would've finished my dissertation." Cissy imagined Sandra writing it while locked in the attic.

"It wasn't for me anyway. But who cares now? Vance is in Africa, you're all free of him, and I'm next to Mexico!"

"You're in Madison, Sandra." Cissy giggled, then beheld the same pear-shaped face and stringy hair, and discerned a new look of determination.

Out of courtesy, Cissy had invited the whole department, minus Sumner Isaacson. Or the remainder of the department, she thought with mixed feelings. At least no one would die from hypothermia at *this* party, nor of heat stroke. It was hot and humid, but not that hot.

The champagne now flowing freely, Cissy finished her glass, then ordered another mineral water, before she got tipsy or sick, plus two more lemonades. Beth introduced her to her partner, as she brought the mineral water.

"Sorry to intrude. I'm just here for the air conditioning," said Verla.

"Oh, it's no intrusion at all. Feel free to have some champagne if you want. There's going to be a toast."

"Thanks, but I'll toast with water."

"And I've taken Beth and Verla under my wing, and am learning a lot that could have helped me understand my latently fertile daughter. And I myself never mind a little champagne." It took Cissy a second to remember Roz's mother.

Cissy hadn't really wanted to have a toast. But as they'd asked her to say a few words, she figured she'd surprise them with the news of her engagement. Everyone seemed to be there except Nick —which was fine with her. Then she remembered Juan and Pepper, and wondered what had happened to them.

As she turned around, Nick burst in, elbowed his way up to the bar and shouted, "There's one major storm brewing all of the sudden out there!"

"Really?" said Cissy, not having noticed through Ho Chi's opaque glass blocks in the guise of windows.

"Another party, another storm," Nick muttered. Across the bar she saw Roz looking on at Nick with a strangeness that seemed to turn to some startling revelation.

Then she noticed that Amelia, with Irv's and Evan's help, was quieting the crowd. At Amelia's side, Davidine gave her characteristic assuring wink at Cissy.

Amelia began to speak: "We all know why we're here today. To celebrate Cissy's tenure. We all know she's worked hard and deserved it." Everyone applauded and, when the noise died down, Amelia proclaimed, "To Cissy's long, successful career!"

"Thanks, Amelia. Thanks to all those who helped me, professionally and otherwise, over the years, including our friend Blake. And, while I'm talking, I have another announcement to make. Evan and I..."

At that moment, a large bolt of lightning struck nearby, and Ho Chi Minh's lights went out.

❧

They'd been standing in the darkness for twenty minutes, when Beth announced, "The beer in the cooler must be getting warm, so you might as well have some on the house!" She started gleefully passing it out to those who could make it up to the bar.

Ginger was glued to the only door with a window, as she interrogated Sandra. Standing several heads behind her, Cissy was able to glimpse boxes, garbage, and tree branches flying down the street.

"You all stand back," Beth came forward a minute later, with a large sheet of cardboard and a flashlight. "This glass could blow out at any minute."

Nick helped Beth affix the cardboard to the glass door, making it even darker. The phones were out, the air conditioning dead.

A minute later, Cissy felt someone pinch her backside. She turned around, ready to slap Nick.

It was Evan, standing next to Irv. "Don't do that in the dark," she said sternly, then to lighten things up, "We're prisoners of Ho Chi Minh's." Perhaps the department should be banned from having parties, as natural disasters seemed to coincide with or follow them.

"Just like in North Vietnam," Irv said, a wry smile barely visible on his face.

"Is that a beer your drinking!?" she said, mildly shocked, to Evan.

"No. Just holding it for Todd. Don't ask me how he got it, but..."

All at once the door flew open, sustained by the wind. Everyone backed away, and Juan and Pepper rushed in, soaked through.

"Irv? Cissy?" Juan yelled, apparently not seeing them. "You'd better come with us. There's been damage to the house!"

"Which house?" Irv hurried up to him in the semi-darkness, with Roz right behind, pulling Dayne, who let out a scream of joy or fear.

"The Willy Street house. The rain's died down a little. You can jump in the car with us."

"Amelia, can you keep an eye on Todd and Danielle?"

"I'm coming too!" Nick announced.

"So am I!" screamed Rhoda.

"No, Mother! We'll be right back."

"Roz, a woman in your condition..."

They rushed out, and Evan, Cissy and Nick all piled into the back of Pepper's small Sunbird, while Irv, Roz and Dayne took off in their own car. They sped away, the traffic lights out, and the car darted branches and unidentifiable debris. A few brave residents were just beginning to emerge into the now-lighter rain to survey the damage. Juan parked the car across the street from the house. Snapped-off branches littered their lawn too.

"You'd better go upstairs," Juan said.

"Is it safe?"

"God almighty!" she heard Evan cry out as he opened the living room door. She scrambled past Irv, Pepper and Roz, and saw... a tree in the kitchen.

"Is the house structurally sound?"

"Who knows?"

"It could be doubtful now."

They ventured into the kitchen and saw a gaping hole in the roof, the top of the tall tree behind the house resting in the middle of the room, water all over the floor, and still running in.

"We'd better get out of here."

Nick bolted into the kitchen. "Irv. I've just been downstairs. Seems to be major water damage. Frankly, I'd been thinking of buying a condo on the west side. I think this makes it definite."

"I understand. You three may be the last inhabitants of this 'historic' house, by the looks of things. At least for a long time."

"Now we're definitely moving," Cissy said to Evan. "And I don't care where."

"Then we can buy on the Isthmus' east side. I'm glad we finally agree." As he spoke, Evan slipped and fell on the kitchen floor. He sat in a puddle of water, chips of bark in his matted blond hair, a leaf stuck to the middle of his forehead.

"I think we'd better get out of here," Evan repeated. Cissy pulled him away, as the roof gave in some more, the top of the tree now grazing her kitchen table.

"The burr oak!" Roz exclaimed outside, as they were contemplating the walk back to Ho Chi Minh's, the storm now over. Irv began to say something, but Roz cut him off: "It's just two blocks to the park. Let's all go see."

"Sure, why not?" Cissy said, looking to Evan for agreement. "Then we'll go back to what's left of our party."

The four of them, plus Dayne, walked toward the park. As they reached it, Cissy didn't see any trees down, though uncountable branches dotted the park's long rectangular lawn.

"It's still standing!" Roz exclaimed from a distance, and they all walked up to the tall, evidently sturdy oak. Cissy noticed a weathered green sign on it and various other trees: "Slated for Imminent Execution." Numbers to call and protest followed.

"Didn't even lose a branch."

"Just because it's slightly diseased is no reason to cut it down," Roz said. "And it withstood the storm better than any other tree in the park."

"You're right, Roz. It's probably got a few more good decades. Too bad the tree behind the Willy Street property didn't." Cissy watched as Irv surveyed the branches and foliage that oddly festooned the park. "Now, a genuine tornado, I don't know if it would have survived that."

"But would we have survived?" Cissy thought aloud.

"If you've survived this year," Evan said, "you can survive anything." He squeezed her hand and Cissy saw Roz gently rubbing her stomach. She looked up at the sky, sun now blazing on them, and wondered what it felt like to be pregnant with twins. At least twins didn't run in her family, if she ever decided to...

"The b'roak," said Dayne.

"Yes, but the burr oak isn't broken, darling." Roz picked him up with motherly tenderness — his weight must have been half of hers — then handed him over to Irv.

Cissy viewed the three of them, an unlikely looking trio, and envisioned herself, Evan and whatever the future might bring, five years from now. On one hand, the prospect was not unappealing.

On the other, it was terrifying.

# FREE freight
# on the original
# tales from MADLANDS!

If you enjoyed reading GOD'S LITTLE ISTHMUS, you'll love the original tales from MADLANDS. Order as many copies as you like at $12.95 each and we'll pay the shipping anywhere in the U.S.

Wisconsin residents please add 5.5% sales tax.